BETWEEN
SISTERS

By Kristin Hannah
Published by Ballantine Books

A HANDFUL OF HEAVEN
THE ENCHANTMENT
ONCE IN EVERY LIFE
IF YOU BELIEVE
WHEN LIGHTNING STRIKES
WAITING FOR THE MOON
HOME AGAIN
ON MYSTIC LAKE
ANGEL FALLS
SUMMER ISLAND
DISTANT SHORES
BETWEEN SISTERS

KRISTIN HANNAH

BALLANTINE BOOKS • NEW YORK

BETWEEN
SISTERS

A Ballantine Book
Published by The Random House Ballantine Publishing Group

Copyright © 2003 by Kristin Hannah

All rights reserved under International and Pan-American Copyright Conventions. Published in the United States by The Random House Ballantine Publishing Group, a division of Random House, Inc., New York, and simultaneously in Canada by Random House of Canada Limited, Toronto.

Ballantine and the Ballantine colophon are registered trademarks of Random House, Inc.

www.ballantinebooks.com

Library of Congress Cataloging-in-Publication Data can be obtained from the publisher upon request.

ISBN 0-345-45073-6

Design by C. Linda Dingler

Manufactured in the United States of America

First Edition: May 2003

10 9 8 7 6 5 4 3 2 1

For my sister, Laura.

And for my father, Laurence.

And, as always, for Benjamin and Tucker.

I love you all.

$\mathcal{A}$CKNOWLEDGMENTS

Thanks to Dr. Barbara Snyder and Katherine Stone . . . again; thanks to Diane VanDerbeek, attorney extraordinaire, for her help with legal matters; and finally, to John and Diane and the wonderful crew of the *Olympus*: Thanks for a fun-filled and memorable boat trip.

"We do not see things as they are,
we see them as we are."
—Anaïs Nin

"If love is the answer, could you please rephrase the question?"
—Lily Tomlin

BETWEEN
SISTERS

Chapter
One

$\mathcal{D}$R. BLOOM WAITED PATIENTLY FOR AN ANSWER.

Meghann Dontess leaned back in her seat and studied her fingernails. It was time for a manicure. Past time. "I try not to feel too much, Harriet. You know that. I find it impedes my enjoyment of life."

"Is that why you've seen me every week for four years? Because you enjoy your life so much?"

"I wouldn't point that out if I were you. It doesn't say much for your psychiatric skills. It's entirely possible, you know, that I was perfectly normal when I met you and you're actually *making* me crazy."

"You're using humor as a shield again."

"You're giving me too much credit. That wasn't funny."

Harriet didn't smile. "I rarely think you're funny."

"There goes my dream of doing stand-up."

"Let's talk about the day you and Claire were separated."

Meghann shifted uncomfortably in her seat. Just when she

needed a smart-ass response, her mind went blank. She knew what Harriet was poking around for, and Harriet knew she knew. If Meghann didn't answer, the question would simply be asked again. "Separated. A nice, clean word. Detached. I like it, but that subject is closed."

"It's interesting that you maintain a relationship with your mother while distancing yourself from your sister."

Meghann shrugged. "Mama's an actress. I'm a lawyer. We're comfortable with make-believe."

"Meaning?"

"Have you ever read one of her interviews?"

"No."

"She tells everyone that we lived this poor, pathetic-but-loving existence. We pretend it's the truth."

"You were living in Bakersfield when the pathetic-but-loving pretense ended, right?"

Meghann remained silent. Harriet had maneuvered her back to the painful subject like a rat through a maze.

Harriet went on, "Claire was nine years old. She was missing several teeth, if I remember correctly, and she was having difficulties with math."

"Don't," Meghann curled her fingers around the chair's sleek wooden arms.

Harriet stared at her. Beneath the unruly black ledge of her eyebrows, her gaze was steady. Small round glasses magnified her eyes. "Don't back away, Meg. We're making progress."

"Any more progress and I'll need an aid car. We should talk about my practice. That's why I come to you, you know. It's a pressure cooker down in Family Court these days. Yesterday, I had a deadbeat dad drive up in a Ferrari and then swear he was flat broke. The shithead. Didn't want to pay for his daughter's tuition. Too bad for him I videotaped his arrival."

"Why do you keep paying me if you don't want to discuss the root of your problems?"

"I have issues, not problems. And there's no point in poking around in the past. I was sixteen when all that happened. Now, I'm a whopping forty-two. It's time to move on. I did the right thing. It doesn't matter anymore."

"Then why do you still have the nightmare?"

She fiddled with the silver David Yurman bracelet on her wrist. "I have nightmares about spiders who wear Oakley sunglasses, too. But you never ask about that. Oh, and last week, I dreamed I was trapped in a glass room that had a floor made of bacon. I could hear people crying, but I couldn't find the key. You want to talk about that one?"

"A feeling of isolation. An awareness that people are upset by your actions, or missing you. Okay, let's talk about that dream. Who was crying?"

"Shit." Meghann should have seen that. After all, she had an undergraduate degree in psychology. Not to mention the fact that she'd once been called a child prodigy.

She glanced down at her platinum-and-gold watch. "Too bad, Harriet. Time's up. I guess we'll have to solve my pesky neuroses next week." She stood up, smoothed the pant legs of her navy Armani suit. Not that there was a wrinkle to be found.

Harriet slowly removed her glasses.

Meghann crossed her arms in an instinctive gesture of self-protection. "This should be good."

"Do you like your life, Meghann?"

That wasn't what she'd expected. "What's not to like? I'm the best divorce attorney in the state. I live—"

"—alone—"

"—in a kick-ass condo above the Public Market and drive a brand-new Porsche."

"Friends?"

"I talk to Elizabeth every Thursday night."

"Family?"

Maybe it was time to get a new therapist. Harriet had ferreted out all of Meghann's weak points. "My mom stayed with me for a week last year. If I'm lucky, she'll come back for another visit just in time to watch the colonization of Mars on MTV."

"And Claire?"

"My sister and I have problems, I'll admit it. But nothing major. We're just too busy to get together." When Harriet didn't speak, Meghann rushed in to fill the silence. "Okay, she makes me crazy, the way she's throwing her life away. She's smart enough to do anything, but she stays tied to that loser campground they call a resort."

"With her father."

"I don't want to discuss my sister. And I *definitely* don't want to discuss her father."

Harriet tapped her pen on the table. "Okay, how about this: When was the last time you slept with the same man twice?"

"You're the only one who thinks that's a *bad* thing. I like variety."

"The way you like younger men, right? Men who have no desire to settle down. You get rid of them before they can get rid of you."

"Again, sleeping with younger, sexy men who don't want to settle down is not a bad thing. I don't want a house with a picket fence in suburbia. I'm not interested in family life, but I like sex."

"And the loneliness, do you like that?"

"I'm not lonely," she said stubbornly. "I'm independent. Men don't like a strong woman."

"Strong men do."

"Then I better start hanging out in gyms instead of bars."

"And strong women face their fears. They talk about the painful choices they've made in their lives."

Meghann actually flinched. "Sorry, Harriet, I need to scoot. See you next week."

She left the office.

Outside, it was a gloriously bright June day. Early in the so-called summer. Everywhere else in the country, people were swimming and barbecuing and organizing poolside picnics. Here, in good ole Seattle, people were methodically checking their calendars and muttering that it was *June, damn it.*

Only a few tourists were around this morning; out-of-towners recognizable by the umbrellas tucked under their arms.

Meghann finally released her breath as she crossed the busy street and stepped up onto the grassy lawn of the waterfront park. A towering totem pole greeted her. Behind it, a dozen seagulls dived for bits of discarded food.

She walked past a park bench where a man lay huddled beneath a blanket of yellowed newspapers. In front of her, the deep blue Sound stretched along the pale horizon. She wished she could take comfort from that view; often, she could. But today, her mind was caught in the net of another time and place.

If she closed her eyes—which she definitely dared not do—she'd remember it all: the dialing of the telephone number, the stilted, desperate conversation with a man she didn't know, the long, silent drive to that shit-ass little town up north. And worst of all, the tears she'd wiped from her little sister's flushed cheeks when she said, *I'm leaving you, Claire.*

Her fingers tightened around the railing. Dr. Bloom was wrong. Talking about Meghann's painful choice and the lonely years that had followed it wouldn't help.

Her past wasn't a collection of memories to be worked through; it was like an oversize Samsonite with a bum wheel. Meghann had learned that a long time ago. All she could do was drag it along behind her.

Each November, the mighty Skykomish River strained against its muddy banks. The threat of flooding was a yearly event. In a dance as old as time itself, the people who lived in the tiny towns along the river watched and waited, sandbags at the ready. Their memory went back for generations. Everyone had a story to tell about the time the water rose to the second floor of so-and-so's house . . . to the top of the doorways at the grange hall . . . to the corner of Spring and Azalea Streets. People who lived in flatter, safer places watched the nightly news and shook their heads, clucking about the ridiculousness of farmers who lived on the flood plain.

When the river finally began to lower, a collective sigh of relief ran through town. It usually started with Emmett Mulvaney, the pharmacist who religiously watched The Weather Channel on Hayden's only big-screen television. He would notice some tiny tidbit of information, something even those hotshot meteorologists in Seattle had missed. He'd pass his assessment on to Sheriff Dick Parks, who told his secretary, Martha. In less time than it took to drive from one end of town to the other, the word spread: *This year is going to be okay. The danger has passed.* Sure enough, twenty-four hours after Emmett's prediction, the meteorologists agreed.

This year had been no exception, but now, on this beautiful early summer's day, it was easy to forget those dangerous months in which rainfall made everyone crazy.

Claire Cavenaugh stood on the bank of the river, her work boots almost ankle-deep in the soft brown mud. Beside her, an out-of-gas Weed Eater lay on its side.

She smiled, wiped a gloved hand across her sweaty brow. The amount of manual labor it took to get the resort ready for summer was unbelievable.

Resort.

That was what her dad called these sixteen acres. Sam Cavenaugh had come across this acreage almost forty years ago, back when Hayden had been nothing more than a gas station stop on the rise up Stevens Pass. He'd bought the parcel for a song and settled into the decrepit farmhouse that came with it. He'd named his place River's Edge Resort and begun to dream of a life that didn't include hard hats and earplugs and night shifts at the paper plant in Everett.

At first he'd worked after hours and weekends. With a chain

saw, a pickup truck, and a plan drawn out on a cocktail napkin, he began. He hacked out campsites and cleaned out a hundred years' worth of underbrush and built each knotty pine riverfront cabin by hand. Now, River's Edge was a thriving family business. There were eight cabins in all, each with two pretty little bedrooms and a single bathroom and a deck that overlooked the river.

In the past few years, they'd added a swimming pool and a game room. Plans for a mini golf course and a Laundromat were in the works. It was the kind of place where the same families came back year after year to spend their precious vacation time.

Claire still remembered the first time she'd seen it. The towering trees and rushing silver river had seemed like paradise to a girl raised in a trailer that only stopped on the poor side of town. Her childhood memories before coming to River's Edge were gray: ugly towns that came and went; uglier apartments in run-down buildings. And Mama. Always on the run from something or other. Mama had been married repeatedly, but Claire couldn't remember a man ever being around for longer than a carton of milk. Meghann was the one Claire remembered. The older sister who took care of everything . . . and then walked away one day, leaving Claire behind.

Now, all these years later, their lives were connected by the thinnest of strands. Once every few months, she and Meg talked on the phone. On particularly bad days, they fell to talking about the weather. Then Meg would invariably "get another call" and hang up. Her sister loved to underscore how successful she was. Meghann could rattle on for ten minutes about how Claire had sold herself short. "Living on that silly little campground, cleaning up after people" was the usual wording. Every single Christmas she offered to pay for college.

As if reading *Beowulf* would improve Claire's life.

For years, Claire had longed to be friends as well as sisters, but Meghann didn't want that, and Meghann always got her way. They were what Meghann wanted them to be: polite strangers who shared a blood type and an ugly childhood.

Claire reached down for the Weed Eater. As she slogged across the spongy ground, she noticed a dozen things that needed to be done before opening day. Roses that needed to be trimmed, moss that needed to be scraped off the roofs, mildew that needed to be bleached off the porch railings. And there was the mowing. A long, wet winter had turned into a surprisingly bright spring, and the grass had grown as tall as Claire's knees. She made a mental note to ask George, their handyman, to scrub out the canoes and kayaks this afternoon.

She tossed the Weed Eater in the back of the pickup. It hit with a clanging thunk that rattled the rusted bed.

"Hey, sweetie. You goin' to town?"

She turned and saw her father standing on the porch of the registration building. He wore a ratty pair of overalls, stained brown down the bib from some long-forgotten oil change, and a flannel shirt.

He pulled a red bandanna out of his hip pocket and wiped his brow as he walked toward her. "I'm fixing that freezer, by the way. Don't you go pricing new ones."

There wasn't an appliance made that he couldn't repair, but Claire was going to check out prices, just the same. "You need anything from town?"

"Smitty has a part for me. Could you pick it up?"

"You bet. And have George start on the canoes when he gets here, okay?"

"I'll put it on the list."

"And have Rita bleach the bathroom ceiling in cabin six. It got mildewy this winter." She closed the pickup's bed.

"You here for dinner?"

"Not tonight. Ali has a Tee Ball game at Riverfront Park, remember? Five o'clock."

"Oh, yeah. I'll be there."

Claire nodded, knowing that he would. He hadn't missed a single event in his granddaughter's life. "Bye, Dad."

She wrenched the truck's door handle and yanked hard. The door screeched open. She grabbed the black steering wheel and climbed up into the seat.

Dad thumped the truck's door. "Drive safely. Watch the turn at milepost seven."

She smiled. He'd been giving her that exact bit of advice for almost two decades. "I love you, Dad."

"I love you, too. Now, go get my granddaughter. If you hurry, we'll have time to watch *SpongeBob SquarePants* before the game."

CHAPTER
TWO

THE WEST SIDE OF THE OFFICE BUILDING FACED PUGET SOUND. A wall of floor-to-ceiling windows framed the beautiful blue-washed view. In the distance lay the forested mound of Bainbridge Island. At night, a few lights could be seen amid all that black-and-green darkness; in the daylight, though, the island looked uninhabited. Only the white ferry, chugging into its dock every hour, indicated that people lived there.

Meghann sat alone at a long, kidney-shaped conference table. The glossy cherry and ebony wood surface bespoke elegance and money. Perhaps money most of all. A table like this had to be custom-made and individually designed; it was true of the suede chairs, too. When a person sat down at this table and looked at that view, the point was clear: Whoever owned this office was damn successful.

It was true. Meghann had achieved every goal she'd set for herself. When she'd started college as a scared, lonely teenager she'd dared to dream of a better life. Now, she had it. Her practice was among the most successful and most respected in the city. She owned an expensive condo in downtown Seattle (a far cry from the broken-down travel trailer that had been her childhood "home"), and no one depended on her.

She glanced down at her watch. 4:20.

Her client was late.

You would think that charging well over three hundred dollars an hour would encourage people to be on time.

"Ms. Dontess?" came a voice through the intercom.

"Yes, Rhona?"

"Your sister, Claire, is on line one."

"Put her through. And buzz me the second May Monroe gets here."

"Very good."

She pushed the button on her headset and forced a smile into her voice. "Claire, it's good to hear from you."

"The phone works both ways, you know. So. How's life in Moneyland?"

"Good. And in Hayden? Everyone still sitting around waiting for the river to flood?"

"That danger's passed for the year."

"Oh." Meghann stared out her window. Below and to her left, huge orange cranes loaded multicolored containers onto a tanker. She had no idea what to say to her sister. They had a past in common, but that was pretty much it. "So, how's that beautiful niece of mine? Did she like the skateboard?"

"She loved it." Claire laughed. "But really, Meg, someday you'll have to ask a salesperson for help. Five-year-old girls don't generally have the coordination for skateboards."

"You did. We were living in Needles that year. The same year I taught you to ride a two-wheeler." Meg immediately wished she hadn't said that. It always hurt to remember their past together. For a lot of years, Claire had been more of a daughter to Meghann than a sister. Certainly, Meg had been more of a mother to Claire than Mama ever had.

"Just get her a Disney movie next time. You don't need to spend so much money on her. She's happy with a Polly Pocket."

Whatever *that* was. An awkward silence fell between them. Meghann looked down at her watch, then they both spoke at once.

"What are you—?"

"Is Alison excited about first grade—?"

Meghann pressed her lips together. It took an act of will not to speak, but she knew Claire hated to be interrupted. She especially hated it when Meg monopolized a conversation.

"Yeah," Claire said. "Ali can't wait for all-day school. Kindergarten hasn't even ended and she's already looking forward to the fall. She talks about it constantly. Sometimes I feel like I'm holding on to the tail of a comet. And she never stops moving, even in her sleep."

Meghann started to say, *You were the same way*, and stopped herself. It hurt remembering that; she wished she could push the memory aside.

"So, how's work going?"

"Good. And the camp?"

"Resort. We open in a little more than two weeks. The Jeffersons are having a family reunion here with about twenty people."

"A week without phone access or television reception? Why am I hearing the *Deliverance* theme music in my head?"

"Some families like to be together," Claire said in that crisp *you've-hurt-me* voice.

"I'm sorry. You're right. I know you love the place. Hey," she said, as if she'd just thought of it, "why don't you borrow some money from me and build a nice little Eurospa on the property? Better yet, a small hotel. People would flock there for a good body wrap. God knows you've got the mud."

Claire sighed heavily. "You just have to remind me that you're successful and I'm not. Damn it, Meg."

"I didn't mean that. It's just . . . that I know you can't expand a business without capital."

"I don't want your money, Meg. *We* don't want it."

There it was: the reminder that Meg was an *I* and Claire was a *we.* "I'm sorry if I said the wrong thing. I just want to help."

"I'm not the baby girl who needs her big sister's protection anymore, Meg."

"Sam was always good at protecting you." Meg heard a tiny flare of bitterness in her voice.

"Yeah." Claire paused, drew in a breath. Meghann knew what her sister was doing. Regrouping, climbing to softer, safer ground. "I'm going to Lake Chelan," she said at last.

"The yearly trip with the girlfriends," Meghann said, thankful for the change in subject. "What do you call yourselves? The Bluesers?"

"Yeah."

"You all going back to that same place?"

"Every summer since high school."

Meghann wondered what it would be like to have a sisterhood of such close friends. If she were another kind of woman, she might be envious. As it was, she didn't have time to run around with a bunch of women. And she couldn't imagine still being friends with people she'd gone to high school with. "Well. Have fun."

"Oh, we will. This year, Charlotte—"

The intercom buzzed. "Meghann? Mrs. Monroe is here."

Thank God. An excuse to hang up. Claire could talk forever about her friends. "Damn. Sorry, Claire, I've got to run."

"Oh, right. I know how much you love to hear about my college dropout friends."

"It's not that. I have a client who just arrived."

"Yeah, sure. Bye."

"Bye." Meghann disconnected the call just as her secretary showed May Monroe into the conference room.

Meghann pulled the headset off and tossed it onto the table,

where it hit with a clatter. "Hello, May," she said, walking briskly toward her client. "Thank you, Rhona. No calls, please."

Her secretary nodded and left the room, closing the door behind
her.

May Monroe stood in front of a large multicolored oil painting,
a Nechita original entitled *True Love*. Meghann had always loved
the irony of that; here, in this room, true love died every day of the
week.

May wore a serviceable black jersey dress and black shoes that
were at least five years out of date. Her champagne-blond hair fell
softly to her shoulders in that age-old easy-care bob. Her wedding
ring was a plain gold band.

Looking at her, you would never know that her husband drove a
jet-black Mercedes and had a regular Tuesday tee-time at the Broad-
moor Golf Course. May probably hadn't spent money on herself in
years. Not since she'd slaved at a local restaurant to put her husband
through dental school. Though she was only a few years older than
Meghann, sadness had left its mark on May. There were shadowy circles under her eyes.

"Please, May, sit down."

May jerked forward like a marionette who'd been moved by
someone else. She sat in one of the comfortable black suede chairs.

Meghann took her usual seat at the head of the table. Spread
out in front of her were several manila file folders with bright pink
Post-it notes fanned along the edges of the paperwork. Meghann
drummed her fingertips on the stack of papers, wondering which of
her many approaches would be best. Over the years, she'd learned
that there were as many reactions to bad news as there were indis-
cretions themselves. Instinct warned her that May Monroe was fragile, that while she was in the midst of breaking up her marriage, she
hadn't fully accepted the inevitable. Although the divorce papers
had been filed months ago, May still didn't believe her husband
would go through with it.

After this meeting, she'd believe it.

Meghann looked at her. "As I told you at our last meeting, May,

I hired a private investigator to check into your husband's financial affairs."

"It was a waste of time, right?"

No matter how often this scene played and replayed itself in this office, it never got any easier. "Not exactly."

May stared at her for a long moment, then she stood up and went to the silver coffee service set out on the cherry wood credenza. "I see," she said, keeping her back to Meghann. "What did you find out?"

"He has more than six hundred thousand dollars in an account in the Cayman Islands, which is under his own name. Seven months ago, he took almost all of the equity out of your home. Perhaps you thought you were signing refinance documents?"

May turned around. She was holding a coffee cup and saucer. The porcelain chattered in her shaking hands as she moved toward the conference table. "The rates had come down."

"What came down was the cash. Right into his hands."

"Oh my," she whispered.

Meghann could see May's world crumbling. It flashed through the woman's green eyes; a light seemed to go out of her.

It was a moment so many women faced at a time like this: the realization that their husbands were strangers and that their dreams were just that.

"It gets worse," Meghann went on, trying to be gentle with her words, but knowing how deep a cut she'd leave behind. "He sold the practice to his partner, Theodore Blevin, for a dollar."

"Why would he do that? It's worth—"

"So you wouldn't be able to get the half you're entitled to."

At that, May's legs seemed to give out on her. She crumpled into her chair. The cup and saucer hit the table with a clatter. Coffee burped over the porcelain rim and puddled on the wood. May immediately started dabbing the mess with her napkin. "I'm sorry."

Meghann touched her client's wrist. "Don't be." She got up, grabbed some napkins, and blotted the spill. "I'm the one who's sorry, May. No matter how often I see this sort of behavior, it still sickens me." She touched May's shoulder and let the woman have time to think.

"Do any of those documents say why he did this to me?"

Meghann wished she didn't have an answer to that. A question was sometimes preferable to an answer. She reached into the file and pulled out a black-and-white photograph. Very gently, as if it were printed on a sheet of plastique explosives instead of glossy paper, she pushed it toward May. "Her name is Ashleigh."

"Ashleigh Stoker. I guess I know why he always offered to pick Sarah up from piano lessons."

Meghann nodded. It was always worse when the wife knew the mistress, even in passing. "Washington is a no-fault state; we don't need grounds for a divorce, so his affair doesn't matter."

May looked up. She wore the vague, glassy-eyed expression of an accident victim. "It doesn't matter?" She closed her eyes. "I'm an idiot." The words were more breath than sound.

"No. You're an honest, trustworthy woman who put a selfish prick through ten years of college so *he* could have a better life."

"It was supposed to be *our* better life."

"Of course it was."

Meg reached out, touched May's hand. "You trusted a man who told you he loved you. Now he's counting on you to be good ole accommodating May, the woman who puts her family first and makes life easy for Dr. Dale Monroe."

May looked confused by that, maybe even a little frightened. Meghann understood; women like May had forgotten a long time ago how to make waves.

That was fine. It was her lawyer's job anyway.

"What should we do? I don't want to hurt the children."

"He's the one who's hurt the children, May. He's stolen money from them. And from you."

"But he's a good father."

"Then he'll want to see that they're provided for. If he's got a shred of decency in him, he'll hand over half of the assets without a fight. If he does that, it'll be a cakewalk."

May knew the truth that Meghann had already surmised. A man like this didn't share well. "And if he doesn't?"

"Then, we'll make him."

"He'll be angry."

Meghann leaned forward. "You're the one who should be angry, May. This man lied to you, cheated on you, and stole from you."

"He also fathered my children," May answered with a calm that Meghann found exasperating. "I don't want this to get ugly. I want him . . . to know he can come home."

Oh, May.

Meghann chose her words carefully. "We're simply going to be fair, May. I don't want to hurt anyone, but you damn sure aren't going to be screwed over and left destitute by this man. Period. He's a very, very wealthy orthodontist. You should be wearing Armani and driving a Porsche."

"I've never wanted to wear Armani."

"And maybe you never will, but it's my job to make sure you have every option. I know it seems cold and harsh right now, May, but believe me, when you're exhausted from raising those two children by yourself and Dr. Smiles is driving around town in a new Porsche and dancing the night away with his twenty-six-year-old piano teacher, you'll be glad you can afford to do whatever you want. Trust me on this."

May looked at her. A tiny, heartbreaking frown tugged at her mouth. "Okay."

"I won't let him hurt you anymore."

"You think a few rounds of paperwork and a pile of money in the bank will protect me from that?" She sighed. "Go ahead, Ms. Dontess, do what you need to do to protect my children's future. But let's not pretend you can make it painless, okay? It already hurts so much I can barely breathe, and it has just begun."

Across the blistered expanse of prairie grass, a row of windmills dotted the cloudless horizon. Their thick metal blades turned in a slow and steady rhythm. Sometimes, when the weather was just

right, you could hear the creaking thwop-thwop-thwop of each ro-
tation.

Today, it was too damn hot to hear anything except the beating
of your own heart.

Joe Wyatt stood on the poured-concrete slab that served as the
warehouse's front porch, holding a now-warm can of Coke, all that
was left of his lunch.

He stared at the distant fields, wishing he were walking along
the wide rows between the trees, smelling the sweet scent of rich
earth and growing fruit.

There might be a breeze down there; even a breath of one would
alleviate this stifling heat. Here, there was only the hot sun, beating
down on the metal warehouse. Perspiration sheened his forehead
and dampened the skin beneath his T-shirt.

The heat was getting to him and it was only the second week of
June. There was no way he could handle summer in the Yakima Valley. It was time to move on again.

The realization exhausted him.

Not for the first time, he wondered how much longer he could
do this, drift from town to town. Loneliness was wearing him down,
whittling him away to a stringy shadow; unfortunately, the alterna-
tive was worse.

Once—it felt long ago now—he'd hoped that one of these
places would feel right, that he'd come into some town, think, *This
is it*, and dare to rent an apartment instead of a seedy motel room.

He no longer harbored such dreams. He knew better. After a
week in the same room, he started to feel things, remember things.
The nightmares would start. The only protection he had found was
strangeness. If a mattress was never "his," if a room remained unfamiliar territory, he could sometimes sleep for more than two hours at
a time. If he settled in, got comfortable, and slept longer, he invariably dreamed about Diana.

That was okay. It hurt, of course, because seeing her face—even
in his dreams—filled him with an ache that ran deep in his bones,

but there was pleasure, too, a sweet remembrance of how life used to be, of the love he'd once been capable of feeling. If only the dreams stopped there, with memories of Diana sitting on the green grass of the Quad in her college days or of them cuddled up in their big bed in the house on Bainbridge Island.

He was never that lucky. The sweet dreams invariably soured and turned ugly. More often than not, he woke up whispering, "I'm sorry."

The only way to survive was to keep moving and never make eye contact.

He'd learned in these vagrant years how to be invisible. If a man cut his hair and dressed well and held down a job, people saw him. They stood in line for the bus beside him, and in small towns they struck up conversations.

But if a man let himself go, if he forgot to cut his hair and wore a faded Harley-Davidson T-shirt and ragged, faded Levi's, and carried a ratty backpack, no one noticed him. More important, no one recognized him.

Behind him, the bell rang. With a sigh, he stepped into the warehouse. The icy cold hit him instantly. Cold storage for the fruit. The sweat on his face turned clammy. He tossed his empty Coke can in the trash, then went back outside.

For a split second, maybe less, the heat felt good; by the time he reached the loading dock, he was sweating again.

"Wyatt," the foreman yelled, "what do you think this is, a damn picnic?"

Joe looked at the endless row of slat-sided trucks, filled to heaping with newly picked cherries. Then he studied the other men unloading the crates—Mexicans mostly, who lived in broken-down trailers on patches of dry, dusty land without flushing toilets or running water.

"No, sir," he said to the florid-faced foreman who clearly got his kicks from yelling at his workers. "I don't think this is a picnic."

"Good. Then get to work. I'm docking you a half an hour's pay."

In his former life, Joe would have grabbed the foreman by

his sweaty, dirty collar and shown him how men treated one another.

Those days were gone.

Slowly, he walked toward the nearest truck, pulling a pair of canvas gloves out of his back pocket as he moved.

It was time to move on.

Claire stood at the kitchen sink, thinking about the phone conversation with Meg yesterday.

"Mommy, can I have another Eggo?"

"How do we ask for that?" Claire said absently.

"Mommy, may I *please* have another Eggo?"

Claire turned away from the window and dried her hands on the dish towel hanging from the oven door. "Sure." She popped a frozen waffle into the toaster. While it was warming, she looked around the kitchen for more dirty dishes—

And saw the place through her sister's eyes.

It wasn't a bad house, certainly not by Hayden standards. Small, yes: three tiny bedrooms tucked into the peaked second floor; a single bathroom on each floor; a living room; and a kitchen with an eating space that doubled as a counter. In the six years Claire had lived here, she'd painted the once moss-green walls a creamy French vanilla and replaced the orange shag carpeting with hardwood floors. Her furniture, although mostly secondhand, was all framed in wood that she'd stripped and refinished herself. Her pride and joy was a Hawaiian koa-wood love seat. It didn't look like much in the living room, with its faded red cushions, but someday, when she lived on Kauai, it would stop people in their tracks.

Meg would see it differently, of course. Meg, who'd graduated high school early and then breezed through seven years of college, who never failed to mention that she had buckets of money, and had the nerve to send her niece Christmas gifts that made the others under the tree look paltry by comparison.

"My waffle's up."

"So it is." Claire took the waffle from the slot, buttered and cut it, then put the plate in front of her daughter. "Here you go."

Alison immediately stabbed a piece and popped it into her mouth, chewing in that cartoon-character way of hers.

Claire couldn't help smiling. Her daughter had had that effect on her since birth. She stared down at the miniature version of herself. Same fine blond hair and pale skin, same heart-shaped face. Although there were no pictures of Claire at five, she imagined that she and Alison were almost carbon copies of each other. Alison's father had left no genetic imprint on his daughter.

It was fitting. The minute he'd heard Claire was pregnant, he'd reached for his running shoes.

"You're in your jammies, Mommy. We're gonna be late if you don't hurry."

"You're right about that." Claire thought about all the things she had to do today: mow the back field; recaulk the showers and bathroom windows; bleach the mildewed wall in cabin three; unplug the toilet in cabin five; and repair the canoe shed. It was early yet, not even 8:00, on the last day of school. Tomorrow, they'd be leaving for a week of rest and fun at Lake Chelan. She hoped she could get everything done in time. She glanced around. "Have you seen my work list, Alison?"

"On the coffee table."

Claire picked up her list from the table, shaking her head. She had absolutely no memory of leaving it there. Sometimes she wondered how she'd get by without Alison.

"I want ballet lessons, Mommy. Is that okay?"

Claire smiled. It occurred to her—one of those passing thoughts that carried a tiny sting—that she'd once wanted to be a ballerina, too. Meghann had encouraged her to dream that dream, even though there had been no money for lessons.

Well, that wasn't quite true. There had been money for *Mama's* dance lessons, but none for Claire's.

Once, though, when Claire had been about six or seven, Meghann had arranged for a series of Saturday-morning lessons with a junior high friend of hers. Claire had never forgotten those few perfect mornings.

Her smile faded.

Alison was frowning at her, one cheek bunched up midbite. "Mommy? Ballet?"

"I wanted to be a ballerina once. Did you know that?"

"Nope."

"Unfortunately, I have feet the size of canoes."

Ali giggled. "Canoes are *huge*, Mommy. Your feet are just really big."

"Thanks." She laughed, too.

"How come you're a worker bee if you wanted to be a ballerina?"

"Worker bee is what Grampa calls me. Really I'm an assistant manager."

It had happened a long time ago, her choosing this life. Like most of her decisions, she'd stumbled across it without paying much attention. First, she'd flunked out of Washington State University—one of the many party casualties of higher education. She hadn't known then, of course, that Meghann was basically right. College gave a girl choices. Without a degree, or a dream, Claire had found herself back in Hayden. Originally, she'd meant to stay a month or so, then move to Kauai and learn to surf, but then Dad got bronchitis and was down for a month. Claire had stepped in to help him out. By the time her father was back on his feet and ready to resume his job, Claire had realized how much she loved this place. She was, in that and in so many things, her father's daughter.

Like him, she loved this job; she was outside all day, rain or shine, working on whatever needed to be done. When she finished each chore, she saw tangible proof of her labor. There was something about these gorgeous sixteen acres along the river that filled her soul.

It didn't surprise her that Meghann didn't understand. Her sister, who valued education and money above everything, saw this place as a waste of time.

Claire tried not to let that condemnation matter. She knew her job wasn't much in the great scheme of things, just managing a few campsites and a couple of cabins, but she never felt like a failure, never felt that her life was a disappointment.

Except when she talked to her sister.

CHAPTER
THREE

*T*WENTY-FOUR HOURS LATER, CLAIRE WAS READY TO LEAVE ON
vacation. She took a last pass through the tiny house, looking for
anything forgotten or left undone, but everything was as it should be.
The windows were locked, the dishwasher was empty, and all the
perishables had been taken out of the fridge. She was straightening
the shower curtain when she heard footsteps in the living room.

"What in the name of a frog's *butt* are you still doing here?"

She smiled and backed out of the minuscule bathroom.

Her father stood in the living room. As always, he dwarfed the
small space. Big and broad-shouldered, he made every room seem
smaller by comparison. But it was his personality that was truly oversize.

She'd first met him when she was nine years old. She'd been
small for her age, and so shy she only spoke to Meghann in those
days. Dad had seemed larger than life when he stepped into their
travel trailer. *Well*, he'd said as he looked down at her, *you must be*

my daughter, Claire. You're the prettiest girl I've ever seen. Let's go home.

Home.

It was the word she'd waited for, dreamed of. It had taken her years—and more than a few tears—to realize that he hadn't offered the same welcome to Meghann. By then, of course, by the time Claire understood the mistake, it was well past the time to rectify it.

"Hey, Dad. I was making sure everything was ready for you to move in."

His grin showed a row of Chiclet-white dentures. "You know damn well I ain't moving in here. I *like* my mobile home. A man doesn't need this much room. I got my fridge and my satellite TV. That's all I need."

They'd been having this discussion ever since Claire had moved back to the property and Dad had given her use of the house. He swore up and down that the mobile home hidden in the trees was more than room enough for a fifty-six-year-old single man.

"But, Dad—"

"Don't talk about my butt. I know it's getting bigger. Now, dance on over here and give your old man a hug."

Claire did as she was told.

His big, strong arms enfolded her, made her feel safe and adored. He smelled faintly of disinfectant today. That was when she remembered the bathroom that needed fixing.

"I'll leave in an hour," she said. "The toilet in cabin—"

He spun her around and pushed her gently toward the door. "Get going. This place isn't going to fall apart without you. I'll fix the damn toilet. *And* I'll remember to pick up the PVC pipe you ordered and to stack the wood under cover. If you remind me again, I'll have to hurt you. I'm sorry, but that's the way it is."

Claire couldn't help smiling. She'd reminded him about the pipe at least six times. "Okay."

He touched her shoulders, forced her to stop long enough to look at him. "Take as long as you want. Really. Take three weeks. I can handle this place alone. You deserve a break."

"*You* never take one."

"I'm on the down side of my life, and I don't want to get out much. You're only thirty-five. You and Alison should kick up your heels a bit. You're too damn responsible."

"I'm a thirty-five-year-old single mother who has never been married. That's not too responsible, and I *will* kick up my heels in Chelan. But I'll be home in a week. In time to check the Jefferson party into their cabins."

He thumped her shoulder. "You've always done exactly what you wanted, but you can't blame a guy for trying. Have fun."

"You, too, Dad. And take Thelma out for dinner while I'm gone. Quit all that skulking around."

He looked genuinely nonplussed. "What—"

She laughed. "Come on, Dad. The whole town knows you're dating."

"We're not dating."

"Okay. Sleeping together." In the silence that followed that re-mark, Claire walked out of the house and into the steely gray day. A drizzling rain fell like a beaded curtain in front of the trees. Crows sat on fence posts and phone wires, cawing loudly to one an-other.

"Come on, Mommy!" Alison's small face poked through the car's open window.

Dad hurried ahead of her and kissed his granddaughter's cheek.

Claire checked the trunk—again—then got into the car and started the engine. "Are we ready, Ali Kat? Do you have every-thing?"

Alison bounced in her seat, clinging to her Mary-Kate-and-Ashley lunch box. "I'm ready!" Her stuffed orca—Bluebell—was strapped into the seat with her.

"We're off to see the Wizard, then," Claire said, shifting into drive as she yelled a final good-bye to her father.

Alison immediately started singing the Barney theme song: "I love you, you love me." Her voice was high and strong, so loud that poodles all across the valley were probably hurling themselves to the ground and whining pitifully. "Come on, Mommy, *sing*."

By the time they reached the top of Stevens Pass, they'd sung forty-two Barney theme songs—in a row—and seventeen Froggy-Went-A-Courtings. When Alison opened her lunch box, Claire rammed a Disney audiotape into the cassette player. The theme music to *The Little Mermaid* started.

"I wish I was like Ariel. I want flippers," Alison said.

"How could you be a ballerina then?"

Alison looked at her, clearly disgusted. "She has feet on *land*, Mommy." Then she leaned back in her seat and closed her eyes, listening to the story of the mermaid princess.

The miles flew by. In no time, they were speeding across the flat, arid land on the eastern side of the state.

"Are we almost there, Mommy?" Alison asked, sucking on a licorice whip, bouncing in her seat. The area around her lips was smudged with black. "I wish we'd get there."

Claire felt the same way. She loved the Blue Skies Campground. She and her girlfriends had first vacationed there a few years after high school graduation. In the early years there had been five of them; time and tragedy had whittled their number down to four. They'd each missed a year now and then, but for the most part, they met there year after year. At first they'd been young and wild and driven to pick up local boys. Gradually, as they'd started dragging bassinets and car seats with them, the vacation had settled down a bit. Now that the kids were old enough to swim and play on the playground alone, the girls—women—had refound a slice of their previous freedom.

"Mommy. You're spacing out."

"Oh. Sorry, honey."

"I *said*, we get the honeymoon cabin this year, remember?" She bounced even harder in her seat. "*Yippee!* We get the big bathtub. And this year I get to jump off the dock, don't forget. You *promised*. Bonnie got to jump when she was five." Alison sighed dramatically and crossed her arms. "Can I jump off the dock or not?"

Claire wanted to go against her overprotective nature, but when you'd grown up in a house where your Mama allowed *anything*, you learned fast how easy it was to get hurt. It made you afraid. "Let's see the dock, okay? And we'll see how you're swimming. Then we'll see."

" 'We'll see' always means no. You *promised*."

"I did not promise. I remember it distinctly, Alison Katherine. We were in the water; you were on my back, with your legs wrapped around me. We were watching Willie and Bonnie jump into the water. You said, 'Next year I'll be five.' And I said, 'Yes, you will.' And you pointed out that Bonnie was five. I pointed out that she was almost six."

"I'm almost six." Alison crossed her arms. "I'm jumping."

"We'll see."

"You're not the boss of me."

Claire always laughed at that. Lately it was her daughter's favorite comeback. "Oh, yes I am."

Alison turned her face toward the window. She was quiet for a long time—almost two minutes. Finally, she said, "Marybeth threw Amy's clay handprint in the toilet last week."

"Really? That wasn't very nice."

"I know. Mrs. Schmidt gave her a *long* time-out. Did you bring my skateboard?"

"No, you're too young to ride it."

"Stevie Wain rides his all the time."

"Isn't that the boy who fell and broke his nose and knocked out two front teeth?"

"They were *baby* teeth, Mommy. He said they were loose anyway. How come Aunt Meg never comes to visit us?"

"I've told you this before, remember? Aunt Meg is so busy she hardly has time to breathe."

"Eliot Zane turned blue when he didn't breathe. The amb'lance came to get him."

"I didn't mean that. I just meant Meg is superbusy helping people."

"Oh."

Claire steeled herself for her daughter's next question. There was *always* a next question with Alison, and you could never predict what it would be.

"Is this the desert already?"

Claire nodded. Her daughter always called eastern Washington the desert. It was easy to see why. After the lush green of Hayden, this yellow-and-brown landscape seemed desolate and scorched. The black ribbon of asphalt stretched forever through the prairie.

"There's the water slide!" Alison said at last. She leaned forward, counting out loud. When she got to forty-seven, she yelled, "There's the lake!"

Lake Chelan filled their view to the left, a huge crystal-blue lake tucked into a golden hillside. They drove over the bridge that led into town.

Two decades ago, this town had been less than three blocks long, without a national franchise to be found. But over time, word of the weather had spread west, to those soggy coastal towns that so prized their plate-size rhododendrons and car-size ferns. Gradually, Seattleites turned their attention eastward. It became a summer tradition, the trek across the mountains toward the flat, scorched plains. As the tourists came, so did the development. Condominium complexes sprouted along the water's edge. As one filled up, another was built beside it, and so on and so on, until, at the millennium, this was a thriving vacation destination, with all the kiddie-required amenities—pools, water-slide parks, and Jet Ski rentals.

The road curved along the lakeshore. They passed dozens of condominium complexes. Then the shore became less inhabited again. They kept driving. A half mile upshore, they saw the sign: *Blue Skies Campground: Next Left.*

"Look, Mommy, look!"

The sign showed a pair of stylized trees bracketing a tent with a canoe in front.

"This is it, Ali Kat."

Claire turned left onto the gravel road. Huge potholes caught the tires and sent the car bouncing right to left.

A mile later, the road took a hairpin turn into a grassy field dotted with trailers and motor homes. They drove past the open field and into the trees, where the few coveted cabins sat in a cluster along the shore. They parked in the gravel lot.

Claire helped Alison out of her car seat, then shut the door and turned toward the lake.

For a split second, Claire was eight years old again, a girl at Lake Winobee, standing at the shoreline, wearing a pretty pink bikini. She remembered splashing into the cold water, shrieking as she went deeper and deeper.

Don't go in past your knees, Claire, Meghann had hollered out, sitting up on the dock.

For Christ's sake, Meggy, quit bein' such an old fuddy-duddy. Mama's voice. *Go on in, sweetums,* she'd yelled to Claire, laughing loudly, waving a Virginia Slims menthol cigarette. *It won't do to be a scaredy-cat.*

And then Meghann was beside Claire, holding her hand, telling her there was nothing wrong with being afraid. *It just shows good sense, Claire-Bear.*

Claire remembered looking back, seeing Mama standing there in her tiny bicentennial bikini, holding a plastic cup full of vodka.

Go ahead, sweetums. Jump in that cold water and swim. It doesn't do a damn bit o' good to be afraid. It's best to get your yuks in while you can.

Claire had asked Meghann, *What's a yuk?*

It's what so-called actresses go looking for after too many vodka collinses. Don't you worry about it.

Poor Meg. Always trying so hard to pretend their life had been ordinary.

But how could it have been? Sometimes God gave you a mama

that made normal impossible. The upside was fun times and parties so loud and crazy you never forgot them . . . the downside was that bad things happened when no one was in charge.

"Mommy!" Alison's voice pulled Claire into the present. "Hurry up."

Claire headed for the old-fashioned farmhouse that served as the campground's lodge. The wraparound porch had been newly painted this year, a forest green that complemented the walnut-stained shingles. Big mullioned windows ran the length of the lower floor; above, where the owners lived, the smaller, original windows had been left alone.

Between the house and the lake was a strip of grass as wide as a football field. It boasted a Lincoln Log–type swing set/play area, a permanent croquet course, a badminton court, a swimming pool, and a boat-rental shed. Off to the left were the four cabins, each with a wraparound porch and floor-to-ceiling windows.

Alison ran on ahead. Her little feet barely made a noise on the steps as she hurried up. She wrenched the screen door open. It banged shut behind her.

Claire smiled and quickened her pace. She opened the screen door just in time to hear Happy Parks say, "—can't be little Ali Kat Cavenaugh. You're too big to be her."

Alison giggled. "I'm gonna be a first grader. I can count to one thousand. Wanna hear?" She immediately launched into counting. "One. Two. Three . . ."

Happy, a beautiful, silver-haired woman who'd run this campground for more than three decades, smiled over Alison's head at Claire.

"One hundred and one. One hundred and two . . ."

Happy clapped. "That's wonderful, Ali. It's good to have you back, Claire. How's life at River's Edge?"

"We got the new cabin done. That makes eight now. I just hope the economy doesn't hurt us. There's that talk of a gas price hike."

"Two hundred. Two hundred and one . . ."

"We sure haven't seen a drop-off," Happy said. "But we're like you—all returning guests. Year after year. Which reminds me: Gina is already here. So is Charlotte. The only one missing is Karen. And this is your year for the honeymoon cabin."

"Yep. The last time Alison slept in the big cabin, she was in a Portacrib."

"We get the TV," Alison said, jumping up and down. Counting was forgotten for the moment. "I brought *tons* of movies."

"Only one hour a day," Claire reminded her daughter, knowing it was a mantra that would be repeated at least ten times a day for the next week. Her daughter could literally watch *The Little Mermaid* 24/7.

Behind them, the screen door screeched open. A group of children burst through the door laughing, followed by six adults.

Happy slid a key across the desk. "You can fill out the paperwork later. I have a feeling this is a group of site hunters. They'll want a photo tour of each site before they commit."

Claire understood. The River's Edge Resort had only a minimum number of campsites—nineteen—and she doled out the good ones carefully. If she liked the guest, she put them near the restrooms and the river. If not . . . well, it could be a long walk to the toilets on a rainy night. She slapped the worn pine counter. "Come over for drinks one night."

"With you crazy girls?" Happy grinned. "I wouldn't miss it for the world."

Claire handed Alison the key. "Here you go, Ali Kat. You're in charge. Show us the way."

With a yelp, Ali was off. She zigzagged through the now-crowded lobby and burst outside. This time her feet slapped the porch steps.

Claire hurried along behind her. As soon as they'd gotten their luggage from the car, they raced across the expanse of lawn, past the boat-rental shed, and plunged into the trees. The ground here was hard-packed dirt, carpeted with a hundred years' worth of pine needles.

Finally, they came to the clearing. A silvery wooden dock floated on the wavy blue water, tilting from side to side in a gentle rocking motion. Far out, across the lake, a white condo grouping sat amid the golden humps of the distant foothills.

"Clara Bella!"

Claire tented a hand over her eyes and looked around.

Gina stood at the shoreline, waving.

Even from here, Claire could see the size of the drink in her friend's hand.

This would be Gina's intervention week. Usually Gina was the conservative one, the buoy that held everyone up, but she'd finalized her divorce a few months ago and she was adrift. A single woman in a paired-up world. Last week, her ex-husband had moved in with a younger woman.

"Hurry up, Ali!" That was Gina's six-year-old daughter, Bonnie.

Alison dropped her Winnie-the-Pooh backpack and peeled off her clothes.

"Alison—"

She proudly showed off her yellow bathing suit. "I'm ready, Mommy."

"Come here, honey," Gina said, pulling out an industrial-size plastic tube of sunscreen. Within moments, she'd slathered Alison all over and released her.

"Don't go in past your belly button," Claire said, dropping their suitcases right there, in the sand.

Alison grimaced. "Aw, Mommy," she whined, then ran for the water, splashing in to join Bonnie.

Claire sat down beside Gina in the golden sand. "What time did you get here?"

Gina laughed. "On time, of course. That's one thing I've learned this year. Your life can fall apart, frigging *explode*, but you're still who you are. Maybe even more so. I'm the kind of woman who gets some-place on time."

"There's nothing wrong with that."

"Rex would disagree. He always said I wasn't spontaneous enough. I thought it meant he wanted sex in the afternoon. Turns out he wanted to skydive." She shook her head, gave Claire a wry smile. "I'd be happy to shove him out of the plane now."

"I'd rig his parachute for him."

They laughed, though it wasn't funny. "How's Bonnie doing?"

"That's the saddest part of all. She barely seems to notice. Rex was never home anyway. I haven't told her that he moved in with another woman, though. How do you tell your kid something like that?" Gina leaned against Claire, who slipped an arm around her friend's ample body. "God, I needed this week."

They were silent for a long moment. The only sound between them was the slapping of the water against the dock and the girls' high-pitched laughter.

Gina turned to her. "How have you done it all these years? Been alone, I mean?"

Claire hadn't thought much about her solitude since Alison's birth. Yes, she'd been alone—in the sense that she'd never been married or lived with a man, but she rarely felt lonely. Oh, she noticed it, ached sometimes for someone to share her life, but she'd made that choice a long time ago. She wouldn't be like her mother. "The upside is, you can always find the TV remote and no one bitches at you to wash the car or park in the perfect spot."

"Seriously, Claire. I need advice."

Claire looked out at Alison, who was standing up to her belly button in the water and jumping up and down, yelling out the ABC song. The sight made Claire's chest tighten. Only yesterday Ali had fit in the crook of her arm. In no time, she'd be asking to have her eyebrow pierced. Claire knew she loved her daughter too much; it was dangerous to need another human being so desperately, but Claire had never known any other way to love. That was why she'd never been married. Men who loved their wives unconditionally were few and far between. In truth, Claire wondered if that kind of true love existed. That doubt was one of many legacies handed down from mother to daughter like an infectious disease. For Mama, divorce had been the answer; for Claire, it was never to say "I do" in the first place.

"You get past being lonely. And you live for your kids," she said softly, surprised to hear regret in her voice. There was so much she'd never dared to reach for.

"Ali shouldn't be your whole world, Claire."

"It's not like I didn't *try* to fall in love. I've dated every single guy in Hayden."

"None of them twice." Gina grinned. "And Bert Shubert is still in love with you. Miss Hauser thinks you're crazy for letting him go."

"It's sad when a fifty-three-year-old plumber with Coke-bottle glasses and a red goatee is considered an eligible bachelor just because he owns an appliance store."

Gina laughed. "Yeah. If I ever tell you I'm going out with Bert, please shoot me." Slowly, her laughter turned to tears. "Aw, *hell*," she said, leaning into Claire's embrace.

"You'll be okay, Gina," Claire whispered, stroking her friend's back. "I promise you will."

"I don't know," Gina said quietly, and something about the way she said it, maybe the softness in a voice that was usually as hard as steel, made Claire feel empty inside. Alone.

Absurdly, she thought about the day her life had changed. When she'd learned that love had a shelf life, a use-by date that could pass suddenly and turn everything sour.

I'm leaving you, her sister had said. Until that moment, Meg had been Claire's best friend, her whole world. More of a mother than Mama had ever been.

And then Claire was crying, too.

Gina sniffed. "No wonder no one wants to sit with me anymore. I'm the princess of darkness. Ten seconds in my company and perfectly happy people start to weep."

Claire wiped her eyes. There was no point in crying about the past. It surprised her, actually, that she had any tears left. She thought she'd made peace with Meg's abandonment long ago. "Remember the year Char fell off the dock because she was crying so hard she couldn't see?"

"Bob's midlife crisis. She thought he was having an affair with their housekeeper."

"And it turned out he was secretly getting hair-plug treatments."

Gina tightened her hold around Claire. "Thank Jesus for the Bluesers. I haven't needed you all this much since I was in labor."

CHAPTER
FOUR

*T*HE INTERCOM BUZZED. "JILL SUMMERVILLE IS HERE TO SEE YOU."

"Send her in."

Meghann grabbed a new yellow legal pad and a pen from the overhead cabinet. By the time Jill was led into the conference room, Meg had returned to her seat and was smiling politely. She rose. "Hello, Jill. I'm Meghann Dontess."

Jill stood near the door, looking ill at ease. She was a pretty woman, thin; maybe fifty. She wore an expensive gray suit with a cream silk shell underneath.

"Come, sit down," Meghann said, indicating the empty chair to her left.

"I'm not certain I want a divorce."

Meghann heard that all the time. "We could talk for a while if you'd like. You could tell me what's going on with your marriage."

Jill sat stiffly in the empty chair. She placed her hands on the table, fingers splayed, as if she were afraid the wood might levitate. "It's not good," she said softly. "I've been married for twenty-six years. But I can't. Do it. Anymore. We don't talk at all. We've become one of those couples who go out to dinner and sit silently across from each other. I saw my parents do that. I swore I never would. I'm going to be fifty next year. It's time I have *my* life."

The second-chance-at-life reason for divorce. It was number two, beaten only by that perennial favorite: He's cheating on me. "Everyone deserves to be happy," Meg said, feeling strangely remote. On autopilot, she reeled off a series of questions and statements designed to elicit solid information as well as inspire trust. Meg could tell that she was doing well on both counts. Jill had begun to relax. Occasionally, she even smiled.

"And how about assets? Do you have an idea of your net worth?"

"Beatrice DeMille told me you'd ask that." She opened her Fendi briefcase and pulled out a packet of papers that were stapled together, then pushed them across the table. "My husband and I started the Internet company Emblazon. We sold out to AOL at the top of the market. That, combined with the lesser companies and homes, puts our net worth at somewhere around seventy-two million."

Seventy-two million dollars.

Meghann held on to her ordinary smile by dint of will, afraid that her mouth would drop open. This was the biggest case ever to fall in her lap. She'd waited her whole career for a case like this. It was supposed to be the trade-off for all of the sleepless nights she'd spent worrying over clients who couldn't pay their bills. Her favorite law professor used to say that the law was the same regardless of the zeroes. Meg knew better: The legal system favored women like Jill.

They should probably hire a media consultant. A case like this could generate a lot of publicity.

She should have been excited by the prospect, energized. Surprisingly, she felt detached. Even a little sad. She knew that, for all her millions, Jill was still a woman about to be broken.

Meg reached for the phone and pressed the intercom button. "Rhona, bring me the lawyer lists. Seattle. L.A. San Francisco. New York and Chicago."

Jill frowned. "But . . . ," she paused when the secretary came into the room, carrying a sheet of paper.

"Thanks." Meghann handed the paper to Jill. "These twenty lawyers are the best in the country."

"I don't understand."

"Once you've spoken to them, they can't represent your husband. It's a conflict of interest."

Jill's gaze flicked over the list, then slowly lifted. "I see. This is divorce strategy."

"Simply planning ahead. In case."

"Is this ethical?"

"Of course. As a consumer, you have every right to get second opinions. I'll need a retainer—say twenty-five thousand dollars—and I'll use ten thousand of that to hire the best forensic accountants in Seattle."

Jill looked at her for a long moment, saying nothing. Finally, she nodded and stood up. "I'll go see everyone on your list. But I assume that if I choose you, you'll represent me."

"Of course." She remembered at the last minute to add, "But hopefully you won't need me."

"Yes," Jill said, "I can see that you're the hopeful type."

Meghann sighed. "I know people all across this country are happily married. They just don't come to see me, but I do hope—honestly—that I won't see you again."

Jill gave her a sad, knowing look, and Meghann knew: The decision might be soft around the edges and filled with regret, but it had been made.

"You go ahead and hope, then," Jill said softly. "For both of us."

"You don't look good."

Sprawled in the black leather chair, Meghann didn't move. "So, that's why I pay you two hundred dollars an hour. To insult me. Tell me I smell, too. Then I'll really get my money's worth."

"Why do you pay me?"

"I consider it a charitable deduction."

Dr. Bloom didn't smile. She sat—as always, chameleon still—watching. If it wasn't for the compassion in her dark brown eyes, she could easily be mistaken for a statue. It was often that compassion—an emotion that bordered on pity—that undid Meghann. Over the past twenty years, Meg had seen a constant stream of shrinks. Always psychiatrists, never counselors or psychologists. First off, she believed in a surplus of education. Second, and more important, she wanted to talk to someone who could dispense drugs.

In her thirties, Meg had gone through a new shrink every two years. She never told them anything that mattered, and they always returned the favor.

Then she'd stumbled across Harriet Bloom, the stone queen who could sit quietly for an entire hour, take the check, and tell Meghann it was her money to spend wisely or throw away.

Harriet, who'd uncovered a few artifacts of the past that mattered, and surmised some of the rest. A dozen times in the past year, Meghann had decided to sever their relationship, but every time she started to actually do it, she panicked and changed her mind.

The silence was gaining weight.

"Okay, I look like shit. I'll admit it. I haven't been sleeping well. I need more pills, by the way."

"That prescription should last for another two weeks."

Meghann couldn't make eye contact. "A couple of times this week, I needed two. The insomnia . . . it really rips me. Sometimes I can't take it."

"Why do you think you can't sleep?"

"Why do *you* think I can't sleep? That's the relevant opinion, isn't it?"

Dr. Bloom studied her. She was so still it seemed impossible that her lungs were functioning. "Is it?"

"I have trouble sleeping sometimes. That's all. Big deal."

"And you use drugs and strangers to help you through the night."

"I don't pick up as many men as I used to. But sometimes . . ." She looked up, saw a sad understanding in Harriet's eyes. It pissed her off. "Don't look at me that way."

Harriet leaned forward, rested her elbows on the table. Her steepled fingers brushed the underside of her chin. "You use sex to dispel loneliness. But what's lonelier than anonymous sex?"

"At least when the guys leave my bed, I don't care."

"Eric again."

"Eric."

Harriet sat back. "You were married for less than a year."

"Don't minimize it, Harriet. He broke my heart."

"Of course he did. And you suck on that candy every day in your practice, as women tell you their sad and similar stories. But the flavor has been gone for years. You're not worried about someone breaking your heart again. You're worried you don't have a heart to break. The bottom line is, you're scared, and fear isn't an emotion that fits well with your need to control."

It was true. Meg was tired of being alone and terrified that her life would be a stretch of empty road. A part of her wanted to nod her head, to say yes, and beg for a way to shed her fear. But that was a thin, reedy voice lost amid the screaming blare of self-preservation. The bedrock lesson of her life was that love didn't last. It was better to be lonely and strong than heartbroken and weak.

Her voice, when she found it, was honed and tight. "I had a difficult week at the office. I'm getting impatient with my clients. I can't seem to feel for them the way I used to."

Harriet was too professional to show her disappointment with something as obvious as a sigh or a frown. Her only reaction was to unsteeple her fingers. That oozing, uncomfortable compassion was back in her eyes, though. That poor-Meghann-so-afraid-of-intimacy look. "Your emotions feel distant and inaccessible? Why do you think that would be?"

"As an attorney, I'm trained to see things dispassionately."

"Yet we both know that the best lawyers are compassionate. And you, Meghann, are an extremely good attorney."

They were on safe ground again, although it could get slippery again in a second. "That's what I've been trying to tell you. I'm not as good as I used to be. I used to *help* people. Even care about them."

"And now?"

"I'm some balance-sheet automaton who moves through the day crunching finances and spitting out settlements. I find myself hashing and rehashing canned speeches to women whose lives are falling apart. I used to be pissed off at the husbands. Now I'm just tired. It's not a game—I take it too seriously still for that—but it's . . . not real life, either. Not to me."

"You might consider a vacation."

"A what?" Meghann smiled. They both knew that relaxation didn't come easily.

"A vacation. Ordinary people take weeks in Hawaii or Aspen."

"Dissatisfaction isn't something you can run away from. Isn't that Psychology 101?"

"I'm not suggesting you run away. I'm suggesting you give yourself a break. Maybe get a tan. You could spend a few days at your sister's place in the mountains."

"Claire and I aren't likely to vacation together."

"You're afraid to talk to her."

"I'm not afraid of anything. Claire's a campground manager in Podunk. We have nothing in common."

"You have history."

"None of it good. Believe me, the tour bus driver of Claire's life would hit the gas and keep driving when he came to our childhood years."

"But you love Claire. That must count for something."

"Yeah," Meg said slowly. "I love her. That's why I stay away." She glanced down at her watch. "Oh, damn. Hour's up. See you next week."

CHAPTER FIVE

JOE STOOD AT THE CORNER OF FIRST AND MAIN, LOOKING DOWN THE street at a town whose name he couldn't remember. He shifted his backpack around, resettled it on his other shoulder. Beneath the strap, his shirt was soaked with sweat and his skin was clammy. In the windless, baking air, he could smell himself. It wasn't good. This morning he'd walked at least seven miles. No one had offered him a ride. No surprise there. The longer—and grayer—his hair got, the fewer rides he was offered. Only the long-haul truckers could be counted on anymore, and they'd been few and far between on this hot Sunday morning.

Up ahead, he saw a hand-painted sign for the Wake Up Café.

He dug into his pocket and pulled out his wallet, a soft, smooth, lambskin artifact from his previous life. Flipping it open, he barely looked at the single photograph in the plastic square as he opened the side slit.

Twelve dollars and seventy-two cents. He'd need to find work today. The money he'd earned in Yakima was almost gone.

He turned into the café. At his entrance, a bell tinkled over-head.

Every head turned to look at him.

The clattering din of conversation died abruptly. The only sounds came from the kitchen, clanging, scraping.

He knew how he looked to them: an unkempt vagrant with shoulder-length silver hair and clothes that needed a heavy wash cycle. His Levi's had faded to a pale, pale blue, and his T-shirt was stained with perspiration. Though his forty-third birthday was next week, he looked sixty. And there was the smell. . . .

He snagged a laminated menu from the slot beside the cash register and walked through the diner, head down, to the last bar stool on the left. He'd learned not to sit too close to the "good people" in any of the towns in which he stopped. Sometimes the presence of a man who'd fallen on hard times was offensive. In those towns it was too damn easy to find your ass on a jail-cell cot. He'd spent enough time in jail already.

The waitress stood back by the grill, dressed in a splotchy, stained pink polyester uniform. Like everyone else in the place, she was staring at him.

He sat quietly, his body tensed.

Then, as if a switch had been flipped, the noise returned.

The waitress pulled a pen out from above her ear and came toward him. When she got closer, he noticed that she was younger than he'd thought. Maybe still in high school, even. Her long brown hair, drawn back in a haphazard ponytail, was streaked with purple, and a small gold hoop clung precariously to her overly plucked eyebrow. She wore more makeup than Boy George.

"What can I getcha?" She wrinkled her nose and stepped backward.

"I guess I need a shower, huh?"

"You could use one." She smiled, then leaned a fraction of an inch closer. "The KOA campground is your best bet. They have a killer bathroom. 'Course it's for guests only, but nobody much watches." She popped her gum and whispered, "The door code is twenty-one hundred. All the locals know it."

"Thank you." He looked at her name tag. "Brandy."

She poised a pen at the small notepad. "Now, whaddaya want?"

He didn't bother looking at the menu. "I'll have a bran muffin, fresh fruit—whatever you have—and a bowl of oatmeal. Oh. And a glass of orange juice."

"No bacon or eggs?"

"Nope."

She shrugged and started to turn away. He stopped her by saying, "Brandy?"

"Yeah?"

"Where could a guy like me find some work?"

She looked at him. "A guy like you?" The tone was obvious. She'd figured he didn't work, just begged and drifted. "I'd try the Tip Top Apple Farm. They always need people. And Yardbirds—they mow lawns for the vacation rentals."

"Thanks."

Joe sat there, on that surprisingly comfortable bar stool, long after he should have gone. He ate his breakfast as slowly as possible, chewing every bite forever, but finally his bowl and plate were empty.

He knew it was time to move on, but he couldn't make himself get up. Last night he'd slept tucked along a fallen log in some farmer's back pasture. Between the howling wind and a sudden rainstorm, it had been an uncomfortable night. His whole body ached today. Now, for once, he was warm but not hot, and his stomach was full, and he was sitting comfortably. It was a moment of Heaven.

"You gotta go," Brandy whispered as she swept past him. "My boss says he's gonna call the cops if you keep hanging around."

Joe could have argued, could have pointed out that he'd paid for breakfast and could legally sit here. An ordinary person certainly had that right.

Instead, he said, "Okay," and put six bucks on the pink Formica counter.

He slowly got to his feet. For a second, he felt dizzy. When the bout passed, he grabbed his backpack and slung it over his shoulder.

Outside, the heat hit him hard, knocking him back. It took a supreme act of will to start walking.

He kept his thumb out, but no one picked him up. Slowly, his strength sapped by the hundred-degree heat, he walked in the direction Brandy had given him. By the time he reached the KOA Campground, he had a pounding headache and his throat hurt.

There was nothing he wanted to do more than walk down that gravel road, duck into the bathroom for a long hot shower, and then rent a cabin for a much-needed rest.

"Impossible," he said aloud, thinking of the six bucks in his wallet. It was a habit he'd acquired lately: talking to himself. Otherwise, he sometimes went days without hearing another human voice.

He'd have to sneak into the bathroom, and he couldn't do it when people were everywhere.

He crept into a thicket of pine trees behind the lodge. The shade felt good. He eased deep into the woods until he couldn't be seen; then he sat down with his back rested against a pine tree. His head pounded at the movement, small as it was, and he closed his eyes.

He was awakened hours later by the sound of laughter. There were several children running through the campsites, shrieking. The smell of smoke—campfires—was heavy in the air.

Dinnertime.

He blinked awake, surprised that he'd slept so long. He waited until the sun set and the campground was quiet, then he got to his feet. Holding his backpack close, he crept cautiously toward the log structure that housed the campground's rest room and laundry facilities.

He was reaching out to punch in the code when a woman appeared beside him. Just . . . appeared.

He froze, turning slowly.

She stood there, wearing a bright blue bathing suit top and a pair of cutoff shorts, holding a stack of pink towels. Her sandy blond hair was a mass of drying curls. She'd been laughing as she approached the bathrooms, but when she saw him her smile faded.

Damn. He'd been close to a hot shower—his first in weeks. Now, any minute, this beautiful woman would scream for the manager.

Very softly, she said, "The code is twenty-one hundred. Here." She handed him a towel, then went into the women's bathroom and closed the door.

It took him a moment to move, that was how deeply her kindness had affected him. Finally, holding the towel close, he punched in the code and hurried into the men's bathroom. It was empty.

He took a long, hot shower, then dressed in the cleanest clothes he had, and washed his dirty clothes in the sink. As he brushed his teeth, he stared at himself in the mirror. His hair was too long and shaggy, and he'd gone almost completely gray. He hadn't been able to shave this morning, so his sunken cheeks were shadowed by a thick stubble. The bags beneath his eyes were carry-on size. He was like a piece of fruit, slowly going bad from the inside out.

He finger-combed the hair back from his face and turned away from the mirror. Really, it was better not to look. All it did was remind him of the old days, when he'd been young and vain, when he'd been careful to keep up appearances. Then, he'd thought a lot of unimportant things mattered.

He went to the door, opened it a crack, and peered out. There was no one nearby, so he slipped into the darkness.

It was completely dark now. A full moon hung over the lake, casting a rippled glow across the waves and illuminating the cabins along the shore. Three of them were brightly lit from within. In one of them, he could see people moving around inside; it looked as if they were dancing. And suddenly, he wanted to be in that cabin, to be part of that circle of people who cared about one another.

"You're losing it, Joe," he said, wishing he could laugh about it the way he once would have. But there was a lump in his throat that made smiling impossible.

He slipped into the cover of the trees and kept moving. As he passed behind one of the cabins, he heard music. "Stayin' Alive" by the Bee Gees. Then he heard the sound of childish laughter. "Dance with me, Daddy," a little girl said loudly.

He forced himself to keep moving. With each step taken, the sound of laughter diminished until, by the time he reached the edge of the woods, he had to strain to hear it at all. He found a soft bed of pine needles and sat down. Moonlight glowed around him, turning the world into a smear of blue-white and black.

He unzipped his backpack and burrowed through the damp, wadded-up clothes, looking for the two items that mattered.

Three years ago, when he'd first run away, he'd carried an expensive suitcase. He still remembered standing in his bedroom, packing for a trip without destination or duration, wondering what a man in exile would need. He'd packed khaki slacks and merino wool sweaters and even a black Joseph Abboud suit.

By the end of his first winter alone, he'd understood that those clothes were the archaeological remains of a forgotten life. Useless. All he needed in his new life were two pair of jeans, a few T-shirts, a sweatshirt, and a rain slicker. Everything else he'd given to charity.

The only expensive garment he'd kept was a pink cashmere sweater with tiny shell buttons. On a good night, he could still smell her perfume in the soft fabric.

He withdrew a small, leatherbound photo album from the backpack. With shaking fingers, he opened the front cover.

The first picture was one of his favorites.

In it, Diana sat on a patch of grass, wearing a pair of white shorts and a Yale T-shirt. There was a stack of books open beside her, and a mound of pink cherry blossoms covered the pages. She was smiling so brightly he had to blink back tears. "Hey, baby," he whispered, touching the glossy covering. "I had a hot shower tonight."

He closed his eyes. In the darkness, she came to him. It was happening more and more often lately, this sensation that she hadn't left him, that she was still here. He knew it was a crack in his mind, a mental defect. He didn't care.

"I'm tired," he said to her, breathing in deeply, savoring the scent of her perfume. Red by Giorgio. He wondered if they made it any-more.

It's no good, what you're doing.

"I don't know what else to do."

Go home.

"I can't."

You break my heart, Joey.

And she was gone.

With a sigh, he leaned back against a big tree stump.

Go home, she'd said. It was what she always said to him.

What he said to himself.

Maybe tomorrow, he thought, reaching for the kind of courage that would make it possible. God knew after three years on the road, he was tired of being this alone.

Maybe tomorrow he would finally—finally—allow himself to start walking west.

Diana would like that.

CHAPTER SIX

*L*IKE SUNSHINE, NIGHT BROUGHT OUT THE BEST IN SEATTLE. THE highway—a bumper-to-bumper nightmare at morning rush hour—became, at night, a glittering red-and-gold Chinese dragon that curled along the blackened banks of Lake Union. The cluster of high-rises in the city's midtown heart, so ordinary in the gray haze on a June day, was a kaleidoscope of sculpted color when night fell.

Meghann stood at her office window. She never failed to be mesmerized by this view. The water was a black stain that consumed nearby Bainbridge Island. Though she couldn't see the streets below, she knew they were clogged. Traffic was the curse Seattle had carried into the new millennium. Millions of people had moved into the once-sleepy town, drawn by the quality of life and the variety of outdoor activities. Unfortunately, after they built expensive cul-de-sac homes in the suburbs, they took jobs in the city. Roads designed for an out-of-the-way port town couldn't possibly keep up.

Progress.

Meghann glanced down at her watch. It was 8:30. Time to head home. She'd bring the Wanamaker file with her. Get a jump on tomorrow.

Behind her, the door opened. Ana, the cleaning woman, pushed her supply cart into the room, dragging a vacuum cleaner alongside. "Hello, Miss Dontess."

Meghann smiled. No matter how often she told Ana to call her Meghann, the woman never did. "Good evening, Ana. How's Raul?"

"Tomorrow we find out if he get stationed at McChord. We keep our fingers crossed, ¿sí?"

"It would be great to have your son so close," Meghann said as she gathered up her files.

Ana mumbled something. It sounded a lot like, "You should have a son nearby, too. Instead of all that work, work, work."

"Are you chastising me again, Ana?"

"I don't know chastising. But you work too hard. Every night you're here. When you gonna meet Mr. Right if you always at work?"

It was an old debate, one that had started almost ten years ago, when Meghann had handled Ana's INS hearing pro bono. Her last moment of peace had ended when she handed Ana a green card and hired her. Ever since, Ana had done her best to "repay" Meghann. That repayment seemed to be an endless stream of casseroles and a constant harangue about the evils of too much hard work.

"You're right, Ana. I think I'll have a drink and unwind."

"Drink isn't what I'm thinking," Ana muttered, bending down to plug in the vacuum.

"Bye, Ana."

Meghann was almost to the elevator when her cell phone rang. She rifled through her black Kate Spade bag and pulled out the phone. "Meghann Dontess," she said.

"Meghann?" The voice was high-pitched and panicky. "It's May Monroe."

Meghann was instantly alert. A divorce could go bad faster than an open cut in the tropics. "What's going on?"

"It's Dale. He came by tonight."

Meghann made a mental note to get a TRO first thing tomorrow. "Uh-huh. What happened?"

"He said something about the papers he got today. He was crazy. What did you send him?"

"We talked about this, May. On the phone, last week, remember? I notified Dale's lawyer and the court that we'd be contesting the fraudulent transfer of his business and demanding an accounting of the Cayman Island accounts. I also told his attorney that we were aware of the affair with the child's piano instructor and that such behavior might threaten his suitability as a parent."

"We never discussed that. You threatened to take away his children?"

"Believe me, May, the temper tantrum is about money. It always is. The kids are a shill game with guys like your husband. Pretend to want custody and you'll get more money. It's a common tactic."

"You think you know my husband better than I do."

Meghann had heard this sentence more times than she could count. It always amazed her. Women who were blindsided by their husband's affairs, lies, and financial gymnastics continually believed that they "knew" their men. Yet another reason not to get married. It wasn't masturbation that made you go blind; it was love. "I don't have to know him," Meghann answered, using the canned speech she'd perfected long ago. "Protecting you is my job. If I upset your"—no good, lying—"husband in the process, that's an unfortunate necessity. He'll calm down. They always do."

"You don't know Dale," she said again.

Meghann's senses pounced on some nuance. Something wasn't right. "Are you scared of him, May?" This was a whole new wrinkle.

"Scared?" May tried to sound surprised by the question, but Meghann knew. Damn. She was always surprised by spousal abuse; it was never the families you expected.

"Does he hit you, May?"

"Sometimes when he's drinking, I can say just the wrong thing."

Oh, yeah. It's May's fault. It was terrifying how often women believed that. "Are you okay now?"

"He didn't hit me. And he never hits the children."

Meghann didn't say what came to mind. Instead, she said, "That's good." If she'd been with May, she would have been able to look in her client's eyes and take a measure of the woman's fragility. If it seemed possible, she would have given her statistics—horror stories designed to drive home the ugly truth. Often, if a man would hit his wife, he'd get around to hitting his children. Bullies were bullies; their defining characteristic was the need to exert power over the powerless. Who was more powerless than a child?

But none of that could be done over the phone. Sometimes a client sounded strong and in control while they were falling apart. Meghann had visited too many of her clients in psych wards and hospitals. She'd grown careful over the years.

"We need to make sure he understands that I'm not going to take his children from him. Otherwise he'll go crazy," May said. There was the barest crack in her voice.

"Let me ask you this, May. Say it's three months from now. You're divorced, and Dale has lost half of everything he owns. He's living with Dance Hall Barbie and they come home drunk one night. Barbie's driving because she only had three margaritas. When they get home, the baby-sitter has let the kids demolish the house and little Billy has accidentally broken the window in Dale's office. Are your children safe?"

"That's a lot of things going wrong."

"Things go wrong, May. You know that. I'm guessing that you've always been a buffer between your husband and kids. A human shock absorber. You probably learned how to calm him down and deflect his attention away from the children. Will Barbie know how to protect them?"

"Am I so ordinary?"

"Sadly, the situation is. The good news is, you're giving yourself—and your children—a new start. Don't weaken now, May. Don't let him bully you."

"So, what do I do?"

"Lock the doors and turn off the phone. Don't talk to him. If you don't feel safe, go to a relative's or friend's house. Or to a motel for one night. Tomorrow we'll get together and come up with a new game plan. I'll file some restraining orders."

"You can keep us safe?"

"You'll be fine, May. Trust me. Bullies are cowards. Once he sees how strong you can be, he'll back down."

"Okay. When can we meet?"

Meghann dug through her bag for her PalmPilot, then checked her schedule. "How about a late lunch—say two o'clock—at the Judicial Annex Café by the courthouse? I'll schedule a meeting with Dale's lawyer for later that afternoon."

"Okay."

"May, I know this is a sensitive question, but do you by any chance have a photograph of yourself . . . you know . . . when he hit you?"

There was a pause on the other end of the line, then May said, "I'll check my photo albums."

"It's simply evidence," Meg said.

"To you, maybe."

"I'm sorry, May. I wish I didn't have to ask questions like that."

"No. *I'm* sorry," May said.

That surprised Meg. "What for?"

"That no man has ever shown you the other side. My father would have killed Dale for all of this."

Before she could stop it, Meghann felt a sharp jab of longing. It was her Achilles' heel. She was sure she didn't believe in love, but still, she dreamed of it. Maybe May was right. Maybe if Meg had had a father who'd loved her, everything would be different. As it was, she knew that love was a rope bridge made of the thinnest strands. It might hold your weight for a while, but sooner or later, it would break.

Oh, there were happy marriages. Her best friend, Elizabeth, had proven that.

There were also forty-eight-million-dollar-lottery winners, five-leaf clovers, Siamese twins, and full eclipses of the sun.

"So, we'll meet at the Annex tomorrow at two?"

"I'll see you there."

"Good." Meghann flipped the phone shut and dropped it in her purse, then pushed the elevator button. When the door opened, she stepped inside. As always, the mirrored walls made it feel as if she were stumbling into herself. She leaned forward, unable to stop herself; when a mirror was near, she had to look into it. In the past few years, she'd begun to search obsessively for signs of aging. Lines, wrinkles, sags.

She was forty-two years old, and since it felt as if she'd been thirty a moment ago, she had to assume it would be a blink's worth of time before she was fifty.

That depressed her. She imagined herself at sixty. Alone, working from dawn to dusk, talking to her neighbor's cats, and going on singles' cruises.

She left the elevator and strode through the lobby, nodding at the night doorman as she passed.

Outside, the night was beautiful; an amethyst sky gave everything a pink and pearlized glow. Lit windows in towering skyscrapers proved that Meghann wasn't the only workaholic in the city.

She walked briskly down the street, bypassing people without making eye contact. At her building, she paused and looked up.

There was her deck. The only one in the building without potted trees and outdoor furniture. The windows behind it were black; the rest of the building was a blaze of light. Friends and families were in those lighted spaces, having dinner, watching television, talking, making love. Connecting with one another.

I'm sorry, May had said, *that no man has ever shown you the other side.*

I'm sorry.

Meghann walked past her building. She didn't want to go up there, put on her old UW sweats, eat Raisin Bran for dinner, and watch a rerun of *Third Watch*.

She went into the Public Market. At this late hour, pretty much everything was closed up. The fish vendors had gone home, and the dewy, beautiful vegetables had been boxed up until tomorrow. The stalls—normally filled with dried flowers, handmade crafts, and homemade food items—were empty.

She turned into the Athenian, the old-fashioned tavern made famous in *Sleepless in Seattle*. It was at this polished wooden bar that Rob Reiner had told Tom Hanks about dating in the nineties.

The smoke in here was so thick you could have played ticktacktoe in it with your finger. There was something comforting in the lack of political correctness in the Athenian. You could order a trendy drink, but their specialty was ice-cold beer.

Meghann had perfected the art of scoping out a bar without being obvious. She did that now.

There were five or six older men at the bar. Fishermen, she'd guess, getting ready to head up to Alaska for the season. A pair of younger Wall Street types were there, too, drinking martinis and no doubt talking shop. She saw enough of that kind in court.

"Hey, Meghann," yelled Freddie, the bartender. "Your usual?"

"You bet." Still smiling, she moved past the bar and turned left, where several varnished wooden tables hugged the two walls. Most were full of couples or foursomes; a few were empty.

Meghann found a place in the back. She sidled into the glossy wooden seat and sat down. A big window was to her left. The view was of Elliot Bay and the wharf.

"Here ye be," Freddie said, setting a martini glass down in front of her. He shook the steel shaker, then poured her a cosmopolitan. "You want an order of oysters and fries?"

"You read my mind."

Freddie grinned. "Ain't hard to do, counselor." He leaned down toward her. "The Eagles are coming in tonight. Should be here any minute."

"The Eagles?"

"The minor league ball team outta Everett." He winked at her. "Good luck."

Meghann groaned. It was bad when bartenders started recommending whole ball teams.

I'm sorry.

Meghann began drinking. When the first cosmo was gone, she ordered a second. By the time she saw the bottom of the glass again, she'd almost forgotten her day.

"May I join you?"

Meghann looked up, startled, and found herself staring into a pair of dark eyes.

He stood in front of her, with one foot up on the seat opposite her. She could tell by the look of him—young, blond, sexy as hell—that he was used to getting what he wanted. And what he wanted tonight was her.

The thought was a tonic.

"Of course." She didn't offer a half smile or bat her eyes. Pretense had never appealed to her. Neither had games. "I'm Meghann Dontess. My friends call me Meg."

He slid into the seat. His knees brushed hers, and at the contact, he smiled. "I'm Donny MacMillan. You like baseball?"

"I like a lot of things." She flagged down Freddie, who nodded at her. A moment later, he brought her another cosmopolitan.

"I'll have a Coors Light," Donny said, leaning back and stretching his arms out along the top of the seat back.

They stared at each other in silence. The noise in the bar grew louder, then seemed to fade away, until all Meghann could hear was the even strains of his breathing and the beating of her heart.

Freddie served a beer and left again.

"I suppose you're a baseball player."

He grinned, and *damn*, it was sexy. She felt the first twinge of desire. Sex with him would be great; she knew it. And it would make her forget—

I'm sorry.

—about her bad day.

"You know it. I'm gonna make it to the show. You watch. Someday I'll be famous."

That was why Meghann gravitated toward younger men. They still believed in themselves and the world. They hadn't yet learned how life really worked, how dreams were slowly strangled and right and wrong became abstract ideas instead of goalposts for all to see. Those truths usually hit around thirty-five, when you realized that your life was not what you'd wanted.

That, of course, and the fact that they never demanded more than she wanted to give. Men her age tended to think sex meant something. Younger men knew better.

For the next hour, Meghann nodded and smiled as Donny talked about himself. By the time she'd finished her fourth drink, she knew that he had graduated from WSU, was the youngest of three brothers, and that his parents still lived in the same Iowa farmhouse that his grandfather had homesteaded. It all went in one ear and out the other. What she really focused on was the way his knee brushed up against hers, the way his thumb stroked the wet beer glass in a steady, sensual rhythm.

He was telling her about a frat party in college when she said, "You want to come to my place?"

"For coffee?"

She smiled. "That, too, I guess."

"You don't screw around, do you?"

"I'd say it's quite clear that I do. I simply like to be direct about it. I'm . . . thirty-four years old. My game-playing days are behind me."

He looked at her then, smiling slowly, and the knowing sensuality in his gaze made her engine overheat. *This is going to be good.* "How far away do you live?"

"As luck would have it, not far."

He stood up, reached his hand down to help her up.

She told herself he was being gallant. As opposed to helping the elderly. She placed her hand in his; at the contact a shivery thrill zipped through her.

They didn't talk as they made their way through the now-dark and empty market. There was nothing to say. The niceties had been exchanged, the foreplay initiated. What mattered from this point on had more to do with bare skin than baring questions.

The doorman at Meghann's building did his job wordlessly. If he noticed that this was the second young man she'd brought home in the last month, he showed no signs of it.

"Evening, Ms. Dontess," he said, nodding.

"Hans," she acknowledged, leading—*Oh, God, what was his name?*

Donny. As in Osmond.

She wished she hadn't made that connection.

They stepped into the elevator. The minute the door closed, he turned to her. She heard the little catch in her breathing as he leaned toward her.

His lips were as soft and sweet as she'd thought they would be.

The elevator pinged at the penthouse floor. He started to pull away from her, but she wouldn't let him. "I'm the only apartment on this floor," she whispered against his mouth. Still kissing him, she reached into her bag and pulled at her keys.

Locked together, they centipeded toward the door and stumbled through it.

"This way." Her voice was harsh, gruff, as she led him toward the bedroom. Once there, she started unbuttoning her blouse. He tried to reach for her but she pushed his hand away.

When she was naked, she looked at him. The room was dark, shadowy, just the way she liked it.

His face was a blur. She opened her nightstand drawer and found a condom.

"Come here," he said, reaching out.

"Oh. I intend to come. Here." She walked toward him slowly, holding her tummy as taut as possible.

He touched her left breast. Her nipple immediately responded. The ache between her legs graduated, deepened.

She reached down, took hold of him, and began stroking.

After that, everything happened fast. They fell on each other like animals, scratching, humping, groaning. Behind them, the headboard banged against the wall. Her orgasm, when it finally happened, was sharp and painful and faded much too quickly.

She was left feeling vaguely dissatisfied. That was happening more and more often. She lay back onto the pillows. He was beside her, so close she could feel the warmth of his bare flesh alongside her thigh.

He was right next to her, and yet she felt alone. Here they were, in bed together, with the scent of their sex still in the air, and she couldn't think of a single thing to say to him.

She rolled over and moved closer to him. Before she quite knew what she was doing, she'd cuddled up alongside him. It was the first time she'd done something so intimate in years.

"Tell me something about you no one knows," she said, sliding her naked leg across his.

He laughed softly. "I guess you live in Bizarro World, where they do everything backward, huh? First you screw my brains out, *then* you want to know me. In the bar, you were practically yawning when I told you about my family."

She drew away from him, pulled back into herself. "I don't like to be ordinary." She was surprised by how okay she sounded.

"You're not, believe me."

He pushed her leg aside and kissed her shoulder. The brush-off. Frankly, she preferred it without the kiss.

"I gotta go."

"So, go."

He frowned. "Don't sound pissed off. It's not like we fell in love tonight."

She reached down to the floor for her Seahawks nightshirt and put it on. She was less vulnerable dressed. "You don't know me well enough to know whether I'm pissed off. And frankly, I can't imagine falling in love with someone who used the term 'ball handling' as often as you did."

"Jesus." He got out of bed and started dressing. She sat in bed, very stiffly, watching him. She wished she had a book on her night-stand. It would have been nice to start reading now.

"If you keep bearing left, you'll find the front door."

His frown deepened. "Are you on medication?"

She laughed at that.

"Because you should be." He started to leave—almost breaking into a run, she noticed—but at the door, he paused and turned around. "I liked you, you know."

Then he was gone.

Meg heard the front door open and click shut. She finally re-leased a heavy breath.

It used to take weeks, months even, before men began to ask if she was medicated. Now she'd managed to completely alienate Danny—*Donny*—in a single night.

She was losing her grip. Life seemed to be unraveling around her. Hell, she couldn't remember the last time she'd kissed a man and felt something more than desire.

And what about loneliness? Dr. Bloom had asked her. *Do you like that, too?*

She leaned sideways and flicked on the bedside lamp. Light fell on a framed photograph of Meghann and her sister, taken years ago.

Meghann wondered what her sister was doing right now. Won-dered if she was awake at this late hour, feeling alone and vulnera-ble. But she knew the answer.

Claire had Alison. And Sam.

Sam.

Meghann wished she could forget the few memories she had of her sister's father. But that kind of amnesia never overtook her. In-stead, Meghann remembered everything, every detail. Mostly, she re-membered how much she'd wanted Sam to be her father, too. When she'd been young and hopeful, she'd thought: *Maybe we could be a family, the three of us.*

The pipe dreams of a child. Still painful after all these years.

Sam was *Claire's* father. He had stepped in and changed every-thing. Meg and Claire had nothing in common anymore.

Claire lived in a house filled with laughter and love. She probably only dated upstanding leaders of the community. No anonymous, dissatisfying sex for Claire.

Meghann closed her eyes, reminding herself that *this* was the life she wanted. She'd tried marriage. It had ended exactly as she'd feared—with his betrayal and her broken heart. She didn't ever want to experience that again. If sometimes she spent an hour or so in the middle of the night with an ache of longing that wouldn't quite go away, well, that was the price of independence.

She leaned across the bed and picked up the phone. There were five numbers on her speed dialer: the office, three take-out restaurants, and her best friend, Elizabeth Shore.

She punched in number three.

"What's the matter?" said a groggy male voice. "Jamie?"

Meghann glanced at the bedside clock. *Damn.* It was almost midnight; that made it nearly three o'clock in New York. "Sorry, Jack. I didn't notice the time."

"For a smart woman, you make that mistake a lot. Just a sec."

Meghann wished she could hang up. She felt exposed by her error. It showed how little a life she had.

"Are you okay?" Elizabeth said, sounding worried.

"I'm fine. I screwed up. Tell Jack I'm sorry. We can talk tomorrow. I'll call before I leave for work."

"Just hang on."

Meghann heard Elizabeth whisper something to her husband. A moment later, she said, "Let me guess. You just got home from the Athenian."

That made her feel even worse. "No. Not tonight."

"Are you okay, Meg?"

"Fine, really. I just lost track of time. I was . . . working on a messy deposition. We'll talk tomorrow."

"Jack and I are leaving for Paris, remember?"

"Oh, yeah. Have a great time."

"I could postpone it—"

"And miss that huge party at the Ritz? No way. Have a wonderful time."

There was a pause on the line, then softly Elizabeth said, "I love you, Meg."

She felt the start of tears. Those were the words she'd needed, even if they came from far away; they made her feel less alone, less vulnerable. "I love you, too, Birdie. Good night."

" 'Night, Meg. Sleep well."

She slowly hung up the phone. The room seemed quiet now; too dark. She pulled the covers up and closed her eyes, knowing it would be hours before she fell asleep.

CHAPTER
SEVEN

$\mathcal{T}$HEIR FIRST GATHERING AT LAKE CHELAN HAD BEEN IN CELEBRA-
tion. Nineteen eighty-nine. The year Madonna urged people to express themselves and Jack Nicholson played the Joker and the first
pieces of the Berlin Wall came down. More important, it was the
year they all turned twenty-one. There had been five of them then.
Best friends since grade school.

That first get-together had happened by accident. The girls had
pooled their money to give Claire a weekend in the honeymoon
cabin for her birthday. At the time—in March—she'd been head
over heels in love with Carl Eldridge. (The first of many head-over-
heels-in-love relationships that turned out to be a plain old kick in
the head.) By mid-July, on the designated weekend, Claire had been
out of love, alone, and more than a little depressed. Never one to
waste money, she'd gone on the trip by herself, intending to sit on
the porch and read.

Just before dinnertime of the first day, a battered yellow Ford
Pinto had pulled into the yard. Her best friends had spilled out of the

car and run across the lawn, laughing, holding two big jugs of margarita mix. They'd called their visit a love intervention, and it had worked. By Monday, Claire had remembered who she was and what she wanted out of life. Carl Eldridge had most definitely not been "the one."

Every year since then, they'd managed to come back for a week. Now, of course, it was different. Gina and Claire each had a daughter; Karen had four children, aged eleven to fourteen; and Charlotte was trying desperately to conceive.

In the past few years, their parties had quieted; less tequila and cigarettes came out of suitcases these days. Instead of getting dressed up and going to Cowboy Bob's Western Roundup to slam tequila and line-dance, they put the kids to bed early, drank glasses of white wine, and played hearts at the round wooden table on the porch. They kept a running score for the week. The winner got the keys to the honeymoon cottage for the next year.

Their vacation had evolved into a sort of slow, lazy merry-go-round rhythm. They spent their days by the lake, stretched out on red-and-white-striped beach towels or sitting on battered old beach chairs, with a portable radio set up on the picnic table. They always listened to the oldies station, and when a song from the eighties came on, they'd jump up and dance and sing along. On hot days—like this one had been—they spent most of their time in the lake, standing neck-deep in the cool water, their faces shielded by floppy hats and sunglasses. Talking. Always talking.

Now, finally, the weather was perfect. The sky was a bright seamless blue, and the lake was like glass. The older kids were in the house, playing crazy eights and listening to Willie's ear-splitting music, probably talking about the latest, grossest R-rated movie that everyone else's mothers allowed their children to see. Alison and Bonnie were pedaling a water bike in the cordoned-off section of the lake. Their giggles could be heard above the others.

Karen sat slouched in her chair, fanning herself with a pamphlet from the water-slide park. Charlotte, completely protected from the sun by a floppy white hat and a diaphanous, three-quarter-sleeved cover-up, was reading the latest Kelly Ripa book club choice and sipping lemonade.

Gina leaned sideways and opened the cooler, rooting noisily through it for a Diet Coke. When she found one, she pulled it out and snapped it open, taking a long drink before she shut the cooler. "My marriage ends and we're drinking Diet Coke and lemonade. When Karen's dickwad first husband left, we slammed tequila and danced the macarena at Cowboy Bob's."

"That was my second husband, Stan," Karen said. "When Aaron left, we ate those pot brownies and went skinny-dipping in the lake."

"My point remains," Gina said. "My crisis is getting the *Sesame Street* treatment. You got *Animal House*."

"Cowboy Bob's," Charlotte said, almost smiling. "We haven't been there in years."

"Not since we started dragging around these undersize humans," Karen pointed out. "It's hard to rock and roll with a kid on your back."

Charlotte looked out at the lake, to where the little girls were pedaling their water bike. Her smile slowly faded. That familiar sadness came into her eyes again. No doubt she was thinking about the baby she wanted so much.

Claire glanced at her friends. It startled her for a moment, as it sometimes did on these trips, to see their thirty-five-year-old selves. This year, more than any other, they seemed quieter. Older, even. Women on the edge of a sparkling lake who had too much on their minds.

That would never do. They came to Lake Chelan to be their younger, freer selves. Troubles were for other latitudes.

Claire pushed herself up on her elbows. The scratchy cotton of her beach towel seemed to bite into her sunburned forearms.

"Willie's fourteen this year, right?"

Karen nodded. "He's starting high school in September. Can you believe it? He still sleeps with a stuffed animal and forgets to brush his teeth. The ninth-grade girls look like Solid Gold Dancers next to him."

"Why couldn't he baby-sit for an hour or two?"

Gina sat upright. "Hot damn, Claire. Why didn't we think of that before? He's fourteen."

Karen frowned. "With the maturity of an earthworm."

"We all baby-sat at his age," Charlotte said. "Hell, I was practically a nanny that summer before high school."

"He's a responsible kid, Karen. He'll be fine," Claire said gently.

"I don't know. Last month his fish died. Lack of food."

"They won't starve to death in two hours."

Karen looked back at the cabin.

Claire understood exactly what her friend was thinking. If Willie was old enough to baby-sit, he wasn't really a little boy anymore.

"Yeah," Karen said finally. "Of course. Why not? We'll leave a cell phone with him—"

"—and a list of numbers—"

"—and we'll tell them not to leave the cabin."

Gina smiled for the first time all day. "Ladies, the Bluesers are going to leave the building."

It took them two hours to shower, change their clothes, and make the kids' dinner. Macaroni and cheese and hot dogs. It took them another hour to convince the kids that their plan was possible.

Finally, Claire took firm hold of Karen and led her outside. As they walked down the long, winding driveway, Karen paused and looked back every few feet. "Are you sure?" she said each time.

"We're sure. The responsibility will be good for him."

Karen frowned. "I keep thinking about those poor little goldfish, floating belly-up in the dirty water."

"Just keep walking." Gina leaned close to Claire and said, "She's like a car in the ice. If she stops, we'll never get her going again."

They were standing across the street from Cowboy Bob's when it hit them.

Claire was the first to speak. "It's not even dark out."

"As party animals, we've lost our touch," Charlotte said.

"*Shit.*" This from Gina.

Claire refused to be thwarted. So what if they looked like sorority girls amid the professional drinkers that populated a place like this in the early evening? They were here to have a good time and Cowboy Bob's was their only choice.

"Come on, ladies," she said, storming forward.

Her friends fell into line behind her. Heads held high, they marched into Cowboy Bob's as if they owned the place. A thick gray haze hung along the ceiling, drifting in thin strands between the overhead lights. There were several regulars along the bar, their hunched bodies planted like soggy mushrooms on the black bar stools. Several multicolored neon beer signs flickered in the gloomy darkness.

Claire led the way to a round, battered table near the empty dance floor. From here they had an unobstructed view of the band—which was now noticeably absent. A whiny Western song played on the jukebox.

They had barely made it to their seats when a tall, thin waitress with leathery cheeks appeared beside them. "What c'n I get for y'all?" she asked, wiping down the table with a gray rag.

Gina ordered a round of margaritas and onion rings, which were promptly served.

"God it feels good to get *out*," Karen said, reaching for her drink. "I can't remember the last time I went out without having to do enough preplanning to launch an air strike."

"Amen to that," Gina agreed. "Rex could never handle getting a sitter. Not even to surprise me with a dinner date. The surprise was always: *We're going out to dinner. Could you plan it?* Like it takes ovaries to pick up the phone." At that, her smile slipped. "It always bugged the hell out of me. But it's a pretty small grievance, isn't it? Why didn't I notice that before?"

Claire knew that Gina was thinking about the changes that were coming in her new, single life. The bed that would be half empty night after night. She wanted to say something, offer a comfort of some kind, but Claire knew nothing of marriage. She'd dated plenty in the last twenty years, and she'd fallen into pseudo-love a few times. But never the real thing.

She'd figured she was missing out, but just now, as she saw the heartbreak in Gina's eyes, she wondered if maybe she'd been lucky.

Claire raised her glass. "To us," she said in a firm voice. "To the Bluesers. We made it through junior high with Mr. Kruetzer, high school with Miss Bass the Wide Ass, through labors and surgeries, weddings and divorces. Two of us have lost our marriages, one hasn't been able to get pregnant, one of us has never been in love, and a few years ago, one of us died. But we're still here. We'll *always* be here for one another. That makes us lucky women."

They clinked their glasses together.

Karen turned to Gina. "I know it feels like you're cracking apart. But it gets better. Life goes on. That's all I can say."

Charlotte pressed a hand on Gina's but said nothing. She was the one of them who knew best that sometimes there were no words to offer.

Gina managed a smile. "Enough. I can mope at home. Let's talk about something else."

Claire changed the subject. At first, it was awkward, a conversation on a one-way road trying to change directions, but gradually, they found their rhythm. They returned to the old days and everything made them laugh. At some point, they ordered a plate of nachos. By the time the second order of food came, the band had started. The first song was a bone-jarringly loud rendition of "Friends in Low Places."

"It sounds like Garth Brooks got caught in a barbed-wire fence," Claire said, laughing.

By the time the band got around to Alan Jackson's "Here in the Real World," the place was wall-to-wall people. Almost everyone was dressed in fake leather Western wear. A group was line-dancing in a thigh-slappin' way.

"Did you hear that?" Claire leaned forward and put her hands on the table. "It's 'Guitars and Cadillacs.' We *gotta* dance."

"Dance?" Gina laughed. "The last time I danced with you two, my butt hit an old man and sent him flying. Give me another drink or two."

Karen shook her head. "Sorry, Charlie. I danced until I hit a size sixteen. Now I consider it wise to keep my ass as still as possible."

Claire stood up. "Come on, Charlotte. You're not as damn old as these two. You want to dance?"

"Are you kidding? I'd love to." She plopped her purse onto her chair and followed Claire to the dance floor. All around them, couples dressed in denim were dancing in patterns. A woman pirouetted past them, mouthing *1-2-3* along the way. She clearly needed all of her concentration skills to keep up with her partner's moves.

Claire let the music pour over her like cool water on a hot summer's day. It refreshed her, rejuvenated her. The minute she started to move in time with it, to swing her hips and stamp her feet and clap her hands, she remembered how much she loved this. She couldn't believe that she'd let so many quiet years accumulate.

The music swept her away and peeled back the layer of motherhood years. She and Charlotte became their teenage selves again, laughing, bumping hips, singing out loud to each other. The next song was "Sweet Home Alabama," and they had to stay for that one. Next came "Margaritaville."

By the time the band took a break, Claire was damp with perspiration and out of breath. A tiny headache had flared behind her left eye; she stuck a hand in her pocket and found an Excedrin.

Charlotte pushed the hair out of her eyes. "That was *great*. Johnny and I haven't danced since . . ." She frowned. "Jeez. Maybe not since our wedding. That's what happens when you try like hell to get pregnant. Romance hits the road."

Claire laughed. "Believe me, honey, it's *after* you get knocked up that romance changes ZIP codes. I haven't had a decent date in years. Come on. I'm so dehydrated I feel like a piece of beef jerky."

Char nodded toward the back. "I need to use the rest room first. Order me another margarita. And tell Karen this round is on me."

"Sure thing." Claire started to head for the table, then remembered the aspirin in her fist. She went to the bar instead and asked for a glass of tap water.

When the water came, she swallowed the single pill, then turned away from the bar. As she started to head back to the table, she saw a man walk onto the stage. He carried a guitar—a regular, old-fashioned guitar that didn't plug in or amp out. The rest of the band had left the stage, but their instruments were still there.

He sat down easily on a rickety bar stool. One black cowboy boot was planted firmly on the floor, the other rested on the stool's bottom rung. He wore a pair of faded, torn jeans and a black T-shirt. His hair was almost shoulder length, and shone blond in the fluorescent overhead lighting. He was looking down at his guitar, and though a black Stetson shielded most of his face, Claire could make out the strong, high bones that defined his cheeks.

"Wow." She couldn't remember the last time she'd seen a man who was so good-looking.

Not in Hayden, that was for sure.

Men like him didn't show up in backwater towns. This was a fact she'd learned long ago. The Toms, the Brads, the Georges of this world lived in Hollywood or Manhattan, and when they traveled, they stood behind blank-eyed bodyguards in ill-fitting black suits. They *talked* about meeting "real people," but they never actually did it. She knew this because they'd once filmed an action movie in Snohomish. Claire had begged her father to take her down to watch the filming. Not one of the stars had spoken to the locals.

The man leaned toward the microphone. "I'm gonna fill in while the band takes a short break. I hope y'all don't mind."

A round of lackluster applause followed his words.

Claire pushed through the crowd, elbowing past a young man in skintight Wrangler jeans and a Stetson as big as a bathtub.

She halted at the edge of the dance floor.

He strummed a few notes on the guitar and started to sing. At first, his voice was uncertain, almost too soft to be heard above the raucous, booze-soaked din.

"Be quiet," Claire was surprised to hear the words spoken out loud; she'd meant only to *think* them.

She felt ridiculously conspicuous, standing there in front of the crowd, only a few feet away from him, but she couldn't move, couldn't look away.

He looked up.

In the smoky darkness, with a dozen people crammed in beside her, Claire thought he was looking at her.

Slowly, he smiled.

Once, years ago, Claire had been running along the dock at Lake Crescent behind her sister. One minute, she'd been laughing and upright; the next second, she was in the freezing cold water, gasping for breath and clawing her way to the surface.

That was how she felt right now.

"I'm Bobby Austin," he said softly, still looking at her. "This song is for The One. Y'all know what I mean. The one I've been lookin' for all my life."

His long, tanned fingers strummed the guitar strings. Then he started to sing. His voice was low and smoky, seductive as hell, and the song had a sad and haunting quality that made Claire think of all the roads she hadn't taken in her life. She found herself swaying in time to the music, dancing all by herself.

When the song ended, he set down the guitar and stood up. The crowd clapped politely, then turned away, heading back to their pitchers of beer and buffalo wings.

He walked toward Claire. She couldn't seem to move.

Directly in front of her he stopped. She fought the urge to look behind her, to see if he was actually looking at someone else.

When he didn't say anything, she said, "I'm Claire Cavenaugh."

A smile hitched one side of his mouth, but it was strangely sad. "I don't know how to say what I'm thinking without sounding like an idiot."

Claire's heart was beating so fast she felt dizzy. "What do you mean?"

He closed the distance between them, small as it had been. Now he was so near she could see the gold flecks in his green eyes, and the tiny half-moon-shaped scar at the edge of his upper lip. She could see, too, that he trimmed his hair himself; the ends were uneven and sloppy.

"I'm The One," he said softly.

"The one what?" She tried to smile. "The way? The light? There is no way to Heaven but through you?"

"No joking. I'm the one you've been looking for."

She ought to have laughed at him, told him she hadn't heard that corny a pick-up line since the year she tried shaping her eyebrows with a Lady Bic.

She was thirty-five years old. Long past her believing-in-love-at-first-sight years. All of that was what she meant to say, the response she framed in her head. But when she opened her mouth, she heard her heart speak. "How do you know that?"

"Because, I've been lookin' for you, too."

Claire took a tiny step backward; just far enough so that she could breathe her own air.

She wanted to laugh at him. She really did.

"Come on, Claire Cavenaugh," he said softly. "Dance with me."

CHAPTER EIGHT

SOME MARRIAGES ENDED WITH BITTER WORDS AND UGLY EPITHETS, others with copious tears and whispered apologies; each proceeding was different. The one constant was sadness. Win, lose, or draw, when the judge's gavel rang out on the wooden bench, Meghann always felt chilled. The death of a woman's dream was a cold, cold thing, and it was a fact, well known in Family Court, that no woman who'd gone through a divorce ever saw the world—or love—in quite the same way again.

"Are you okay?" Meghann asked May.

Her client sat rigidly upright, her hands clasped tightly in her lap. To an outside observer, she might have appeared serene, almost unconcerned about the heartbreaking drama that had just played out in this courtroom.

Meghann knew better. She knew that May was close to the breaking point. Only sheer force of will kept her from screaming.

"I'm fine," May said, her breathing shallow. That was common, actually. In times like these, women often began Lamaze-type breathing.

Meghann touched May's arm. "Let's go next door and get something to eat, okay?"

"Food," was May's reply, neither an agreement to nor a rejection of the idea.

In the front of the courtroom, the judge stood up. She smiled at Meghann; then at George Gutterson, the opposing counsel; then left the courtroom.

Meghann helped May to her feet. She held on to her arm to keep her steady as they headed toward the door.

"You *bitch!*"

Meghann heard May's sharply indrawn breath, felt her client's body tense. May stumbled to a halt.

Dale Monroe surged forward. His face was a deep, purply red. A blue vein throbbed down the middle of his forehead.

"Dale," George said, reaching for his client. "Don't be stupid—"

Dale shook his lawyer's arm away and kept coming.

Meghann sidestepped easily, putting herself between Dale and May. "Step back, Mr. Monroe."

"That's *Dr.* Monroe, you avaricious bitch."

"Excellent word usage. You must have gone to a good liberal arts college. Now, please, step back." She could feel May trembling behind her, breathing too fast. "Get your client out of my face, George."

George lifted his hands, palms up. "He isn't listening to me."

"You took my children away from me," Dale said, looking right at Meghann.

"Are you suggesting that *I* was the one who fraudulently transferred assets out of my wife's reach . . . or that *I* stole money and equity from my family?" She took a step toward him. "Or wait. Maybe you're suggesting that *I* was the one who banged my daughter's piano teacher every Tuesday afternoon."

He paled. It made that vein look even more pronounced. He edged sideways, tried to make eye contact with his wife.

Ex-wife.

"May, come on," he said. "You know me better than that. I didn't do all of those things. I would have given you everything you asked for. But the kids . . . I can't see them only on weekends and two weeks in the summer."

He sounded sincere, actually. If Meghann hadn't seen the ugly truth in black and white, she might have believed he was upset about the children.

She spoke quickly, so May wouldn't have to. "The separation of your assets was entirely fair and equitable, Dr. Monroe. The custody issues were also fairly resolved, and when you calm down, I'm sure you'll agree. We all read the depositions that reflected your lifestyle. You were gone in the morning by six A.M.—before the children woke up—and you rarely returned home before ten P.M.—after they were in bed. Weekends you spent with the guys, playing golf and poker. Hell, you'll probably see your children more now than you did while you resided at the family home." Meghann smiled, pleased with herself. That had been a smart, well-thought-out argument. He couldn't disagree. She glanced at George, who stood silently beside his client. The attorney looked like he was going to be sick.

"Who do you think you are?" Dale whispered harshly, taking a step toward her. At his sides, his fingers curled into fists.

"You going to hit me, Dale? Go ahead. Lose what little custody you have."

He hesitated.

She took a step toward him. "And if you *ever* hit May again, or even touch her too hard, you'll find yourself back in this courtroom, only it won't be money at risk. It'll be your freedom."

"Are you *threatening* me?"

"Am I?" Her gaze found his. "Yes. I am. Are we clear on that? You stay the hell away from my client or I'll make sure your life turns into a shower scene from *Oz*. And I don't mean Munchkinland. Every other Friday you can park in front of the house and wait for the kids to come out. You return them on time, as stipulated, and that's the sum of your contact with May. We're all clear on that, right?"

May touched her arm, leaned close, and whispered, "Let's go."

Meghann heard the tired strain in May's voice. It reminded Meghann of her own divorce. She'd tried so hard to be strong, but the moment she'd stepped out of the courtroom, she'd broken like an old drawbridge, just crumbled. There was a big part of her that had never stood upright again.

She grabbed her briefcase off the oak library table and slipped her other arm around May's waist. Linked together, they walked out of the courtroom.

"You'll pay for this, you bitch," Dale screamed to their backs. Then something crashed against the floor.

Meghann guessed it was the other oak table.

She didn't look back. Instead, she kept a steadying hand on May's waist and led her to the elevator. In the small cubicle, they stood side by side.

The moment the door closed, May burst into tears.

Meghann held May's hand, squeezing it gently. "I know it seems impossible now, but life will get better. I promise. Not instantly, not even quickly, but it will get better."

She led May down the courthouse steps and outside. The sky was heavy and gray with clouds. A dismal rain spit itself along the car-clogged streets. The sun was nowhere to be seen. No doubt it had followed the geese south, to places like Florida and California. It wouldn't return to western Washington full-time until after the Fourth of July.

They walked down Third Street to the Judicial Annex, the favorite lunch spot for the Family Court gang.

By the time they reached the front door, Meghann's suit was more than a little damp. Gray streaks marred the collar of her white silk blouse. If there was one accessory no local owned, it was an umbrella.

"Hey, Meg," said a few colleagues as she walked through the restaurant to an empty table at the back. She pulled out a chair for May, then sat down opposite her.

Within moments, a harried-looking waitress was beside them. She pulled a pencil out from her ponytail. "Is this a champagne or a martini day?" she asked Meghann.

"Definitely champagne. Thanks."

May looked across the table at her. "We aren't really going to drink champagne, are we?"

"May. You are now a millionaire. Your children can get Ph.D.s from Harvard if they want. You have a beautiful waterfront home in Medina and no mortgage payment. Dale, on the other hand, is living in a thirteen-hundred-square-foot condo in Kirkland. And you got full custody of the kids. Hell yes, we're celebrating."

"What happened to you?"

"What do you mean?"

"My life has been hit by a Scud missile. The man I love is gone. Now I find out he might have existed only in my mind, anyway. I have to live with the fact that not only am I alone, but, apparently, I've been stupid, too. My children will have to live all their lives knowing that families break, that love is impermanent, and, most of all, that promises get broken. They'll go on, of course. That's what children and women do—we go on. But we won't ever be quite whole again. I'll have money. Big fat deal. You have money, I assume. Do you sleep with it at night? Does it hold you when you've awakened from a nightmare?"

"Did Dale?"

"A long time ago, yes. Unfortunately, that's the man I keep remembering." May looked down at her hand. At the wedding ring on her finger. "I feel like I'm bleeding. And there you sit. Drinking champagne." She looked up again. "What's wrong with you?"

"This can be a harsh job," she answered truthfully. "Sometimes, the only way I can get through it is—"

A commotion broke out in the restaurant. Glass shattered. A table crashed to the floor. A woman screamed.

"Oh, no," May breathed. Her face was pale.

Meghann frowned. "What in the—?" She turned around in her chair.

Dale stood in the open doorway, holding a gun in his left hand. When Meghann looked at him, he smiled and stepped over a fallen chair. But there was no humor in that smile; in fact, he appeared to be crying.

Or maybe that was the rain.

"Put down the gun, Dale." She was surprised to hear the calmness in her voice.

"Your turn at the mike is over, counselor."

A woman in a black pinstripe suit crawled across the floor. She moved slowly until she made it to the door. Then she got up and ran.

Dale either didn't notice or didn't care. He only had eyes for Meghann. "You ruined my life."

"Put the gun down, Dale. You don't want to do something stupid."

"I already did something stupid." His voice broke, and Meghann saw that he *was* crying. "I had an affair and got greedy and forgot how much I love my wife."

May started to get to her feet. Meghann grabbed her, forced her down, then stood up herself.

She raised her hands into the air. Her heart was a jackhammer trying to crack through her rib cage. "Come on, Dale. Put the gun down. We'll get you some help."

"Where was all your help when I tried to tell my wife how sorry I was?"

"I made a mistake. I'm sorry. This time we'll all sit down and talk."

"You think I don't know how screwed I am? Believe me, lady, I *know*." His voice caught again. Tears rolled down his cheeks. "Jesus, May, how did I get here?"

"Dale," Meghann said his name in a calm, even voice. "I know how—"

"Shut *up*. It's your fault, you bitch. You're the one who did all of this." He raised the gun, aimed, and pulled the trigger.

Joe awoke with a fever and a stinging throat. A dry, hacking cough brought him upright before he'd even fully opened his eyes.

When it was over, he sat there, bleary-eyed, in desperate need of some water.

A glittering layer of frost coated his sleeping bag, its presence a testament to the altitude. Though the days in this part of the state were as hot as hell, the nights were cold.

He coughed again, then climbed out of the sleeping bag. His fingers were trembling as he rolled up the bag and tied it onto his backpack. He stumbled out of the still-dark forest and emerged molelike and blinking into a sunny day. Already the sun was angry as it climbed the cloudless sky.

Joe dug the toothbrush, soap, and toothpaste out of his pack and, squatting by the rushing rapids of Icicle Creek, readied himself for the day.

By the time he finished, he was breathing hard, as if the exertion of brushing his teeth was on par with running the Boston Marathon.

He stared at himself in the river. Though his reflection wavered in the current, the clear water captured his image in surprising detail. His hair was far too long and as tangled as the underbrush that had formed his bed for the last two nights. A thick beard covered the lower half of his face; it was a quiltlike combination of gray and black. His eyelids hung low, as if in tired defeat.

And today was his birthday. His forty-third.

In another time—another life—this would have been a day for celebration, for family. Diana had always loved a party; she'd throw one at the drop of a hat. The year he'd turned thirty-eight, she'd rented the Space Needle and hired a Bruce Springsteen impersonator to sing the soundtrack of their youth. The place had been packed with friends. Everyone wanted to celebrate Joe's birthday with him.

Then.

With a sigh, he pushed to his feet. A quick check of his wallet and pockets revealed that he was nearly broke again. The money he'd made last week mowing lawns had all but disappeared.

Slinging his backpack into place, he followed the winding river out of the National Forest. By the time he reached Highway 2, he was sweating so hard he had to keep wiping his eyes. His forehead was on fire. He knew he had a fever. One hundred degrees, at least.

He stared at the black river of asphalt that flowed down to the tiny town of Leavenworth. On either side, spindly green pine trees stood guard.

Town was only a mile or so away. From this distance, he could see the Bavarian-themed buildings, the stoplights and billboards. It was, he knew, the kind of town that sold handmade Christmas ornaments year-round and had a quaint bed-and-breakfast on every corner. The kind of place that welcomed tourists and visitors with open arms.

Unless you looked or smelled like Joe.

Still, he was too tired to walk uphill, so he turned toward town. His feet hurt and his stomach ached. He hadn't had a good meal in several days. Yesterday, he'd survived on unripe apples and the last of his beef jerky.

By the time he reached town, his headache was almost unbearable. For two hours, he went from door to door trying to find temporary work.

There was nothing.

Finally, at the Chevron station, he spent his last two dollars on aspirin, which he washed down with water from the rusty sink in the public rest room. Afterward, he stood in the candy aisle, staring blindly at the products.

Corn Nuts would be good now . . .

Or barbecue potato chips.

Or—

"You gotta get a move on, Mister," said the young man behind the cash register. He wore a tattered brown T-shirt that read: *We interrupt this marriage to bring you elk-hunting season.* "Unless you're gonna buy something else."

Joe glanced up at the clock, surprised to see that he'd been there more than an hour. Nodding at the kid, he took his canteen into the rest room and filled it with water, then used the facilities and headed out. At the cash register, he paused. Careful not to make eye contact, he asked if there was a place he could find part-time work.

"The Darrington farm hires transients sometimes. Usually at harvesttime. I dunno about now. And the Whiskey Creek Lodge needs maintenance men during the salmon run."

Picking fruit or gutting fish. He'd done plenty of both in the past three years. "Thanks."

"Hey. You look sick." The kid frowned. "Do I know you?"

"I'm okay. Thanks." Joe kept moving, afraid that if he stopped for too long he'd stumble, then fall. He'd wake up in a hospital bed or on a jail-cell cot. He wasn't sure which fate was worse. Each brought too many bad memories.

He was outside the mini mart, unsteady on his feet, trying to will the aspirin to take effect when the first raindrop hit. It was big and fat and splatted right in his eye. He tilted his chin up, saw the sudden blackness of the sky overhead.

"Shit."

Before he finished the word, the storm hit. A pounding rain that seemed to nail him in place.

He closed his eyes and dropped his chin.

Now his flu would escalate into pneumonia. Another night outside in wet clothes would seal it.

And suddenly he couldn't live like this anymore. He was sick and tired of being sick and tired.

Home.

The idea came to him like a balmy breeze, took him far away from this ugly spot in the driving rain. He closed his eyes and thought of the small town where he'd been raised, where he'd played shortstop for the local ball team and worked at a garage after school and every summer until he went away to college. If any town would still accept him after what he'd done, it would be that one.

Maybe.

Moving slowly, his emotions a convoluted mixture of fear and anticipation, he went to the phone booth and stepped inside its quiet enclosure. Now the rain was only noise; it was like his heartbeat: fast, breathless.

He let out a long breath, then picked up the phone, punched 0 and placed a collect call.

"Hey, little sister," he said when she answered. "How are you?"

"Oh, my God. It's about damn time. I've been worried sick about you, Joey. You haven't called in—what? Eight months? And then you sounded awful."

He remembered that call. He'd been in Sedona. The whole town had seemed to be draped in crystals and waiting for otherworld contact. He'd thought Diana had called him there, but of course she hadn't. It had just been another town to pass through. He'd called his sister on her birthday. Back then, he'd thought he'd be home any day. "I know. I'm sorry."

She sighed again, and he could picture her perfectly: standing at her kitchen counter, probably making a list of things to do—shopping, carpool, swimming lessons. He doubted she'd changed much in the last three years, but he wished he knew for sure. Missing her blossomed into an ache; it was the reason he never called. It hurt too much. "How's my beautiful niece?"

"She's great."

He heard something in her voice. "What's the matter?"

"Nothing," she said, then more softly. "I could use my big brother right about now, that's all. Has it been long enough?"

There it was, the question upon which everything rested. "I don't know. I'm tired, I know that. Have people forgotten?"

"I don't get asked so much anymore."

So some had forgotten, but not everyone. If he returned, the memory would tag along. He didn't know if he was strong enough to stand up to his past. He hadn't been when it was his present.

"Come home, Joey. It has to be time. You can't hide forever. And . . . I need you."

He heard the sound of her crying; it was soft and broken and it pulled something out of him. "Don't cry. Please."

"I'm not. I'm chopping onions for dinner." She sniffed. "Your niece is going through a spaghetti phase. She won't eat anything else." She tried to laugh.

Joe appreciated the attempt at normalcy, however forced.

"Make her some of Mom's spaghetti. That should end it."

She laughed. "Gosh, I'd forgotten. Hers was awful."

"Better than her meat loaf."

After that, a silence slipped through the lines. Softly, she said, "You've got to forgive yourself, Joey."

"Some things are unforgivable."

"Then at least come home. People care about you here."

"I want to. I can't . . . live like this anymore."

"I hope that's what this phone call means."

"I hope so, too."

It was that rarest of days in downtown Seattle. Hot and humid. A smoggy haze hung over the city, reminding everyone that too many cars zipped down too many highways in this once-pristine corner of the country. There was no breeze. Puget Sound was as flat as a summer lake. Even the mountains appeared smaller, as if they, too, had been beaten down by the unexpected heat.

If it was hot outside, it was sweltering in the courthouse. An old air-conditioning unit sat awkwardly in an open window, making soft, strangled noises. A white flap of ribbon, tied to the frontpiece, fluttered every now and then, defeated.

Meghann stared down at the yellow legal pad in front of her. A neat stack of black pens were lined up along one side. The desktop, scarred by decades of clients and attorneys, wobbled on uneven legs.

She hadn't written a word.

That surprised her. Usually her pen was the only thing that worked as fast as her brain.

"Ms. Dontess. Ahem. *Ms. Dontess.*"

The judge was speaking to her.

She blinked slowly. "I'm sorry." She got to her feet and automatically smoothed the hair back from her face. But she'd worn it back this morning, in a French twist.

The judge, a thin, heronlike woman with no collar peeking out from the black vee of her robes, was frowning. "What are your thoughts on this?"

Meghann felt a flare of worry, almost panic. She looked again at her blank legal pad. Her right hand started to shake. The expensive pen fell from her fingers and clattered on the table.

"Approach the bench," said the judge.

Meghann didn't glance to her left. She didn't want to make eye contact with her opposing counsel. She was weak right now—shaking, for God's sake—and everyone knew it.

She tried to look confident; perhaps it worked. As she crossed the wooden floor, she heard her heels clacking with each step. The sound was like an exclamation mark on the sentence of her every breath.

At the high oak bench, she stopped and looked up. It took an act of will to keep her hands open and at her sides. "Yes, Your Honor?" Her voice, thank God, sounded normal. Strong.

The judge leaned forward to say softly, "We all know what happened last week, Meghann. That bullet missed you by inches. Are you certain you're ready to be back in a courtroom?"

"Yes." Meghann's voice was softer now. Her right hand was trembling.

The judge frowned down at her, then cleared her throat and nodded. "Step back."

Meghann headed back to the desk. John Heinreid stepped in beside her. They'd tried dozens of cases against each other. They often shared a glass of wine and a plate of oysters after a long day in court.

"You sure you're okay? I'd be willing to shove this back a few days."

She didn't look at him. "Thanks, John. I'm fine." She went back to the table, slid into her seat.

Her client, a Mercer Island housewife who couldn't possibly live on nineteen thousand dollars a month, stared at her. "What's going on?" she mouthed, twisting the gold chain of her Chanel handbag.

Meghann shook her head. "Don't worry."

"I'll restate, Your Honor," John said. "My client would like to stay these proceedings for a short time so that he and Mrs. Miller can obtain counseling. There are, after all, small children involved. He'd like to give the marriage every opportunity to succeed."

Meghann heard her client whisper, "No way," as she planted her hands on the desk and slowly rose.

Her mind went blank. She couldn't think of a single argument. When she closed her eyes, trying to concentrate, she heard a different voice, gruff and desperate. *It's your fault, you bitch.* Then she saw the gun pointed at her, heard an echoed blast. When she opened her eyes, everyone was looking at her. Had she flinched or cried out? *Shit.* She didn't know. "My client believes that the marriage is irretrievably broken, Your Honor. She sees no benefit to counseling."

"No benefit?" John argued. "Certainly, after fifteen years of living together, it couldn't hurt to spend a few hours with a therapist. My client believes that the children's welfare should be paramount here. He's merely asking for an opportunity to save his family."

Meghann turned to her client. "It's a reasonable request, Celene," she whispered. "You won't look good if we fight this battle in front of the judge."

"Oh. I guess . . ." Celene frowned.

Meghann returned her attention to the bench. "We'd ask for a time limit and a follow-up court date to be set now."

"That's acceptable to us, Your Honor."

Meghann stood there, a little unsteady on her feet as the details were worked out. Her right hand was still trembling and a tic had begun spasming in her left eyelid. On autopilot, she packed up her briefcase.

"Wait. What just happened?" Celene whispered.

"We agreed to counseling. A few months or so. No more. Maybe—"

"Counseling? We've tried counseling—or did you forget that? We've also tried hypnosis and romantic vacations and even a week-long couples' self-help seminar. None of it worked. And do you know why?"

Meghann had forgotten all of that. The information that should have been at her fingertips had vanished. "Oh" was all she could manage.

"It didn't work because he doesn't love me," Celene's voice cracked. "Mr. Computer Software likes male prostitutes, remember? Blow jobs under the Viaduct and in X-rated theaters."

"I'm sorry, Celene."

"Sorry? *Sorry.* My children and I need to start over, not relive the same old shit."

"You're right. I'll fix this. I promise I will." And she could. A phone call to John Heinreid that threatened to reveal Mr. Miller's preferred sex partners and it'd be handled instantly. Quietly.

Celene sighed. "Look, I know what happened last week. It was on every channel. I feel sorry for that lady—and for you. I know that husband tried to kill you. But I need to worry about myself. For once. Can you understand that?"

For a terrible moment, Meghann thought she was going to lose it. How in God's name had she glanced at Celene Miller and seen just another pampered, spoiled housewife? "You *should* be taking care of yourself first. I did you a disservice in here. I screwed up. But I'll fix it, and you won't be paying a dime for this divorce. Okay? Can you trust me again?"

Celene's frown released. "Trusting people has always been easy for me. It's part of why I'm here."

"I'll catch up with John right now. We'll talk tomorrow about what I came up with."

Celene tried valiantly to smile. "Okay."

Meghann put a hand down on the desk to steady herself as she stood there, watching her client walk out of the courtroom. When Celene was gone, Meghann sighed heavily. She hadn't realized that she'd been holding her breath.

She reached for her yellow pad, noticed her trembling fingers and thought: *What's wrong with me?*

A hand pressed against her shoulder, and she jumped at the contact.

"Meg?"

It was Julie Gorset, her partner.

"Hey, Jules. Tell me you weren't in the courtroom today."

Julie looked at her sadly. "I was. And we need to talk."

The Pike Place Public Market was wall-to-wall people on a sunny summer's day. Now, at nighttime, it was quiet. Sweaty vendors in gauzy clothes were busy packing up their homemade crafts and loading them onto trucks parked outside on the cobblestone street. The night air rang out with the ping-ping-ping of delivery trucks in reverse gear.

Meghann stood outside the Athenian's open door. The bar was hazy with cigarette smoke; the expansive Puget Sound view sparkled in the few open spaces between patrons. There were at least two dozen people at the bar, no doubt shooting oysters—drinking them raw from a glass jigger. It was a house tradition.

She glanced from table to table. There were plenty of possibilities. Single men in expensive suits and college boys in cutoff shorts that showed their lean torsos and checkered boxers.

She could go in there, put on her *kiss me* smile and find someone to spend time with her. For a few blessed hours, she could be part of a couple, no matter how false and fragile that pairing might be. At least she wouldn't have to think. Or feel.

She started to take a step forward. Her toe caught on the threshold and she stumbled sideways, skimming the door's side.

And suddenly, all she could think about was what would really happen. She'd meet some guy whose name wouldn't matter, let him touch her body and crawl inside of her . . . and then be left more alone than when she'd started.

The tic in her left eye started again.

She reached into her handbag and pulled out her cell phone. She'd already left a desperate-sounding *call me* message on Elizabeth's answering machine, when she remembered that her friend was in Paris.

There was no one else to call. Unless . . .

Don't do it.

But she couldn't think of anywhere else to turn.

She punched in the number, biting down on her lip as it rang. She was just about to hang up when a voice answered.

"Hello? Hello?" Then: "Meghann. I recognize your cell phone number."

"I'm going to sue whoever invented Caller ID. It's ruined the time-honored tradition of hanging up on someone."

"It's eight thirty at night. Why are you calling me?" Harriet asked.

"My left eyelid is flapping like a flag on the Fourth of July. I need a prescription for a muscle relaxer."

"We talked about a delayed reaction, remember?"

"Yeah. Post-traumatic stress. I thought you meant I'd get depressed; not that my eyelid would try to fly off my face. And . . . my hands are shaking. It would *not* be a good week to start quilting."

"Where are you?"

Meghann considered lying, but Harriet had ears like a bloodhound; she could probably hear the bar noises. "Outside of the Athenian."

"Of course. I'll be in my office in thirty minutes."

"You don't have to do that. If you could just call in a prescription—"

"My office. Thirty minutes. If you aren't there, I'll come looking for you. And nothing scares off drunk college boys like an angry shrink named Harriet. Understood?"

Honestly, Meghann was relieved. Harriet might be a pain in the ass, but at least she was someone to talk to. "I'll be there."

Meghann hung up the phone and put it back in her purse. It took her less than fifteen minutes to get to Harriet's office. The doorman let her in and, after a short question-and-answer routine, pointed to the elevator. She rode up to the fourth floor and stood outside the glass-doored office.

At precisely 9:00, Harriet showed up, looking rushed and poorly put together. Her normally smoothed black hair had been drawn back in a thin headband and her face shone pink without makeup. "If you make a crack about the headband, I'll charge you double."

"Me? Be judgmental? You must be joking."

Harriet smiled at that. They'd often discussed avid judgmentalism as one of Meghann's many flaws. "I had to choose between being on time and looking decent."

"Clearly, you're on time."

"Get inside." Harriet unlocked the door and pushed it open.

Even now, late at night, the office smelled of fresh flowers and worn leather. The familiarity of it immediately put Meghann at ease. She walked through the reception area and went into Harriet's large corner office, going over to stand in front of the window. Below her, the city was a grid of moving cars and stoplights.

Harriet took her usual seat. "So, you think a prescription will help you."

Meghann slowly turned around. Her eyelid was thumping like a metronome. "Either that or a Seeing Eye dog. If the other one starts, I'll be blind."

"Sit down, Meghann."

"Do I have to?"

"Well, no. I could go home and finish watching *Friends*."

"You watch *Friends*? I would have guessed you tuned in to PBS. Maybe the Discovery Channel."

"Sit."

Meghann did as she was told. The comfortable chair enfolded her. "I remember when I hated this chair. Now it seems made for me."

Harriet steepled her fingers and peered at Meghann over her

short, clear-polished nails. "It was a week ago today, wasn't it? When your client's husband tried to shoot you."

Meghann's left foot started to tap. The plush gray carpet swallowed the sound. "Yes. The funny thing is, the publicity has gotten me clients. It seems women *want* a lawyer who makes a man that crazy." She tried to smile.

"I told you you needed to deal with it."

"Yes, you did. Remind me to put a gold star next to your name on the door."

"Are you sleeping?"

"No. Every time I close my eyes, I see it all again. The gunshot whizzing past my ear . . . the way he dropped the gun afterward and sank to his knees . . . May rushing to him, holding him, telling him everything would be all right, that she'd stand behind him . . . the police taking him away in handcuffs. Today, I relived it in court." She looked up. "That was lovely, by the way."

"It's not your fault. He's the one to blame."

"I know that. I also know that I handled their divorce badly. I've lost my ability to really *feel* for people." She sighed. "I don't know . . . if I can do this job anymore. Today I completely screwed a client. My partner has asked me—ordered me, really—to take a vacation."

"That might not be a bad idea. It wouldn't hurt you to develop a real life."

"Will I feel better in London or Rome . . . alone?"

"Why don't you call Claire? You could go stay at her resort for a while. Maybe try to relax. Get to know her."

"That's a funny thing about visiting relatives. You need an invitation."

"Are you saying Claire wouldn't want you to visit?"

"Of course I'm saying that. We can't talk for more than five minutes without getting into an argument."

"You could visit your mother."

"I'd rather contract the West Nile virus."

"How about Elizabeth?"

"She and Jack are in Europe, celebrating their anniversary. I don't think they'd appreciate a guest."

"So, what you're saying is, you have nowhere to go and no one to visit."

"All I said was, Where would I go?" It had been a mistake to come here. Harriet was making her feel worse. "Look, Harriet," her voice was softer than usual, and cracked. "I'm falling apart. It's like I'm losing myself. All I want from you is a drug to take the edge off. You know me, I'll be fine in a day or two."

"The Queen of Denial."

"When something works for me, I stick with it."

"Only denial isn't working anymore, is it? That's why your eyelid is spasming, your hands are shaking, and you can't sleep. You're breaking apart."

"I won't break. Trust me."

"Meghann, you're one of the smartest women I've ever known. Maybe too smart. You've handled a lot of trauma in your life and succeeded. But you can't keep running away from your own past. Someday you're going to have to settle the tab with Claire."

"A client's husband tries to blow my brains out, and you manage to make my breakdown about my family. Are you sure you're really a doctor?"

"All I have to do is mention Claire and the walls go up. Why is that?"

"Because this isn't about Claire, damn it."

"Sooner or later, Meg, it's always about family. The past has an irritating way of becoming the present."

"I once had a fortune cookie that said the same thing."

"You're deflecting again."

"No. I'm rejecting." Meghann got to her feet. "Does this mean you won't write me a prescription for a muscle relaxant?"

"It wouldn't help your tic."

"Fine. I'll get an eye patch."

Harriet slowly stood up. Across the desk, they faced each other. "Why won't you let me help you?"

Meghann swallowed hard. She'd asked herself the same question a hundred times.

"What do you want?" Harriet asked finally.

"I don't know."

"Yes, you do."

"Well, if you know the answer, why ask the question?"

"You want to stop feeling so alone."

A shudder passed through Meghann, left her chilled. "I've always been alone. I'm used to it."

"No. Not always."

Meghann's thoughts spooled back to those years, so long ago now, when she and Claire had been inseparable, the best of friends. Then, Meg had known how to love.

Enough. This was getting Meg nowhere.

Harriet was wrong. This wasn't about the past. So Meg felt guilty about the way she'd abandoned her sister, and she'd been hurt when Claire rejected her and chose Sam. So what? That water had flowed under the bridge for twenty-six years. She wasn't likely to drown in it now. "Well, I'm alone now, aren't I? And I sure as hell better figure out how to get my shit together. Thanks for the help with that, by the way." She grabbed her purse off the floor and headed for the door. "Send tonight's bill to my secretary. Charge whatever you want. Good-bye, Harriet." She said good-bye instead of good night because she didn't intend to come back.

She was at the door when Harriet's voice stopped her.

"Be careful, Meghann. Especially now. Don't let loneliness consume you."

Meghann kept walking, right out the door and into the elevator and across the lobby.

Outside, she looked down at her watch.

9:40.

There was still plenty of time to go to the Athenian.

CHAPTER NINE

$\mathscr{I}$N THE PASSENGER SEAT OF AN EIGHTEEN-WHEELER, JOE SAT slumped against the window. The truck's air conditioner had gone out about forty miles ago, and it was as hot as hell in the cab.

The driver, a long-hauler named Erv, hit the Jake Brakes and shifted gears. The truck groaned and shuddered and began to slow down. "There's the Hayden exit."

Joe saw the familiar sign and didn't know how to feel. He hadn't been here in so long. . . .

Home.

No. It was where he'd grown up; home was something else—or, more accurately, some*one* else—and she wouldn't be waiting up for him to return.

The off-ramp looped over the freeway and flattened out onto a tree-lined road. On the left side was a small shingled gas station and a mini mart.

Erv pulled up in front of the pump and came to a creaking stop. The brakes wheezed loudly and fell silent. "The store there makes some mighty fine egg-salad samiches, if you're hungry." Erv opened his door and got out.

Joe wedged the handle down and gave the door a good hard push. It creaked wearily open, and he stepped down onto the pavement of western Washington for the first time in three years. He broke out in a cold sweat—whether from the fever or his arrival home, he didn't know.

He looked at Erv, who was busy pumping gas. "Thanks for the ride."

Erv nodded. "You don't talk much, but you were good company. The road can get lonely."

"Yeah," Joe said. "It can."

"You sure you don't want to go to Seattle? It's only an hour and a half away. There ain't much here."

Joe looked down the long, tree-lined road. Though he could only make out the barest hint of town, his memories compensated. "You'd be surprised," he said softly.

His sister was just down that road, waiting for him in spite of everything, hoping he'd knock on her door. If he did, if he found that courage, she'd pull him into her arms and hold him so tightly, he'd remember how it felt to be loved.

The thought galvanized him.

"Bye, Erv." He slung his backpack over his shoulder and started walking. In no time, he came to the small green sign that welcomed him to *Hayden, population 872. Home of Lori Adams, 1974 State Spelling Bee Champion.*

The town where he'd been born, where he'd grown up and moved on from, hadn't changed at all. It looked precisely as he remembered, a pretty little collection of Western-themed buildings dozing peacefully beneath this warm June sun.

The buildings all had false fronts, and there were hitching posts stationed here and there along a wooden boardwalk. The stores were mostly the same—the Whitewater Diner and the Basket Case Florist Shoppe, then Mo's Fireside Tavern and the Stock 'Em Up grocery store. Every sign sparked some memory, every doorway had once welcomed him. He'd bagged groceries for old Bill Turman at the grocery store one summer and ordered his first legal beer at Mo's.

Once, he'd been welcomed everywhere in town.

Now . . . who knew?

He let out a long sigh, trying to understand how he felt at this moment. He'd dreaded and longed for this return for three years, but now that he'd actually come home, he felt curiously numb. Maybe it was the flu. Or the hunger. Certainly a homecoming ought to be sharper. Returning after so long an absence, after all that he had done.

He made a valiant effort to *feel*.

But nothing seized hold of him, and so he began to walk again, past the four-way stop sign that introduced the start of town, past the Loose Screw Hardware Shop and the family-owned bakery.

He felt people looking at him; it beat him down, those looks that turned into frowns of recognition. Whispers followed him, nipped at his heels.

Jesus, is that Joe Wyatt?

Did you see that, Myrtle? It was Joe Wyatt.

He's got some nerve—

How long has it been?

Every one made him hunch a little farther. He tucked his chin close to his chest, rammed his hands in his pockets, and kept moving.

On Azalea Street, he veered left, then, on Cascade he turned right.

Finally, he could breathe again. Here, only a few blocks from Main Street, the world was quiet again. Quaint wood-framed houses sat on impeccably trimmed lawns, one after another for a few blocks, and then the signs of inhabitation grew sparse.

By the time he reached Rhododendron Lane, the street was almost completely deserted. He walked past Craven Farms, quiet this time of year before the fall harvest, and then turned into the driveway. Now the mailbox said *Trainor*. For years and years, it had read: *Wyatt*.

The house was a sprawling log-built A-frame that was set amid a perfectly landscaped yard. A mossy split-rail fence outlined the property. Flowers bloomed everywhere, bright and vibrant, and glossy green boxwoods had been shaped into a rounded hedge that paralleled the fencing. His father had built this house by hand, log by log. One of the last things Dad had said to them, as he lay in his hospital bed dying of a broken heart, was: *Take care of the house. Your mother loved it so . . .*

Joe felt a sudden tightening in his throat, a sadness almost too sweet to bear. His sister had done as she'd been asked. She'd kept the house looking exactly as it always had. Mom and Dad would be pleased.

Something caught his eye. He looked up, caught a fluttering, incorporeal glimpse of a young woman on the porch, dressed in flowing white as she giggled and ran away. The image was shadowy and indistinct and heartbreaking.

Diana.

It was a memory; only that.

Halloween. Nineteen ninety-seven. They'd come here to take his niece trick-or-treating for the first time. In her Galadriel costume, Diana had looked about twenty-five years old.

Someday soon, she'd whispered that night, clinging to his hand, *we'll take our own child trick-or-treating.* Only a few months later, they found out why they'd been unable to conceive. . . .

He stumbled, came to a stop at the bottom of the porch steps, and glanced back down the road, thinking, *Maybe I should turn around.*

The memories here would ruin what little peace he'd been able to find. . . .

No.

He'd found no peace out there.

He climbed the steps, hearing the familiar creaking of the boards underfoot. After a long pause in which he found himself listening to the rapid hammering of his heart, he knocked on the door.

For a moment, there was no sound within; then the clattering of heavy-soled shoes and the called-out "Coming!"

The door swung open. Gina stood there, dressed in baggy black sweats and green rubber clogs, breathing hard. Her cheeks were bright pink, her chestnut brown hair a bird's nest of disarray. She took one look at him, mouthed *Oh*, then burst into tears. "Joey—"

She pulled him into her arms. For a moment, he was dazed, too confused to respond. He hadn't been touched in so long, it felt wrong somehow.

"Joey," she said again, putting her face in the crook of his neck. He felt her warm tears on his skin and something inside of him gave way. He brought his arms around her and held on. The whole of his childhood came back to him then, drifted on the baking-bread smell of the house and the sweet citrusy scent of her shampoo. He remembered building her a stick fort by the fish pond long after he'd outgrown it himself, and baby-sitting her on Saturday mornings and walking her home from school. Though they were seven years apart in age, they'd always been a pair.

She drew back, sniffling, wiping her red-rimmed eyes. "I didn't think you'd really come back." She patted her hair and made a face. "Oh, shit, I look like the undead. I was planting flowers in the backyard."

"You look beautiful," he said, meaning it.

"Pretend that Grandma Hester's ass hasn't moved onto my body." She reached out for him, took hold of his hand, and dragged him into the sunlit living room.

"I should take a shower before I sit—"

"Forget it." Gina sat down on a beautiful butter-yellow sofa and pulled him down beside her.

He felt uncomfortable suddenly, out of place. He could smell his own scent, feel the clammy dampness of his skin.

"You look sick."

"I am. My head is pounding."

Gina popped up and hurried from the room. All the while she was gone, she talked to him from another room. No doubt she was afraid he'd vanish again.

"—some water," she called out, "and aspirin."

He started to say something—he had no idea what—when he saw the photo on the mantel.

He got slowly to his feet and walked toward it.

The photograph was of five women crowded together; four of them wore matching pink dresses. They were all smiling broadly and holding up wineglasses, most of which, he noticed, were empty. Gina was front and center, the only woman in white. Diana was beside her, laughing.

"Hey, Di," he whispered. "I'm home."

"That's one of my favorite pictures," Gina said, coming up behind him.

"At the end," he said softly, "she talked about you guys. The Bluesers. She must have told me a hundred Lake Chelan stories."

Gina squeezed his shoulder. "We all miss her."

"I know."

"Did you find it out there . . . whatever you were looking for?"

He thought about that. "No," he said at last. "But now that I'm here, I want to be gone again. Everywhere I look, I'll see her."

"Tell me that wasn't true out there, too."

He sighed. His sister was right. It didn't matter where he was. Diana filled his thoughts, his dreams. Finally, he turned around and looked down at his sister. "What now?"

"You're home. That counts for something."

"I'm lost, Gigi. It's like I'm stuck in the ice. I can't move. I don't know how to start over."

She touched his cheek. "Don't you see? You already have. You're here."

He placed his hand over hers and stared down at her, trying to think of something to say. Nothing came to mind, so he tried to smile instead. "Where's my beautiful niece? And my brother-in-law?"

"Bonnie's over at River's Edge, playing with Ali."

Joe frowned, took a step back. "And Rex? He doesn't work on Sundays."

"He left me, Joey. Divorced me."

She didn't say, *While you were gone*, but she could have. His baby sister had needed him and he hadn't been there for her. He pulled her into his arms.

She burst into tears. He stroked her hair and whispered that he was here, that he wasn't going anywhere.

For the first time in three years, it was the truth.

Meghann's desk was clean for the first time in more than a decade. All her pending cases had been portioned out to the other attorneys. She'd promised Julie that she'd take at least three weeks of vacation, but already she was having second thoughts. What in the hell would she do with all the hours that made up an ordinary day?

Last night and the night before, she'd gone out for dinner and drinks with some lawyer friends. Unfortunately, it had become obvious that they were worried about her. No one mentioned the drama with the gun, and when Meg made a joke about her near-death experience, it fell flat. The two evenings had only served to make her feel more alone.

She thought about calling Harriet, then discarded the idea. She'd studiously avoided her therapist in the past few days, even going so far as to cancel her regular appointment. Their late-night session had been depressing and disturbing; frankly, Meghann was doing a good enough job at depressing herself. She didn't need to pay a professional to help her.

She retrieved her briefcase and handbag from the bottom desk drawer and headed for the door. She allowed herself a last look at the room that was more of a home to her than her condo and quietly closed the door.

As she walked down the wide marble hallway, she noticed that her colleagues were avoiding her. Success was a virus everyone longed to catch. Not so failure. The watercooler whispers had been rampant in the past weeks. *Dontess is losing it . . . cracking up . . . just shows you what happens when you have no life.*

The comments were quietly made, of course, in hushed and hurried tones. She was a senior partner, after all, the second name on the door in a business where pecking order was everything. Still, for the first time in her career, they were questioning her, wondering if the Bitch of Belltown had lost her edge. She sensed the same curiosity from her lawyer friends.

At the closed door of Julia's corner office, she paused and knocked gently.

"Come in."

Meghann opened the door and entered the bright, sunlit office. "Hey, Jules."

Julie looked up from her paperwork. "Hey, Meg. You want to go out for a drink? Maybe celebrate your first vacation in a decade?"

"How about celebrating my decision to stick around?"

"Sorry, Charlie. I've taken a month a year for the last decade. Your only time off generally comes with novocaine." She stood up. "You're tired, Meg, but you're too stubborn to admit it. What happened last week would mess with anyone's mind. Let yourself feel it. You need a rest. I recommend at least a month."

"Have you ever *seen* me rest?"

"No. That makes my point, not yours, counselor. Where are you going to go?"

"Bangladesh, maybe. I hear the hotels are dirt cheap."

"Funny. Why don't you use my condo in Hawaii? A week by the pool is just what the doctor ordered."

"No, thanks. I can't drink anything that comes with an umbrella. I think I'll just watch Court TV or CNN. Listen for my voice on *Larry King Live*."

"I won't change my mind, no matter how pathetic you seem. Now, go. Your vacation time can't start if you don't leave."

"The O'Connor case—"

"Continuance."

"Jill Summerville—"

"Settlement conference on Friday. I'm handling it personally, and I'll conduct the Lange deposition next Wednesday. Everything is handled, Meg. Go."

"Where?" she asked quietly, hating the neediness in her voice.

Julie moved toward her, touched her shoulder. "You're forty-two years old, Meg. If you don't have anywhere to go and no one to visit, it's about time you reassessed. This is a job. A damn good one, to be sure, but just a job. You've made it your life—I let you, I'll admit it— but it's time to make some changes. Go find *something*."

Meghann pulled Julie into her arms, gave her a fierce hug. Then, feeling awkward with the uncharacteristic display of emotion, she stumbled backward, turned around, and strode out of the office.

Outside, night was closing in, drawing the warmth from a sur- prisingly hot day. As she neared the Public Market, the crowds in- creased. Tourists stood in front of flower shops and outside bakery windows. She cut through Post Alley toward her building. It wasn't a route she often chose, but she didn't want to walk past the Athe- nian. Not now, when she felt vulnerable. This was the kind of night where it would be easy to slip from grace and, honestly, she was tired of the fall. It hurt too much to land.

In the lobby of her building, she waved at the doorman and went up to her condo.

She'd forgotten to leave the radio playing. The place was jar- ringly silent.

She tossed her keys on the entryway table. They clanged into a floral-carved Lalique bowl.

Her place was beautiful and neat, with not so much as a paper clip out of place. The cleaning lady had been here today and care- fully removed all evidence of Meghann's natural disorder. Without the books and folders and papers piled everywhere, it had the look of an expensive hotel room. The kind of place people visited, not where they lived. A pair of blue-black brocade sofas faced each other, with an elegant black coffee table in between. The west-facing walls were solid glass. The view was a blue wash of sky and Sound.

Meghann opened the antique black-and-gold lacquered armoire in the television room and grabbed the remote. As sound blared to life, she slumped into her favorite suede chair and planted her feet on the ottoman.

It took less than five seconds to recognize the theme music.

"Oh, shit."

It was a rerun of her mother's old television show—*Starbase IV*. She recognized the episode. It was called "Topsy-Turvy"; in it, the crew of the floating biodome was accidentally transformed into bugs. Mosquito-men took control of the laboratories.

Mama hurried on-screen wearing that ridiculous lime-green stretch suit with black thigh-high boots. She looked alive and vibrant. Beautiful. Even Meg had trouble looking away.

"Captain Wad," Mama said, her overly plucked eyebrows frowning just enough to convey emotion but not enough to create wrinkles. "We've received an emergency message from the boys in the dehydratin' pod. They said somethin' about mosquitos."

Dehydratin'.

As if a microbotanist on a Martian space station had to be from Alabama. Meg hated the fake accent. And Mama had used it ever since. Said her fans expected it of her. Sadly, they probably did.

"Don't think about it," Meghann said aloud.

But, of course, it was impossible. Turning away from the past was something Meg could do when she was strong. When she was weak, the memories took over. She closed her eyes and remembered. A lifetime ago. They'd been living in Bakersfield then. . . .

"Hey, girls, Mama's home."

Meghann huddled closer to Claire, holding her baby sister tightly. Mama stumbled into the trailer's small, cluttered living room, wearing a clinging red-sequined dress with silver fringe and clear plastic shoes.

"I've brought Mr. Mason home with me. I met him at the Wild

Beaver. You girls be nice to him now," she said in that boozy, lilting voice that meant she'd wake up mean.

Meghann knew she had to act fast. With a man in the trailer, Mama wouldn't be able to think about much else, and the rent was long past due. She reached down for the wrinkled copy of Variety that she'd stolen from the local library. "Mama?"

Mama lit up a menthol cigarette and took a long drag. "What is it?"

Meghann thrust out the magazine. She'd outlined the ad in red ink. It read: Mature actress sought for small part in science fiction television series. Open call. Then the address in Los Angeles.

Mama read the ad out loud. Her smile froze in place at the words mature actress. After a long, tense moment, she laughed and gave Mr. Mason a little shove toward the bedroom. When he went into the room and closed the door behind him, Mama knelt down and opened her arms. "Give Mama a hug."

Meghann and Claire flew into her embrace. They waited days for a moment like this, sometimes weeks. Mama could be cold and distracted, but when she turned on the heat of her love, it warmed you to the bone.

"Thank you, Miss Meggy. I don't know what I'd do without you. I'll surely try out for that part. Now, you two scamper off and stay out of trouble. I've got some entertaining to do."

Mama had read for the role, all right. To her—and everyone else's—amazement she'd nailed the audition. Instead of winning the small part she'd gone up for, she'd won the starring role of Tara Zyn, the space station's microbotanist.

It had been the beginning of the end.

Meghann sighed. She didn't want to think about the week Mama had gone to Los Angeles and left her daughters alone in that dirty trailer . . . or the changes that had come afterward. Meghann and Claire had never really been sisters since.

Beside her, the phone rang. It was jarringly loud in the silence. Meghann pounced on it, eager to talk to *anyone*. "Hello?"

"Hey, Meggy, it's me. Your mama. How are you, darlin'?"

Meg rolled her eyes at the accent. She should have let the answering machine pick up. "I'm fine, Mama. And you?"

"Couldn't be better. The Fan-ference was this weekend. I have a few photos left over. I thought y'might like a signed one for your collection."

"No thanks, Mama."

"I'll have m'houseboy send you one. Lordy, I signed s'many autographs, my fingers ache."

Meghann had been to one of the *Starbase IV* Fan Conference weekends. One had been enough. Hundreds of starry-eyed geeks in cheap polyester costumes, clamoring for photographs with a bunch of has-beens and never-really-weres. Mama was the only cast member who'd had a career since the show was canceled, and it wasn't much. A few bad made-for-TV movies in the eighties and a cult horror classic in the late nineties. It was reruns that had made her rich and famous. A whole new generation of nerds had latched on to the old show. "Well, your fans love you."

"Thank God for small miracles. It surely is nice to talk to you, Meggy. We should do it more often. Y'all should come down and visit me."

Mama always said that. It was part of the script. A way to pretend they were something they weren't—family.

It was understood that she didn't mean it.

Still . . .

Meghann took a deep breath. *Don't do it. You're not that desperate.*

But she couldn't sit alone in this condo for three weeks. "I'm taking a vacation," she said in a rush. "Maybe I could come stay with you."

"Oh. That would be . . . fine." Mama exhaled heavily; Meghann swore she could smell smoke coming through the phone. "Maybe this Christmas—"

"Tomorrow."

"Tomorrow?" Mama laughed. "Honey, I've got a photographer from *People* magazine comin' over at three o'clock, and at my age I wake up lookin' like one o' those hairless dogs. It takes ten women all day to make me beautiful."

Her accent was getting pronounced. That always happened when her emotions were strong. Meghann wanted to hang up, say forget it, but when she looked around her empty, photo-free apartment, she felt almost sick. "How about Monday, then? Just for a few days. Maybe we could go to a spa."

"Don't you *ever* watch the E! channel? I'm leavin' for Cleveland on Monday. I'm doin' Shakespeare in some park with Pamela Anderson and Charlie Sheen. Hamlet."

"*You? You're* doing Shakespeare?"

Another dramatic pause. "I'm gonna forget I heard that tone in your voice."

"Cut the accent, Mama. It's me. I know you were born in Detroit. Joan Jojovitch is the name on your birth certificate."

"Now you're just being rude. You always were a prickly child."

Meghann didn't know what to say. The last place in the world she wanted to go was to her mother's, and yet being studiously noninvited rankled her. "Well. Good luck."

"It's a big break for me."

For me. Mama's favorite words. "You better get a good night's sleep before the magazine shoot."

"That's the God's honest truth." Mama exhaled again. "Maybe y'all could come down later in the year. When I'm not so busy. Claire, too."

"Sure. Bye, Mama."

Meghann hung up the phone and sat there in her too-quiet home. She called Elizabeth, got the answering machine, and left a quick message. Then she hung up.

What now? She had no idea.

For the next hour, she paced the apartment, trying to formulate a plan that made sense.

The phone rang. She dived for it, hoping it was Elizabeth. "Hello?"

"Hi, Meg."

"Claire? This is a nice surprise." And for once it was. She sat down. "I talked to Mama today. You won't believe this. She's doing—"

"I'm getting married."

"—Shakespeare in—*married?*"

"I've never been so happy, Meg. I know it's crazy, but that's love, I guess."

"Who are you marrying?"

"Bobby Jack Austin."

"I've never even heard his name." Not since *Hee Haw* went off the air, anyway.

"I met him ten days ago in Chelan. I know what you're going to say, but—"

"Ten days ago. You have sex with men you just met, Claire. Sometimes you even sneak away for a wild weekend. What you don't do is marry them."

"I'm in love, Meg. Please don't ruin it for me."

Meg wanted to give advice so badly she had to curl her hands into fists. "What does he do for a living?"

"He's a singer/songwriter. You should hear him, Meg. He sounds like an angel. He was singing in Cowboy Bob's Western Roundup when I first saw him. My heart stopped for a second. Have you ever felt that way?"

Before Meghann could answer, Claire went on, "He's a ski instructor in Aspen in the winter and he travels around in the summer, playing his music. He's two years older than I am, and he's so good-looking you won't believe it. Better than Brad Pitt, I kid you not. He's going to be a star."

Meghann let it all soak in. Her sister was marrying a thirty-seven-year-old ski bum who dreamed of being a Country and Western singer. And the best gig he could get was Cowboy Bob's in Nowheresville.

"Don't be yourself, Meg," Claire said evenly when the pause had gone on too long.

"Does he know what the campground is worth? Will he sign a prenuptial agreement?"

"Damn you, Meg. Can't you be happy for me?"

"I want to be," Meghann said, and it was true. "It's just that you deserve the best, Claire."

"Bobby is the best. You haven't asked about the wedding."

"When is it?"

"Saturday, the twenty-third."

"Of *this* month?"

"We thought, Why wait? I'm not getting any younger. So we booked the church."

"The church." This was crazy. Too fast. "I need to meet him."

"Of course. The rehearsal dinner—"

"No way. I need to meet him *now*. I'll be at your house tomorrow night. I'll take you guys out to dinner."

"Really, Meg, you don't have to do that."

Meg pretended not to hear Claire's reluctance. "I want to. I have to meet the man who stole my sister's heart, don't I?"

"Okay. I'll see you tomorrow." Claire paused, then said, "It'll be good to see you."

"Yeah. Bye." Meg hung up, then punched in the number for her office and left a message for her secretary. "Get me everything we've got on prenuptial agreements. Forms, cases, even the Ortega agreement. I want it all delivered to my house by ten o'clock tomorrow morning." As an afterthought, she added, "Thanks."

Then she headed for her computer to do some checking up on Bobby Jack Austin.

This was what she'd do on her idiotic vacation. She'd save Claire from making the biggest mistake of her life.

CHAPTER
TEN

*C*LAIRE HUNG UP THE OFFICE PHONE. IN THE SILENCE THAT FOL-
lowed, doubt crept into the room.

She and Bobby *were* moving awfully fast. . . .

"Damn you, Meg."

But even as she cursed her sister, Claire knew the doubt had been
there all along, a little seed inside of her, waiting to sprout and grow.
She was too old to be swept away by passion.

She had a daughter to think about, after all. Alison had never
known her biological father. It had been easy so far, bubble-wrapping
Ali's world so that none of life's sharp edges could hurt her. Marriage
would change everything.

The last thing Claire wanted to do was marry a man who had
itchy feet.

She knew about men like that, men who smiled pretty smiles and
made big promises and disappeared one night while you were brushing your teeth.

Claire had had four stepfathers before she'd turned nine. That number didn't include the men she'd been asked to call Uncle, the men who'd passed through Mama's life like shots of tequila. There and gone, leaving nothing behind but a bitter aftertaste.

Claire had had such high hopes for each new stepfather, too. *This one,* she'd thought each time. *He'll be the one to take me roller-skating and teach me how to ride a bike.* Of course, it had been Meg who'd taught her those things; Meg, who never once called one of Mama's husbands Daddy and refused to have any hopes for them at all.

No wonder Meghann was suspicious. Their past had given her reason to be.

Claire walked across the main lobby of the registration office. On her way to the window, she picked up a fallen flyer, no doubt dropped by one of the guests, and tossed it into the cold fireplace.

Outside, the sun was just beginning to set. The camp lay bathed in a rose-gold light in which every leaf edge seemed sharper, every green distinct. Sunlight sparkled on the blue water in the swimming pool, empty now as the guests were firing up their camp stoves and barbecues.

As she stood there, feeling vulnerable and uncertain, she saw a shadow fall across the grass.

Dad and Bobby strolled into view. Dad wore his summertime uniform: blue overalls and a black T-shirt. A tattered River's Edge baseball cap shaded his eyes; beneath it, his brown hair was a mass of fuzzy curls.

And Bobby.

He wore a pair of faded jeans and a blue T-shirt that read: *Cowboy Up for Coors.* In this fading light, his long hair was the color of eighteen-carat gold, rich and warm. He carried their Weed Eater in one hand and a can of gasoline in the other. In the days he'd been here, Bobby had pitched in with the work. He was good at it, though she knew he wouldn't be happy at River's Edge forever. Already, he'd mentioned going on the road for a few weeks this summer. The three of them. "The Austins' road trip" was how he put it. Claire thought it sounded great, traveling from town to town for a while, listening to her new husband sing. She hadn't broached the idea with her father, but she knew he'd be all for it. As for what would become of the camp next season, they'd have to cross that bridge together when the time came.

Dad and Bobby stopped in front of cabin number five. Dad pointed up toward the eaves and Bobby nodded. A minute later, they were both laughing. Dad put his hand on Bobby's shoulder. They moved away, toward the laundry room.

"Hey, Mommy. Whatcha lookin' at?"

Claire turned around. Ali stood at the bottom of the stairs, clutching her Tickle Me Elmo doll. "Hey, Ali Kat. Come over here a minute, will you?" She sat down in the blue-and-white striped chair-and-a-half by the fireplace, putting her feet up on the matching ottoman.

Alison crawled onto her lap, settling comfortably in place. Heart to heart, the way they always sat.

"I was just watching Grandpa talk to Bobby."

"Bobby's gonna teach me to fish. He says I'm old enough to go to the trout farm in Skykomish." Alison leaned closer and whispered, "There's a trick to catching the big ones. He's gonna teach it to me. An' he says we can float down the river in inner tubes by August. Even me. Did you ever put a worm on a hook? Yeech. But I'm gonna do it. You'll see. Bobby said he'd help me if it was too wriggly or snotty."

"I'm glad you like him," Claire said softly, trying not to smile.

"He's great." Alison wiggled around until she was facing Claire. "What's the matter, Mommy? You look like you're gonna cry. The worms don't feel anything. Honest."

She stroked Alison's soft cheek. "You're my whole world, Ali Kat. You know that, don't you? No one could ever take your place in my heart."

Alison and Elmo kissed Claire. "I know that." Alison giggled and scampered out of Claire's lap. "I gotta go. Grandpa's taking me to Smitty's Garage. We're gonna get the truck fixed."

As she watched her daughter run out the front door, heard her yell "*Grandpa! Bobby!* I'm here!" Claire felt the pressing weight of responsibility again. How did a woman know if she was being selfish, and was that necessarily a bad thing, anyway? Men were selfish all the time and they built multibillion-dollar corporations and rockets that flew to the moon.

But what if the marriage didn't work?

There it was. The clay beneath it all.

She needed to talk to someone about this. Not her sister, of course. A friend. She dialed Gina's number.

Gina answered on the first ring. "Hello?"

Claire slumped back into the oversize chair and put her feet up. "It's me. The Insta-Marry Queen."

"Yeah, Claire. That's you."

"Meghann thinks I'm being an idiot."

"Since when do we care what *she* thinks? She's an attorney, for God's sake. That's below invertebrates on the evolutionary chain."

Claire's chest eased. She smiled. "I knew you'd put it in perspective."

"That's what friends are for. Would you like me to sing that?"

"Please, no. I've heard you sing. Just tell me I'm not being a selfish bitch who is going to ruin her daughter's life by marrying a stranger."

"Oh, so it's your mother we're talking about."

"I don't want to be like her." Claire's voice was suddenly soft.

"I've known you since all five of us showed up for the first day of school in the same blue shirt. I remember when you bought cream to make your boobs grow and still believed in sea monkeys. Honey, you've never been selfish. And I've never seen you this happy. I don't care that you've known him less than two weeks. God has finally given you the gift of love and passion. Don't return it unopened."

"I'm scared. I should have done this when I was young and optimistic."

"You *are* young and optimistic, and of course you're scared. If you'll remember, I had to drink two tequila straight shots to marry Rex—and we'd lived together for four years." She paused. "I probably shouldn't have used us as an example. But the point remains. A smart person is afraid of marriage. You made it past the marriage-for-marriage's-sake years and you haven't reached the nursing-home-desperation years. You met a man and fell in love. So it happened fast. Big deal. If you're not ready to marry him, by all means, wait. But don't wait because your big sister made you question yourself. Follow your heart."

Claire's gut was clenched, her mind was clouded, but her heart was crystal clear. "What would I do without you?"

"The same thing I'd do without you—drink too much and whine to strangers."

Claire heard the tiny thread of depression in Gina's voice. It made her love her friend all the more for listening to her problems while her own whole world was caving in. "How are you doing?"

"This day or this week? I've got more mood swings than a teenager, and my ass is starting to look like a Buick."

"No jokes, Gigi. How are you?"

She sighed. "Shitty. Rex came by last night. The son of a bitch has lost about ten pounds and dyed his hair. Pretty soon he'll ask me to call him the Rexster again." She paused. "He wants to marry that woman."

"Ouch."

"Ouch with a blowtorch. I'm remembering the day he proposed to me, and he's pricing diamonds. It hurts like hell. But you haven't heard the real news: Joey's back."

"You're kidding. Where's he been?"

There was a pause, the sound of movement, then Gina lowered her voice. "I don't know. Here and there, he says. He looks bad. Older. He got home yesterday. He's been asleep for almost thirteen hours. Honestly, I hope I never love anyone as much as he loved Diana."

"What's he going to do?"

"I don't know. I said he could stay here, but he won't. He's like some animal that's been in the wild too long. And this house brings back a lot of memories. He stared at the picture of my wedding for almost an hour. Honest to God, I wanted to cry."

"Give him my love."

"You got it."

They talked for a few more minutes about ordinary, everyday things. By the time they hung up, Claire felt better. The ground beneath her feet felt firm again. Thinking about Joe and Diana helped, too. With everything that had gone wrong between those two, they still were proof that love could be real.

She looked down at her left hand, at the engagement ring she wore. It was a strip of silver foil, carefully folded and twisted around her finger.

She refused to think of what her sister would say about it, and remembered instead how she'd felt when Bobby put it there.

Marry me, he'd said, on bended knee. She'd known she should smile gently, say, *Oh, Bobby, of course not. We barely know each other.*

But she couldn't say those words. His dark eyes had been filled with the kind of love she'd only dreamed of, and she'd been lost. Her rational self—the part that had been alone for almost three dozen years and become a single parent—had warned her not to be a fool.

Ah, but her heart. That tender organ would not be ignored. She *was* in love. So much so that it felt like drowning.

Gina was right. This love was a gift she'd been given, one she'd stopped looking for and almost stopped believing in. She wouldn't turn away from it because she was afraid. One thing motherhood had taught her—love required boldness. And fear simply came with the package.

She grabbed her sweater off the back of the sofa and slipped it over her shoulders, then she went outside.

Night had almost completely fallen now; darkness enveloped the salmon-hued granite peaks. To the tourists who sat around their campfires making s'mores and roasting hot dogs, it seemed like a quiet time in this patch of green tucked up against the mountains' vertical walls. The locals knew better. Within walking distance, there was a whole world unseen by the casual observer, unheard by those who spent their lives listening on telephones and watching computer screens.

On peaks nearby, ones with names like Formidable, Terror, and Despair, the glaciers were never still, never silent. They slid forward, groaning, creaking, crunching every rock in their path. Even the heat of an August sun couldn't melt them away, and along the banks of the mighty Skykomish, just beyond where the humans walked, a thousand species of wildlife preyed on one another.

Yet the night felt still and calm; the air smelled of pine needles and drying grass. It was that time of year when, for a few weeks, the lawns in town would turn brittle and brown. That rarest of times in the Northwest—a patch of dry.

She heard the quiet buzz of the campers' dinner conversations, punctuated every now and then by a barking dog or a child's high-pitched giggle. Underneath it all, as steady and familiar as the beating of her heart, was the chattering of the river. These sounds had become the music of her youth, long ago replacing the jumbled cacophony of raucous music that had been Mama's soundtrack.

She didn't bother with shoes. Barefoot, her soles toughened by summers spent along this river's banks, she strolled past the empty pool. In the small, shingled pool house, the filter's motor thumped on, buzzing. A pair of inner tubes—one shocking pink and one lime green—floated on the darkening water.

She made her nightly rounds slowly, stopping to talk to several of their guests, even sharing a glass of wine with Wendy and Jeff Goldstein at campsite thirteen.

It was completely dark by the time she reached the small row of cabins on the property's eastern edge. All of the windows glowed with fuzzy golden light.

At first, she thought the sound she heard was crickets, gearing up for a nightly concert. Then she heard the sweet sound of strings being strummed.

Cabin four had a pretty little porch that faced the river. They had taken the cabin off the market this summer because of rain damage to the roof; the vacancy had given Bobby a place to stay until the wedding. *Destiny*, Dad had said when he gave Claire the key.

Now, destiny sat on the edge of the porch, cross-legged, his body veiled in shadows, a guitar across his lap. He stared out at the river, plucking a slow and uncertain tune.

Claire eased into the darkness beneath a giant Douglas fir. Hidden, she watched him. The music sent shivers skimming along her flesh.

Almost too quietly to hear, he started to sing. "I've been walkin' all my life . . . on a road goin' nowhere. Then I turned a corner, darlin' . . . and there you were."

Claire's throat tightened with an emotion so sweet and powerful she felt the start of tears. She stepped out of the shadows.

Bobby looked up and saw her. A smile crinkled the suntanned planes of his face.

She stepped toward him, her bare feet making a soft, thumping beat on the hard, dried grass.

He began to sing again, his gaze on her face. "For the first time in my life . . . I believe in God almighty . . . in the Lord my grandpa promised me . . . 'cause, honey, I see Heaven in your eyes." He strummed a few more chords, then thumped his hand on the guitar and grinned. "That's all I've written so far. I know it needs work." He put down the guitar and moved toward her.

With every footstep, she felt her breathing shorten until, by the time he was standing in front of her, she couldn't seem to draw a full breath. It was almost embarrassing to feel this much.

He took her left hand in his, looked down at the strip of foil that was supposed to be a diamond ring. When he looked at her again, he was no longer smiling.

"Pathetic," he whispered, and her heart ached for the shame she saw in his dark eyes. "Not every woman would accept a ring like this."

"I love you, Bobby. That's all that matters. I know it's crazy, impossible even, but I love you." The words freed something inside her. She could breathe again.

"I'm no prize, Claire. You know that. I've made mistakes in my life. Three of 'em, to be exact."

Claire could practically hear Meg's voice in the breeze. But the sound meant nothing when she saw how Bobby looked at her. No one had ever looked at her like that before, as if she were the most precious woman on earth. "I'm a single mother who never got married. I know about mistakes, Bobby."

"I've never felt this way before," he said softly, a catch in his voice. "Honest to God."

"What way?"

"As if my heart doesn't belong to me anymore, as if it can't beat without you. You're inside me, Claire, holding me up. You make me want to be more than I am."

"I want us to grow old together," she whispered the words. It was her deepest dream, her most treasured hope. All her life, she'd imagined herself alone in old age, one of those white-haired women who sat on the porch, waiting for the phone to ring or a car to drive up. Now, finally, she allowed herself to imagine a better future, one filled with love and laughter and family.

"I want to hear our kids fight about who's touching who in the smelly backseat of a minivan."

Claire laughed. It felt so good to dream with someone.

He pulled her into his arms, danced with her to the music of the river and the crickets.

Finally, Claire said, "My sister, Meghann, is coming up to meet you tomorrow."

He drew back. Taking her hand, he led her to his porch. They sat down in the creaky oak swing and rocked gently. "I thought you said she'd boycott the wedding."

"Wishful thinking." She looked up at him. "She was predictably underwhelmed by our decision to get married."

"This is the sister Gina called Cruella De Vil?"

"Jaws is really the preferred nickname."

"Does her opinion matter?"

"It shouldn't."

"But it does."

Claire felt like a fool. "It does."

"Then I'll win her over. Maybe I'll write a song for her."

"It better go platinum. Meg doesn't like second best. She should be here by early evening tomorrow."

"Should I go down to the army surplus and check out some Kevlar?"

"At the very least."

Bobby's smile faded after a moment. "She won't be able to change your mind about me, will she?"

She was moved by his vulnerability. "She's never been able to change my mind about anything. It's what makes her foam at the mouth."

"As long as you love me, I can take anything."

"Well, Bobby Austin," she put her arms around him and leaned over for a kiss. Just before their lips touched, she whispered, "Then you can take anything. Even my sister."

CHAPTER
ELEVEN

CLAIRE STOOD AT THE KITCHEN SINK, WASHING THE BREAKFAST dishes. It was a gray, not-quite-rainy day, the kind where the sky was so low it seemed to bump you in the forehead when you dared to venture outside. Perfect weather for a visit with Meghann.

The thought made her head pound. She dried her hands and reached for the bottle of Excedrin on the windowsill.

"Mary Kay Acheson gets to have Cap'n Crunch for breakfast."

It was a common early-morning argument. "She'll probably have false teeth in time for eighth grade. You don't want to have to take your teeth out at bedtime, do you?"

Ali banged her feet rhythmically on the rungs at the base of her chair. "Willie has all his teeth and he's gonna be in ninth grade. He's practically a grown-up."

"That's because Karen feeds him Raisin Bran for breakfast. If he ate Cap'n Crunch, it'd be a different story."

Ali frowned, thinking about that.

Claire washed down the aspirin.

"Do you have a headache again, Mommy?"

"Aunt Meg's coming over tonight. She wants to meet Bobby."

Ali's frown deepened. Obviously, she was trying to understand the connection between Mom's headache and Aunt Meg's visit. "I thought she was too busy to breathe."

Claire went to the table and sat down beside her daughter. "You know why Meghann wants to meet Bobby?"

Alison rolled her eyes. "Duh, Mommy."

"Duh?" Claire bit back a smile. At some point, she'd have to address the issue of respectful responses, but she'd better wait until she could do it without cracking up. She held out her hand instead. "You know what this ring means?"

"It's not a ring. It's foil."

"This kind of ring is a symbol. The ring isn't what matters. The words that come with it are what matters. And Bobby asked me to marry him."

"I know that, Mommy. C'n I have some cheddar Goldfish?"

"Let's eat in a second. I want to talk to you about this. No one is more important to me than you. No one. I'll always love you, even if I'm married."

"Jeez, Mommy. I know that. Now c'n I have—"

"Forget the Goldfish." No wonder *It's like talking to a five year old* was a common expression of frustration. "Do you mind if I marry Bobby?"

"Oh." Ali's little face scrunched up. She bunched up her left cheek, then her right. Then she looked up at Claire. "C'n I call him Daddy?"

"He'd like that."

"So at school, on family day, he'll come for the sack races and help Brittani's dad barbecue the hot dogs?"

Claire released a breath. It wasn't easy for her to make blanket promises for another human being. That kind of faith lived in the hearts of women who'd grown up in safer homes, where Mom and Dad could be counted on. But she believed in Bobby as much as one of her mother's daughters could believe in any man. "Yes. We can count on him."

Alison grinned. "Okay. I want him to be my dad. Daddy." She was obviously testing the word, weighing how it felt to say aloud. It was amazing how many little girls' dreams could be contained in those few letters.

Big girls' dreams, too, for that matter.

Alison gave Claire a quick kiss, then scampered off, dragging a dirty Elmo on the floor behind her. She went upstairs to her bedroom. Seconds later, *The Little Mermaid* theme music started.

Claire stared down at her engagement ring. As makeshift as it was, it gave her a warm feeling of hopefulness.

"One down," she said aloud. Actually, it was two. Both her father and her daughter had put their stamp of approval on the wedding plans.

That left only two blood-related holdouts. Meghann, who definitely hadn't sounded approving, and Mama, who probably wouldn't much care. Claire had been putting off the call. No good ever came from talking to Mama.

Still, she was her mother, and she had to be called.

The funny part was, when Claire thought of her "mother," the face that came to her was Meg's. In every childhood memory, it was her sister who'd been there . . . until, of course, the day she decided she'd had enough of caring for Claire.

And Mama. Well. Truth be told, Claire's memories of Mama were sketchy at best. Claire was lucky in that; the brunt of mama's flightiness had fallen on Meg. Still, they all pretended that they were family.

Claire picked up the phone and punched in the number. It rang and rang. Finally, an answering machine clicked on. Mama's thick-as-honey-and-twice-as-sweet Southern drawl was accompanied by music. "I do so appreciate your call on m'private number. Unfortunately, I'm too darn busy to answer, but leave me a message and I'll return your call just as soon as I can. And look for my interview in *People* magazine, on newsstands in late June. Bye, y'all."

Only Mama would self-promote on her answering machine.

"Hey, Mama," she said at the beep, "It's Claire here. Your daughter. I've got some big news and I'd like to talk to you. Call me." She left her number, just in case, and hung up.

She was still holding the phone, listening to the dial tone when she realized her mistake. She was getting married in less than two weeks. If she waited for Mama to call, the wedding would be long past. The point was to *invite* Mama, not to simply inform. You had to invite your mother to your wedding, even if the woman who bore you had the parenting instincts of a mosquito, and there was little chance she'd actually show up.

By the time Mama had managed to fly from Los Angeles to Seattle to see her only granddaughter, Alison had been four years old.

Claire still remembered the day vividly. They'd met at the Woodland Park Zoo in downtown Seattle. Mama had been in the middle of a *Starbase IV* promotional tour (yet again) that touched down there.

Claire and Alison had been sitting on the wooden bench by the zoo's entrance for more than an hour, waiting.

Claire had almost given up when she'd heard a familiar high-pitched screech. She'd looked up just in time to see Mama, dressed in a bronze silk caftan, bearing down on them like a Thanksgiving Day parade float.

Lordy it's good to see my girl again, she'd cried out loudly enough that everyone nearby stopped to stare. A hushed buzz of recognition twittered through the crowd.

It's her, someone said. *Tara Zyn from* Starbase IV.

Claire had fought the urge to roll her eyes. She stood up, her hand clasped tightly around Alison's. *Hey, Mama. It's good to see you again.*

Mama had swooped down on one knee in a movement that sent silk wings flying up on either side of her. *Is this darlin' little thing my granddaughter?*

Hello, Mrs. Sullivan, Alison had said, stumbling awkwardly over the name she'd practiced for a week. Claire had been sure that

Mama wouldn't appreciate the word *Grandma*. In print, she claimed to be looking forward to her fiftieth birthday.

Mama had studied Alison carefully. For a moment, only that, a kind of sadness passed through her blue eyes. Then that smile was back. *You can call me Nanna.* She reached out one bejeweled hand, stroked Ali's curly hair. *You're the spittin' image of your mama.*

I'm not allowed to spit, Mrs. . . . Nanna.

Mama had looked up. *She's spunky, Claire-Bear. Just like Meggy. Good for you. It's the spunky ones that make it in life. I think she's the most well spoken two-year-old I've ever had the pleasure o' meetin'.*

That's because she's four, Mama.

Four? Mama popped to her feet. *Oh, honey, I don't think so. Y'all were just in the hospital. Now, let's hurry along to the snake house. That's m'favorite. And I've got to be back t'my hotel in an hour for an interview with* Evenin' Magazine. Later that afternoon, Meghann had shown up and the four of them had walked silently through the Seattle Center, pretending they had something in common.

It used to hurt Claire to remember that day. Not so much anymore. The wound had healed over, grown a layer of thicker skin. She'd long ago quit wishing for a different mother. It was a hope that had once crippled her; she'd had to let it go. Like her dream of a sister who was also a best friend. Some things just didn't turn out the way you wanted, and a girl could only cry for so many years.

She glanced up at the clock on the oven. It was almost one o'clock.

In only a few hours, Meghann would be here.

"Great," Claire muttered.

"My sister called me last night."

Harriet sat back in her chair. It made a squeaking sound at the movement. "Ah. No wonder you actually kept this appointment. I'd begun to despair."

"I missed one appointment. That's hardly a big deal. I called to cancel and I paid for it."

"You always assume that money is the answer."

"What's your point, Harriet? Today you're being so obscure even Freud couldn't follow you."

"I understand that you were upset at our last appointment."

Meghann's eye started to twitch. "Not really."

Harriet stared at her. "Don't you understand that being upset is part of healing? You need to stop running from your emotions."

"That's what I'm trying to do, if you'll listen. I *said*, my sister called last night."

Harriet sighed. "Is that unusual? I was under the impression that you spoke to Claire quite often; you just never talk about what matters."

"Well, that's true. We call each other every few months. Always on holidays and birthdays."

"So what is remarkable about last night's conversation?"

Meghann's eye twitch kicked into high gear. She could barely see. For no reason at all, she found it difficult to sit still. "She's getting married."

"Take a deep breath, Meg," Harriet said softly.

"My eye is batting like an Evinrude motor."

"Breathe."

Meghann felt like an idiot. "What in the hell is wrong with me?"

"You're scared, that's all."

Identifying the emotion helped. She *was* scared. She released a pent-up breath slowly and looked at Harriet. "I don't want her to get hurt."

"Why do you assume that marriage will hurt her?"

"Oh, please. I notice you're no longer wearing that one-karat solitaire on your left hand. I don't suppose taking it off was a song-inspiring moment of joy."

Harriet fisted her left hand. "Many sisters rejoice when they hear this kind of news."

"Not the ones who handle the divorces."

"Can you separate yourself from your job?"

"This isn't about my job, Harriet. My sister is in trouble. I have to save her."

"Is she in love?"

Meghann waved her hand impatiently. "Of course."

"You don't think that matters?"

"They're always in love in the beginning. It's like going out to sea on a huge throat lozenge. The water disintegrates it. After a few floating years, you're swimming with nothing to hold you up. Then the sharks move in."

"That would be people like you."

"This is no time for lawyer jokes. I have to save my sister before she marries the wrong man."

"How do you know he's the wrong man?"

Meghann fought the urge to say, *They all are.* That admission would only fill up another round of observations and questions. "He's practically jobless. They've known each other less than a month. He's a *musician.* He lets people call him Bobby Jack. Take your pick."

"Are you jealous?"

"Yeah. I want to marry an itinerant Country and Western singer who can't even headline at Cowboy Bob's Western Roundup in Lake Chelan. Yes, Harriet, you've hit the core of it this time. I'm jealous." She crossed her arms. "He's probably marrying her for the so-called resort. He'll try to talk her into building condos or dentists' offices."

"That would show some initiative."

"Claire *loves* that tired piece of land. She would hate to pave over it."

"I thought you said the land was underdeveloped and that Claire was wasting her life there. I believe you mentioned building a spa on the property."

"You're completely missing the point."

"The point being that you need to ride in on a white horse and save her."

"Someone has to protect her. I want to be there for her this time."

"This time."

Meghann looked up sharply. Of course Harriet had pounced on the two words that mattered. "Yes."

Harriet leaned forward. "Tell me about the day you weren't there for your sister."

Meghann stiffened, drew back. The chair squeaked as it rolled backward. "That's not what this is about."

"You're smarter than that, Meg. I don't have to remind you that everything between you and Claire is about the past. What happened?"

Meghann closed her eyes. Obviously, she was in a weakened state, because the sour memories were there, waiting to crowd to the front of her mind. She shrugged, tried to appear casual as she opened her eyes and looked at Harriet. "You know it all. You just want to hear me go through it."

"Do I?"

"I was sixteen. Claire was nine. Mama went to Los Angeles for the *Starbase IV* audition and had so much fun she forgot about the kids she left in Bakersfield. For her, it was a common oversight. Then Social Services started poking around. They threatened to put us into foster care. I was old enough to run away, but Claire . . ." She shrugged. "So I pulled a Nancy Drew and tracked down Sam Cavenaugh—her biological dad. I called him. Sam couldn't save his daughter fast enough." Meg heard the adolescent hurt in her voice. Even now, all these years later, the memories of that summer were hard to bear. She hated to remember how much she'd wanted Sam to be her father, too. Meg straightened. "None of this old shit matters. Sam was a great father to Claire. Everyone ended up happier."

"Everyone? How about the girl who lost her mother and sister and had no father to turn to?"

The observation hurt. Meghann had never been able to discover her own father's name; all Mama ever called him was *That loser*. "Enough. Tell me this, Harriet. Is it smart to marry a man you've known a few weeks? Would you like it if your daughter did what Claire is doing?"

"I'd have to trust her, wouldn't I? We can't live other people's lives for them. Even if we love them."

"I do love Claire," Meghann said quietly.

"I know you do. That's never been the issue, has it?"

"We have nothing in common. It doesn't mean I want to see her throw her life away."

"Oh, I think you have something in common. You lived together for nine years. That's a lot of shared memories. I get the feeling that you used to be best friends."

"Before I dumped her off with a man she barely knew and then ran away? Yeah. We were best friends before that. But Claire wanted a daddy, and once she got one . . . well . . ." Meghann glanced at the intricately cast crystal desk clock. It was 4:00. "It'll take me almost two hours to reach Hayden at this time of day. Our traffic is just terrible, don't you think? If we would elect a mayor instead of—"

"Meg. Don't go off on one of your rants. Today is important. Claire may harbor certain animosities against you."

"I've *told* you she does."

"And yet you're going to race up to Hayden in your expensive car and butt into her life."

"I'd characterize my involvement as saving her from herself. Just handing out some obviously overlooked information."

"Do you think she'll appreciate your help?"

Meghann winced. Claire would probably *not* be pleased. Some people had trouble accepting certain facts. "I'll be pleasant about it."

"You'll pleasantly tell her that she shouldn't marry a singer with no real prospects."

"Yes. I know I can be abrasive at times, and opinionated to the point of oppression, but this time I intend to choose my words carefully. I won't say *loser* or *gold digger* or *stupid*. She'll be hurt, but she'll see that I'm only trying to look out for her."

Harriet seemed to wait an inordinately long time before she asked, "Do you remember how love feels?"

Meghann couldn't follow the segue, but she was glad to quit talking about Claire. "I married Eric, didn't I?" *Number two on the hit parade of bad decisions.*

"What do you remember about your marriage to Eric?"

"The end of it. I've had headaches that lasted longer than my marriage."

"Why did it end?"

"You know this. He cheated on me. With most of the Seahawks' cheerleaders and half the wait staff at the Bellevue Hooters. He was absolutely *ardent* in his pursuit of silicone. If only he'd shown so much drive in his career."

"Do you remember when he proposed?"

Meghann sighed. She didn't want to think about that day. It had all happened so long ago. The candlelit room, the trail of white rose petals that led to the king-size bed, the music coming from another room, a soft, instrumental version of Air Supply's "All Out of Love" that was playing on the radio. "I proposed to him, if you must know. I've never been good at waiting, and it took Eric an hour to pick out a pair of socks."

Harriet looked pained. "Meghann."

"What?"

"Why don't you try that story again? My memory is not as poor as you'd like to think."

Meghann looked down at her fingernails. For years she'd told stories about Eric's infidelities. The remark about his ardent pursuit of silicone always got a laugh. It was better that way, she'd learned; better to think of him as a villain. The truth hurt too much. Even Elizabeth didn't know what had really happened in Meghann's marriage. But now, somehow, Harriet had ferreted out the facts. "I don't want to talk about this."

"Of course you don't," Harriet said gently. "That's why you should."

Meghann released her breath slowly. "He didn't go after waitresses. Not as far as I know, anyway. He was faithful to me . . . until he met Nancy." She closed her eyes, remembering that terrible day when he'd come home crying. *I can't do it anymore, Meg. You're killing me. Nothing I do is good enough for you. And your love . . . it's a cold place.*

And then, just when she'd felt the start of her own tears and tasted the desperate plea in her mouth, he said, *I've met someone. She loves who I am, not who I could be if I were more ambitious. And . . . she's pregnant.*

The memories twisted Meghann's insides, made her feel needy and weak. She couldn't hold it all inside anymore. "It was so romantic," she said softly. "The night he proposed to me. The white rose petals were true. So was the music. He poured a glass of champagne and told me that I was his whole world, that he wanted to love me forever and be the father of my children. I cried when he said it." She wiped her eyes of tears that should have dried long ago. "I should have known how fragile love was, given my family history, but I was reckless. I handled a glass bubble as if it were made of steel. I couldn't believe how quickly it broke. He left because I didn't know how to love him enough." On that, her voice cracked. "You can't blame him."

"So, you did love him."

"Oh, I loved him," Meghann said quietly, feeling the dormant pain well up and become fresh again.

"It's interesting that you readily remember the pain of your divorce, but you have to be reminded of the love."

"No more," Meg said, standing up. "This is like open-heart surgery without anesthesia." She looked at her watch. "Besides, we're out of time. I told Claire I'd be there this evening. I need to go."

Harriet slowly removed her glasses and looked up at Meghann. "Think this thing through, Meg. Maybe this wedding could bring you and Claire together, give you some new ground to stand on."

"You think I should just let her marry Bobby Jack Tom Dick and say nothing?"

"Sometimes love means trusting people to make their own decisions. In other words, shutting up."

"Women pay me handsomely to tell them the truth."

"*Your* version of the truth. And Claire is not one of your clients. She's a woman who is getting married for the first time. A thirty-five-year-old woman, I might add."

"So I should just smile and hug her and tell her I think it's great that she's marrying a stranger?"

"Yes."

"What if he breaks her heart?"

"Then she'll need her sister. But she won't turn to someone who'll say, *I told you so.*"

Meghann thought about that. She was opinionated and abrasive, but she wasn't a dimwit. "Sorry, Harriet," she said at last. "I don't agree. I can't let him hurt her. Claire's the best person I know."

"The best person you don't know, you mean. Clearly, you want to keep it that way. You want to keep her at arm's length."

"Whatever. Good-bye." Meghann hurried from the office.

Harriet was wrong. It was that simple.

Meghann had let Claire down once; she wouldn't do it again.

It's stupid to marry a man you just met.

" 'Stupid' is not a good word choice."

It's inadvisable to—

"You're her sister, not her lawyer."

Meghann had been carrying on this demented conversation with the rearview mirror for more than an hour. How was it that she came up with closing arguments that would bring a jury to tears and she couldn't find a simple, compelling way to warn her sister of impending doom?

She drove through the stop-and-go traffic of downtown Seattle and into the flat green farmland of the Snohomish valley. Towns that in her youth had been sleepy little dairy towns now wore the glitzy facade of bedroom communities. Big, brick-fronted, porticoed suburban homes sat on chopped-up pieces of land, their driveways cluttered with SUVs and recreational vehicles. The original clapboard farmhouses had been torn down long ago; only rarely did one peek out from behind a billboard or beside a strip mall.

But as the highway began to climb, that yuppie sheen disappeared. Here, in the shadow of the lavender-gray peaks of the central Cascade Mountains, the towns were untouched by the march of progress. These towns, with names like Sultan, Goldbar, and Index, were too far out of the way to be gentrified. For now.

The last stop before Hayden wasn't a town at all; rather, it was a collection of buildings on the side of the road, the final place to get gas and supplies before the top of the pass. A run-down tavern—the Roadhouse—sat huddled beneath a blinking neon sign that recommended Coors Light.

Honest to God, she wanted to pull over, walk into that crowded tavern, and lose herself in the smoky darkness. It would certainly be better than saying to Claire after being separated all these years, *You're making a mistake.*

But she didn't slow down. Instead, she drove the nine miles to Hayden, veered into the exit lane and turned off the freeway. The road immediately telescoped down to two lanes bordered on either side by towering evergreens. The mountains were jagged and cruel-looking. Even in the summer months, snow lay atop their inaccessible peaks.

A small green sign welcomed her to *Hayden, population 872. Home of Lori Adams, 1974 State Spelling Bee Champion.*

Nineteen seventy-four.

Meghann had first seen this sleepy little town only three years later. Back then, Hayden had been nothing more than a few run-down buildings. The city fathers hadn't stumbled across the Western motif as a tourist attraction idea yet.

The memory of driving into town was still fresh. She could practically smell the musty odor of Sam's old pickup truck, practically feel Claire's thin body tucked in close beside her. *Does he really want us?* her sister had whispered every time Sam got out to pump gas or check them into a cheap motel. They'd driven from California to Washington in two days; in that time, almost no words had been exchanged between them. Meghann had felt sick to her stomach the whole time. Each passing mile had made her more afraid that calling Sam had been the wrong thing to do. By the time they'd actually reached Hayden, Meg had run out of optimistic answers to her sister's questions, so she'd simply tightened her hold on Claire. Sam must have been uncomfortable in the silence, too. He'd cranked the radio up. Elton John's "Goodbye Yellow Brick Road" had been playing when they'd pulled up to the resort.

Funny, the things one remembered.

She slowed down. Hayden still looked like the kind of place that welcomed newcomers, where women brought homemade tuna casseroles to the families who moved in across the street.

But Meghann knew better.

She'd lived here long enough to know how cruel these nice-looking people could be to a girl who ran with the wrong crowd. Sure, a small town could comfort a person; it could also turn cold fast. When you'd been raised by a stripper and grown up in a trailer on the wrong side of town, you couldn't move to Mayberry and fit in.

At least, Meghann hadn't been able to. Claire had been a different story.

Meghann came to the one and only stoplight. When it turned green, she hit the gas and sped through town.

A few miles later she came to the sign.

River's Edge Resort. Next Left.

She turned onto the gravel road. The trees on either side were gigantic. Salal and Volkswagen-size ferns grew in their immense shadows.

At the first driveway, she slowed again. A cute mailbox, painted to look like a killer whale, read: *C. Cavenaugh.*

The once-wild yard had been tamed, trimmed, and planted; it now looked like an English country garden. The house was Martha Stewart perfect—pale, butter-yellow clapboard siding and glossy white trim, a pretty white wraparound porch decorated with hanging pots of geraniums and lobelia.

Meg had been here only once, after Ali was born. All she remembered about that day was sitting on a shabby sofa, trying to make conversation with her sister. Then the Bluesers had descended—Claire's friends—they'd swarmed into the house like locusts, chattering and buzzing.

For an endless hour, Meg had sat there, sipping weak lemonade, thinking about a deposition that had gone badly. Finally, she'd made some idiotic excuse and slipped away. She hadn't been back since.

Now she parked and got out of the car. Lugging gifts, she walked up to the front door and knocked.

No one answered.

After a long wait, she walked back to the car and drove the five hundred or so yards to the campground's main office.

She walked past the swimming pool, where kids were playing Marco Polo, toward the long, narrow log building that served as the registration office. A bell tinkled overhead as she opened the door.

Sam Cavenaugh stood behind the desk. At her entrance, he looked up. His ready smile faded slowly, then reinforced itself. "Hey, Meg. It's good to see you. It's been too damn long."

"Yeah, I'm sure you missed me." As always, she felt uncomfortable around Sam; angry. Harriet claimed it was because Claire had rejected Meghann in favor of him, but that wasn't right. She still remembered the day he told her, *Go, just leave.* He'd thought she was a bad influence on *his daughter.* But what she'd really hated, the one that stayed with her was *just like your damn mother.*

They stared at each other. Thankfully, he kept his distance.

"You look good," he said at last.

"You, too." Meghann glanced down at her watch. The last thing she wanted to do was stand around not talking with Sam.

"Claire told me to watch out for you. She's running a little late. The Ford family, over in campsite seventeen, had a little emergency with their stove. She had to go help them out, but she should be back any minute."

"Good. I'll wait for her at the house, then."

"She should be there any minute."

"You just said that."

"You're still tough, aren't you, Meghann?" he said, his voice soft, a little tired even.

"I had to be, Sam. You know that better than anyone."

"I didn't kick you out, Meghann, I—"

She turned and walked away, let the door slam shut behind her. She was halfway to the car when she heard his voice again.

"She's happy, you know. With this fella," he said.

Meghann slowly turned around. "If I remember correctly, you were happy when you married Mama. I was happy when I married Eric."

Sam walked toward her. "Your mama is a piece of work, that's for sure, and I was mad at her for a lot of years, but I'm glad I married her."

"You must be on drugs."

"Claire" was all he said.

"Oh." Meghann felt a pinch of jealousy. There it was again—the Claire father-daughter thing. It pissed her off. She ought to be long past that.

"Be careful with her," he said. "You're her sister."

"I know I'm her sister."

"Do you?"

"Yeah, I do." Once again, she walked away. She strolled through the campground, surprised at the number of guests who were there. All of them seemed to be having a good time. The place was well maintained and perfectly situated. Every view was a picture postcard of mountain, trees, and water. Finally, she returned to her car and drove to Claire's house.

This time when she knocked on the front door, she heard the patter of feet come from inside. The door burst open.

Alison stood there, dressed in daisy-festooned denim overalls and a pretty yellow eyelet blouse.

"You can't be Alison Katherine Cavenaugh. She's a baby."

Ali beamed at that. "I'm a big girl now."

"Yes, you are."

Alison frowned up at her. "Your hair is longer and there's gray in it."

"Why, thank you for noticing. Can you give your Aunt Meg a hug?"

"You look like you're breathing okay."

Meg had no idea what the child meant by that. "I am."

Alison moved forward and gave her a lukewarm hug. When she stepped back, Meg said, "I brought you a present."

"Let me guess." Claire emerged from the shadows at the end of the hallway. "You thought every five year old needs a Swiss Army Knife."

"No. A BB gun."

"You didn't."

Meghann laughed. "I went into the bowels of Hell—a toy store at Northgate—and found the dullest-looking salesperson. She recommended this instead." She handed Alison a brightly wrapped box.

Ali ripped it open. "It's a Groovy Girl, Mommy. A Groovy Girl!" She flung herself at Meghann, this time hugging for real. She showed the doll to Claire, then ran upstairs.

Meghann handed Claire a bottle of wine—Far Niente 1997. "This is one of my favorites."

"Thank you."

They stared at each other. Their last meeting had been a year ago, when Mama was in town for the Fan-ference. Mama had taken Claire and Ali to the zoo, then later, Meghann had joined them at the Seattle Center. They'd spent most of their time taking Alison for rides in the Fun Forest. That way, they didn't need to talk.

Finally Claire surged forward, pulled Meghann into a quickie hug, then let her go.

Meghann stumbled back, too surprised by the gesture to respond. Afterward, she wished she'd hugged Claire in return. "Dinner smells good, but you didn't have to cook. I wanted to take you out."

"The Chuck Wagon smorgasbord isn't exactly your style. I didn't want to hear about it."

"Oh."

"Anyway, come in. It's been too long since you were here."

"You've never been to my place."

Claire looked at her. "It's called small talk, Meg. I wasn't picking a fight."

"Oh," Meghann said again, feeling like an idiot.

She followed Claire to the sofa and sat down beside her. She couldn't help noticing the ridiculous engagement ring—a band of tinfoil, for God's sake. It was good she'd come up here. There was no point in putting it off. "Claire, I think—"

Then *he* walked into the room. Meghann knew instantly why her sister had fallen so hard. Bobby might be a loser as a singer, but he was a winner in the looks department. He was tall and lean, but broad-shouldered, with blond hair that fell almost to his shoulders. When he smiled, it was with his whole face.

A man like this didn't just sweep you off your feet; he twirled you into the air so far and fast there was nowhere to go but down.

He and Claire exchanged a look that radiated love. Meg was reminded of *The Way We Were*, that paean to the bittersweet truth that sometimes the wrong man could look so good he took your breath away.

But sooner or later a woman had to breathe.

"I'm Bobby Austin," he said, smiling.

Meghann rose to her feet and shook his hand. "Meghann Dontess."

"Claire says folks call you Meg."

"My friends do, yes."

He smiled. "I'm judging by that bite-on-a-lemon look of yours that you'd like me to stick with Miz Dontess."

"I imagine those mountain girls in Arkansas think you're charming."

"The Texas girls sure did." He put an arm around Claire. "But those days are behind me now. I've found the girl I want to grow old with." He kissed Claire lightly on the cheek and squeezed her hand, then he took the wine bottle and walked into the kitchen.

In the few moments he was gone, Meghann stood there, staring at her sister, trying to choose her words with care, but nothing seemed quite right.

Bobby returned with two glasses of wine and handed one to Meghann. "I imagine you have some questions for me," he said, sitting down.

His forthrightness threw Meghann off. Slowly, feeling a little uncertain, she sat down in the chair opposite the sofa. They were separate entities now: Bobby and Claire versus Meghann. "Tell me about yourself."

"I love Claire."

"Something substantive."

"You're a facts-and-figures, gal, huh? I'm thirty-seven years old. Graduated from Oklahoma State. Degree in music appreciation. Rodeo scholarship. I was a calf roper. Which is why my knees are gone. I've . . . been married."

Meghann leaned forward, on alert. "How many times?"

He glanced at Claire. "Three."

"Oh, *shit.*" Meghann looked at Claire. "You've got to be kidding. If marriages were felonies, he'd be in prison for life."

He scooted forward. "I married Suellen when we were eighteen years old. She was pregnant, and where I come from—"

"You've got kids?"

"No." His voice grew soft. "Miscarriage. After that, there wasn't much reason to stay married. We lasted less than three months. I'm a slow learner, though. I got married again at twenty-one. Unfortunately, it turned out that she wanted a different life than I did. Nice cars, nice jewelry. I got arrested when they busted her for selling cocaine out of our house. I lived with her for two years and never noticed it. I just thought she was moody as hell. Nobody believed I wasn't a part of it. Laura was the only one who counted. She was—is—a pediatrician who loves country music. We were married for ten years. It broke up about a year ago. I could tell you why, but it's none of your business. Claire knows everything, though."

A three-time loser and a felon.

Perfect.

And now the bad sister had to break the good sister's heart.

How?

That was the $64,000 question. How did you say the things that needed to be said at a time like this? Especially with Mr. Better-Looking Than God sitting there? Harriet had been right about one thing: Meghann and Claire had been poised on a cliff of politeness and pretense for years. The wrong approach could send them over the edge.

Claire got off the sofa, moved toward her. She sat on the carved Chinese chest that served as a coffee table.

"I know you can't be happy for me, Meg."

"I want to be." It was the truth. "It's just that—"

"I know. He wouldn't get a platinum rating. I know. And you handle divorces for a living. I know that, too. Most of all, I know that you grew up in Mama's house." She leaned forward. "I *know*, Meg."

Meghann felt the weight of those few words. Her sister had thought of all the same reasons, had seen all the possible outcomes. There wasn't anything Meghann could say that Claire didn't already know.

"It won't ever make sense and I know it's crazy and risky and—worst of all—Mama-like. I don't need you to tell me these things. What I need is for you to trust me."

Trust. Exactly what Harriet had predicted. But Meghann had forgotten long ago how to trust people. If she'd ever known.

"It's hard for you, I know. The leader of the pack never makes a good follower. But it would mean a lot to me if you'd let this go. Maybe hug me and say you're happy for me. Even if it's a lie."

Meghann looked into her sister's pale green eyes. Claire looked frightened right now; expectant, too. She was obviously preparing herself to be wounded by Meghann's response, but a slim part of her couldn't help believing. . . .

It reminded Meghann of their childhood. Whenever Mama had brought a new "friend" home, Claire had let herself believe that *finally* there would be a daddy in her life. Meghann had tried to protect Claire from her own optimism, but she'd never succeeded, and so, each stepfather had broken a tiny piece of Claire's heart. And yet, when the next man arrived, her sister found a way to believe again.

Of course Claire believed in Bobby Austin.

There was no way Meghann would change her sister's mind, or—more important—her heart. Thus, she had two choices: pretend to give her blessing or stick to her guns. The first choice allowed her and Claire to remain the almost sisters they were. The second choice risked even that tenuous relationship.

"I trust you, Claire," Meghann said at last. She was rewarded with a small, uncertain smile. "If you say Bobby Austin is the man you love, that's good enough for me."

Claire released a sharp breath. "Thank you. I know that wasn't easy for you." She leaned forward and hugged Meghann, who was too surprised by it to hug her back.

Claire drew back and stood up. She went over to the sofa and sat down by Bobby, who immediately put an arm around her and pulled her in close.

Meghann tried to think of what to say in the awkward silence that followed. "So, what's the wedding plan? Justice of the peace? I have a friend who's a judge. . . ."

"No way." Claire laughed. "I waited thirty-five years for this. I'm having the whole enchilada. White dress. Formal church wedding. Cake. Reception with dancing. All of it."

Meghann didn't know why she was surprised. Claire had been one of those children who played bride endlessly. "There's a consultant in my building. I think she planned Bill Gates's wedding."

"This is Hayden, not Seattle. I'll rent the VFW hall and everyone will pitch in with potluck. The Bon Marché has a bridal department now. It'll be great. You'll see."

"Potluck? *Potluck?*" Meghann got to her feet. Apparently there was something of her mother in her after all. She wasn't going to let her sister have a Wal-Mart wedding. "I'll organize the wedding and reception," she said impulsively. Once she'd offered, she felt steady again. In control of something.

Claire's smile faded. "You?"

"I'm not a social moron. I can do this."

"But . . . but . . . your job is so hectic. I couldn't ask you to take time out of your busy schedule for this."

"You didn't ask. I offered. And it so happens that I find myself . . . underutilized at work." The idea seized hold of her. Maybe it could bring them together. "This would be perfect, really. I'd *like* to do this for you, Claire."

"Oh." Claire sounded underwhelmed. Meghann knew what her sister was thinking—Meghann was a bull in a small-town china shop.

"I'll listen to you and do what you want. It'll be *your* wedding. I promise."

"I think it sounds great," Bobby said, smiling broadly. "You're very generous, Meghann."

Claire frowned at Meghann. "Why am I seeing *Father of the Bride* playing in my head? You never do anything in a small way, Meg."

Meghann felt awkward suddenly, vulnerable. She wasn't certain why she wanted this so badly. "I will this time. Honest."

"Okay," Claire said finally. "You can help me plan my wedding."

Meghann grinned and clapped her hands. "Good. Now, I better get started. Where's a local phone book? And what's the date again—the twenty-third? Next Saturday? That's not much time to pull this together." She headed for the kitchen, where she found a scrap of paper and began a to-do list.

"Oh, man," she heard her sister say. "I've created a monster."

CHAPTER
TWELVE

By the second night in his sister's house, Joe felt as if he were suffocating. Everywhere he looked he saw glimpses of his old life. He didn't know how he was going to go forward, but he knew he couldn't stay here.

He waited until Gina left to go grocery shopping, then crammed his things—including several framed photographs of Diana that he'd taken from the house—into the old backpack and headed for the door. He left a note on the kitchen counter.

Can't stay here. Sorry. Hurts too much.
I know this is a rough time for you, so
I won't go far. Will call soon. Love you.
Thank you.
J.

He walked the few miles back to town. By the time he reached Hayden, it felt as if he were slogging through mud. He was tired again, weary.

He didn't want to run away, didn't want to hunker down in some shitty little motel room and gnaw on the old guilt.

He looked up and saw a sign for the Mountain View Cemetery. A shiver passed through him. The last time he'd been there it had been pouring rain. There had been two policemen beside him, shadowing his every move. The mourners had kept their distance. He'd felt their condemnation, heard their whispers.

He'd tried to walk away during the ceremony, but the police yanked him back in line. He'd whispered, *I can't watch this* in a broken voice. One of his guards had said, *Too bad* and held him in place.

He should go there now, to the cemetery. But he couldn't do it, couldn't kneel on the sweet green grass in front of her headstone.

Besides, he wouldn't find her at the cemetery. There was more of her in his heart than beneath any gray stone.

He skirted town and hiked across an empty field toward the river. The soft, gurgling sounds sparked a dozen memories of their youth. Days they'd picnicked along the water's edge and nights they'd parked there, making love in the dark interior of the Dodge Charger he'd once owned.

He knelt there.

"Hey, Di." He squeezed his eyes shut, battling a wave of guilt. "I'm home. What now?"

No answer came to him on the summer breeze, no scent of Red wafted his way. And yet, he knew. She was glad he'd come back.

He opened his eyes again, stared at the silver caps of the current. "I can't go to the house." The thought of it made him almost ill. Three years ago, he'd walked out of their home on Bainbridge Island and never looked back. Her clothes were still in the closet. Her toothbrush was still by the sink.

No way he could go there. His only hope—if there was any hope at all—lay in baby steps. He didn't have to move *toward* his old life; he simply had to stop running from it.

"I could get a job in Hayden," he said after a long silence.

Staying in town would be difficult, he knew. So many people remembered what he'd done. He'd have to endure the looks . . . the gossip.

"I could try it."

With that, he found that he could breathe again.

He spent another hour there, kneeling in the grass, remembering. Then, finally, he climbed to his feet and walked back to town.

There were a few people milling around the streets, and more than one face peered frowningly up at him, but no one approached him. He saw when he was recognized, saw the way old friends lurched at the sight of him, drew back. He kept his head down, kept moving. He was about to give up on the whole damn idea of finding a job here when he came to the end of town. He stood across the street from Riverfront Park, staring at a collection of cars, all lined up on a patch of gravel behind a sagging chain-link fence. A metal Quonset hut advertised *Smitty's, The Best Auto Shop in Hayden.*

On the chain-link fence was a sign: *Help Wanted. Experience requested, but who am I kidding?*

Joe crossed the street and headed toward the entrance.

A dog started barking. He noticed the *Beware of Dog* sign. Seconds later, a miniature white poodle came tearing around the corner.

"Madonna, stop that damn yapping." An old man stepped out from the shadowed darkness of the Quonset hut. He wore oil-stained overalls and a Mariners baseball cap. A long white beard hid the lower half of his face. "Don't mind the dog. What can I do ya for?"

"I saw your help-wanted sign."

"No kiddin'." The old man slapped his thigh. "That thing's been up there since Jeremy Forman went off to college. Hell, that's been pret near on two years now. I—" He paused, stepped forward, frowning slowly. "Joe Wyatt?"

He tensed. "Hey, Smitty."

Smitty blew out a heavy breath. "I'll be damned."

"I'm back. And I need a job. But if it'd cost you customers to hire me, I understand. No hard feelings."

"You want a job *wrenching?* But you're a doctor—"

"That life is over."

Smitty stared at him a long time, then said, "You remember my son, Phil?"

"He was a lot older than me, but yeah. He used to drive that red Camaro."

"Vietnam ruined him. Guilt, I think. He did stuff over there. . . . Anyway, I've seen a man run before. It isn't good. Of course I'll hire you, Joe. The cabin still comes with the job. You want it?"

"Yes."

Smitty nodded, then led the way through the Quonset hut and out the other end. The backyard was big and well maintained. Flowers grew in riotous clumps along the walkway. There, a thicket of towering evergreens stood clustered behind the small log cabin. Moss furred the roof; the front porch sagged precariously.

"You were a teenager the last time you lived here. I couldn't keep track of all the girls you dated."

"That was a long time ago."

"Yeah," Smitty sighed. "Helga still keeps it spick-'n'-span clean. She'll be glad to have you back."

Joe followed Smitty to the cabin.

Inside, it was as clean as always. A red-striped woolen blanket covered an old leather sofa and a rocking chair sat next to the river-rock fireplace. The yellow Formica-clad kitchen appeared well stocked for appliances and pots and pans, and a single bedroom boasted a queen-size four-poster bed.

Joe reached out and shook Smitty's bear-claw hand. "Thank you, Smitty," he said, surprised at how deep his gratitude ran. His throat felt tight.

"There are a lot of people in this town who care about you, Joe. You seem to have forgotten that."

"That's nice to hear. Still, I'd be happier if no one knew I was here, for a while, anyway. I don't . . . feel comfortable around people anymore."

"It's a long road back from something like that, I guess."

"A very long road."

After Smitty left, Joe burrowed through his backpack for one of the framed photographs that he'd taken from his sister's house. He stared down at Diana's smiling face. "It's a start," he said to her.

Meghann woke up disoriented. In the first place, the room was dark. Second, it was quiet. No honking horns and sirens and the beep-beep-beep of trucks in reverse gear. At first she thought a radio was on, in a room down the hall. Then she realized that the noise was birdsong. Birdsong, for God's sake.

Claire's house.

She sat up in bed. The beautifully decorated guest room was oddly comforting. Everywhere were handmade trinkets—proof of time spent on the little things—as well as Ali's artwork. Framed photographs cluttered every surface. In another time and place, Meghann might have laughed at the crudely painted macaroni-coated egg carton that acted as a jewelry box. Here, in her sister's house, it made her smile. When she looked at it, she pictured Ali, with her pudgy little fingers, gluing and placing and painting. And Claire, clapping with pride when the project was done; then proudly displaying it. All the things their own mama wouldn't have had time for.

There was a knock at the door, then a hesitantly called out "Meg?"

She glanced at the bedside clock.

Ten fifteen.

Oh, man. She rubbed her eyes, which felt like a sandpit from lack of sleep. As usual, she'd tossed and turned all night. "I'm up," she said, throwing the covers back.

"Breakfast is on the table," Claire said through the closed door. "I'm going to go clean the swimming pool. We'll leave at about eleven, if that's still okay?"

It took Meghann a second to remember. She'd promised to join Claire and her friends in town. Wedding-dress shopping in Hayden with grown women who called themselves the Bluesers.

Meghann groaned. "I'll be ready."

"See you then."

Meghann listened to the footsteps as Claire walked away. How long could she keep up this charade of *I'm your sister, I support your wedding*? Sooner or later, her head would pop off, or—worse—her mouth would open and her opinion would explode, bomblike: *You can't marry him. You don't know him. Be smart.*

None of these opinions would sit well.

And yet, because Meghann couldn't return to work, had no friends to call, and no true vacation plans, she found herself preparing to plan her sister's wedding. Honestly, who could possibly be worse for the job?

She couldn't even remember the last wedding she'd attended. Oh, yes she could.

Hers.

Of course, it hadn't been the wedding that sent them on the wrong road; it was the pairing up that had done it.

She got out of bed and went to the door. Opening it a crack, she peeked out. Everything was quiet. She hurried down the hallway to the small second-floor bathroom. An unopened traveler's toothbrush lay on the side of the sink, no doubt a quick repossession from the "resort's" mini store. She brushed her teeth, then took a quick, very hot shower.

Thirty minutes later, she was ready to go, re-dressed in yesterday's clothes—a white Dolce & Gabbana blouse, a pair of low-rise Marc Jacobs jeans, and a wide brown belt with a silver circle buckle.

She quickly picked up the bathroom, made her bed, and left the house.

Outside, the sun shone brightly on the well-tended yard. It was late June, a glorious time of year in the Northwest. So much was in bloom. There was color everywhere in the yard, all of it backed and bordered by glossy green bushes and a thicket of trees. At the far end, looking almost close enough to touch, the granite triangle of Formidable Peak pushed up toward a high layer of clouds.

Meghann tossed her purse onto the passenger seat of her Porsche and got inside. The engine growled to life. She drove toward the resort slowly, careful not to stir up too much dust on the gravel road. It was a short distance, maybe five hundred yards between the house and the registration office, but her high-heeled sandals couldn't handle the loose stone.

Finally, she pulled up in front of the registration building and parked. Choosing a careful path through the dewy grass, she went into the building.

It was empty.

She went to the desk and found the Hayden phone book, then flipped to *Wedding Consultants*. There was one listing. *Royal Event Planning*. In fine print it read: *Pretend you'll only get married once.*

Meghann couldn't help smiling at that. A cynic with humor. Who better to help Meghann plan a wedding? She wrote down the number and put it in her purse.

She found Claire in the campground's rest room, plunging a backed-up toilet. At Meghann's horrified expression, Claire laughed. "Go on outside, hotshot. I'll be out in a sec."

Meghann backed out and stood on the edge of the grass.

True to her word, Claire was out in no time. "I'll wash up and we'll go." She looked at the Boxster. "You *drove* over here?" Laughing, she walked away.

Meghann got in the car and started it up. The stereo immediately came on, too loud. "Hotel California." She put the convertible top down and waited.

Finally Claire reappeared, wearing a pair of jeans and a River's Edge Resort T-shirt. She tossed her canvas handbag behind the seat and climbed in. "Now, this is going to town in style."

Meghann didn't know if Claire intended that remark as a put-down or not, so she kept silent. Actually, that was her new mantra: *Shut up and smile.*

"You sure slept late," Claire said, turning down the music. "I thought you usually got to the office by seven."

"I had trouble sleeping last night."

"Please don't worry about me, Meg. Please."

Meghann was trapped by that quiet *please*. She couldn't let her sister think the insomnia was because of the wedding. "It's not the wedding. I never sleep."

"Since when?"

"I guess it started in college. Cramming all night for exams. You know how it is."

"No, I don't."

Meghann had been trying to protect Claire, to hide the fact that the insomnia had started when their family fell apart, but college had been the wrong tack. To Claire, it was another reminder of everything between them, one more instance of Meghann lording it over her sister. Over the years, Claire had made dozens of remarks about her brainiac older sister who started college early. It was a touchy subject. "From what I hear, motherhood causes a few all-nighters, too."

"You know something about babies. Mama said I was colicky. A real pain in the ass."

"Yeah, like Mama would know. You didn't have colic. You had ear infections. When you were sick, you wailed like a banshee. I used to carry you, screaming, down to the Laundromat. If I sat on top of the dryer, holding you, you'd finally fall asleep. Mama always wondered what happened to all her quarters."

Meghann felt Claire's gaze on her. She tried to think of something to say, a way to change the conversation, but she came up empty.

Claire finally laughed, but the sound was brittle. "No wonder I don't mind doing the laundry. Turn here."

They were on safe land once again, she and Claire; each standing on her separate shore.

"This is it." Claire pointed to an old Victorian house, painted Pepto-Bismol pink with lavender trim. A gravel walkway cut through a perfectly shorn lawn. On either side were bright red roses in full bloom. The white picket fence bore a hand-painted sign that read: *Miss Abigail's Drawers. Come on in.*

Meghann looked up at the ridiculously cute house. "We could zip down to Escada or Nordstrom. . . ."

"Don't be yourself, Meg."

"Okay." She sighed. "I'll be Tammy Faye. Or better yet, Small-Town Sally. Lead on. I'll shut my mouth."

They walked up the rickety stairs and entered the store. There was merchandise everywhere—plastic flowers and seashell picture frames, and Christmas ornaments made of painted dough. The fireplace screen was alight with votive candles.

"Hello!" Claire called out.

There was an immediate response. A gaggle of women's voices, then a herd of running footsteps.

A large, older woman barreled around the corner, her gray sausage-curled hair bobbing like Cindy's on *The Brady Bunch.* She wore a floral muumuu and white pom-pomed mule slippers. "Claire Cavenaugh. I'm so glad to *finally* be able to show you the second floor."

"Wedding dresses are on the second floor," Claire said to Meghann. "Abby had given up on me."

Before Meghann could respond, two other women hurried into the room. One was short and wore a baggy, waistless dress and white tennis shoes. The other was tall, perhaps too thin, and dressed flawlessly in beige silk.

Two of the Bluesers. Meg recognized the women but couldn't have matched a name to a face for all the prize money in the world.

Waistless dress, she learned, was Gina, and beige silk was Charlotte.

"Karen couldn't make it today," Gina said, eyeing Meghann suspiciously. "Willie had an orthodontist appointment and Dottie sat on her glasses."

"In other words," Charlotte said, "an ordinary Karen day."

They all started talking at once.

Meghann watched Claire fall in beside Charlotte and Abigail. They were talking about lace and beadwork and veils.

All Meg could think was: *The perfect accessory is a prenup.* It made her feel decades older than these women, and distinctly apart.

"So. Meghann. The last time I saw you, Alison was a newborn." Gina stood beside a cast-iron statue of a crane. "Now you're back for the wedding."

Claire's friends had always been good at the not-so-subtle reminder than Meghann didn't belong here. "Hello, Gina. It's nice to see you again."

Gina looked at her. "I'm surprised you could get away from the office. I hear you're the best divorce attorney in Seattle."

"I wouldn't miss Claire's wedding."

"I know a divorce attorney. She's good at breaking up families."

"That's what we do."

A look passed through Gina's eyes. Her voice softened. "Do you ever put them back together?"

"Not often."

Gina's face seemed to fall; it crumpled like an old paper bag, and Meghann understood. "You're going through a divorce."

Gina tried valiantly to smile. "Just finished it, actually. Tell me it'll get better."

"It will," Meg said softly. "But it may take a while. There are several support groups that might help you." She started to reach into her purse.

"I've got the Bluesers to cry with, but thank you. I appreciate the honesty. Now let's go upstairs and find your sister the perfect wedding dress."

"In Hayden?"

Gina laughed at that and led Meg upstairs. By the time they got there, Claire was already wearing the first dress. It had huge leg-of-mutton sleeves, a sweetheart neckline, and a skirt that looked like an upside-down teacup. Meg sat down in an ornate white wicker chair. Gina stood behind her.

"Oh, my. That's lovely," Abigail said, "and it's thirty-three percent off."

Claire stood in front of a three-paneled full-length mirror, turning this way and that.

"It's very princesslike," Charlotte said.

Claire looked at Meg. "What do you think?"

Meghann wasn't sure what was expected of her. Honesty or support. She took another look at the dress and knew support was impossible. "Of course the dress is on sale. It's hideous."

Claire climbed down from the platform and went in search of a different dress.

At her exit, Charlotte and Abigail looked at Meghann. Neither woman was smiling.

She'd been too honest—a common flaw—and now she was suspect. The outsider.

She would *not* comment on the next dress. She absolutely would not.

"What do you think?" Claire asked a few moments later.

Meg squirmed in her chair. Was this a joke? The dress looked like something you'd wear to a formal hoedown. Maybe the Country Music Awards. The only thing missing was a beaded milking pan. The dress was ugly. Period. And cheap-looking, to boot.

Claire studied herself in the mirror, again turning this way and that. Then she turned to look at Meghann. "You're awfully quiet."

"It's the vomit backing up in my throat. I can't talk."

Claire's smile froze. "I take it that's a negative."

"A cheap dress from the Bon Marché is a negative. That piece of lace-festooned shit is a get-me-the-hell-out-of-here-you've-lost-your-mind thing."

"I think you're being a bit harsh," Abigail said, puffing up like a colorful blowfish.

"It's her *wedding*," Meg said. "Not a tryout for *Little House on the Prairie*."

"My sister is always harsh," Claire said quietly, walking back into the dressing room.

Meghann sighed. She'd screwed up again, wielded her opinion

like a blunt instrument to the back of the head. She hunkered down in her chair and clamped her mouth shut.

The remainder of the afternoon was a mind-wrecking parade of cheap dresses. One after another, Claire zipped in, got opinions, and zipped out. She didn't again ask for Meghann's opinion, and Meghann knew better than to offer it. Instead, she leaned back in her chair and rested her head against the wall.

A jab in the rib cage woke her up. She blinked, leaned forward. Charlotte, Abigail, and Claire were walking away from her, talking animatedly until they disappeared into a room marked *Hats and Veils*.

Gina was staring at her. "I'd heard you could be a bitch, but falling asleep while your sister tries on wedding dresses is pretty rude."

Meghann wiped her eyes. "It was the only way I could keep quiet. I've seen better-looking dresses on Denny's waitresses. Believe me, I was doing her a favor. Did she find one?"

"No."

"I want to say thank God, but I'm afraid there's another shop in town." Meghann frowned suddenly. "What do you mean I'm a bitch? Is that what Claire says?"

"No. Yes. Sometimes. You know how it is when you're drinking margaritas on a bad day. Karen calls her sister Susan the Soulless Psychopath. Claire calls you Jaws."

Meghann wanted to smile but couldn't. "Oh."

"I remember when she moved here, you know," Gina said softly. "She was quiet as a mouse and cried if you looked at her the wrong way. All she'd say for years was that she missed her sister. I didn't find out until after graduation what had happened to her."

"What I'd done, you mean."

"I'm not one to judge. Hell, I've waded through some ugly shit in my life, and motherhood is the hardest job in the world. Even if you're grown-up and ready for it. My point is this: Claire was wounded by all of that, and sometimes, when she hurts the most, she turns into Polly Politeness. She's really nice, but the temperature in the rooms drops about twenty-five degrees."

"I've pretty much needed a coat all day."

"Stick with it. Whether she admits it or not, it means a lot to her that you're here."

"I told her I'd plan the wedding."

"You seem perfectly suited for it."

"Oh, yeah. I'm a real romantic." She sighed.

"All you have to do is listen to Claire. Really listen, and then do whatever you can to make her dream come true."

"Maybe you could get the info and report back to me. Sort of a CIA-like mission."

"When was the last time you sat down for a drink with your sister and just *talked*?"

"Let's put it this way: We wouldn't have been old enough to have wine with our meal."

"That's what I thought. Go with her now."

"But Alison—"

"Sam can take care of Ali. I'll let him know." She opened her purse and dug through it, finally pulling out a scrap of paper. She wrote something down and handed it to Meghann. "Here's my cell phone number. Call me in an hour and I'll let you know Ali's schedule."

"Claire won't want to go with me. Especially not after I nixed the dresses."

"And fell asleep. The snoring was especially poignant. Anyway, I got the impression from Claire that other people's needs or wants didn't matter much to you."

"You don't pull any punches, do you?"

"Thus, the divorce. Take Claire out for dinner. Go see a movie. Look at wedding flowers. Do *something* sisterly. It's about time."

CHAPTER THIRTEEN

CLAIRE KNEW HER LIPS WERE DRAWN IN A TIGHT, UNYIELDING LINE that communicated displeasure. She'd honed that skill; the ability to convey anger without having to form the words that would make her feel regret afterward. Her dad often remarked on this talent of hers. *Lordy, Claire,* he'd say, *no one else can yell at me without saying a word. Someday all that silent anger of yours is gonna back up in your throat and choke you.*

She glanced sideways at her sister, who was behind the wheel, driving too fast, her black hair flapping behind her like some celebrity starlet's. Sunglasses that probably cost more than Claire's net worth covered her eyes. "Where are we going?" she asked for the fourth time.

"You'll see." Always the same answer. Clipped and unadorned. As if Meghann were afraid to say more.

She'd fallen asleep.

It wasn't as if Claire asked much of her sister. Hell, nothing was farther from the truth. She hadn't expected her sister to join in the fun of buying a wedding gown. God, no. Meghann enjoy a day with girlfriends? Hardly.

What galled most was that Claire had asked Meg's opinion first, even with Gina and Charlotte right there. Claire had put her neediness on the table: *What do you think, Meghann?*

She'd asked her *twice*. After the second time, she rectified her mistake and ignored Meghann completely.

Then she'd heard the snores.

That was when she'd felt the sting of tears.

It hadn't helped, of course, that all of the dresses had been wrong, or that even ugly dresses were expensive these days, or that, by the end of the afternoon, she'd actually begun to think that a white sundress might be more practical. That had only brought the tears closer. But now Claire was just plain mad. Meghann would ruin this wedding; there was no doubt about it. Her sister was like an airborne virus. Ten seconds in the room with her and you began to feel sick.

"I need to get back to Ali," Claire said, also for the fourth time.

"You will."

Claire took a deep breath. Enough was enough. "Look, Meg, about planning my wedding. Honestly, you—"

"We're here." Meg tucked the silver Porsche into an empty parking spot on the street. Before Claire could respond, Meghann was out of the car and standing by the meter. "Come on."

They were in downtown Seattle now. Her sister's territory. Meg probably wanted to show off her hugely expensive condo.

Claire frowned. They were parked at the base of a long, slowly rising hill. Up ahead—maybe six blocks away—she could see the Public Market. Behind them, also several blocks away, was the ferry terminal. A street musician played a sad tune on a saxophone; the music floated above the traffic noises. To their left, a waterfall of concrete steps spilled down the courtyard of a condo complex. Across the street was a Diamond Parking lot, the stalls mostly empty on this non-game day.

"Do you live here?" Claire asked as she grabbed her bag and

climbed out of the sports car. "I always pictured you in some sleek high-rise."

"I invited you to my place a ton of times."

"Twice. You invited me over once that day Mama was in town for the el creepo convention and once for Christmas dinner. You canceled the Christmas dinner because you got the flu, and Mama took us out for dinner at Canlis instead."

Meghann looked surprised by that. "Really? I thought I was always asking you to see my place."

"You were. You just never set up a day and time. I was always supposed to stop by when I was in town. News flash: I'm never in town."

"You seem a little hostile today."

"Do I? I can't imagine why." Claire slung her purse strap over her shoulder and fell into step beside Meghann, who was marching up-hill like Patton. "We need to talk about the wedding. Your performance this morning—"

"Here," Meghann said, stopping suddenly in front of a narrow white door flanked by windows on either side. A small iron-scrolled sign read: *By Design.* A man in a severe black suit was busily undressing a mannequin behind the glass. He saw Meghann and waved her in.

"What *is* this place?"

"You said I could plan your wedding, right?"

"Actually, that's what I've been trying to discuss with you. Unfortunately, your listening skills are seriously underdeveloped."

Meg opened the door and went inside.

Claire hesitated.

"Come on." Meghann waited for her in front of an elevator.

Claire followed.

A second later, the elevator pinged and the doors slid open. They went in; the doors closed.

Finally, Meghann said, "I'm sorry about this morning. I know I screwed up."

"Sleeping is one thing. Snoring is another."

"I know. I'm sorry."

Claire sighed. "It's the story of our lives, Meg. Don't you get tired of it? One of us is always sorry about something, but we never—"

The elevator doors opened.

Claire gasped.

Meg had to lay a hand on her shoulder and gently shove her forward. She stumbled over the off-kilter threshold and into the store.

Only it wasn't a store. That was like calling Disneyland a carnival.

There were mannequins everywhere, poised perfectly, and dressed in the most beautiful wedding dresses Claire had ever seen. "Oh, my God," she breathed, stepping forward. The gown in front of her was an off-the-shoulder creation, nipped at the waist. Ivory silk charmeuse fell in folds to the floor. Claire felt the fabric—softer than anything she'd ever touched—and peeked at the price tag. It read: *Escada $4,200.*

She let go of it suddenly and turned to Meghann. "Let's go." Her throat felt tight. She was a little girl again, standing in the hallway of a friend's house, watching a family have dinner together.

Meg grabbed her wrist, wouldn't let her go. "I want you to try on dresses *here.*"

"I can't. I know you're just being you, Meg. But this . . . hurts a little. I work at a campground."

"I don't want to say this twice, Claire, so please listen and believe me. I work eighty-five hours a week, and my clients pay almost four hundred dollars an hour. I'm not showing off. It's a fact: Money is something I have. It would mean a lot to me to buy you this wedding gown. You don't belong in the dresses we saw this morning. I'm sorry if you think I'm a bitch and a snob, but that's how I feel. Please. Let me do this for you."

Before Claire had come up with her answer, a woman cried out, "Meghann Dontess. In a wedding shop. Who would *ever* believe it?"

A tall, rail-thin woman in a navy blue sheath dress strode forward, her impossibly high heels clacking on the marble floor. Her hair, a perfect combination of white-blond and silver, stood out from her face in a Meg Ryan–type cut.

"Hello, Risa," Meg said, extending her hand. The women shook hands, then Risa looked at Claire.

"This is the great one's baby sister, yes?"

Claire heard the barest hint of an Eastern European accent. Maybe even Russian. "I'm Claire."

"And Meghann is letting you marry."

"She's advised against it, actually."

Risa threw back her head and laughed. "Of course she advised against it. I have heard such advice from her twice. Both times I should have listened, yes, but love will have its way." She took a step back, studying Claire from head to toe.

Claire fisted her left hand, hiding the tinfoil ring.

Risa tapped a long, dark fingernail against her front teeth. "This is not what I expected," she said, glancing pointedly at Meghann. "You said your sister was a country girl. Getting married in the middle of nowhere."

Claire didn't know whether to smile or smack Meghann in the head. "I am a small-town girl. Meghann used to be."

"Ah. That must be where she left her heart, yes?" Risa tapped her teeth again. "You are beautiful," she said at last. "Size ten or twelve, I expect. We won't need to pad your bra." She turned to Meghann. "Can she get an appointment with Renaldo? The hair . . ."

"I can try."

"We must accentuate those beautiful eyes. So blue. It makes me think of Brad Pitt's wife. The nervous one from *Friends*. Yes. This is who your sister looks like. For her, I think the classics. Prada. Valentino. Armani. Wang. Maybe a vintage Azzaro. Come." She turned and began marching away. Her hand snaked out now and then to grab a dress.

Claire looked at Meghann. "Armani? Vera Wang?" She shook her head, unable to say, *You can't do this.* They were the right words, the thing she should say, but the denial of this moment caught in her throat. What little girl hadn't dreamed of this? Especially a girl who had believed in love even after so many broken promises.

"We can always leave without buying anything," Meghann said. "Try them on. Just for fun."

"Just for fun."

"Hurry up, you two! I haven't the whole day." Risa's voice rang out, startling Claire, who hurried forward.

Meghann hung back as Risa went from rack to rack, piling one dress after another into her arms.

A few minutes later, Claire stepped into a dressing area that was bigger than her bedroom. Three floor-to-ceiling mirrors fanned out in front of her. A small wooden platform stood in the center.

"Go on. The dresses are in there. Try one on," Risa gave her a gentle shove.

Claire went into the dressing room, where several gowns hung waiting. The first one was a stunning white silk Ralph Lauren with an intricate lace-and-beadwork patterned bodice. Another was a romantic peach-tinged ivory Prada with ruffled, capped sleeves and a slightly asymmetrical hemline. There was a white silk Armani sheath: simplicity itself with a plunging V neck and a draped, sexy back.

Claire didn't allow herself to look at the prices. This was her make-believe moment. She could afford anything. She peeled out of her wrinkled jeans and work T-shirt and tossed them on the floor. (She did *not* look at her faded, overwashed JCPenney bra and Jockey-for-Her underwear.)

The Ralph Lauren gown floated over her shoulders like a cloud and fell down her nearly naked body. From the neck down, she looked like Kim Basinger in *L.A. Confidential*.

"Come on, honey. Let's see," Risa said.

She opened the door and stepped into the dressing area.

There was a gasp at her entrance. Then Risa shouted, "Shoes!" and ran off.

Meg stood there, holding an armful of dresses. Her lips parted in a soft sigh.

Claire couldn't help smiling. At the same time, she had the oddest urge to cry. "That Ralph Lauren is no slouch. Of course, my car cost less than this dress." She stepped up onto the platform and looked at herself in the mirror. No wonder Meghann had hated the gowns this morning.

Risa came back, brandishing a pair of strappy high-heeled sandals.

Claire laughed. "Who do you think I am—Carrie Bradshaw? My nose would bleed if I wore heels that high. Not to mention the fact that I'd break a hip when I fell."

"Hush. Put them on."

Claire did as she was told, then stood very still. Every breath threatened to send her toppling off the block.

"*Aagh.* Your mother, she did not teach you to stand in heels. A crime. I get you pumps." Her mouth twisted slightly at the last word.

When Risa disappeared, Meghann laughed. "The only thing Mama taught us was how to walk in shoes you'd outgrown."

"She always had a new pair."

"Funny thing."

A look passed between them, a moment of perfect understanding; when it passed, and they were back in ordinary time, Claire felt a tug of regret.

"I think the fabric is too flimsy, don't you?" Claire said. Her job was to find a flaw in each dress, a reason her sister shouldn't spend this much money.

Meghann frowned. "Too flimsy? You look gorgeous."

"It hangs on every bulge. I'd have to wear undergarments made by Boeing."

"Claire. It's a size ten. One more comment like that and you'll qualify for the Hollywood Wives Eating Disorder League."

After that, Claire tried on a succession of dresses, each one more beautiful than the last. She felt like a princess, and it didn't ruin the day at all that she had to decline each one. She could always find one tiny thing that made the dress less than perfect. *The sleeves are*

too short, too wide, too ruffled. . . . The neckline is too sweet, too sexy,
too traditional. . . . The feel of this one isn't right.

She could tell that Meghann was getting frustrated. She kept de-
livering armfuls of gowns. "Here, try these," she said every time. Meg
and patience had never known each other well.

Risa had long ago gone on to other customers.

Finally, Claire came to the last dress of the day. Meghann had
chosen it. An elegant white gown with a heavily beaded tank bodice
and a flowing taffeta silk skirt.

Claire unhooked her bra and stepped into the dress. She was still
fastening the back as she stepped out of the dressing room.

Meghann was completely silent.

Claire frowned. She heard Risa in another part of the store, chattering loudly to another customer.

Claire looked at her sister. "You're uncharacteristically quiet.
Should I begin the Heimlich?"

"Look."

Claire lifted the heavy skirt off the ground and stepped up onto
the platform. Slowly, she faced the trifold mirror.

The woman who stared back at her wasn't Claire Cavenaugh.
No. This woman hadn't partied her way out of a state college and decided that cosmetology was a viable career choice, only to quit at-
tending those classes as well . . . she hadn't borne a child out of
wedlock because her lover refused to marry her . . . and she certainly
didn't manage a campground that pretended it was a resort.

This woman arrived in limousines and drank champagne from
fluted glasses. She slept on high-thread-count sheets and always had
a current passport.

This was the woman she could have been, if she'd gone to college in New York and done graduate work in Paris. Maybe it was the
woman she could still become.

How could a dress highlight everything that had gone wrong
with your life and subtly promise a different future? She imagined the
look on Bobby's face when she walked down the aisle. Bobby, who'd

knelt on one knee when he asked her to please, please be his wife. If he saw her in this dress . . .

Meghann came up behind her, stood on the platform.

There they were, side by side. Mama's girls, who'd once been closer than sisters and were now so far apart.

Meghann touched Claire's bare shoulder. "Don't even try to find something wrong with this dress."

"I didn't look at the price tag, but—"

Meghann ripped the tag in half. "And you won't." She turned, raised a hand. "Risa. Get over here."

Claire looked at her sister. "You knew, didn't you? You hand-picked it."

Meg tried not to smile. "It's Vera Wang, honey. Of course I knew. I also knew your defenses were a bit high at the outset. You don't want me to buy your dress."

"It's not that I don't want you to."

"It's okay, Claire. It means a lot to me that you've included me in your wedding."

"We're family," Claire answered after a long pause. It felt awkward, this conversation, and vaguely dangerous. As if they were skating on a frozen pond that couldn't possibly hold their weight. "Thank you for the dress. It's what . . ." Her voice cracked a little. "I always dreamed of."

Meg finally smiled. "Just because I don't believe in marriage doesn't mean I can't plan a kick-ass wedding, you know."

Risa stepped into the dressing room, her face flushed, her arms full of gowns. "The Wang," she said softly, looking at Meg. "You said this would be her choice."

"A good guess."

"She is the picture of love, yes?" Risa hung up the unnecessary gowns and went to Claire. "We'll need to take in the bust a little— just to there, don't you think?—and let out the waist. We'll also need to choose a veil. Something elegant, yes? Not too ornate. What shoes will you wear?" She began pinning and pulling.

"These pumps are fine."

Risa knelt down to pin the hemline. "I'll keep the skirt long. In case you change your mind, which you must do. It'll be ready in time," she promised when she was finished, then hurried off.

After she'd been gone for a moment, Claire said, "How did you know I'd choose this dress?"

"At my wedding, I overheard you talking to Elizabeth. You said a wedding dress should be simple. You were right. Mine looked like something a circus performer would wear." Meghann seemed determined to smile. "Maybe that's why Eric left me."

Claire heard the hurt in her sister's voice. It was thin and quiet, a thread fluttering. It surprised her. Claire always imagined her sister's defenses to be solid granite. "He hurt you, didn't he?"

"Of course he hurt me. He broke my heart and then wanted my money. It would have been a lot easier if I'd had a prenuptial agreement. Or better yet, if I'd lived with him instead of marrying him."

Claire couldn't help smiling at the not-so-subtle reminder. This time it made sense. "If marrying Bobby is a mistake, it's one I want to make."

"Yeah. That's the thing about love. It's inherently optimistic. No wonder I stick to sex instead. Now, how about if we pick up some takeout from the Wild Ginger and eat at my place?"

"Alison—"

"—is having dinner at Zeke's Drive-In and joining Sam and Bobby for date night at the Big Bowl. I called Gina from Everett."

Claire smiled. "Bobby is going to date night at the bowling alley? And you don't believe in true love. Now, help me out of this dress." Claire hiked up the falling dress and picked her way carefully to the dressing room. She was just about to shut the door when she remembered to say, "Your wedding dress was beautiful, Meghann, and you were beautiful. I hope I didn't hurt your feelings when I said that to Elizabeth. We'd had a few drinks by then."

"My sleeves looked like open umbrellas. God knows why I picked it. No, that's not true. Sadly, I inherited Mama's style sense. As soon as I started making money, I hired a personal shopper. Anyway, thanks for the apology."

Claire closed the dressing-room door and changed back into her clothes. They spent another hour trying on veils and then shoes. When they had chosen everything, Meghann took Claire by the arm and led her out of the boutique.

In front of the Wild Ginger, Meghann double-parked, ran into the restaurant, and came out three minutes later with a paper sack. She tossed it into Claire's lap, jumped into the driver's seat, and stomped on the gas.

They turned down Pike Street and veered left hard, into an underground parking lot.

Claire followed her sister into the elevator, up to the penthouse floor, and into the condo.

The view was breathtaking. An amethyst almost-night sky filled every picture window. To the north, the sleepy community of Queen Anne sparkled with multicolored light. The Space Needle, decked out in summertime colors, filled one window. Everywhere else, it was the midnight-blue Sound, its dark surface broken only by the streamers of city lights along the shore.

"Wow," Claire said.

"Yeah. It's some view," Meghann said, plopping the paper sack on the kitchen's black granite countertop.

Everywhere Claire looked, she saw perfection. Not a painting was askew on the silk-covered walls, not a piece of paper cluttered a table. Of course there was no dust.

She walked over to a small Biedermeier desk in the corner. On its shiny surface stood a single framed photograph. It was the only one in the room, as far as she could tell.

It was a photograph of Claire and Meghann, taken long ago. In it, they were kids—maybe seven and fourteen—sitting at the end of a dock with their arms looped around each other. In the corner, a glowing cigarette tip identified Mama as the photographer.

Surprisingly, Claire found that it hurt to see them this way. She glanced over at Meg, who was busily dividing up the food.

She put the photograph back and kept moving through her sister's condo. She saw the white-on-white bedroom that only a woman without pets or children would possibly choose and the bathroom that contained more beauty products than the cosmetics counter at Rite Aid. All the while, Claire found herself thinking that something was wrong.

She made her way back to the kitchen.

Meg handed her a margarita in a frosted glass. "On the rocks. No salt. Is that okay?"

"Perfect. Your home is gorgeous."

"Home." Meg laughed. "That's funny. I never think of it that way, but it is, of course. Thanks."

That was it. This wasn't a home. It was a really nice hotel suite. Definitely four-star, but cold. Impersonal. "Did you decorate it yourself?"

"You're kidding, right? The last thing I chose for myself was the wedding gown with parachute sleeves. I hired a decorator. German woman who didn't speak English." She set out the plates. "Here. Let's eat out on the deck." She carried her plate and drink outside. "We'll have to sit on the floor. The decorator chose the most uncomfortable outdoor furniture in the world. I returned it all and haven't found the time to buy new stuff."

"How long have you lived here?"

"Seven years."

Claire followed her sister outside. It was a beautiful night. Stars everywhere.

As they ate, silence fell between them. Meg said a few odd, awkward things, clearly designed to break the quiet, but like seawater in a rising tide, the silence always returned.

"Did I thank you for the gown?"

"Yes. And you're welcome." Meg put her empty plate down on the deck and leaned back.

"It's funny," Claire said. "It's loud out here at night—between the traffic and the ferry horns and the railroad, but it still feels . . . empty. Kind of lonely."

"The city can be that way."

Claire looked at Meghann and, for once, she didn't see the harsh, judgmental older sister who was always right. Neither did she see the older sister who'd once loved her so completely. Now, she saw a pale, rarely smiling woman who seemed to have no life apart from work. A lonely woman who'd had her heart broken long ago and now wouldn't allow herself to believe in love.

She couldn't help remembering the old days, when they'd been best friends. For the first time in years, she wondered if that could happen again. If so, one of them would have to make the first move.

Claire took a chance. "Maybe you'd like to come stay at my house for a few nights, while you're planning the wedding."

"Really?" Meghann looked up, obviously surprised.

"You're probably too busy."

"No, actually. I'm . . . between cases right now. And I do need to spend some time in Hayden. Getting stuff ready, you know. I have a meeting there tomorrow, in fact. With the wedding consultant. But I wouldn't want to intrude."

Big mistake, Claire. Incredible Hulk big. "It's settled, then. You'll spend a few nights at my house."

CHAPTER
FOURTEEN

𝓜EGHANN PARKED THE CAR AND STEPPED OUT ONTO THE CURB.
She checked her instructions again, then looked up the street.

Hayden shimmered in the warm, lemony sunlight. People drifted
across the street and along the boardwalks, gathering now and then
in gossipy circles, waving to one another as they moved on.

Across the street, standing all by herself, was a magenta-haired
teenager wearing pants that would have been big on Shaquille
O'Neal.

Meghann knew how that girl felt, the outsider in this pretty little town. The girl who didn't fit in. Trailer parks, Meghann had
learned early on, were always on the wrong side of the tracks, regardless of where they'd been built. And when your clothes were
wrong and your address was even worse, you were always treated like
a slut, whether you were or not. Sooner or later—and with
Meghann, it had been sooner—you gave in and started being what
everyone already thought you were.

No wonder Mama had never stopped in towns like Hayden. *One tavern and four churches? I think we'll pass this burg right on by.* She liked the kind of place where nobody knew your name . . . where nobody knew how to find you when you snuck off in the middle of the night, with three months' back rent due.

Meghann walked two blocks, then turned right on Azalea Street.

Her destination was easy to spot: a narrow Victorian house painted canary yellow with purple trim. A sign hung askew on the white picket fence out front: *Royal Event Planning.* There were glittery roses all around the pink letters.

Meghann almost kept walking. There was no way that someone who painted with glittery paint could plan a classy wedding.

But it was Claire's day, and she wanted a small, casual wedding. *Do you hear me, Meg? I mean it.*

Claire had said it three times last night and twice this morning.

What, no swing bands or ice sculptures? she'd teased.

Ice sculptures? I hope you're kidding. I mean it, Meg. Simple is the adjective you should remember. We don't need it catered, either. Everyone will bring something to eat.

Meghann had drawn the line there. *It's a wedding, not a funeral, and while I see certain similarities in the two events, I am not—repeat not—going to let you have a potluck wedding.*

But—

Hot dogs wrapped in Kraft cheese and pink Jell-O in wedding-ring molds? She shuddered. *I don't think so.*

Meg, Claire had said, *you're being you again.*

Okay. I'm a lawyer. I can compromise. The food will be casual.

And the reception has to be outside.

Outside. Where it rains? Where bugs breed? That outside?

Claire had been smiling by then. *Outside. In Hayden,* she added.

It's a good thing you mentioned that. I might have accidentally booked the Bloedel Reserve on Bainbridge Island. It is beautiful there. And not a horrible drive, she'd added hopefully.

Hayden.

Okay. But a bird will probably crap on your head during the ceremony.

Claire had laughed, then sobered. *You don't have to do this, you know. Really. It's a lot of work to have a wedding ready in nine days.*

Meg knew Claire didn't really want her planning this, and that knowledge stung. As with all opposition, it strengthened her resolve to do a great job. *I have a meeting in town, so I'd better run.* As Meg started to leave, Claire had said, *Don't forget the bridal shower. Tomorrow night at Gina's.*

Meghann had forced herself to keep smiling. A "couples'" shower. No doubt she'd be the only single woman in the room besides Gina.

What fun.

She unlatched the picket gate and stepped into a surreal Candy Land yard, half expecting Pee-wee Herman and his pals to jump out at her. A green Astro Turf walkway led her to the porch steps, which sagged beneath her weight. At the salmon-pink door, she knocked.

The door started to open, then thunked into something. A voice cursed thickly, "Damn door."

This time the door opened all the way.

An old woman with pink hair sat in a motorized wheelchair, a canister of oxygen beside her. Clear tubes slipped into each nostril, rode across her high, hollow cheekbones, and tucked behind her ears.

"Am I supposed to guess?" she said, frowning.

"Excuse me?"

"What you want, for Henry's sake. You knocked on the damn door, dintcha?"

"Oh. I'm here to see the event coordinator."

"That's me. Whaddaya want? Male strippers?"

"Now, Grandma," came a thin male voice from the other room. "You know you retired twenty years ago."

The woman backed up, spun her wheelchair around, and headed away. "Erica is in trouble. I better go."

"Forgive Granny," said the tall man who came to the door. He had curly bottle-blond hair and a California-dark tan. His glasses were heavy and black-rimmed. He wore skintight black leather pants and a teal green muscle-shirt, which showed off scarecrow-thin arms. "She has a little memory loss now and then. You must be Meghann Dontess. I'm Roy Royal."

She tried not to smile.

"Go ahead, have a good laugh. I'm just lucky my middle name isn't Al." He swung one hip out, planted a hand on it. "Those are some pretty sharp clothes, Ms. Dontess. We don't see much Marc Jacobs in Hayden. Our labels of choice are Levi's and Wrangler. I can't imagine what brings you here."

"I'm Claire Cavenaugh's sister. I'm here to plan her wedding."

He actually jumped into the air and screeched. "Claire! All right, girl! Well, let's get going. Only the best for Claire." He ushered her into the sitting room, toward a pink velvet settee. "Wedding at the Episcopal Church, of course. Reception at the Moose Lodge, catering by the Chuck Wagon. We can get tons of silk flowers from Target. Then they can be reused."

Meg thought, *Simple and casual, simple and casual.*

She couldn't do it. "Wait."

Roy stopped in mid-excited-utterance. "Yes."

"That's a wedding in Hayden, huh?"

"Top drawer. Only Missy Henshaw's was better, and she sprang for the clubhouse at the golf course in Monroe." He leaned forward. "They had champagne, not just beer."

"And what does a wedding cost around here?"

"Not like Missy's, but a good, solid event? Say . . . two thousand dollars." He looked at her. "Maybe a little less if one of the community college kids takes the photos."

Meg was the one who leaned forward now. "Do you read *People* magazine, Roy? Or *In Style*?"

He laughed. "Are you kidding? Cover to cover."

"So you know what a celebrity wedding is like. Especially the kind they call 'simple and elegant.'"

He waved his hand in the air, snapped his fingers. "Are you kidding, honey? Denise Richard's wedding was supposedly simple and they had enough fresh flowers to cover a Rose Parade float. Simple in Hollywood just means really, really expensive but no bridesmaids and an outdoor reception."

"Can you keep a secret, Roy?"

"I stayed in the closet during the Reagan years. Believe me, honey, these lips know when to close."

"I want the kind of wedding this town has never seen. But—and this is important—no one but you and I can know that it's a big deal. You have to master the phrase *It was on sale*. Deal?"

"No kidding," he grinned and clapped. "What's your budget?"

"Perfection. Every little girl's dream."

"In other words—"

"Money isn't something we should worry about."

He shook his head, still smiling. "Honey, that's a sentence I've *never* heard before. I do believe you're the best-looking woman I've ever seen." He reached out to the coffee table and grabbed a copy of *Bride's* magazine. "We should start with the gown. It's—"

"She's got it."

He looked up.

"Vera Wang."

"Vera Wang," he repeated it in a reverent tone of voice and closed the magazine. "Okay. Let's get to work."

"It has to be outside."

"Ah. A tent. Perfect. We should start with the lighting. . . ."

Meghann barely listened as his voice droned on and on about a zillion details. Lighting. Flowers. Table dressings. Grooms' cakes, for goodness' sake.

She had *definitely* made the right decision in coming here. All she had to do was write the checks.

Joe was elbow-deep in the undercarriage of an old Kubota tractor, changing the oil, when he heard a car drive up. He listened for

Smitty's booming voice, always loud when he welcomed customers to the garage, but now there was nothing except the tinny, scratchy strains of an old Hank Williams song on the radio.

"Anyone here?" someone called out. "Smitty?"

Joe rolled out from under the tractor and got to his feet. He was just putting his baseball cap on, pulling the brim low on his eyes, when a florid, heavyset man walked into the garage.

Joe recognized the man. It was Reb Tribbs, an old-time logger who'd lost an arm on the job.

Joe pulled his cap down lower and didn't make eye contact. "What can I do for you?"

"My truck's dyin' again. I just brought the damn thing to Smitty. He said he fixed it. Some job, he done. I ain't payin' for it till it runs."

"You'll have to take that up with Smitty. But if you want to drive into the garage, I'll—"

"Do I know you?" Reb frowned, pushed the cowboy hat back on his head, and stepped closer. "I don't never forget a voice. Can't see for shit, but I got the hearin' of a damn wolf."

Do I know you? It was the question Joe had heard in every town in Washington. "I've got one of those faces. People always think they know me. Now, if you'll bring the truck around—"

"Joe Wyatt. Ho-ly shit." Reb made a whistling sound. "It's you, ain't it?"

Joe sighed, beaten. "Hey, Reb."

There was a long pause, during which Reb studied Joe, his head cocked to the side as if he were listening to someone. "You got some nerve comin' back here, boy. Folks around here remember what you done. Hell, I thought you were in prison."

"No." Joe fought the urge to walk away. Instead, he stood there, listening. He deserved every word.

"You'd best get a move on. Her daddy don't need to hear that you're back in town."

"I haven't seen her dad."

"Course not. Chickenshit piece of crap like you don't have the guts. You'd best move on, Joe Wyatt. This town doesn't need a man like you."

"That's enough, Reb." It was Smitty's voice. He stood at the open garage door, holding a half-eaten sandwich in one hand and a can of Coke in the other.

"I can't believe you'd hire this piece of garbage," Reb said.

"I said, that's enough."

"I won't bring my truck here if he's gonna work on it."

"I imagine I can lose your business and still survive," Smitty said.

Reb made a sputtering sound, then turned on his heel and marched out. As he got into his truck, he yelled out, "You'll be sorry, Zeb Smith. Trash like him don't belong in this town."

After he drove away, Smitty placed a hand on Joe's shoulder. "He's the trash, Joe. Always has been. Mean as a badger."

Joe stared out the window, saw the beat-up red truck buck down the road. "You'll lose customers when word gets out that I'm here."

"Don't matter. My house is paid for. My land's paid for. I own a rental house in town that brings in five hundred a month. Helga and I both have Social Security. I don't need a single damn customer. Ever."

"Still. Your reputation is important."

Smitty squeezed his shoulder. "Last Helga and I heard about our Philly, he was living in Seattle. Under the Viaduct. Heroin. Every day I hope someone offers him a helping hand."

Joe nodded. He didn't know what to say.

Finally, Smitty said, "I gotta make a Costco run. You think you can handle the garage for the next two hours?"

"Not if Reb is any indication."

"He isn't." Smitty tossed him the keys. "Close up anytime you want." Then he left.

Joe finished out the workday, but he couldn't forget the incident with Reb. The old man's words seemed to hang in the garage, poisoning the air.

This town doesn't need a man like you.

By the time he closed up shop, he felt empty again. Gutted by the truth of Reb's observations.

Then he remembered Gina. He had family here now; he didn't have to be alone.

He went into the office and called her. The answering machine picked up. He hung up without leaving a message.

Instead, he locked up for the night. He was just about to turn toward his cabin when he happened to glance down the street.

The neon *Redhook* sign in Mo's window caught his attention.

And suddenly he was thirsty. He wanted to sneak into that smoky darkness and drink until the ache in his chest went away.

He pulled the baseball cap low on his forehead and crossed the street. Outside the tavern he paused just long enough to pray that no one he knew was inside, then he pushed through the scarred wooden door.

He glanced around, saw no familiar faces, and finally breathed easily. He made his way to a table in the back, the one tucked farthest from the overhead lights. A few minutes later, a tired-looking waitress appeared. She took his order for a pitcher, then left. In no time, she was back with his beer.

He poured himself a schooner. Unfortunately, the three empty chairs around the table reminded him of other times, of another life, in fact. Back then, he never drank alone.

Meghann hadn't been to a bridal shower in more than a decade. Her friends and colleagues lived with their boyfriends for years and then—sometimes—quietly got married. She had no idea how to blend in to this small-town crowd, how to adapt to their coloration. The last thing she wanted to do was stand out.

Yesterday, after her four-hour meeting with Roy, Meghann had spent another hour in Too Many Cooks. Although she wasn't much of a cook, she was familiar with all the gadgets and gizmos. Sometimes, when she couldn't sleep, she'd watch cooking shows on TV. So she knew what every kitchen needed. She bought Claire (and

Bobby, although she didn't think of them as a couple, really) a Cuisinart food processor.

She'd been tired by the time she made it back to Claire's house, and dinner hadn't helped. As the meal progressed, she'd felt increasingly separate, a woman distinct in her solitude even among her so-called family.

She'd tried to make mealtime conversation, but it had been difficult. Claire and Bobby rarely took their eyes off each other, and Alison talked continually—mostly to her mother and Bobby. On the few rare instances in which Meghann had been able to wedge a word in between the child's soliloquies, she'd discovered what a yawning silence was.

What? Bobby had asked twice, blinking slowly as he peeled his gaze away from Claire.

Meghann couldn't remember now what she'd said. All she recalled for sure was that it had been wrong. She knew for a fact that she shouldn't have mentioned her work. One innocent little remark about a deadbeat dad, and Alison asked loudly, "Will you and Bobby ever get divorced, Mommy?"

Claire had not been amused. "No, honey. Don't listen to Aunt Meg. She's the Antichrist when it comes to marriage."

"The what?"

Bobby had laughed so hard he spilled his milk. That had made Alison laugh, then Claire. It was remarkable how alienating other people's laughter could be.

Meghann had been the only one not laughing as they sopped up the milk. She'd excused herself quickly from the table—pleaded a headache—and ran upstairs.

But now, nearly an hour later, she felt better. A quick glance at the bedside clock told her it was 6:40.

Come on, Meg. It's time—again—to celebrate your sister's decision to marry a three-time loser. Wait! Give them gifts! She went down the hall and ducked into the bathroom, where she twisted her abundant black hair into a knot and applied enough makeup to hide the lack-of-sleep lines around her eyes. Then she went back into the bedroom and opened her closet. It took her a while to figure out what to wear. Fortunately, she'd packed a lot of choices.

In the end, she decided on a plain black dress. Armani was never wrong. She added sheer black hose and a pair of pumps, then went downstairs.

The house was quiet.

"Claire?"

No answer.

Then she saw the note on the kitchen table:

Dear Meg, Sorry you're feeling sick. Stay home and rest, xxoo, C.

They'd left without her. She glanced at her watch. It was 7:00. Of course they'd left. They were the guests of honor. They couldn't be late.

"Damn it."

She considered staying right here.

I'm sorry, Claire. I—

—lost the directions.

—felt sick after dinner.

—couldn't get my car started.

Each excuse would work. In truth, Claire would probably love it if Meg stayed away. And yet, it would be one more brick in the wall that separated them.

There were enough bricks already.

She dug through her purse for the pale lavender invitation. It read *Couples' Shower for Claire and Bobby, 7:00.* The directions were on the back.

She couldn't remember the last time she'd walked so slowly to her car, or when she'd followed the speed limit signs so precisely. Even so, Hayden was a small town and the directions on the invitation were easy to follow. It took her less than ten minutes to find Gina's house. She pulled up behind a battered red pickup with a gun rack in the cab window and a bumper sticker that read: *Screw the Spotted Owl.*

Clearly a member of Greenpeace.

She got out of the car and walked up the slanted concrete driveway that led to a sprawling log house with a wraparound porch. Bright red geraniums and purple lobelia cascaded from hanging pots. Rhododendrons sporting plate-size red blooms were everywhere. She could hear the buzz of conversations through the open windows. From somewhere came the pounding beat of an old Queen song. "Another One Bites the Dust."

Meghann smiled at the choice. Holding the gift firmly under one arm, she climbed the porch steps and knocked on the front door. *You can do this. You can fit in with her friends. Just smile and nod and ask for a pitcher of margaritas.*

There was a rush of footsteps, then the door opened.

Gina stood there, her face creased in laughter. Until she saw Meghann. "Oh." She stepped back to allow entry. "I'm glad you're feeling better."

Meghann stared at Gina, who was dressed in a pair of denim capri pants and an oversize black T-shirt. Her feet were bare. *Great.* "I'm overdressed."

"Are you kidding? If I hadn't gained fifteen pounds since Rex left I'd be dressed up, too. Come on. You're my date for the evening." Gina smiled. "I thought I'd been stood up."

She took Meghann by the arm and led her down a wide hallway, toward the noise. They finally reached the great room—a living room/dining room combination—that overlooked a beautifully landscaped backyard. "Claire! Look who made it," she said loudly enough to be heard above the din.

Everyone stopped talking and turned toward them. The crowd was a sea of T-shirts and jeans.

Except for Meghann, of course, who looked ready for a night of dancing at the Space Needle.

Claire extricated herself from Tentacle Boy and hurried toward her. She looked gorgeous in a pair of ice-blue cotton pants and white boat-neck cotton sweater. Her long blond hair had been pulled back from her face and gathered in a white scrunchy. She smiled brightly.

"I'm so glad you could make it. I thought you had a migraine. When I get a headache, I can't move for hours."

Meghann felt like Jackie O at a keggar. "I shouldn't have come. I'll go."

"Please don't," her sister said. "I'm glad you're here. Really."

Bobby sauntered through the crowd and sidled up to Claire, slipping an arm around her hips. Meghann had to admit that he looked good. Damn good. He was going to bypass breaking her sister's heart and just plain shatter it.

"Heya, Meghann," he said, smiling broadly. "I'm glad you could make it."

It stuck in her craw to be welcomed to her own sister's party by country boy. She had to force herself to smile. "Thanks, Bobby."

They stood there in an uncomfortable silence. Finally, Gina said, "I'll bet you could use a drink."

Meghann nodded. "By all means."

"Come to the kitchen with me," Gina said. "We'll get you a jumbo margarita."

"Hurry back," Claire said. "We were just going to start the games."

Meghann actually stumbled.

Games.

Meghann really did have a headache now.

She sat on the edge of the sofa, her knees tucked primly together, a paper plate of homemade cookies on her lap. The rest of the guests (in pairs, like on Noah's ark) sat sprawled against one another, in a circle on the hardwood floor. They were all talking at once, resurrecting memories and moments from a lifetime Meghann didn't know.

Remember when Claire fell off the high dive at Island Lake Camp—

Or when she hid Mrs. Testern's favorite ruler—

When she called Poison Control because she caught Ali eating the diaper-pail deodorant—

The junior and senior high school years, the girls-just-want-to-have-fun years, the Alison years. They were all a mystery to Meghann. She had stories to tell, of course, stories about a girl who once cut all of her hair so she could look like Buffy on *Family Affair*, who cried every night that Mama forgot to come home, and who slept curled in her big sister's arms on a cot that was too small.

"Claire's big sister," said a brown-haired woman in faded jeans and an Old Navy T-shirt. Her wedding ring sported a diamond the size of a pencil eraser. She plopped down beside Meghann. "I'm Karen, by the way. We met several years ago. Your dress is beautiful."

"Thank you."

"I hear you want Claire to sign a prenuptial."

"That was it for small talk, huh?"

"We watch out for one another."

In truth, Meghann was glad for that. God knew she'd failed Claire in the watching-over department. That was why she was sitting here, overdressed and separate, pretending to love the cookies. "That's nice. She's lucky to have you as friends."

"We're all lucky. She won't sign anything, you know. I gave her the same advice."

"You did?"

She fluttered the fingers of her left hand. "Divorce wars survivor. That guy over there—the one chewing like a squirrel—that's Harold."

"Maybe you could talk to Claire. It's not smart for her to go into this thing unprotected."

"This thing is marriage, and it's all about faith. Your sister is one of the believers in this world. Don't take that away from her."

"In law school faith is surgically removed."

"My guess is that yours was lost long before that. Don't look so shocked. I'm not a psychic or anything. We tell each other everything. You guys had a rough time of it growing up."

Meghann shifted uncomfortably. She wasn't used to people knowing so much about her. Not friends, and certainly not strangers. Her childhood was something she'd never shared with a girlfriend, not even Elizabeth. She remembered how people had looked at her when she was child, as if she were white trash; she hadn't wanted that judgment to follow her into adulthood.

Karen seemed to be waiting for a response. The moment lengthened between them. Meg's heartbeat accelerated. She didn't want this conversation to continue. These Bluesers were too damn blunt.

"Okay, everyone, it's time for the games!" Gina yelled suddenly, jumping to her feet.

Meghann let out her breath in a relieved sigh.

"Gina loves games," Karen said. "I just hope no one has to humiliate themselves. It was nice to see you again. I better run. Harold just started hyperventilating." And she was gone, back to her husband in a blink.

"Outside," Gina said, clapping her hands again and ushering everyone outside, where a row of powdered-sugar doughnuts hung at intervals along a sagging clothesline. "Everyone pick a doughnut and stand in front of it.

The guests surged forward, lining up.

Meghann hung back in the doorway.

"Come on, Meg," Gina called out. "There's a place for you, too."

Everyone turned to look at her.

She hurried across the porch and out into the yard. The sweet smell of honeysuckle and roses filled the night air. Somewhere nearby there must be a pond, because frogs were croaking en masse. It gave the evening an odd, surreal edge—or maybe that came from the swinging doughnuts.

"When I start the stopwatch, everyone starts licking the sugar off the doughnuts. This will tell us who is the best kisser."

A man laughed. Meghann thought it was Charlotte's husband. "If you want to know who has the best tongue, we should be licking—"

"Don't you *dare* finish that sentence," Charlotte said, laughing.

"Go. And no fair using hands."

The group went at it. Within seconds, everyone was laughing.

Meghann tried, she really did, but at her first pass, the doughnut hit her in the nose and white sugar fluttered down the front of her black Armani.

"Done!" Bobby yelled, throwing his hands in the air as if he'd just scored the game-winning run.

Claire put her arms around him. "And there you have it, the *real* reason I'm marrying him."

Meghann stepped back from the undulating doughnut. Once again, she was the only one not laughing, and her silence settled on her chest like Hester Prynne's scarlet A.

Gina handed Bobby a CD. "You win. And I must say, none of us will ever look at you quite the same again." She rushed back into the house, then came out with a big white porcelain bowl. "The next game is called Truth in M&M's. Everybody take as many as you want, then find a seat." She went around the group, handing out candy.

Meghann could tell that she wasn't the only suspicious person. No one took a handful. Meg chose two, then sat down on the top porch step. Everyone else pulled up a patch of grass and sat down.

"For each M&M, you have to tell one thing about the bride or groom and make a prediction for the future."

A groan moved through the men.

Harold rolled his eyes; Karen elbowed him.

"I'll start," Charlotte said. "I have three. Claire has a beautiful smile, and I predict Bobby will keep it on her face. Also, she is a great cook, so I predict he'll be fat by forty. And finally, she hates to do laundry, so I predict Bobby will learn to like the stained, rumpled look."

Claire laughed the loudest of all of them.

"My turn," Karen said. "I'm on a diet—as usual—so I only picked one. Claire has developed a . . . fondness for electrical devices. I predict she won't need one anymore."

"Karen!" Claire cried out, her face turning red even as she laughed.

They continued around the circle, and with each comment,

Meghann felt herself edging toward uneasiness. Even the husbands here seemed to know more about Claire's everyday life than Meghann did, and she was terrified that when her turn came to make a prediction, she'd blurt out, *I predict he breaks her heart.* She finished her second margarita in gulps.

"Meg? Meg?" It was Gina. "Your turn."

Meghann looked down in her palm. Sweat had turned the candies into red smudges. "I have two." She tried to smile. "Claire is . . . the best mother I know, so I predict she'll have another child."

Claire smiled at her, then leaned lovingly against Bobby, who whispered something in her ear.

"Another one, Meg."

She nodded. "Claire loves well, but not necessarily easily, so I predict," she barely paused, "that this is the real thing." When she looked up, Claire was frowning.

Meghann didn't know what she'd said wrong. It had seemed cheery and optimistic to her, romantic even. But Claire looked ready to cry.

"I'm last," Gina said in the sudden silence. "I have only one. Claire is completely tone-deaf. So I predict that Bobby will never let her be his backup singer."

That got them all laughing and talking again. They got to their feet and closed ranks around Claire and Bobby.

Absurdly, Meghann felt the start of tears. She got clumsily to her feet, realizing when she stood up that those margaritas had been stronger than she'd thought. She turned away from the party. Getting drunk would be the last straw. When no one was looking, she ducked into the house and ran for her car.

She meant to go home, wait up for Claire, and apologize for whatever wrongs she'd uttered.

Then she saw the tavern.

CHAPTER
FIFTEEN

*M*EGHANN EASED HER FOOT OFF THE ACCELERATOR. THE PORSCHE
slowed to a crawl.

Through the smoke-grayed glass of the tavern's window, she
could make out the shadowy bodies inside, pressed in close together
along the bar.

It was easy to get lost in a crowd like that, where no one asked
your name or why you were there. She knew that if she went inside
and had a drink—or two or three—she would feel better.

Maybe she would meet someone . . . and he would take her to his
place for a few hours and help her forget. Help her sleep.

Experience had taught her that on a night like this, when her in-
adequacies felt as sharp as bits of glass embedded in her skin, she
would lie in her lonely bed and stare up at the ceiling, unable to
sleep. In the morning, she would awaken to a face that was wrinkled
and stare into eyes that were tired and sad.

Meghann hit the gas. The car roared to life. She sped down two
blocks, found a parking space, and pulled in. When she shut down

the engine and got out of the car, she noticed how quiet the night was. The Big Dipper pointed toward the river.

Most of the stores were closed. Only a few kept their signs illuminated. Every twenty feet or so a green wrought-iron streetlamp tossed light downward, creating a lacy, scalloped pattern along the darkened boardwalk.

Meghann settled her shoulder strap in place, clamped her elbow tightly against her purse, and started for the tavern. She didn't falter when she reached the open door, just turned and walked in.

It was like a hundred other taverns she'd been in. Smoke collected along the acoustical tile ceiling, trailing like ghostly sleeves below the inset lighting. The bar ran the length of the room on the right side, a huge mahogany piece that had to be a hundred years old. The mirror behind it was at least six feet long, veined in strands of gold and aged to a tarnished silver. In it, the patrons looked taller and thinner, a fun-house mirror for people too drunk to notice.

She saw the people clustered along the bar, seated on wooden stools. The pitchers outnumbered the people, and there was a lit cigarette in every hand.

Those were the hardcore drinkers, the folks who found their bar stools at 10:00 A.M. and climbed aboard.

Scatted throughout the left side of the room were round tables; most of them were full. In the smoky background, she saw the faded outline of a pool table, heard the clackety-thump of a game in progress. An old Springsteen song played on the jukebox. "Glory Days."

Perfect. It had probably been chosen by the guy sitting at the bar who wore a red-and-white letterman's jacket. He'd long ago lost all his hair.

She moved into the haze. Her heart beat faster: Smoke and anticipation made her eyes water. She walked to the closest empty space on the bar, where a tired-looking man was busily wiping up a spill. At her arrival, he sighed and looked up. If he was surprised by her—after all, women like her didn't show up alone in seedy taverns every day—he hid it well.

"Whaddaya want?" He threw down the rag and grabbed his cigarette from an ashtray.

She smiled. "Dirty martini."

"This is a *tavern*, lady. We don't have an H license."

"It was a joke. I'll take a glass of white wine. Vouvray, if you have it."

"We have Inglenook and Gallo."

"Inglenook."

He turned and headed down the other way. In a moment, he returned with a glass of wine.

She slapped her Platinum credit card on the bar. "Open a tab."

The jukebox clicked, then buzzed. An old Aerosmith song came on. She had a sudden flashback to her youth—standing front and center in the Kingdome, screaming out her love for Steven Tyler.

She took her card back from the bartender, slipped it in her bag, and headed toward the nearest table, where three men sat, talking loudly.

Normally, she'd find an empty table, sit down, and wait to see who came on to her, but she felt jittery tonight, nervous. She was tired of being alone.

"Hey, boys," she said, gliding into an empty space between two of the men.

Their conversation stopped. The sudden silence made her teeth ache. That was when she noticed that they each wore a wedding ring.

She kept her smile in place. It wasn't easy.

"Hi," one of the men said, shifting uncomfortably in his seat.

"Hi."

"Hi." The others followed suit. None of them made eye contact.

"I have to run, guys," the first one said, pushing back from the table.

"Me, too."

"Me, too."

And just like that, they were gone.

Meghann waved at their backs, said brightly, "See you again, soon. Drive safely." Just in case anyone had witnessed her humiliation.

She counted silently to five, then turned around. There was another table, not too far away. This one had only one man seated at it. He was writing on a yellow legal pad, obviously taking notes from an open textbook. He was staring so intently at the work that he hadn't seen her debacle at the table.

She walked over to him. "May I join you?"

When he looked up, she saw that he was young. Maybe twenty-one or twenty-two. His eyes were unguarded, filled with the kind of open-ended hope that came with youth. She felt drawn to that optimism, warmed by it. "I'm sorry, Ma'am. What did you say?"

Ma'am.

"Call me Meg."

He frowned. "You look familiar. Are you a friend of my mother's? Sada Carlyle."

She felt like the old lady from *Titanic*. "No. I don't know her. And I . . . thought I knew you, but I was mistaken. Sorry."

She tightened her grip on the wineglass. Desperation came for her, tapped her on the shoulder.

Get a grip.

She headed toward another table. As she came within range, a woman slipped into the empty chair and leaned in to kiss the man.

Meghann spun to her left and ran into a shaggy, derelict-looking guy who was obviously on his way back from the bar. "I'm sorry," she said. "I should have signaled before I made a turn like that."

"No harm done."

He went back to his table and sat down. She saw that he was slightly unsteady on his feet.

She stood there, alone in the midst of the crowded bar. There were three men back at the pool table. Two of them looked dangerous, dressed as they were in black leather and chains. The third man had so many tattoos on his bald head that it looked like earth as seen from space.

She felt the press of desperation, but it was useless. This wasn't going to be her night. She'd have to return to Claire's homey, comfortable guest room, climb into bed alone, and spend the night tossing and turning and wanting. Wanting, most of all.

She looked at the derelict. His shoulders were broad; his black T-shirt stretched taut along the top of his back. The waistband of his worn, faded Levi's veed out, as if he'd lost weight and hadn't bothered to buy jeans that fit.

It was him . . . or loneliness.

She went to his table, stood beside him. "May I sit down?"

He didn't look up from his beer. "What am I, your lucky fifth choice?"

"You're *counting?*"

"It isn't hard, lady. You're clearing out the place faster than a cop at a frat party."

She pulled out a chair and sat down across from him. The song "Lookin' for Love" came on the jukebox. *In all the wrong places . . .*

Finally, he looked up. Beneath the silvery fringe of hair that must have been trimmed with a pocket knife, a pair of blue eyes stared at her. With a start, she realized that he wasn't much older than she was, and he was almost handsome, in a Sam Elliott stranger-in-town kind of way. He looked like the kind of man who'd walked down a few dark alleys in his time.

"Whatever you're looking for," he said, "you won't find it here."

She started to flirt, to say something funny and impersonal, but before her tongue had even formed the first word, she paused. There was something about him. . . .

"Have we met?" she asked, frowning. She prided herself on her memory. Faces, she rarely forgot. Unless they belonged to the men she sometimes picked up; *those* she forgot immediately. *Please God, tell me I haven't screwed him already.*

"People say that all the time." He sighed. "Just an ordinary face, I guess."

No, that wasn't it. She was sure she'd seen him before, but it didn't matter, really. Besides, anonymity was her goal here, not making friends. "It's far from ordinary. Are you from around here?"

"I am now."

"What do you do for a living?"

"Do I *look* like I make a living? I get by, that's all."

"That's all any of us do, really."

"Look, lady—"

"Meghann. Friends call me Meg."

"Meghann. I'm not going to take you home. Is that clear enough for you?"

That made her smile. "I don't remember asking to be taken home. I asked if I could sit down. You're making quite an assumption."

He pulled back a little, looked uncomfortable. "Sorry. I've been . . . alone for a while. Makes a man poor company."

Poor company. It had the ring of education to it.

She leaned closer, studying him. Though the light was dim in here, and the air clogged with cigarette smoke, she liked his face. Enough for one night, at least.

"What if I *did* want to go home with you?"

When he looked up again, she would have sworn that he'd gone pale. His eyes were swimming-pool blue.

It was an eternity before he answered. "I'd say it wouldn't mean anything." His voice sounded tight. He looked scared.

She frowned. "The sex?"

He nodded.

She felt it suddenly, the thrill of the chase, the revving up of her heart. She reached out, pressed her forefinger along the back of his hand. "What if I said that was okay? That I didn't want it to mean anything?"

"I'd say that was sad."

She pulled her hand back, stung by the observation. She felt transparent suddenly, as if those blue eyes could see straight into her. "Do you want to get laid or not? No strings. No future. Just tonight. A little time together." She heard her voice spike; it was a small, desperate kind of sound, and it shamed her into sudden silence.

Another eternity passed. Finally, he spoke. "I don't know if I'd be any good at it."

"I am." She pressed her lips together to keep from saying something stupid. It was ridiculous, really, but she was nervous. She wanted him to want her, wanted it more than she understood. He was nothing, just another link in the chain of unavailable, ultimately forgettable men she'd slept with since her divorce. As far as she could tell, he had nothing to recommend him, nothing that would account for the odd fluttering in her chest. But she was afraid he'd turn her down. "Maybe we could just get each other through this one night."

He stood up so quickly the chair wobbled and almost fell. "I live down the street."

She didn't touch him, didn't take his hand or otherwise lay claim to him. None of the usual pretense of affection. "I'll follow you" was all she said.

Joe felt her beside him, the warmth of her body, the way her hand brushed accidentally against his every now and then.

Stop this now, he thought. *Just turn to her and say, "I made a mistake, I'm sorry."* But he kept walking forward, putting one foot in front of the other.

He could smell her perfume. Something musty and sweet and sexy; it reminded him of summer in the deep South. Of fragrant blossoms and hot, dark nights.

He was losing his grip. Must be drunker than he'd thought.

He couldn't do this. Didn't even remember how. (Not the sex part—*that* he remembered; it was the rest of it that eluded him, the talking, the touching, the being with another person.)

Suddenly he was standing in front of his cabin. Three blocks they'd walked, and he hadn't managed a single word of conversation. Neither had she, and he didn't know if he was thankful or not. If she'd chattered ridiculously on about nothing, perhaps he would have had the strength to turn away from her, to make his excuses. Her silence was his undoing.

"This is where I live right now," he said, rather stupidly he thought, as they were standing at the front door.

"Right now, huh?"

That surprised him. She'd picked up on the one thing in the sentence that revealed something. He'd need to be careful around her.

He opened the door and stepped aside to let her enter first.

She frowned briefly, then walked past him, into the darkness.

He followed her, leaving the lights off on purpose. There were photos of Diana everywhere. He didn't want to explain why he lived this way, not to this woman in her designer dress and expensive gold-and-platinum jewelry. In fact, he didn't want to talk at all.

He went to the kitchen and grabbed some candles. There were dozens available, kept on hand for winter storms when the power went out. Wordlessly, he carried them into the bedroom and placed them wherever he could; then, one by one, he lit them. When he was finished, he turned around and there she was, standing at the end of the bed, holding her purse as if she thought he might steal it.

He released a pent-up breath. She was beautiful. Jet-black hair, pale skin, green eyes that slanted upward, lips that seemed reluctant to smile. What in the hell was she doing here with him? And what was he doing here with her? He hadn't been with a woman since Diana.

She reached into her purse for something—

A condom. Oh, God.

—and then dropped her bag on the floor. As she walked toward him, hips swaying slightly, she unzipped her dress. It fell halfway down her arms, revealing a lacy black bra and creamy cleavage.

He meant to say, *Go away*, but instead he reached for her, pulled her against him. Her body molded to his and began slowly, slowly to move.

When he found the strength to pull back, he was trembling.

"Are you okay?" she asked.

He didn't think, didn't speak, just swept her into his arms and carried her toward the bed.

They fell onto the rumpled bedding together, she beneath him.

His body lay possessively on top of hers, and it felt good. Her hips came up to meet him.

Groaning, he bent down to kiss her. The soft, pliant feel of her mouth jolted him back in time.

Diana.

"What did you say?"

He drew back, looked down at her.

Meghann.

This time, when he kissed her, he kept his eyes open. She kissed him with a ferocity that left him breathless.

She shoved her hands underneath his T-shirt. Her fingertips grazed his nipples. "Take off your pants." Her voice was coarse. "I want to touch you."

They broke apart. He slid off the bed and undressed, his fingers too shaky to unbutton his jeans on the first try.

Naked, they fell together on the bed again. He rubbed his erection against her, kissing her open mouth, her chin, her closed eyes. She wrapped her leg over his and pressed in close. He felt her moisture against his thigh.

Then she reached down and touched him, wrapped her fingers tightly around him. Up and down. Up and down. He felt the condom slide into place in one practiced move.

He groaned as he thrust into her grasp one sweet, aching time, then pulled away before it was too late. He slid down her body, kissing her chin, her throat, her breasts. He tasted one nipple, drew it into his mouth, and sucked its sweetness. His hands pushed her legs apart as he moved downward, kissing her navel, her pubic hair.

She tried to push him away.

He held her in place, lowered his kisses until he was inside her. Moaning, she clutched his head and spread her legs wider apart. His tongue explored her, tasted her, glided up and down and in and out.

"Oh. My. God." She said it brokenly. "*Now.*"

He pulled her toward him in one swift motion and entered her.

She clung to him, arched up to meet him. She matched him thrust for thrust.

Joe's climax was like nothing he'd ever experienced before.

"Whew," she said, pushing the damp hair away from her face. "That was definitely an E-ticket ride."

He leaned back against the wobbly headboard. His whole body felt weak, trembling.

She looked up at him, smiling broadly, still breathing hard. "What's your name?"

"Joe."

"Well, Joe. That was great."

After a long minute, he dared to slide his arm around her, draw her closer. Holding her, he closed his eyes.

For the first time in years, he went to sleep with a woman in his arms.

When he woke up, he was alone again.

CHAPTER
SIXTEEN

"WHEW!" CLAIRE FLOPPED BACK ONTO THE PILLOWS. "I CAN'T RE-member the last time I got lucky in the morning." She pushed the hair out of her eyes and smiled at Bobby. "You must really love me if you'll kiss me before I brush my teeth."

He rolled onto his side. His handsome face was crisscrossed with tiny pink sleep lines. "You still wonder, don't you?"

"No," she said too quickly.

He touched her cheek in a caress so soft it made her sigh. "I love you, Claire Cavenaugh. I'd like to kick the ass of the man who made you so afraid to believe me."

She knew her smile was more than a little sad. There was noth-ing she could do about it. "It's not just men."

"But I can't beat up your mother or your sister."

She laughed at that. "Just prove Meg wrong. Nothing will make her crazier."

"She's trying, you know."

Claire sat up in bed. "Yeah. I noticed. She made that crack about me not loving people, then left the party early."

"She also bought you a dress that cost more than my car."

"Money's easy for Meg. She's got tons. Just ask her."

Bobby leaned back against the headboard. The blankets slid down his naked chest and pooled across his lap.

"She grew up with your mother, too, and she didn't have a dad to pick up the slack. It had to be hard on her, raising you all those years and then watching Sam step in to replace her."

"I can't believe you're defending her. She told me I was stupid to marry you."

He gave her that slow-growing smile that always made her go weak in the knees. "Darlin', you can't hold that against her. She's just trying to protect you."

"Control me is more like it."

"Come here," he whispered.

She leaned toward him. Her bare breasts breezed against his chest as they kissed. He slipped a hand around her neck and held her there, kissing her until she forgot their whole conversation. When she finally drew back, she was dizzy and breathing too hard.

"I'm getting to know you, Claire Cavenaugh-soon-to-be-Austin," he whispered against her lips. "You had a headache after the wedding dress screwup and again last night. When Meghann hurts your feelings, you say you don't care and start chewing aspirin. I've been there, darlin'. I know what matters is that she's your sister. The only one you've got."

Claire wanted to disagree but knew it was pointless. She *did* want to be close to Meg again. More and more often in the past few days, she'd found herself remembering the old Meg. The way they used to love each other. "I'm tired of the way we are together," she admitted.

"Well?"

"No one can push my buttons like Meghann. She has a true gift for saying exactly the wrong thing."

"Yeah. My dad was like that. We never could quite make it work between us. Now he's gone, and I wish we'd tried harder."

"Okay, Sigmund Freud. I'll try talking to her. Again."

"No more aspirin."

She gave him another long, lingering kiss, then walked naked into the bathroom. By the time she'd finished showering and gotten dressed, he was gone.

She made her bed and walked across the hall to Ali's room. Her daughter lay in bed, hidden beneath a blue-and-green pile of Little Mermaid sheets and comforters.

"Hey, sweetie," she said, sitting on the edge of the twin bed. "Time to wake up."

Alison stretched and rolled onto her back. "Did we get a kitten?"

"No. Why?"

"I thought I heard a kitty meowing this morning."

Claire bit her lower lip to keep from smiling. *Note to self: Come quietly.* "Nope, no kitty. You must have been dreaming."

"An' I heard someone on the stairs."

"I . . . uh . . . went down to make coffee."

"Oh. Well, *could* we get a puppy? Amy Schmidt has one and her mom is 'lergic to dogs."

"How about a goldfish?"

"Mo-om. The last goldfish got flushed down the toilet."

"I'll think about it, okay? Now hurry downstairs. I'm making blueberry pancakes for breakfast."

Claire went down to start the coffee. By the time Alison came into the kitchen, dragging her Groovy Girl doll behind her, the eggs and pancakes were ready.

Alison climbed up onto her chair, positioned the doll in her lap, and started pouring syrup.

"That's enough syrup," Claire said as she flipped another pancake on the Teflon griddle.

"You and Bobby and Aunt Meghann took a shower together last night. How'dya all fit?"

Claire laughed. "It's not a shower with water. It's a party for people who are going to be married. You know, like a birthday party."

"Didja play games?"

"Of course."

"Get presents?"

"You bet."

"Like what?"

Thong underwear. Chocolate body paint. A giant box of rubbers.
"Aunt Meghann gave us a Cuisinart." At Ali's confused look, she
added, "It's a way-cool blender."

"Oh. Grandpa is taking me fishing today. Up at Tidwell Pond."

"That'll be fun."

"He said you had wedding shit to do."

"Alison Katherine. You know better than to repeat Grandpa's
bad words."

"Oops." Ali bent forward and started licking the syrup off her
plate. In no time, it was clean. "Did you know that if you cut a worm
in half, it'll grow back?"

"I did know that."

She pushed back from her seat. "But Lily France got her finger
cut off an' it didn't grow back." She frowned. "I think God likes
worms better than Lily. It's cuz she cuts in line at lunch."

"Well, I don't—"

"Bye, Mom!" Alison threw her a kiss and scampered off. The
screen door banged shut behind her. A moment later, Claire heard
her daughter's high-pitched voice yell out, "I'm here, Grandpa. Were
you lookin' for me?"

Claire smiled and turned off the griddle, then poured herself a
second cup of coffee and went out to the back porch. The slatted
swing welcomed her.

She sat there, rocking gently, staring out at the silver curve of
water that defined her back property line. The house was set well
back from the river, on a rise of safety, but on a day like today, with
the sky as blue as forget-me-nots and the grass turning golden from

an unexpected week of sunlight, it was almost impossible to remember how dangerous the river could be.

The screen door screeched open and banged shut. Meghann stepped out onto the porch. She wore a fringed black peasant top and flare-legged jeans. Her hair, unbound, fell down her back in a riot of curls. She looked beautiful. "Morning."

Claire pulled the woolen blanket tighter around her legs, hiding the ratty, torn sweats she'd put on. "You want some pancakes?"

Meg sat down on the wooden Adirondack chair across from the swing. "No, thanks. I'm still trying to metabolize last night's cake."

"You sure left the party early." Claire hoped she sounded casual and not hurt.

"It was a nice party. Your friend Gina has a great sense of humor."

"Yeah, she does."

"It must be hard on her—watching your wedding so soon after her own divorce."

Claire nodded. "She's going through a really difficult time."

"It's always hard to find out you married the wrong man."

"They were married for fifteen years. Just because they got divorced doesn't mean he was the wrong man to marry."

Meg looked at her. "I would say it meant exactly that."

"Eric really played a number on you, didn't he?"

"I guess."

Claire took a sip of coffee. It occurred to her to drop the whole thing, to do what she'd always done around Meg—shut up and pretend it didn't hurt. Then she remembered her conversation with Bobby. Slowly, she said, "You didn't answer my question: How come you left the shower early?"

"It wasn't that early. How were your presents?"

"They were great. Thank you for the Cuisinart, by the way. Now: Why did you leave early?"

Meg closed her eyes, then slowly opened them. She looked . . . scared.

It shocked Claire so much she straightened. "Meg?"

"It was the M&M game," she answered. "I tried to be a good sport and play the game, but I barely know you, so I said something wrong. I still don't know what the hell it was."

"You said I loved well but not easily."

"Yes."

"I don't think it's true, that's all, and it hurt my feelings."

"It's true for me," Meg said.

Claire leaned forward. They were finally circling something that mattered. "Sometimes it's hard to love you, Meg."

"Believe me, I know." She laughed, but it was a bitter, throaty sound.

"You judge people—me—so harshly. Your opinions are like bull-whips. Every one leaves a bloody mark."

"People, yes. But you? I don't judge you."

"I flunked out of college. I dropped out of cosmetology school. I never left Hayden. I dress poorly. I had a child out of wedlock with a man whom I discovered was already married. Now I'm marrying a three-time loser and I'm too stupid to protect myself with a prenuptial agreement. Stop me when it sounds familiar."

Meg frowned. "Have I hung all that on you?"

"Like a suit of armor. I can't talk to you without feeling like a poor-white-trash loser. And, of course, you're rich and perfect."

"That part is true." Meg saw that her attempt at humor failed. "My therapist thinks I have control issues."

"Well, *duh*. You're a lot like Mama, you know. You both need to run the show."

"The difference is, she's psychotic. I'm neurotic. But God knows she handed down bad luck with men." Meghann looked at her. "Have you broken the curse?"

Even yesterday, Claire would have been angered by the question. Now, she understood it. Claire's legacy from Mama was a belief that sooner or later love walked out on you. Meg had inherited something else entirely: She didn't believe in love at all. "I have, Meg. Honestly."

Meg smiled, but there was a sadness in her eyes. "I wish I had your faith."

For once, Claire felt like the stronger sister. "I know love is real. It's in every moment I share with Ali and Dad. Maybe if . . . you'd had a father, you'd be able to believe in it." Claire saw the way her sister went pale; she knew she'd gone too far.

"You were lucky to have Sam," Meg said slowly.

Claire couldn't help thinking about the summer Dad had tried to be there for Meg. It had been a nightmare. Meg and Sam had had screaming fights about who loved Claire more, who knew what was best for her. It had been Claire herself who'd ended the worst of the battles. She'd cried out to Meg, *Quit yelling at my daddy.* That was the first time she'd seen her sister cry. The next day, Meg had gone. Years later, she'd finally called Claire. By then, Meg was in college and had her own life.

"He wanted to be there for you, too," Claire said gently.

"He wasn't my father."

They fell silent after that. The quiet bothered Claire, compelled her to stack up words between them, but she didn't know what to say.

She was saved by the phone. When it rang, she jumped up and ran inside the house to answer it.

"Hello?"

"Hold for Eliana Sullivan, please."

Claire heard Meg come up behind her. She mouthed: *Mama.*

"This should be good," Meg said, pouring herself a cup of coffee.

"Hello?" Mama said. "Hello?"

"Hey, Mama, it's me, Claire."

Mama laughed, that throaty, carefully sexy sound she'd cultivated over the years. "I believe I know which of my own daughters I called, Claire."

"Of course," Claire answered, although Mama confused the two of them all the time. Her memories were completely interchangeable. When called on it, Mama would say airily, *Whatever; y'all were thick as thieves back then. How'm I supposed to keep every little detail straight?*

"Well, honey, speak up. M'houseboy said you left me a message. What's goin' on?"

Claire hated the faux Southern accent. Every elongated vowel reminded her that she was ultimately "the audience" to Mama. "I called to tell you I'm getting married."

"Well, I'll be damned. I thought for sure you were going to die an old maid."

"Thanks, Mama."

"So, who is he?"

"You'll love him, Mama. He's a nice Texas boy."

"Boy? I thought that was your sister's way."

Claire actually laughed. "He's a man, Mama. Thirty-seven years old."

"How much money does he make?"

"That isn't important to me."

"Broke, huh? Well, I'll give you my best advice, honey. It's easier to marry the rich ones, but what the hell. Congratulations. When's the wedding?"

"Saturday the twenty-third."

"Of June? You mean this comin' Saturday?"

"That's what I mean. You would have had plenty of notice if you'd called me back."

"I was doing Shakespeare in the park. With Charlie Sheen, I might add."

"All night?"

"Now, honey. You *know* I have to take care of my fans. They're my life's blood. Did you see my picture in *People*, by the way? Just me and Jules Asner, sharin' a little girl talk."

"I missed that. Sorry."

"I *gave* you a subscription. What do y'all do, just let it sit around?"

"I've been busy with the wedding plans."

"Oh. Right. Well, Saturday's difficult for me, honey. How about the first weekend in August?"

Claire rolled her eyes. "As interested as I am in your schedule, Mama, the invitations have already gone out. Meg's busy planning the big day. It's too late to change the date."

Mama laughed. "*Meg* is planning your wedding? Honey, that's like asking the pope to plan a bar mitzvah."

"The wedding is Saturday. I hope you'll be able to attend." There she was, getting stiff and formal again, her usual reaction to stress.

Meghann handed her an aspirin.

Claire couldn't help smiling.

"She gives *me* a migraine every time," Meg said. "Is she still babbling?"

Claire nodded, whispered, "I think I heard the name Anna Nicole Smith."

Meg grinned. "Another nice Southern girl with intimacy issues."

"Claire?" Mama said sharply. "Are you listening to me?"

"Of course, Mama. Every word is a pearl."

"What time on Saturday? I asked you twice."

"The wedding is at seven P.M. Reception to follow."

Mama sighed. "Saturday. I've been waitin' three months for my hair appointment with José. Maybe he can take me early."

Claire couldn't take any more. "I've got to run, Mama. I'll be at the Hayden Episcopal Church at seven this Saturday. I hope you can make it, but I'll certainly understand if you're too busy."

"I *am* busy. But how often does a woman's daughter get married?"

"In our family, not often."

"Tell me straight up, honey. D'you think this one'll last? I'd hate to give up my hair appointment for—"

"I've got to go, Mama. Bye."

"Okay, honey. Me, too. And congratulations. I couldn't be happier for you."

"Thanks, Mama. Bye."

Claire tried to smile as she looked up at Meghann. "Saturday's a bad day for her."

"What? An audition for the $25,000 *Pyramid?*"

"A hair appointment with José."

"We should have sent her the invite after it was over."

"I don't know why I keep expecting something different from her."

Meg shook her head. "Yeah, I know. Even a mother alligator sticks around the eggs."

"Mama would make herself an omelette."

They actually laughed at that.

Claire looked out the window. Sunlight streamed onto her yard, made the flowers glow. She took peace from that view; it reminded her of all that was right with her world. It was best to forget about Mama. "Let's talk about the wedding plans," she said at last.

"Perfect. Maybe we could go over the menu."

Claire straightened. "Of course. I was thinking about those foot-long submarine sandwiches. They really feed a lot of people, and the men love them. Gina's potato salad is a perfect side dish."

Meghann was staring at her. "Potato salad and submarine sandwiches. That would be . . ." She paused. "Delicious."

"You paused."

"Did I? I think I took a breath."

"I know that pause. It's judgment talking."

"No. No. I had just talked to a girlfriend of mine. Carla. She's a struggling chef—just graduated—and she's broke. Can't pay her rent. She offered to do up some hors d'oeuvres for cost plus a tiny amount. She needs the word of mouth; you know how it is. But don't worry. I'll be happy to go to Safeway for the food, if that's what you'd rather do."

Claire frowned. "Would it really help your friend out? Catering the reception?"

"It would, but that's not what matters. What I care about is that you get the wedding *you* want."

"How much would it cost?"

"The same as submarine sandwiches and potato salad."

"No kidding. Well. I guess that would be okay. As long as we include those little hot dogs wrapped in the popover dough. Bobby *loves* those."

"Pigs in blankets. Of *course*. I'm sure I would have thought of that."

Claire thought her sister paused again, but she couldn't be sure.

Meg smiled. It was only a little forced. "Now, oddly enough, I also know an out-of-work baker who could make a four-layer cake with fresh flowers. She recommends violets, but of course, it's up to you."

"You know, Meg, you're a complete pain in the ass."

"I know. Judgmental and unforgiving."

"Absolutely. But you take charge well."

Meghann's smile faded. Claire knew her sister was thinking of that summer, so many years ago, when Meg had taken charge and changed all their lives.

"I didn't mean anything bad by that," Claire said softly. "It's such a damn minefield between us."

"I know."

"Now, about the cake . . ."

CHAPTER
SEVENTEEN

"I've gotten the permit for the park, and the tent is reserved from the party rental store. I'll go over the final details of setup with them tomorrow on my way to Costco." Roy sat back with a flourish. "That's it."

"And the lights?" Meghann asked, checking off the tent from her list.

"Ten thousand white Christmas lights, forty-two Chinese lanterns, and twenty hanging lights. Check."

Meghann marked her list accordingly. That was it. Everything on her list had been taken care of. In the past two days, she'd worked her ass off, checking and rechecking each detail. She'd arranged for every single thing that Roy had wanted. It was going to be, he declared at least three times a day, the best wedding ever to take place in Hayden.

Meghann didn't think that was much of a standard, but she was learning to keep her cynical thoughts to herself. She'd even been working so hard that she slept at night. The only problem now was her dreams.

They all seemed to be about Joe. When she closed her eyes, she remembered everything about that night. The blue eyes that were so sad . . . the way he'd whispered something—a name, maybe—while they were making love.

Making love.

She'd never thought of it that way, not with anyone.

"Meghann? You're getting that mushy look again. Are you thinking about the hors d'oeuvres?"

She smiled at Roy. "You should have seen Carla's face when I told her she'd have to do up a tray of pigs in blankets."

"I hate to admit it, but . . . they are tasty, you know. Dipped in ketchup. Even better dragged in baked beans. They'll probably disappear long before the Brie and pâté."

"I didn't let her do pâté." Meghann consulted her list again. It was a habit, checking and rechecking everything.

Roy touched her arm. "Sweetheart, you're done. All you have to do is show up at the rehearsal tonight and then get a good night's sleep."

"Thanks, Roy. I don't know what I would have done without you on all of this."

"Believe me, it has been an unexpected pleasure to work on this wedding. My next event is a potluck keggar in the Clausens' cow field to celebrate little Todd's acceptance to community college."

After the meeting, she headed back toward her car. She'd walked several blocks before she realized she was going in the wrong direction. She was just about to turn around when she saw the garage. There, tucked back in a thicket of trees and runaway salal, was Joe's cabin.

She had a sudden urge to walk up to the door, say, *Hey, Joe,* and follow him to the bedroom. The sex had been great. Hell, it had been better than great. So good that she'd sneaked off in the middle of the night. She'd always been better at good-bye than good morning.

The light in his kitchen went on. She saw a shadow cross the window, a flash of silvery hair.

She almost went to him.

Almost.

The one thing she knew for certain—had learned from hard-won experience—was that anonymous sex was all she could handle.

She turned and walked back to her car.

Joe stood at the kitchen sink, listening to the water running. It gargled down the rusty pipes. He was supposed to be washing his lunch dishes—that's why he'd come over here, after all—but he couldn't make his hands work.

She was standing across the street, looking at his house.

Meghann. *Friends call me Meg.*

She stood perfectly still, her arms crossed, her pointy chin held up just the slightest bit. Beside her, a huge hanging pot of flowers sent a red trailer of blossoms along her upper arm. She didn't seem to notice. Probably didn't notice their scent, either. She didn't strike him as a romantic woman.

"Meghann." He said her name softly, surprised by the unexpected rush of longing that came with it. He'd thought about her too often in the hours since their meeting.

He told himself it meant nothing, was simply an excess of hormones in a body that had been cold for years. But now, looking at her, wanting her again, he knew he was lying to himself.

Across the street, she took a step toward him.

His heartbeat sped up, his hands clenched.

Then she turned and walked away, quickly.

"Thank God," he said, wishing he meant it.

He shut the water off and dried his hands. Slowly, he went to the mantel and stood in front of a picture of Diana. In it, she stood at the base of the Arc de Triomphe in Paris, waving at him. She was smiling brightly.

"I'm sorry," he whispered, touching the glass.

The phone rang, startling him.

He knew who it was, of course. "Hey, Gina," he answered, reaching for his work gloves.

"Hey, big brother. I know it's late notice, but I'm having a rehearsal dinner at my house tonight. I thought you might like to come."

A rehearsal dinner. Prelude to a wedding. "Sorry, no."

"It's for Claire Cavenaugh. She's finally getting married."

Joe closed his eyes, remembering Claire. "I'm sorry, Gigi," he said at last. "I can't do that." The only thing worse than celebrating a marriage would be walking into a hospital.

"I understand, Joey. Really. I'll call you next week."

Claire sat in the doctor's waiting room, reading the newest issue of *People* magazine. There it was, a picture of her mother in some city park, surrounded by fans dressed in full space-traveler regalia. The caption read: *Eliana Sullivan mobbed by fans on the twenty-fifth anniversary of* Starbase IV's *first show.*

"Oh, please. I had better Halloween costumes in second grade."

"What, Mommy?"

Claire smiled down at her daughter, who sat cross-legged on the taupe-colored carpet, playing with a Cat in the Hat doll. "Nothing, honey."

"Oh. How much longer? I'm hungry."

"Not much longer. Dr. Roloff is busy with people who are really sick. You saw Sammy Chan go in—he has a broken arm."

Alison frowned. "You're not sick, right?"

"Of course not. This is my yearly appointment. You always come with me."

"Yeah." Ali went back to playing.

A few minutes later, the receptionist—Monica Lundberg—came out into the waiting room. As always, she looked beautiful, this time in a pale celery-colored sundress. "Doctor will see you now."

Claire looked down at Alison. "Stay right here, honey. I'll be right back."

"I'll watch her," Monica said. "You go on into room four."

"Thanks." Claire went down the hallway and turned into the last room on the left.

"Hey, Claire, how're the wedding plans going?"

She smiled at Bess, the nurse who had worked for Dr. Roloff for as long as anyone could remember.

"Great. We're having something simple."

"Of course you are." Bess took Claire's blood pressure and temperature. "Good blood pressure, kiddo. You must be living right." She took a quick blood sample, then burrowed through the cupboard over the sink and withdrew a plastic specimen cup. "You know the drill. Leave a sample in the door in the rest room. Doctor will be in as soon as he can."

"Thanks, Bess."

Bess winked. "See you tomorrow. Bye." And she was gone.

Claire hurried across the hall, left a urine sample in the bathroom, then returned to the room, where she dressed quickly in the hospital gown and climbed up onto the paper-covered examination table.

Moments later, Dr. Roloff walked in. He was a tall, gray-haired man with stern eyes and a ready smile. He'd been Claire's doctor for most of her life. He'd tended her through ear infections, acne, and pregnancy. Now he was Alison's doctor. Sam's, too.

The doctor sat down on a rolling stool and moved toward her. "How're the wedding plans going?"

"Great. Will you and Tina be able to make it?"

"Wouldn't miss it for the world." He paused, looked down for a minute. Claire knew he was thinking about the daughter he'd lost. "Diana would have loved your wedding."

Claire swallowed hard. It was true. One of the hardest parts of this wedding was doing it without Diana. The Bluesers had always done everything together. "She always said I was saving myself for royalty."

He finally looked up. The smile he offered was tired and more than a little worn. "Did you hear about Joe? He's back in town."

"I know. How is he?"

Henry sighed heavily. "I don't know. He hasn't been to see Tina and me." It was obvious how hurt the doctor was by that.

"I'm sure he will."

"Yeah. I'm sure." Dr. Roloff pushed the glasses higher on his nose and straightened. "Well, enough of that." Opening her chart, he studied it. "Everything okay?"

"Yeah."

"You're not due to see me for another two months. Why so early, Claire? Usually we have to send three notices and make a phone call to get you in here."

"Birth control pills," she said, feeling her cheeks heat up. It was ridiculous; she was thirty-five years old. There was no reason to be embarrassed. But she was. "We want to wait awhile before we get pregnant."

He studied her chart again, then nodded. "I wouldn't want you on them for too many years, but for now you'll be okay. We'll start you on the mini pill."

"Great."

Dr. Roloff set her chart aside. "Let's do your Pap smear."

When he was finished, Claire sat up.

"Your dad told me you had a headache last week," he said, stripping off his gloves. "And that you twisted your left ankle."

Life in a small town. Claire sighed. For as long as she could remember, her dad had run to the doctor whenever she had a hangnail or a loose tooth. Her arrival at adulthood hadn't changed his behavior. "Last year he thought I had Ménière's disease after a ride on the Ferris wheel made me dizzy."

He smiled at that. "Sam is certainly vigilant in terms of health care, that's true. You should have seen him when you were little. I got three calls a week asking if such-and-such was normal. Things like three sneezes in a row would set him off. Nonetheless, that doesn't mean he's a fool. Do the headaches seem to be triggered by your cycles?"

"I'm thirty-five," she said with a laugh. "It seems like I'm always ovulating or flowing. So, yeah, maybe."

"Did you ever start exercising?"

"*Ever?* Ninth grade was a good year for me. I went out for track and volleyball."

He wrote something in her chart. Probably *couch potato*.

"Are you sleeping well?"

"Like a baby. Since I met Bobby . . ." She blushed again. "Well, you know. I sleep great."

"I'm glad to hear that. Stress?"

"I'm a single mother who is about to get married for the first time. The sister I barely know is planning the wedding, *and* my mother is threatening to come. So, yes, I'm a little stressed out."

"Okay. Tell your dad I said everything is fine. No worries. But get some exercise. It's the best treatment for stress. Also, you're a little anemic again. That can cause headaches, too. So start taking some iron, okay?"

"You got it."

"Now get that beautiful little girl of yours home and start doing that woman-wedding thing. The whole town is looking forward to it."

"That's what happens when you wait fifteen years after everyone else in your class."

"You were only moments away from being labeled the town spinster. I don't know who Bess and Tina will worry about now." His eyes sparkled behind the small round glasses.

"Thanks, Doc."

He patted her shoulder. "I'm happy for you, Claire. We all are."

CHAPTER EIGHTEEN

THE AFTERNOON TURNED GRAY AND COLD. RAIN FELL IN TINY staccato bursts that were all but invisible to the naked eye.

Claire spent the rest of the day pretending to work.

"Go home, Claire," her father said to her whenever he happened to walk into the office and see her.

"I've got work to do," was her standard answer, and every time she said it, he laughed.

"Yeah. You're a big help today. Go take a bath. Do your nails."

She was too nervous to take a bath or do her nails. Thirty-five was too old to marry for the first time. How could she possibly be doing the right thing?

But every time her worries threatened to overwhelm her, she'd turn a corner or open a door and see Bobby. He was painting the fence around the laundry room the first time she saw him, scrubbing canoes the second.

He'd looked up at her approach both times. *Hey, darlin'*, he'd said, smiling. *I love you.*

Just that, those few and precious words, and Claire breathed easier again, for an hour or so, until the doubts once again welled up.

Finally, at around three in the afternoon, she gave up and walked back to her house. Toys lay scattered on the grass in the front yard; a Barbie that was half dressed, a pink plastic bucket and tiny shovel, a red Fisher-Price barn, complete with farm animals. She picked everything up and headed for the house.

"There you are," Meghann said when she walked in.

"Hey," she said, sighing as she walked over to the toy box and dumped her load in.

"Are you okay?"

"I'm fine." She certainly didn't want to discuss her wedding jitters with Miss Prenup.

Meghann got up. Claire could feel her sister's gaze; it was lawyerly and intense. Not a sister-to-sister look at all. "I was just going to have some iced tea. Would you like one?"

"A margarita would be better."

"You got it. Sit."

Claire sank onto the sofa and put her feet up on the magazine-covered coffee table.

Meg was back in no time, holding two glasses. "Here you are."

Claire took the glass and tried the margarita. "This is good. Thanks."

Meg sat in the bentwood rocker by the fireplace. "You're scared," she said gently.

Claire jumped as if she'd been shouted at. "Anyone would be." She took another drink, careful not to make eye contact. She felt like a squirrel in the presence of a cobra.

Meg moved to the sofa and sat down beside Claire. "It's normal, believe me. If you weren't scared right now, I'd take your pulse."

"You think I *should* be scared."

"I remember when Elizabeth and Jack got married. They were as in love as any two people I've ever seen. And she *still* needed two martinis to walk down the aisle. Only a fool wouldn't be afraid,

Claire. Maybe that's why weddings take place in churches—because each one is an act of faith."

"I love him."

"I know you do."

"But I should sign a prenuptial agreement to protect my assets in case we get divorced."

"I'm a lawyer. Protecting people is what I do."

"You protect strangers. Members of your family are a different thing."

Meghann looked down at her drink, then said softly, "I guess."

Claire wished she could take back that little cruelty. What was it about their past that made them wound each other so consistently? "I know you're trying to help, but how can you? You don't believe in love. Or marriage."

It was a moment before Meg answered, and when she did speak, her voice was soft. "I've never seen a baby crow."

"What?"

"On my way to work, I see crows clustered along the phone lines in the waterfront park. So I know that every spring there are nests somewhere, filled with tiny newborn crows."

"Meg, are you having a seizure?"

"My point is: I know things exist that I never see. Love has to be one of them. I'm trying to believe in it for you."

Claire knew how much it cost her sister to say something like that. No one who'd grown up in Mama's shadow found it easy to believe in love. That Meghann would try, for Claire's sake, really meant something. "Thank you. And thanks for planning the wedding. Even if you are keeping every detail a secret."

"It's been more fun that I thought. Kinda like being on the prom committee—not that I ever would have been on such a thing."

"I was Prom Queen." Claire grinned. "No kidding, and Rhododendron Princess, too, at Mountaineering Days."

Meghann laughed. Obviously she was relieved by a return to casual conversation. "What does the rhodie princess do?"

"Sit in the back of a 1953 Ford pickup in a dress the color of Pepto-Bismol and wave at the crowd. The 4-H Goat Club walked behind us in the parade. It was raining so hard that I ended up looking like Tim Curry at the end of *The Rocky Horror Picture Show.* Dad took about three dozen photos and put them all in an album."

Meghann looked down at her drink again. It was a moment before she spoke. "That's a nice memory."

Claire immediately regretted her comment. All it did was highlight Meghann's fatherlessness. "I'm sorry."

"You were lucky to have Sam. And Ali is lucky to have you. You're a great mother."

"Do you regret it?" Claire said, surprising both of them with the intimate question. "Not having kids, I mean."

"Being a divorce lawyer made me sterile."

"Meghann," she said evenly.

Meg finally looked at her. "I don't think I'd be any good at it. Let's just leave it at that."

"You were a good mother to me. For a while."

"It's the 'for a while' that matters."

Claire leaned toward her sister. "I'd like you to baby-sit Alison next week. While Bobby and I are on our honeymoon."

"I thought you weren't taking a honeymoon."

"Dad insisted. His wedding gift was a week's trip to Kauai."

"And you want *me* to baby-sit?"

Claire smiled. "It would mean a lot to me. Ali needs to know you better."

Meghann released a fluttery breath. She looked nervous. "You'd trust me?"

"Of course."

Meg sat back. A tremulous smile curved her lips. "Okay."

Claire grinned. "No taking her to the shooting range or teaching her to bungee-jump."

"So, skydiving lessons are out. Can I take her for a pony ride?"

They were still laughing when Dad pushed through the door and came into the living room. He was already dressed for the rehearsal in black pants—freshly ironed—and a pale blue denim shirt with a River's Edge logo on the pocket. His brown hair had been recently cut and was combed back from his forehead. If Claire didn't know better, she'd think he'd moussed it.

"Hey, Dad. You look great."

"Thanks." He flashed an uncomfortable smile at her sister. "Meg."

"Sam," Meg said stiffly as she got to her feet. "I need to get dressed. Good-bye."

When Meghann had disappeared upstairs, Sam sighed and shook his head. "I feel about two feet tall when she looks at me."

"I know the feeling. What's going on, Dad? I need to get dressed." She looked past him. "I thought you were playing checkers with Ali?"

"Bobby is trying to French-braid her hair."

Claire laughed at that and started for the stairs. "I'll redo it before we leave. You want to pick me up in forty-five minutes?"

"I need to talk to you first. Just for a minute. I didn't know if I should talk to Bobby at the same time—"

She smiled. "I hope this isn't my long-overdue sex talk."

"I talked to you about sex."

"*Don't do it* is not a talk."

"Wiseass." He nodded toward the couch. "Sit down. And don't give me any lip. This'll just take a second."

He sat down on the coffee table. "Margaritas, already?" he said, glancing at Meg's glass.

"I was a little nervous."

"It makes me think of when I married your mama."

"Let me guess, she was power-drinking all day."

"We both were." He smiled, but it was a little sad, that smile, and it excluded Claire somehow.

After a short pause, he reached into his pocket, pulled out a small black box, and opened it.

Inside was a marquise-cut yellow diamond set on a wide platinum band. "It's your grandma Myrtle's diamond. She wanted you to have it."

The ring sparked a dozen sweet memories. Whenever her grandmother had dealt a hand of cards, this diamond had splashed tiny colored reflections on the walls.

Dad reached out, took her hand. "I couldn't let my baby get married with a tinfoil ring."

She tried it on. The ring fit as if it had been made for her. She leaned over and pulled him into her arms. "Thanks, Dad."

He smelled of woodsmoke and bay rum aftershave, as he had for the whole of her life, and in that moment, as she held him with her face pressed against his cheek, she remembered a dozen times from her girlhood. Nights they'd gone bowling and had dinner at Zeke's Drive-In . . . the way the porch light flickered ten seconds after she and her date pulled into the driveway . . . the stories he used to tell her at bedtime when she felt scared and alone and missed her big sister.

After tomorrow, she would be a married woman. Another man would be the center of her life, another arm would keep her steady. She would be Bobby's wife from now on; not Sam Cavenaugh's little girl.

When Dad drew back, there were tears in his eyes, and she knew he'd been thinking the same thing.

"Always," she whispered.

He nodded in understanding. "Always."

CHAPTER
NINETEEN

*M*EGHANN WISHED TO GOD SHE'D NEVER AGREED TO LET GINA host and plan the rehearsal dinner. Every moment was pure hell.

Are you here by yourself?

Where's your husband?

You don't have children? Well. That's lucky, sometimes I wish I could give mine away. This one was followed by a clearly uncomfortable laugh.

No husband, huh? It must be great to be so independent. This one was always followed by a frown.

Meghann knew that Claire's friends were trying to make conversation with her; they just didn't know what to say. How could they? This was a group of women who talked endlessly about their families. Summer camp start-times were a big topic of conversation; also resorts that were "kid friendly" on Lake Chelan and along the Oregon Coast. Meghann had no idea what *kid friendly* even meant. That they served ketchup with every meal, maybe.

They were trying to include her, especially the Bluesers, but the more they tried to make her a part of the group, the more alienated she felt. She could talk about a lot of things—world politics, the situation in the Mideast, where to get the best deal on designer clothes, real estate markets, and Wall Street. What she couldn't talk about were family things. Kid things.

Meghann stood at the fireplace in Gina's beautifully decorated house, sipping her second margarita. This one, like the first, was disappearing much too quickly. There were pods of people everywhere—on the deck, in the living room, sitting at the dining-room table—all talking and laughing among themselves. Across the room, Claire stood at the kitchen bar/counter, eating potato chips and laughing with Gina. As Meghann watched, Bobby came up behind Claire and whispered something in her ear. She immediately turned into his arms. They came together like puzzle pieces, fitting perfectly, and when Claire looked up at Bobby, her face glowed.

Love.

There it was, in all its quicksilver glory.

Please, God, she found herself praying for the first time in years, *let it be real.*

"Okay, everyone," Gina said, coming into the room. "Now it's time for the second part of the evening."

A hush fell. Everyone looked up.

Gina smiled. "Hector is opening the bowling alley just for us! We leave in fifteen minutes."

Bowling. Rented shoes. Polyester shirts. The division of people into teams.

Meg eased away from the wall. Taking a sip of her cocktail, she realized that she'd finished it. "Damn."

"We haven't really met yet. I'm Harold Banner. Karen's husband."

Meghann was startled by the man's presence. She hadn't heard him approach. "Hello, Harold."

He was a tall, thin man with bushy black eyebrows and a smile that was just a bit too wide, as if maybe he had too many teeth. "I hear you're a lawyer."

"Yes."

"Let me ask you then—"

She tried not to groan.

He barked out a braying laugh. "Just kidding. I'm a doctor. I get the same thing all the time. Everyone I meet mentions a pain somewhere."

In the ass, maybe. She nodded and looked down into her empty glass again.

"I guess you left your husband at home, huh? Lucky guy. Karen makes me show up at everything."

"I'm single." She tried not to grit her teeth, but this was about the tenth time she'd had to reveal that tonight.

"Ah. Footloose and fancy-free. Lucky you. Kids?"

She knew he was just being nice, trying to find some common ground for conversation, but she didn't care. Tonight had been brutal. One more reminder that she was a woman alone in the world and she'd probably scream. Normally she was proud of her independence, but this small-town crowd made her feel as if she lacked something important. "I'm sorry, Harold. I need to go now."

"What about bowling?"

"I don't bowl." She walked across the living room and came up beside Claire, gently putting her hand on her sister's shoulder.

Claire turned. She looked so happy right then it took Meghann's breath away. When she saw Meghann, she laughed. "Let me guess. You're not a bowler."

"Oh, I love bowling. Really," she added at her sister's skeptical look. "I have my own ball." She knew immediately that she'd gone too far with that one.

"You do, huh?" Claire leaned against Bobby, who was talking animatedly to Charlotte's husband.

"Unfortunately, I have a few last-minute details I need to go over for tomorrow. I have to get up early."

Claire nodded. "I understand, Meg. I really do."

"I thought I'd call Mama again, too."

Claire's happy look faded. "Do you think she'll show up?"

Meghann wished she could protect Claire from Mama. "I'll do my best to get her here."

Claire nodded.

"Well. Bye. I'll tell Gina why I'm leaving."

Fifteen minutes later, Meghann was in her car, speeding down the country road toward Hayden. She had the top down, and the cool night air whipped through her hair.

She tried to forget the rehearsal dinner, get the hurtful memories out of her mind, but she couldn't do it. Her sister's well-meaning friends had managed to underscore the emptiness of Meg's life.

She saw the sign for Mo's Fireside Tavern and slammed on the brakes.

It was a bad idea to go in, she knew. There was nothing but trouble in there. And yet . . .

She parked on the street and went inside the smoky bar. It was crowded tonight.

Friday. Of course.

Men sat on every barstool, at every table. There were a few women scattered throughout the crowd, but damn few.

She made her way through the place, boldly checking out every man. She got enough smiles to know that she could definitely find one here tonight.

She had toured the whole place and made her way back to the front door when she realized why she was really here.

"Joe," she said softly, surprised. She honestly hadn't known that she wanted him.

That wasn't good.

She left the bar. Out on the street, she took a deep breath of sweet mountain air. She never slept with a man twice. Or rarely, anyway. As her friend Elizabeth had once pointed out, Meghann would sometimes make a New Year's resolution to quit screwing college kids, and then date men without hair for a week or two, but that was pretty much the extent of her so-called dating life.

The amazing thing was, she didn't want to cull through the possibilities in the bar and bring home a stranger.

She wanted . . .

Joe.

She stood at her car, looking down the street at his small cabin. Light glowed from the windows.

"No," she said aloud. She shouldn't do it, but she was walking anyway, crossing the street, and entering his yard, which smelled of honeysuckle and jasmine. At the door, she paused, wondering what in the hell she was doing.

Then she knocked. There was a long silence. No one answered.

She twisted the knob and went inside. The cabin was dark and quiet. A single lamp glowed with soft light, and a fire crackled in the hearth.

"Joe?" Cautiously, she stepped forward.

No answer.

A shiver crept along her spine. She sensed that he was here, close by, burrowed into the darkness like a wounded animal, watching her.

She was being ridiculous. He simply wasn't home. And she shouldn't be here.

She started to turn for the door when she saw the photographs. They were everywhere—on the coffee table, the end tables, the windowsills, the mantel.

Frowning, she walked from place to place looking at the pictures. They were all of the same woman, a lovely blond with a Grace Kelly kind of elegance. There was something familiar about her. Meghann picked one up, smoothed her finger across the cheap Plexiglas frame. In this photograph, the woman was clearly trying to make pie dough from scratch. There was flour everywhere. She wore an apron that read: *Kiss the Cook.* Her smile was infectious. Meghann couldn't help smiling along with her.

"Do you always break into other people's homes and paw through their things?"

Meghann jumped back. Her fingers went numb—just for a second, but it was time enough. The picture crashed to the floor. She turned around, looking for him. "Joe? It's me, Meghann."

"I know it's you."

He was slumped in the corner of the room, with one leg bent and the other stretched out. Firelight illuminated his silvery hair and half of his face. She didn't know if it was the dim lighting, but she noticed the lines etched around his eyes. Sadness clung to him, made her wonder if he'd been crying.

"I shouldn't have come in. Or come here, for that matter," she said, uncomfortably. "I'm sorry." She turned and headed for the door.

"Have a drink with me."

She released a breath, realizing just then how much she'd wanted him to ask her to stay. Slowly, she faced him.

"What can I get you?"

"Martini?"

He laughed. It was a dry, rustling sound that bore no resemblance to the real thing. "I've got scotch. And scotch."

She sidled past the coffee table and sat down on the worn leather sofa. "I'll have a scotch."

He got up, shuffled across the room. She saw now why he'd been so invisible; he had on worn black jeans and a black T-shirt.

She heard a splash of liquid, then a rattling of ice. As he poured her drink, she looked around the room. All those photographs of the Grace Kelly look-alike made her uncomfortable. These pictures weren't decoration; they were obsession, naked and unashamed. She tried to figure out where she'd seen this woman but couldn't.

"Here."

She looked up.

He stood in front of her. The top two buttons of his Levi's were undone, and the T-shirt was ripped at the collar, revealing a dark patch of chest hair.

"Thank you," she said.

He took a drink straight from the bottle, then wiped his mouth with the back of his hand. "Sure." He didn't move away, just stood there, staring down at her. He was unsteady on his feet.

"You're drunk," she said, finally getting it.

"Iss June twenty-second." He smiled, or tried to, but the sadness in his eyes made it impossible.

"Do you have something against the twenty-second?"

His gaze darted to the end table beside her. To the photographs clustered there. He looked quickly back at her. "You were here the other day. You didn't come in."

So he'd seen her, standing on the street that afternoon, looking at his house. She couldn't think of how to answer, so she drank instead.

He sat down beside her.

She twisted around to face him, realizing an instant too late how close they were. She could feel his breath against her lips. She tried to edge away.

He reached out, grabbed her wrist. "Don't go."

"I wasn't leaving. But maybe I should."

He let go of her wrist suddenly. "Maybe you should." He took another swig from the bottle.

"Who is she, Joe?" Her voice was soft, but in the quiet room, it seemed too loud, too intimate. She flinched, wishing she hadn't asked, surprised that she cared.

"My wife. Diana."

"You're married?"

"Not anymore. She . . . left me."

"On June twenty-second."

"How'jou know?"

"I know about divorces. The anniversaries can be hell." Meghann stared into his sad, sad eyes and tried not to feel anything. It was better that way, safer. But sitting here beside him, close enough to be taken into his arms, she felt . . . needy. Maybe even desperate. Suddenly she wanted something from Joe; something more than sex.

"Maybe I should go. You seem to want to be alone."

"I've been alone."

She heard the ache of loneliness in his voice and it drew her in. "Me, too."

He reached out, touched her face. "I can't offer you anything, Meghann."

The way he said her name, all sad and drawn out and slow, sent a shiver along her spine. She wanted to tell him that she didn't want anything from him except a night in his bed, but amazingly, she couldn't form the words. "It's okay."

"You should want more."

"So should you."

She felt fragile suddenly, as if this man she didn't know at all had the power to break her heart. "We're talking too much, Joe. Kiss me."

In the fireplace, a log fell to the hearth floor with a thud. Sparks flooded into the room.

With a groan, he pulled her into his arms.

CHAPTER TWENTY

$\mathcal{T}$HE NEXT MORNING, THE WEATHER IN HAYDEN WAS PERFECT. A bright sun rode high in the cornflower blue, cloudless sky. A thin, cooling breeze rustled through the trees, making music on the deep green maple leaves. By five o'clock, Claire was ready to begin dressing. The problem was, she couldn't move.

Behind her, there was a knock at the door.

"Come in," she said, thankful for the distraction.

Meghann stood in the doorway, holding a pile of plastic-sheathed dresses. She looked nervous, uncharacteristically uncertain. "I thought maybe we'd get dressed together." When Claire didn't answer instantly, Meghann said, "You probably think it's a stupid idea." She backed out of the room.

"Stop. I think it would be great."

"You do?"

"Yeah. I just need to shower."

"Me, too. I'll meet you back here in ten minutes."

True to her word, Meghann was back in ten minutes, wearing a towel around her naked body. Once inside the room, she changed into a bra and panties, then dried her hair and fashioned it into a beautiful French twist.

"That looks great," Claire said.

"I could do your hair if you'd like."

"Really?"

"Sure. I did it all the time when you were little."

Claire didn't remember that, and yet she crossed the room and automatically knelt in front of the bed.

Meghann settled in behind her, began brushing her hair. She hummed as she worked.

Claire closed her eyes. It felt so good to have someone brushing her hair.

It came to her then, floating on the lullaby of her sister's humming, a memory.

You'll be the prettiest girl in all of Barstow kindergarten, Claire-Bear. I'll put this pink ribbon all through your braids and it'll protect you.

Like a magic ribbon?

Yes. Just exactly like that. Now sit still and let me finish.

"You *did* do my hair when I was little."

The hairbrush paused, then began stroking again. "Yes."

"I wish I remembered more of those years."

"I wish I remembered less."

Claire didn't know what to say to that, so she changed the subject. "Have you heard from Mama?"

"No. I left three messages yesterday. Her *houseboy* told me she'd call back at a better time."

"There's no point getting mad at her. She is who she is."

"Yeah. A has-been actress and a never-was mother."

Claire laughed. "She'd debate 'has-been actress' with you."

"That's true. After all, she's done Shakespeare in Cleveland. There. All done."

Claire climbed to her feet and started to head for the bathroom.

"Wait." Meghann pulled her back to the bed. "Sit down here. No one is supposed to do their own wedding makeup." Meg got up, ran to her bedroom, and returned a minute later with a box big enough to hold fishing tackle.

Claire frowned as she sat down. "Not too much. I don't want to look like Tammy Faye."

"Really? I thought you did." Meghann opened the tackle box. Inside lay dozens of shiny black compacts emblazoned with the interlocked Chanel Cs.

Claire smiled. "I think you spend too much time at Nordstrom."

"Close your eyes."

Claire did as she was told. Whisper-soft bristles breezed across her eyelids and along her cheekbones.

Fairy kisses, that's what I call 'em.

Halloween. The year they lived in Medford, Oregon. Mama had been waiting tables during the day and dancing in a strip club at night.

Can you make me look like a princess, Meggy? Claire had asked, eyeing Mama's oh-so-off-limits bag of makeup.

Of course I can, silly. Now, close your eyes.

"Okay. You're done."

Claire's legs were unsteady as she got to her feet. She looked at Meghann, sitting there on her knees with the makeup box open beside her and, for a split second, Claire was a six-year-old princess, holding her big sister's hand on Halloween night.

"Go look."

Claire went into the bathroom and looked in the mirror.

Her blond hair had been loosely drawn back from her face and twisted into an elegant roll. The hairstyle emphasized her cheekbones and made her eyes look huge. She'd never looked this pretty. Never.

"Oh" was all she said.

"You don't like it. I can change it. Come over here."

Claire turned to her sister. They were always doing that to each other, misinterpreting, imagining the worst. No wonder every conversation bruised one or the other. "I love it," she said.

Meghann's smile was dazzling. "Really?"

Claire took a step toward her. "What happened to us, Meg?"

Meghann's smile faded. "You know what happened. Please. Let's not talk about it now. Not today."

"We've been saying 'not today' for years. I don't think it's a strategy that's worked, do you?"

Meghann released a heavy sigh. "Some things hurt too much to talk about."

Claire knew about that. It was the principle that had guided their whole relationship. Unfortunately, it had kept them strangers to each other. "Sometimes silence hurts most of all." She heard the ache in her voice; there was no way to mask it.

"I guess we're living proof of that."

They stared at each other.

Suddenly the door banged open. "Mommy!" Ali raced into the room, already wearing her beautiful ice-blue silk bridesmaid dress. "Hurry, Mommy, come look." She grabbed Claire's hand, dragged her toward the door.

"Just a second, honey." Claire threw Meghann a bathrobe, then slipped a nightgown over her own head and followed Ali downstairs. Outside in the driveway, Dad, Bobby, and Alison stood around a candy-apple-red convertible.

Claire moved toward them, frowning. That was when she noticed the pink bow on the hood. "What in the world?"

Dad handed her a note. It read:

Dear Claire and Bobby,
Best of luck on your big day. I'm
still hoping to make it up there.
Hugs and kisses,
Mama

Claire stood there a long time, staring down at the car. She knew what it meant: Mama wasn't going to make it to the wedding. Probably, she chose the hard-to-get hair appointment instead.

Meg came up beside her, laid a hand on her shoulder. "Let me guess: Mama's wedding gift."

Claire sighed. "Leave it to Mama to give me a car with two seats. Am I supposed to have Ali run along behind?"

Then she laughed. What else could she do?

Claire stood in the dressing room at the small Episcopal church on Front Street. The last hour had been nonstop action. She and Meghann hadn't found five minutes to talk.

The Bluesers had been in and out of the dressing room every few minutes, oohing and aahing over her dress, and Meghann had been busily checking details, clipboard in hand. Ali had asked at least a dozen times which step she was supposed to stand on.

But now, the room was mercifully quiet. Claire stood in front of the full-length mirror, unable to quite grasp that the woman in the glass was her. The gown fit perfectly, flowing to the floor in a cascade of white silk, and the veil made her look every bit the princess.

Her wedding day.

She couldn't quite believe it. Every night since meeting Bobby, she'd gone to sleep wondering if he'd be there in the morning. When the sun came up, she was quietly amazed to find him still there.

Another lovely legacy from childhood, she supposed.

But soon, she would be Mrs. Robert Jackson Austin.

There was a knock at the door.

It was Meghann. "The church is packed. Are you ready?"

Claire swallowed hard. "I am."

Meghann took her sister's arm and led her out to the small area behind the closed church doors. Dad was already there, waiting with Ali.

"Oh, Ali Kat, you look like a princess," Claire said, kneeling down to kiss her daughter.

Alison giggled, twirled. "I love my dress, Mommy."

Behind the doors, the music started. It was time.

Meghann bent down to Alison. "Are you ready, sweetie? You walk slow—like we practiced, okay?"

Ali hopped up and down. "I'm ready."

Meghann eased the door open a crack. Ali slipped through and disappeared.

Dad turned to Claire. His eyes filled slowly with tears. "I guess you're not my little girl anymore."

"Get ready," Meghann said; a second later, the organ started "Here Comes the Bride," and she opened the doors.

Claire slipped her arm through her dad's and they walked slowly down the aisle. At the end of it, Bobby, dressed in a black tuxedo, waited. His brother, Tommy Clinton, stood beside him. Both men were smiling broadly.

Dad stopped, turned to Claire. He lifted the veil and kissed her cheek, then eased away from her, and suddenly Bobby was there beside her, taking her arm, leading her up to the altar.

She looked up at him, loving him so much it scared her. It wasn't safe to love someone this much. . . .

Don't be scared, he mouthed, squeezing her hands.

She focused on the feel of his hand in hers, the comfortable stability of him beside her.

Father Tim droned on and on, but Claire couldn't really hear anything except the beating of her own heart. When it came time for her to say her lines, she panicked that she wouldn't be able to hear or remember them.

But she did. When she said, "I do," it felt as if her heart were actually expanding inside her chest. In that moment, standing in front of her friends and family and staring into Bobby's blue eyes, she started to cry.

Father Tim smiled down at each of them, then said, "I now pronounce you husband and—"

The doors to the church banged open.

A woman stood in the doorway, arms out-flung, a cigarette in one hand. She wore a silver lamé dress that showcased her curves. Behind her, there were at least a dozen people: bodyguards, reporters, and photographers. "I can't *believe* y'all started without me."

A gasp of recognition moved through the church. Someone whispered, "It's *her*."

Bobby frowned.

Claire sighed and wiped her eyes. She should have expected this. "Bobby, you're about to meet Mama."

"I am going to *kill* her." Meghann wiped the unexpected tears from her eyes and shot to her feet. Mumbling *Excuse me* to the shell-shocked guests beside her, she sidled out of the pew and stepped into the aisle.

"There's my other girl." Mama threw open her arms. Again the flashbulbs erupted in spasms of blinding light.

Meghann grabbed her mother by the arm and yanked her back through the doors. The paparazzi followed, all talking at once. There was one terrifying moment when Mama wobbled on her ridiculous heels and Meghann feared a California-freeway-type pileup of bodies on the red-carpeted aisle, but she tightened her grip and staved off disaster.

Through the now-closed doors, she could hear Father Tim's stumbling second attempt to pronounce Bobby and Claire husband and wife. A moment later, applause thundered through the church.

Meghann pulled Mama into the dressing room and shut the door behind them.

"What?" Mama whined, obviously unable to frown but wanting to. Too much Botox, no doubt.

A dog barked. Mama looked down at a small St. John beaded travel carrier in her arms. "It's okay, honey. Meggy's makin' a mountain out of a molehill."

"You brought your *dog?*"

Mama pressed a hand to her ample breast. "You know Elvis hates to be left alone."

"Mama, you haven't been alone in years. Forget whatever poor fool you're currently sleeping with, you employ three gardeners, two housekeepers, a personal assistant, and a houseboy. Certainly one of them could dog-sit."

"I don't have to clear my lifestyle with you, Miss Meggy. Now why in the *hell* did you throw me out of my own daughter's weddin'?"

Meghann felt a surge of impotent anger. It was like dealing with a child. There was no way to make Mama understand what she'd done wrong. "You're late."

Mama waved a hand. "Darlin', I'm a celebrity. We're *always* late."

"Today was Claire's day to be a star. Can you get that, Mama? *Her* day. And you walked in right at the moment of glory and stole the show. What were you doing out here, *waiting* for the perfect moment to make your entrance?"

Mama looked away for just a second, but it was enough to confirm Meghann's suspicion. Her mother *had* timed her entrance. "Oh, Mama," she said, shaking her head. "That's a new low. Even for you. And who are all those people? Do you think you need bodyguards at a wedding in Hayden?"

"You always pooh-pooh my career, but my fans are everywhere. They scare me sometimes."

Meghann laughed at that. "Save the acting for *People* magazine, Mama."

"Did you see the article? I looked good, don't you think?" Mama immediately went to the mirror and began checking her makeup.

"As soon as the church empties out, I'm going to talk to your entourage. They arrived in cars; they can sit in them until it's time to leave. I'll protect you from your stampeding fans."

"Dang it, Meggy. Who'll take my picture at the weddin'? A woman my age needs filters." Mama reached into her crystal-encrusted evening bag and pulled out a black tube of lipstick. She leaned closer to the mirror.

"Mama," Meghann said slowly, "Claire has waited a long time for this day."

"That's for sure. I was startin' to think she and those friends of hers were gay." Mama snapped the lipstick shut and smiled at her reflection.

"The point is, we need to focus on *her* today. Her needs."

Mama spun around. "Now, that hurts. When have I *ever* put my needs ahead of my children's?"

Meghann was speechless. The most amazing part of this science-fiction moment was that her mother actually believed what she just said. Meghann forced a smile. "Look, Mama, I don't want to argue with you on this special day. You and I are going to walk over to the reception and tell Claire how happy we are for her."

"I am happy for her. Bein' married is the most wonderful feelin' in the world. Why I remember when I married her daddy, I felt swept away by him."

You get swept away more often than a muddy riverbank. Meghann kept her lips sealed and her smile tacked in place. She didn't remind Mama that the marriage to Sam had lasted less than six months, or that Mama had run out on him in the middle of the night, *after* sending him to the store for tampons. For years, Meghann had had a mental picture of Sam, returning to the Chief Sealth Trailer Park in Concrete, Washington, on that rainy night, standing at the empty site, holding a box of tampons. He hadn't known for almost ten years—until Meghann called—that his marriage had produced a daughter. "That's the way, Mama. Pour it on. But," she stepped closer, looked up into her mother's surgically wrinkle-less face, "you may bring one photographer. One. No bodyguards and no dog. These rules are not negotiable."

"You are a pain in the ass, Meghann," Mama said. Her accent was so thick only a trained ear could understand it. "No wonder you can't keep a man for long."

"This from the woman whose been married what—six times? Pretty soon you and Elizabeth Taylor will have to start swapping husbands or you'll run out."

"You have no romance in your soul."

"I can't imagine why, growing up as I did with so much love."

They stood there, inches apart, staring at each other.

Then Mama laughed. The real thing this time, not that sexy

kitten-laugh she used in Hollywood, but the deep, tavern sound she'd been born with. "Meggy, darlin', you always did bust my ass. You flipped me off when you were eight months old—did I ever tell you that?"

Meghann smiled in spite of herself. It was always this way between them. How could you stay angry with a woman as shallow as Mama? In the end, sometimes there was nothing to do but laugh and go on. "I don't think so, Mama."

She put her arm around Meghann and pulled her close. It reminded Meghann of so many childhood and adolescent times. She and Mama had always fought like cats and dogs, and then ended up laughing. Probably because both of them would rather laugh than cry. "No. You looked right up, smiled, and flipped me off. It was the funniest damn thing ever."

"I've done it a few times since."

"I imagine you have. It's the nature of the beast. You'd know this if you'd had children."

"Don't go there, Mama."

"Oh, fiddle-dee-dee. You don't tell me what to do or say, Missy. It takes guts to be a mother. You just don't have 'em, that's all. Look at the way you pawned off your sister. Nothin' to be ashamed of."

"Mama, I don't think you ought to tell me what it takes to be a mother. I might have to remind you of a few things you pretend to forget. Like how it was your job to raise Claire, not mine."

"So, are we goin' to this reception or not? I have a midnight flight home. But don't worry, there's none of that two-hours-ahead stuff for stars like me. I need to be at SeaTac by eleven."

"That means you need to leave here about eight-thirty. So let's go. And I mean it, Mama, best behavior."

"Now, darlin', you know that social etiquette is bred into us Southern girls."

"Oh, *please.* You're as Southern as Tony Soprano."

Mama sniffed. "I swear, I should have left you by the side of the road in Wheeling, West Virginia."

"You *did* leave me there."

"You always were a hard and unforgiving person. It's a flaw, Meggy. Truly. So I miscounted my children. It happens. My *mistake* was in comin' back for you."

Meghann sighed. There was no way to get the last word with Mama. "Come on, Mama. Claire probably thinks I killed you."

CHAPTER
TWENTY-ONE

CLAIRE REFUSED TO THINK ABOUT THE DEBACLE WITH MAMA. SHE clung to Bobby's arm and let herself be carried away. She was the center of a laughing, talking, congratulatory crowd. She had never felt so special, so completely loved in her life. Most of the town had turned out for this wedding, and everyone stopped Claire to tell her that she was the prettiest bride ever.

It went straight to a woman's head, that kind of thing. You forgot sometimes, in the middle of a hectic, single-mother life, how it felt to be the center of attention.

Bobby slipped an arm more tightly around her waist, pulled her close. "Have I told you how beautiful you look?"

She stopped and turned to him, letting her body melt against his. The wedding guests kept moving past them, jostling them. "You have."

"When you came down that aisle, you took my breath away. I love you, Mrs. Austin."

She felt tears start again. It came as no surprise. She'd been weepy all day.

They kept their arms around each other and followed the crowd, walking slowly this time. "I don't see why everyone had to park at Riverfront Park. There's usually plenty of room at the church. We can all carpool to the campground."

Bobby shrugged. "I'm just following the crowd. Gina said the limo was waiting for us at the park."

Claire laughed. "Leave it to Meghann to rent a limo to drive us six miles." But she couldn't deny that she was excited. She'd never been in a limousine.

In front of them, the crowd stopped; as if on cue, they parted, forming a dark aisle.

"Come on," Gina yelled out, waving them forward.

Claire grabbed Bobby's hand and pulled him forward. Around them, the guests clapped and cheered them on. A shower of rice seemed to fall from the sky; it sprinkled their faces and crunched beneath their feet.

They came to the end of the crowd.

"Oh, my God." Claire turned around, searched the crowd for Meghann, but her sister was nowhere to be seen.

She couldn't believe her eyes. Riverfront Park, the very place where she'd spent her childhood, where she'd broken her ankle playing red rover, where she'd tasted her first kiss, had been transformed.

Night turned the thick lawn jet-black. Off to the right, the now-quiet river was a tarnished silver ribbon that caught the moonlight and held it.

A huge white tent had been set up in the park. Thousands of tiny white Christmas lights twined up the poles and across the makeshift ceilings. Even from here, Claire could see the tables set up within the tent. Silvery, shimmery tablecloths draped each one. Chinese lanterns cut the light into shapes—stars and crescents that patterned the floor and walls.

She moved forward. The scent of roses filled the night air, turned it sweet. She saw that each table had a floral centerpiece, a simple glass bowl filled with fresh white roses. A long, silver-clothed table ran along one side, its surface cluttered with elegant sterling chafing dishes and pewter trays of food. In the corner, a trio of men in white tuxedos played a World War II love song in soft, haunting tones.

"Wow," Bobby said, coming up beside her.

The band struck up a beautiful rendition of "Isn't It Romantic?"

"Would you like to dance, Mrs. Austin?"

Claire let him take her in his arms and lead her to the dance floor. There, with all her friends and family watching, she danced with her husband.

When, at last, the song came to an end, Claire finally saw her sister. She was tagging after Mama, who was clearly in her meet-and-greet mode. "Come on, Bobby," she said, taking his hand and pulling him off the dance floor. It felt as if it took them hours to get through the well-wishers, each of whom had something to say. But finally, they were near the bar, where Mama was regaling a starstruck crowd with stories of life aboard the USS *Star Seeker*.

Mama saw her coming and stopped talking midsentence. A genuine smile curved her lips. "Claire," she said, reaching for her with both hands. "I'm sorry I was late, darlin'. A star's life is run by others. But you were the most beautiful bride I've ever seen." Her voice cracked just a bit. "Really, Claire," she said, softer this time, for Claire's ears alone, "you made me so proud."

Their gazes met. In her mother's dark eyes, Claire glimpsed a genuine joy, and it touched her.

"Now," Mama said quickly, smiling again, "where's my new son-in-law?"

"Here I am, Miz Sullivan."

"Call me Ellie. All my family does." She moved toward him, whistling softly. "You're good-looking enough for Hollywood."

It was Mama's highest compliment.

"Thank you, Ma'am."

A look of irritation crossed Mama's face; it was there and gone in a flash. "Really. Call me Ellie. I hear you're a singer. Meggy doesn't know if you're any good."

"I'm good."

She took his hand. "If you sing half as good as you look, you'll be on the radio in no time. Come. Tell me about your career while we dance."

"I'd be honored to dance with my new mother-in-law." Tossing Claire a quick smile, he was off.

Claire turned at last to Meghann, who'd stood silently by for the whole exchange. "Are you okay?"

"Mama brought her dog. Not to mention an entourage of body-guards."

"She could be overcome by the hoards of her fans at any moment," Claire said in her best pseudo-Southern voice.

Meghann laughed. Then sobered. "She has to leave at eight-thirty."

"A manicure with Rollo?"

"Probably. Whatever it is, I believe a prayer of thanks is in order."

The band shifted into a sweet, soulful version of "As Time Goes By."

Claire stared at her sister, trying to come up with words to match her emotions. "This wedding," she started but her voice cracked. She swallowed hard.

"I did something wrong, didn't I?"

Claire ached then for the whole of their relationship, for the years that had been lost and those that had never been.

"You spent a fortune," Claire said.

"No." Meghann shook her head. "Almost everything was on sale. They're my Christmas lights. The tent—"

Claire touched her sister's lips, shut her up. "I'm trying to say thank you."

"Oh."

"I wish . . ." She didn't even know how to word it, this sudden longing of hers. It seemed too big to stand on something as thin as words.

"I know," Meghann said softly. "Maybe things can be different now. This time together . . . it's made me remember how things used to be between us."

"You were my best friend," Claire said, wiping her eyes carefully, so she didn't smear her makeup. "I missed that when you . . ." *Left.* She couldn't say the harsh word, not now.

"I missed you, too."

"Mommy! Mommy! Come dance with us."

Claire twisted around and saw her dad and Alison, standing a few feet away.

"I believe it's customary for the bride to dance with her father," he said, smiling, holding out his calloused hand.

"And her daughter! Grandpa'll carry me." Alison was hopping up and down with excitement.

Claire gave her champagne glass to Meghann, who mouthed: *Go.* She let herself be pulled onto the dance floor. As they made it to the center of the crowd, Dad whispered in her ear, "Someday Ali will get married and you'll know how this feels. It's every emotion at once."

"Pick me up, Grandpa!"

He bent down and scooped Alison up. The three of them clung to one another, swaying gently in time to "The Very Thought of You."

Claire looked away quickly—before Ali could ask why Mommy was crying. To her left, Mama was spinning poor Bobby around as if he were a top. Claire laughed out loud and knew exactly what her dad meant.

Every emotion.

That was what tonight was. All her life she'd look back on this night and remember how good her life was, how much she loved and was loved in return.

That was what Meghann had given her.

Meghann gazed at the black velvet lawn of Edgar Peabody Riverfront Park. Across the street, the Quonset hut sat bathed in moonlight. Behind her, the band was breaking down their equipment. Only a few die-hard guests were still here. Mama had left hours ago, as had Sam and Ali. Everyone else, including the bride and groom, had drifted away at around midnight. Meghann had stayed late, supervising the cleanup, but now that job was done.

Meghann sipped her champagne and looked across the street again. Her car was parked in front of Joe's house. She wondered now if that had been a conscious choice.

He was probably sleeping.

She knew it was ridiculous to go to him, maybe even dangerous, but there was something in the air tonight. A heady combination of romance and magic. It smelled like roses and made a woman believe that anything was possible. For tonight, anyway.

She didn't let herself think about it. If she did, she'd call herself a fool and stay put. So she hummed along with the music and walked down the gravel road. When she reached the black ribbon of asphalt, she turned right.

At his gate, she paused. The lights were on.

This was so unlike her.

She pushed the thought away and went to his door. There, she debated for another minute or two, then knocked.

Moments later, Joe opened the door. His hair was messed up, as if he'd been asleep; all he wore was a pair of black jeans. He waited for her to say something, but her voice had pulled a full retreat. She just stood there like an idiot, staring at his naked chest.

"You just going to stand there?"

She lifted her right hand, showing him the bottle of champagne she'd carried over.

He stared at her, saying nothing. When the silence became uncomfortable, he grabbed a black T-shirt from the sofa and put it on, then came back to the door. "I suppose you're horny. That's why you came by, right?"

She flinched at that. She thought about pulling herself up, slapping him, even, but it would be for show. A woman who screwed strangers had lost that right long ago. He was being honest, but there was something else, too. It felt as if he were angry with her. She couldn't imagine why. Even more disconcerting was the realization that she cared. "No. I thought maybe we could go out."

"You want us to go on a *date*? At one o'clock in the morning?"

"Sure. Why not?"

"A better question is why."

She looked up at him. When their gazes locked, she felt a flutter in her pulse. She couldn't possibly put the answer into words. She didn't dare look too closely at her own motivations. "Look, Joe. I was in a good mood. Maybe I had too much to drink." Her voice stumbled; need tripped her up. Humiliated, she closed her eyes. "I shouldn't have come. I'm sorry." When she opened her eyes, she saw that he'd moved closer. It would take nothing at all for him to kiss her now, barely a movement.

"I'm not much for going out."

"Oh."

"But I wouldn't mind if you wanted to come in."

She felt the start of a smile. "Great."

"What I *mind*," he said, "is waking up alone. It's okay if you don't want to spend the night, but don't sneak out like a hooker."

So that was it. "I'm sorry."

He smiled. It lit up his whole face, made him look ten years younger. "Okay. Come on in."

She touched his arm. "That's the first time I've seen you smile."

"Yeah," he said softly, maybe sadly. "It's been a while."

Meghann slept through the night. When dawn came to the small, dingy cabin windows and peered inside, she woke with a start. Instead of feeling nervous and cranky—her normal moods after a sleepless night—she felt rested and relaxed. She couldn't remember the last time morning had been so sweet.

She felt the heavy weight of Joe's bare leg against her own. His arm was around her, anchoring her in place. Even in sleep, his forefinger brushed possessively against her skin.

She should move away. It was a maneuver she'd perfected over the years—the intimacy-evading sideways roll, the silent plop to the floor, the soundless dressing and unseen exit.

What I mind, he'd said last night, *is waking up alone.*

She couldn't sneak out.

The surprising part was that she didn't want to, not really. She sensed that she *should*, in that basic self-preservation kind of way, but really, it felt good to be in a man's arms again. As she lay here, listening to his slow, even breathing, feeling his arm around her, she couldn't help but realize how little intimacy she'd known in her life. She was always so in control, moving forward on the path she saw for herself, she never let herself slow down enough to feel anything. It wasn't real, of course, this intimacy she felt with Joe. They didn't know or care deeply about each other, but for Meghann, even this approximation of emotion was more than she'd felt in years.

The sex had been different last night, too. Softer, gentler. Instead of their previous I'm-going-as-fast-as-I-can coupling, they'd acted as if they had all the time in the world. His long, slow kisses had made her crazy with wanting. It wasn't simple horniness, either; at least that's what she'd thought when he'd swept her away. She'd imagined that there was something more between them.

That worried her. Need was something she understood, accepted. In a gray world, it was jet-black.

Emotion was something else entirely. Even if it wasn't a lead-up to love, it was trouble. The last thing Meghann wanted was to care for someone.

Still . . .

She had never been one to deceive herself and, just now, lying naked in his arms, she had to admit that there was something between them. Not love, surely, but *something*. When he kissed her, it felt as if she'd never been kissed before.

There it was, as clear to her as the colors of the rising dawn: the prelude to heartache.

The beginning.

It had sneaked up on her. She'd opened a door called anonymous sex and found herself standing in a room filled with unexpected possibilities.

Possibilities that could break a woman's heart.

If she left him behind, he would fade into a pretty memory. It might hurt to remember him, but it would be a bittersweet pain, almost pleasurable. Certainly preferable to the kind of heartache that was sure to follow if she tried to believe in something more than sex.

She had to end this thing right now, before it left a mark.

The realization saddened her, made her feel even lonelier.

She couldn't help herself; she leaned over and kissed him. She wanted to whisper, *Make love to me,* but she knew her voice would betray her.

So she closed her eyes and pretended to sleep. It didn't help. All she could think about was later, when she would leave him.

She knew she wouldn't say good-bye.

Joe awoke with Meghann in his arms, their naked bodies tangled together. Memories of last night teased him, made him feel strangely light-headed. Most of all, he remembered the hoarse, desperate sound of her voice when she'd cried out his name.

He shifted his weight gently, moved just enough so that he could look down at her. Her black hair was a tangled mess; he remembered driving his hands through it in passion, then stroking it as he fell asleep. Her pale cheeks looked even whiter against the grayed cotton pillowcase. Even in sleep, he saw a kind of sadness around her eyes and mouth, as if she worried her troubles both day and night.

What a pair they were. They'd spent three nights together now and had exchanged almost no secrets about each other.

The amazing thing was, he wanted her again already. Not just her body, either. He wanted to get to know her, and just that—the wanting—seemed to change him. It was as if a light had gone on in a place that had been cold and dark.

And yet it frightened him.

The guilt was so much a part of him. In the last few years it had wrapped around him, bone and sinew. For more nights than he wanted to count, it had been his strength, the only thing holding him together; the first thing he remembered in the morning and the last thing on his mind when he fell asleep.

If he let go of the guilt—not all of it, of course, but just enough to reach for a different life, a different woman—would he lose the memories, too? Had Diana become so intertwined with his regret that he could have both or neither? And if so, could he *really* make a life that was separate from the woman he'd loved for so much of his life?

He didn't know.

But just now, looking down at Meghann, feeling the whisper softness of her breath against his skin, he wanted to try. He reached out, brushed a silky strand of hair from her face. It was the kind of touch he hadn't dared in years.

She blinked awake. "Morning," she said, her voice scratchy and raw.

He kissed her gently, whispered, "Good morning."

She pulled back too quickly, turned away. "I need to go. I'm supposed to pick up my niece at nine o'clock." She threw the covers back and got out of bed. Naked, she yanked a pillow up to cover herself and hurried into the bathroom. By the time she reemerged, dressed once again in her expensive lavender silk dress, he was dressed.

She picked up her strappy sandals in one hand and draped her panty hose over one shoulder. "I've really got to go." She glanced at the front door and started to turn toward it.

He wanted to stop her, but didn't know how. "I'm glad you came last night."

She laughed. "Me, too. Twice."

"Don't," he said, moving toward her. He had no idea what—if anything—was between them, but he knew it wasn't a joke.

She looked at the door again, then up at him. "I can't stay, Joe."

"See you later, then. Good-bye." He waited for her to answer, but she didn't. Instead, she kissed him. Hard. He was breathless by the time she pulled back, whispered, "You're a good man, Joe."

Then she was gone.

Joe went to the window and watched her leave. She practically ran to her car, but once she was there, she paused, looking back at the house. From this distance, she looked oddly sad. It made him realize how little he knew her.

He wanted to change that, wanted to believe there was a future for him after all. Maybe even one with her.

But he'd have to let go of the past.

He didn't know how to do all of it, how to start a life over and believe in a different future, but he knew what the first step was. He'd always known.

He had to talk to Diana's parents.

CHAPTER
TWENTY-TWO

MEGHANN PARKED THE CAR AND GOT OUT. A QUICK GLANCE UP at the house told her that no one was home. The lights were all out. She rammed her panty hose into her handbag and ran barefoot across the lawn, then slipped quietly into the darkened house.

Thirty minutes later, she was showered, dressed in a T-shirt and jeans, and packed. On her way out, she paused long enough to write Claire a quick note, which she left on the kitchen counter.

Claire and Bobby
Welcome home.
Love, Meg.

She drew a funny picture of a pair of martini glasses alongside her name, then paused, took one last look at the house that was so much a home. It was unexpectedly difficult to leave. Her condo was so cold and empty by comparison.

Finally, she went to her car and drove slowly through the campground.

The place was quiet this early on a Sunday morning. There were no children in the pool, no campers walking around. A lonely pair of fishermen—father and son by the looks of them—stood at the riverbank, casting their lines toward the water.

At the property line she turned right onto a rutted gravel road. Here, the trees grew closer together, their towering limbs blocking out all but the hardiest rays of morning sunlight. Finally, she came to the clearing, a horseshoe-shaped yard full of oversize rhododendrons and humongous ferns. A gray mobile home squatted on cement blocks in the middle of the yard, its front end accentuated by a pretty cedar deck. Pots of red geraniums and purple petunias were everywhere.

Meghann parked the car and got out. As always, she felt a tightening in her stomach when she thought about meeting Sam. It took a concerted effort to look at him and not remember their past.

Go. Just leave.

You're just like your Mama.

She gripped her purse strap and walked up the gravel walkway and onto the porch, which smelled of honeysuckle and jasmine on this June morning.

She knocked, too softly at first. When no one answered, she tried again. Harder this time.

The door swung open, hinges creaking, and there he was, filling the doorway, dressed in shabby overalls and a pale blue T-shirt that read: *River's Edge.* His brown hair was Albert Einstein wild.

"Meg," he said, clearly forcing a smile. He stepped back. "Come on in."

She sidled past him and found herself in a surprisingly cozy living room. "Good morning, Sam. I'm here to pick up Alison."

"Yeah." He frowned. "Are you sure you want to take her this week? I'd be happy to keep her."

"I'm sure you would," she answered, stung. It was too much like the other time.

"I didn't mean anything by that."

"Of course not."

"I know how busy you are, though."

She looked at him. "You still think I'm a bad influence, is that it?"

He took a step toward her, stopped. "I should never have thought that. Claire's told me how good you were to her. I didn't know about kids back then, and I sure as hell didn't know about teenage girls who—"

"Please. Don't finish that sentence. Do you have a list for me? Allergies. Medications. Anything I should know?"

"She goes to bed at eight. She likes it if you read her a story. *The Little Mermaid* is her favorite."

"Great." Meg looked down the hallway. "Is she ready?"

"Yeah. She's just telling the cat good-bye."

Meg waited. Somewhere in the trailer a clock ticked past a minute, then another.

"She has a birthday party to go to on Saturday. If you get her here by noon, she'll make it," Sam said finally. "That way she'll already be here when Claire and Bobby get home on Sunday."

Meghann knew the arrangements. "She'll be on time. Do I need to take her shopping for a gift?"

"If you don't mind."

"I don't."

"Nothing too expensive."

"I think I can handle shopping, thank you."

Another silence fell, marked by the clock's passing minutes.

Meghann was trolling for something innocuous to say when Alison came racing down the hallway, carrying a black cat whose body stretched almost to the ground. "Lightning wants to come with me, Grandpa. He meowed me. Can I take him with me, Aunt Meg, can I?"

Meg had no idea whether cats were allowed in her building.

Before she could answer, Sam knelt down in front of his granddaughter and gently eased the cat from her arms. "Lightning needs to stay here, honey. You know he likes to play with his friends and hunt for mice in the woods. He's a country cat. He wouldn't like the city."

Alison's eyes looked huge in the heart-shaped pallor of her face. "But I'm not a city girl, either," she said, puffing out her lower lip.

"No," Sam said. "You're an adventurer, though. Just like Mulan and Princess Jasmine. Do you think they'd be nervous about a trip to the big city?"

Ali shook her head.

Sam pulled her into his arms and hugged her tightly. When he finally let her go, he got slowly to his feet and looked at Meghann. "Take good care of my granddaughter."

It was not unlike what she'd said to Sam all those years ago, just before she left for good. *Take care of my sister.* The only difference was, she'd been crying. "I will."

Alison grabbed her Little Mermaid backpack and her small suitcase. "I'm ready, Aunt Meg."

"Okay, let's go." Meg took the suitcase and headed for the door. They were in the car and moving forward down the gravel driveway when Alison suddenly screamed, "Stop!"

Meg slammed on the brakes. "What's wrong?"

Alison climbed out of her seat, opened the door, and ran back into the trailer. A moment later she was back, clutching a ratty pink blanket to her chest. Her eyes glistened with tears.

"I can't go 'venturing without my wubbie."

Claire would always remember her first sight of Kauai.

As the jet banked left and dipped down, she saw the turquoise-blue water that ringed the white sand beaches. Reefs glittered black beneath the surface.

"Oh, Bobby," she said, turning to look at him. She wanted to tell him what this moment meant to the girl who'd grown up in trailers, dreaming of palm trees. But the words she came up with were too small, too trite.

An hour later, they were settled in their rental car—a Mustang convertible—and driving north.

Amazingly, with every mile driven, the island grew greener, lusher. By the time they reached the famous Hanalei Bridge, where huge green patchwork taro fields lay tucked against the rising black mountains, it was another world completely. On one side of the two-lane road, the local farmers stood in water, tending their taro crops. There wasn't a house or a road to be seen for miles. On the right side, the winding Hanalei River, hemmed on either side by thick, flowering green vegetation, calmly carried kayakers downstream. In the distance, the dark mountains stood in stark contrast to the blue sky; a few diaphanous clouds hinted at rain for tomorrow, but now, it was perfect weather.

"Here! Turn here," she said a block after a church.

The houses along the beach road sat on huge waterfront lots. Claire had braced herself for Bel Air–type mansions. She needn't have bothered. Most of the houses were old-fashioned, unpretentious. At the park, they turned again, and there it was: the house her dad had rented. Only a block from the beach and tucked as it was in a cul-de-sac, it ought to feel ordinary.

It was anything but. Painted a bright tropical blue with glossy white trim, the house looked like a jeweled box hidden in a tropical landscape. A thick green hedge ran down three borders of the property, effectively blocking the neighbors from view.

Inside, the house had white walls, pine plank floors, and bright Hawaiian furniture. Upstairs, the bedroom, done in more bright colors, led to a private balcony that overlooked the mountains. As she stood there, staring out at the waterfall-ribboned mountain, Claire could hear the distant surf.

Bobby came up behind her, slipped his arms around her. "Maybe someday I'll make it big, and we'll live here."

She leaned back against him. It was the same dream she'd had for years, but now its hold had loosened. "I don't care about making it big or someday, Bobby. We have this right now, and really, it's more than I ever dreamed of."

He turned her around so that she was facing him. There was an uncharacteristic sadness in his eyes. "I won't leave you, Claire. How can you not know that?"

Claire wanted to smile, shake the words off. "I do know that."

"No. You don't yet. I love you, Claire. I guess all I can do is keep saying it. I'm not going anywhere."

"How about to the beach?"

They walked hand in hand down the road toward the beach. At the pavilion, one of the many public access points, a large group of Hawaiians were celebrating a family reunion. Dark-haired, copper-skinned children in brightly colored swimsuits played running games on the grass while the adults set out a buffet inside. Someone somewhere was playing a ukelele.

Hanalei Bay fanned out from her on either side, a mile of white-sand beach shaped in a giant horseshoe. To the north stood the mountains, turned pink now by the sinking sun.

Small, white-tipped waves rolled forward, carrying laughing children toward the sand. Farther back, some teenage boys lay on oversize surfboards. Their instructor, a good-looking guy in a straw hat, gave them each a shove when a wave seemed promising.

They spent the rest of the day on the warm sands of Hanalei Bay and watched the sunset and talked. When the beach fell silent and lay in darkness, with stars glittering on the black water, they finally went back to their house. Together, they made dinner and ate it on a picnic table on the back lanai, with lanterns and mosquito-repellant candles lighting their way. By the time dinner was finished and the dishes were done, they couldn't keep their hands off each other anymore.

Bobby swept Claire into his arms and carried her upstairs. She laughed and clung to him, letting go only when he dropped her onto the bed. She immediately came up to her knees and looked at him.

"You're so beautiful," he said, reaching out to slip a finger beneath her bathing-suit bra strap. She felt the heat of that touch against her cold, goosefleshed skin and found it hard to breathe.

He bent down and stripped out of his suit, then straightened again. The sight of his naked body, hard and ready, made her shiver and reach out.

He moved to the bed. She could feel the eager trembling in his hands as he removed her swimsuit and touched her breasts. At last he kissed her—her mouth, her eyelids, her chin, her nipples.

She wrapped her arms around him and pulled him down on top of her. She felt his hand slip between her legs, finding her wetness. With a groan, she opened herself to him. When he finally climbed on top of her, she dug her fingers into his hard backside and arched up to meet him. They came at the same time, each crying out the other's name.

Afterward, Claire curled up against her husband's damp, hot body and fell asleep to the quiet evenness of his breathing and the steady drone of the ceiling fan.

Meg took Alison on a whirlwind tour of downtown Seattle. They went to the aquarium and watched the feeding of the otters and seals. Meg even dared to roll up her designer sleeves and plunge her bare hands into the exploration tank, where, alongside a busload of out-of-town children, she and Alison touched sea anemones and mussels and starfish.

After that, they got hot dogs at a frankfurter stand and walked down the wharf. At Ye Olde Curiosity Shoppe they saw shrunken heads and Egyptian mummies and cheap souvenirs. (Meg didn't point out the eight-foot-long petrified whale penis that hung suspended from the ceiling; she could just imagine what Ali would tell her friends.) They had dinner at the Red Robin Hamburger Emporium and finished off the day with a Disney movie at the Pacific Place Theater.

By the time they made it back to the condo, Meg was exhausted.

Unfortunately, Alison had energy to spare. She ran from room to room, picking up stuff, looking at it, yelling *Wow!* over things like a Sonicare toothbrush.

Meg was on the couch, sprawled out with her feet on the coffee table, when Alison skidded into the room, carrying the Lalique bowl from the front entry.

"Did you see this, Aunt Meg? These girls have no clothes on."
She giggled.

"They're angels."

"They're *naked*. Billy says his dad has magazines with naked girls
in 'em. Gross."

Meg got up and very gently took the bowl from Alison. "Gross is
in the eye of the beholder." She returned it to its spot on the entry
table. When she walked back into the living room, Alison was
frowning.

"What's a bee holder? Is that like a hive?"

Meg was too tired to come up with a smart answer. "Kind of."
She collapsed onto the couch again. How had she done this when
she was a teenager?

"Didja know that baby eagles eat their daddy's barf?"

"No kidding. Even *my* cooking is better than that."

Alison giggled. "My mommy's a good cook." The minute she said
it, her lower lip wobbled. Tears glistened in her green eyes, and just
then, standing there on the verge of crying, Alison looked so much
like Claire that Meghann couldn't breathe. She was thrown back in
time to all the nights she'd comforted her little sister, held her
tightly, and promised that *Soon, soon things will get better . . . and
Mama will come home.*

"Come here, Ali," she said, her throat tight.

Alison hesitated for a moment, just that, but the pause reminded
Meghann of how little she and her niece knew each other.

Alison sat down on the sofa, about a foot away.

"Do you want to call your mommy? She's going to call at six
o'clock, but—"

"Yeah!" Alison yelled, bouncing up and down on the cushion.

Meghann went in search of the phone. She found it on the
nightstand by her bed. After a quick consultation in her day plan-
ner, she dialed the Kauai house's direct number, then handed the
phone to her niece.

"Mommy?" Alison said after a few seconds. Then, "Hi, Mommy.
It's me, Ali Kat."

Smiling, Meg walked into the kitchen and began unpacking the bags of groceries and goodies she'd picked up today. Stuff she hadn't bought in years—Frosted Flakes, Pop-Tarts, Oreo cookies—and stuff she'd never seen before, like juice that came in silver bags and mix-your-own yogurt. The most important purchase was an activity book for children. She intended to make this a week Alison wouldn't forget.

"She wants to talk to you, Aunt Meg," Alison said, bouncing into the kitchen.

"Thanks." Meg took the phone, said, "Hello?"

"Hey, big sis, how's it going? Has she stopped talking yet?"

Meg laughed. "Not even when she's eating."

"That's my Ali."

Alison tugged on Meg's pant leg. "Mommy said the sand is like sugar. *Sugar.* Can I have some cookies?"

Meg handed her an Oreo. "Only one before bed," she said to her niece. To Claire, she said, "I need a margarita."

"You'll be fine."

"I know. It makes me think. . . ."

"What?" Claire asked softly.

"About us. You. Sometimes I look at Ali and all I can see is us."

"Then, she'll love you, Meg."

Meg closed her eyes. It felt so good to talk to Claire this way, as true sisters who had something more than a sordid childhood in common. "She misses you."

"Bedtime might be hard. You'll need to read her a story." Claire laughed. "I warn you, she has quite an attention span."

"I'll try *Moby-Dick*. You'd have to be on speed to stay awake for that."

Alison grabbed her pant leg again. "I think I'm gonna be—" And she puked all over Meg's shoes.

"I need to go, Claire. Have a great trip. We'll talk to you tomorrow."

She hung up the phone and set it on the counter.

Alison looked up at her, giggling. "Oops."

"Maybe the double banana split was a bad idea." She eased out of her shoes and scooped Alison into her arms and carried her to the bathroom.

Alison looked so tiny in the big marble tub.

"This is like a swimming pool," she said, sucking up a mouthful of water and spitting it on the tile wall.

"Let's not drink our own bathwater, shall we? It's one of the things that separates us from the lesser primates. Like men."

"Grandpa lets me."

"My point exactly. Now come here, let me wash your hair." She reached for the brand-new baby shampoo. The scent made her smile. "I used to wash your mom's hair with this shampoo."

"You're getting it in my eyes."

"That's what she used to say." Meghann was still smiling when she rinsed Alison's hair and helped her out of the tub. She dried off the little girl, dressed her in pink flannel pajamas, and carried her into the guest room.

"It's a big bed," Alison said, frowning.

"That's because it's for princesses only."

"Am I a princess?"

"You are." Meghann curtsied. "Milady," she said in a solemn voice. "What command have you for me?"

Alison giggled and climbed under the covers. "Read me a story. I want . . . *Professor Wormbog in Search of the Zipperump-a-Zoo.*"

Meg dug through the toys and books in the suitcase, found the right one, and started to read.

"You gotta be on the bed," Alison said.

"Oh." Meghann climbed onto the bed and settled in comfortably. Alison immediately snuggled in beside her, resting her cheek on the precious wubbie.

Meg started to read again.

An hour and six books later, Alison was finally asleep. Meg kissed her niece's sweet pink cheek and left the room, careful to leave the door open.

Afraid to turn on the television or the stereo—she didn't want to wake Alison—she tried to read a magazine. Within minutes she was falling asleep, so she padded into her bedroom, changed into her Seahawks nightshirt, brushed her teeth, and got into bed.

Closing her eyes, she thought of all the things she had to do tomorrow. There was no way she'd fall asleep tonight.

Woodland Park Zoo.

The BFG at the Children's Theater.

GameWorks.

F.A.O. Schwarz.

Fun Forest at Seattle Center.

Her mind skipped from Fun Forest to National Forest to Hayden to Joe.

Joe.

He'd kissed her good-bye so gently on that last morning they were together. It had made her feel inexplicably vulnerable.

She wanted to see him. And not just for sex.

For what, then?

She'd chosen him in the first place for his unavailability. What had been his first words to her, or practically the first?

I won't take you home with me.

Or something like that. Right off the bat he'd declared his unavailability.

And so she'd gone for him. But where could they go beyond the bedroom? He was a small-town mechanic who still cried over his divorce.

There was no future for them.

Still . . . when she closed her eyes he was there, waiting to kiss her in the darkness of her own mind.

"Aunt Meg?"

She sat upright, flicked on the light. "What is it?"

Alison stood there, clutching her wubbie. Her face was moist with tears; her eyes were red. She looked impossibly small in the open doorway. "I can't sleep."

She looked so much like Claire. . . .

"Come on up here, honey. Come sleep with me. I'll keep you safe."

Alison bolted across the room and clambered up into the bed, then snuggled close against Meg, who held her tightly. "Your mommy used to sleep with me when she was scared, did you know that?"

Alison popped a thumb in her mouth and closed her eyes. Almost immediately, she was asleep.

Meghann loved the smell of her, the little girl/baby shampoo sweetness. She cuddled in close to her niece and closed her eyes, expecting to start thinking about tomorrow again.

Amazingly, she fell asleep.

The telephone woke Claire up. She sat up fast. "What time is it?" She looked around for the bedside clock, found it. Five forty-five A.M. *Oh, God.* "Bobby, the phone—"

She scrambled over him and picked it up. "Hello? Meghann? Is Ali okay?"

"Hey, darlin', how are you?"

Claire released a heavy breath and climbed out of bed. "I'm fine, Mama. It's five-forty-five on Kauai."

"Is that right? I thought y'all were the same time zone as California."

"We're halfway to Asia, Mama."

"You always did exaggerate, Claire. I *do* have a reason for callin', you know."

Claire grabbed her robe out of the closet and slipped it on, then went out onto the balcony. Outside, the sky was just turning pink. In the backyard, a rooster strutted across the lawn; hens clucked along behind. The morning smelled of sweet tropical flowers and salt air. "What is it?"

"I know you don't think I'm much of a mother."

"That's not true." She yawned, wondering if there was any chance of falling asleep again. She looked through the windows at Bobby, who was sitting up now, frowning at her.

"It is so. You and Miss Perfect are constantly remindin' me that I did a poor job raisin' you. I consider it ungrateful to say the least, but motherhood has its burdens, as you know, and misunderstanding is mine."

"It's a little early for drama, Mama. Maybe you could—"

"The point is, I do some things poorly and some things well. I'm like ordinary people in that way."

Claire sighed. "Yes, Mama."

"I just want you to remember that. And tell your bigmouthed sister. No matter what y'all remember, or think you do, the truth is that I love you. I always have."

"I know, Mama." She smiled at Bobby, mouthed: *Mama*, then: *coffee.*

"Now put your husband on the phone."

"Excuse me?"

"You do have a man in your bed right now?"

Claire laughed. "I do."

"Let me talk to him."

"Why?"

Mama sighed dramatically. "It's another of my burdens to be saddled with suspicious daughters. It's about a weddin' gift, if you must know. I heard y'all didn't like the car."

"There's no room for Alison."

"Does she have to go *everywhere* with y'all?"

"Mama—"

"Put Bobby on. This present is for him, since you were so ungrateful."

"Okay, Mama. Whatever. Just a second." She went back inside. "She wants to talk to you."

Bobby sat up. *This can't be good*, he mouthed as he took the phone from Claire. "How's the sexiest mother-in-law in the world?" After a moment, his smile faded. "What?" Then: "You're kidding me. How did you do it?"

Claire moved toward him, placed her hand on his shoulder. "What's going on?"

He shook his head. "That's incredible, Ellie. Really. I don't know how to thank you. When?" He frowned. "You know we're here—oh. Yeah. I understand. At the ticket counter. Yes. Okay. Of course we'll call right away. And thank you. I can't tell you how much this means. Yes. Good-bye."

"What did she do?" Claire asked when he hung up the phone.

Bobby's smile was so big it creased his whole face into pleats. "She got me an audition with Kent Ames at Down Home Records. I can't *believe* it. I've been playing shit-ass honky-tonk joints for ten years waiting for a break like this."

Claire threw herself at him, holding him tightly in her arms. She told herself it was foolish to have been afraid, worried, but still her hands were shaking. Too many bad years with Mama, she supposed. She always expected the worst. "You'll knock 'em dead."

He twirled her around until they were both laughing. "This is it, Claire."

She was still laughing when he eased her back to her feet.

"But . . . ," he said, not smiling now.

That worry came back. "What?"

"The audition is Thursday. After that, Kent is leaving for a month."

"This Thursday?"

"In Nashville."

Claire looked up at her husband, who wore his heart in his eyes right now. She knew that if she said no, said, *Our honeymoon won't be over by then,* he'd kiss her and say, *Okay, maybe call your Mama back and see if the audition can be rescheduled in a month.* Knowing all that made her answer easy.

"I've always wanted to see Opryland."

Bobby pulled her into his arms, gazed down at her. "I'd given up," he admitted quietly.

"Let that be a lesson," she answered happily. "Now, hand me that phone. I better let Dad and Meghann know that we'll probably add a day or two on to the trip."

• • •

The days with Alison settled into a comfortable routine. By the third afternoon, Meghann had let go of her obsessive need to show her niece every child-friendly venue in the city. Instead, they did simple things. They rented movies and made cookies and played Candy Land until Meg cried out for mercy.

Each night Meg slept with Ali tucked in her arms, and each morning she awoke with an unexpected sense of anticipation. She smiled easier, laughed more often. She'd forgotten how good it felt to care for someone else.

When Claire called to extend the length of her honeymoon, Meg knew she'd shocked her sister by offering—gladly—to keep Alison for a few extra days. Unfortunately, the oh-so-important birthday party ruined that option.

When Saturday finally came, Meghann was surprised by the depth of her emotions. All the way to Hayden she had to work to keep smiling, while Ali chattered nonstop and bounced in her seat. At Sam's house, Ali flew into her grandfather's arms and started telling him about the week. Meg kissed her niece good-bye and hurried out of the trailer. That night, she hardly slept at all. She couldn't seem to stave off the loneliness.

On Monday, she went back to work.

The hours stacked on top of one another, growing heavier than usual. By 3:00, she was so tired she could hardly function.

She hoped that Harriet wouldn't notice.

A useless hope, of course.

"You look bad," Harriet said when Meghann slumped into the familiar chair.

"Thank you."

"How did the wedding go?"

"It was nice," Meg said, looking down at her hands. "Even Mama couldn't ruin it. I planned the wedding, you know."

"You?"

"Don't sound so shocked. I followed your advice and kept my mouth shut. Claire and I . . . connected again. I even baby-sat my niece during the honeymoon. But now . . ."

"Now, what?"

Meg shrugged. "The real world is back." She looked up. "My condo is quiet. I never noticed that before."

"Your niece was loud?"

"She never stopped talking. Except when she was asleep." Meg felt a tightening in her chest. She would miss sleeping with Ali, miss having a little girl to care for.

"It reminded you of Claire."

"Lately, everything reminds me of those days."

"Why?"

"We were best friends," Meg said softly.

"And now?"

Meghann sighed. "She's married. She has her family. It's just like before. I probably won't hear from her until my birthday."

"The phone works both ways."

"Yeah." Meghann looked down at her watch. She didn't want to talk about this anymore. It hurt too much. "I gotta go, Harriet. Bye."

Meghann stared at her client, hoping the smile she managed to form wasn't as plastic as it felt.

Robin O'Houlihan paced in front of the window. Stick-thin and wearing more makeup than Terence Stamp in *The Adventures of Priscilla, Queen of the Desert*, she was the clichéd Hollywood wife. Too thin, too greedy, too everything. Meg wondered why none of these women noticed that at a certain age thin became gaunt. The more weight they lost, the less attractive their faces became, and Robin's hair had been dyed and redyed blond so often and so long it looked like a straw wig. "It's not enough. Period. End of story."

"Robin," she said, striving for a calm and even voice. "He's offering twenty-thousand dollars a month, the house on Lake Washington, and the condo in La Jolla. Frankly, for a nine-year marriage that produced no children, I think—"

"I *wanted* children." She practically hurled the words at Meg. "He was the one who didn't. He should have to pay for that, too. He took away the best reproductive years of my life."

"Robin. You're forty-nine years old."

"Are you saying I'm too *old* to have a child?"

Well, no. But you've been married six times and frankly, you have the mental and emotional stability of a two-year-old. Believe me, your never-conceived children thank you. "Of course not, Robin. I'm simply suggesting that the children approach won't help us. Washington is a no-fault state, you remember. The whys of a divorce don't matter."

"I want the dogs."

"We've discussed this. The dogs were his before you got married. It seems reasonable—"

"*I* was the one who reminded Lupe to feed and water them. Without me, those Lhasa Apsos would be hairy toast. Dead by the side of the pool. I want them. And you should quit fighting with me. You're *my* lawyer, not his. I can hardly live on twenty grand a month." She laughed bitterly. "He still has the jet, the place in Aspen, the Malibu beach house, and all our friends." Her voice cracked and, for just a moment, Meghann saw a flash of the woman Robin O'Houlihan had once been. A now-frightened, once-ordinary girl from Snohomish who'd believed a woman could marry her way to the top.

Meghann wanted to be gentle, say something soothing. In the old days, it would have been easy. But those days were gone now, stamped into muddy nothingness by the stiletto heels of a hundred angry wives who didn't want to work and couldn't possibly live on twenty grand a month.

She closed her eyes briefly, wanting to clear her mutinous mind. But instead of a quiet darkness, she flashed on an image of Mr. O'Houlihan, sitting quietly in the conference room, his hands clasped on the table. He'd answered all her questions with a sincerity that surprised her.

No prenuptial, no. I believed we'd last forever.

I loved her.

My first wife died. I met Robin nearly ten years later.

Oh. Yes. I wanted more children. Robin didn't.

It had been one of those uncomfortable moments that occasionally blindsided an attorney. That sickening realization that you were leading the wrong team.

Simply put, she'd believed him. And that was no good.

"Hel-*lo*. I'm talking here." Robin pulled a cigarette from her quilted Chanel bag. Remembering suddenly that she couldn't smoke in here, she jammed it back in her purse. "So, how do I get the house in Aspen? And the dogs."

Meghann rolled the pen between her thumb and forefinger, thinking. Every now and then the pen thumped on the manila folder open in front of her. It sounded vaguely like a war drumbeat. "I'll call Graham and hash this through. Apparently your husband is willing to be very generous, but trust me on this, Robin. People get pissed off over a lot less than a beloved dog. If you're going to go to the mat for Fluffy and Scruffy, be prepared to give up a lot. Your husband could yank the houses from the table in an instant. You better decide how important those dogs are."

"I just want to hurt him."

Meghann thought of the man she'd deposed more than a month ago. His look had been sad—worn, even. "I think you already have, if that's any consolation."

Robin tapped a long scarlet fingernail against her teeth as she stared out toward Bainbridge Island. "I shouldn't have slept with the pool guy."

Or the meat delivery boy or the dentist who bleached your teeth. "This is a no-fault state, remember."

"I'm not talking about the divorce. I'm talking about the marriage."

"Oh." There it was again, that flash of a real person hiding behind the decoupage of expensive makeup. "It's easy to see your life in retrospect. It's too bad we don't live life backward. I think it was Kierkegaard who said that."

"Really." Robin was clearly disinterested. "I'll think about the dogs and let you know."

"Act fast. Graham said this offer lasts for thirty-six hours. After that, he said it was ring time. Round one."

Robin nodded. "You seem awfully timid for someone they call the Bitch of Belltown."

"Not timid. Practical. But if you'd prefer other representation—"

"No." Robin slung her purse over her shoulder and headed for the door. As she opened it, she said, "I'll call you tomorrow." Without looking back, she left. The door clicked shut.

Meg let out a heavy sigh. She felt pummeled, smaller somehow.

She set the file aside, and as she did, she thought of Mr. O'Houlihan's sad face again.

No prenuptial, no. I believed we'd last forever.

This was going to rip his heart out. It wouldn't be enough to break his heart. Oh, no. Meghann and Robin were going to take it one step further and show him the true character of the woman he'd married. He'd find it damn near impossible to trust his heart the next time.

With a sigh, she checked her schedule. Robin had been her last appointment. Thank God. Meghann didn't think she could handle another sad story of failed loved right now. She packed up her papers, grabbed her purse and briefcase, and left the office.

Outside, it was a balmy early-summer night. The hustle and bustle of rush hour traffic clogged the streets. In the market, tourists were still crowded around the fish stand. White-aproned vendors threw thirty-pound king salmons through the air to one another: at every toss, tourists snapped photographs.

Meghann barely noticed the familiar show. She was past the fish market and down to the vegetables when she realized what route she'd chosen.

The Athenian was the next doorway.

She paused outside, smelling the pungent familiar odors of cigarette smoke and frying grease, listening to the buzz of conversations that were always the same, ultimately circling back to *Are you here alone?*

Alone.

It was certainly the most accurate adjective to describe her life. Even more so now that Ali was gone. It was amazing how big a hole her tiny niece had left behind.

She didn't want to go into the Athenian, pick up some man she didn't know, and bring him back to her bed. She wanted—

Joe.

A wave of melancholy came with his name, a deepening of the loneliness.

She pushed away from the doorway and headed home.

In the lobby of her building, she waved to the doorman, who started to say something to her. She ignored him and went into the elevator. On the penthouse floor, the elevator bell clanged, and she got out.

Her apartment door was open.

She frowned, wondering if she'd left it that way this morning.

No.

She was just about to slink back into the elevator when a hand appeared in her doorway; it held a full bottle of tequila.

Elizabeth Shore stepped out into the hallway. "I heard your transatlantic cry for help, and I brought the preferred tranquilizer for the slutty, over-the-hill set."

To Meghann's complete horror, she burst into tears.

CHAPTER
TWENTY-THREE

*J*OE WAS ALMOST FINISHED FOR THE DAY. IT WAS A GOOD THING BE-
cause he actually had places to go and people to see.

It felt good to look forward to something, even if that something
would ultimately cause him pain. He'd been drifting and alone for so
long that simply having an itinerary was oddly calming.

Now he lay on his back, staring up at the dirty underside of an
old Impala.

"Hey there."

Joe frowned. He thought he'd heard something, but it was hard
to tell. The radio on the workbench was turned up loud. Willie Nel-
son was warning mamas about babies that grew up to be cowboys.

Then someone kicked his boot.

Joe rolled out from underneath the car.

The face looking down at him was small, freckled, and smiling.
Earnest green eyes stared down at him. She squinted just a bit,
enough to make him wonder if she needed glasses, then he realized
that his worklight was shining in her face. He clicked it off.

"Smitty's in the office," he said.

"I know that, silly. He's always there. Did you know that the sand in Hawaii is like sugar? Smitty lets me play with the tools. Who are you?"

He stood up, wiped his hands on his coveralls. "I'm Joe. Now, run along."

"I'm Alison. My mom mostly calls me Ali. Like the gator."

"It's nice to meet you, Ali." He glanced up at the clock. It was 4:00. Time to get going.

"Brittani Henshaw always says, 'See you later, Ali Gator,' to me. Get it?"

"I do. Now—"

"My mom says I'm not 'posed to talk to strangers, but you're Joe." She scrunched up her face and stared up at him. "How come your hair is so long? It's like a girl's."

"I like it that way." He went to the sink and washed the grease from his hands.

"My backpack has Ariel on it. Wanna see?" Without waiting for an answer, she scampered out of the garage. "Don't go anywhere," she yelled back at him.

He was halfway to his cabin when Alison skidded in beside him. "See Ariel? She's a princess on this side and a mermaid on the other."

He missed a step but kept moving. "I'm going into my house. You better run along."

"Do ya hafta poop?"

He was startled into laughter by that. "No."

"You wouldn't tell me anyway."

"I definitely would not. I need to get ready to go somewhere. It was nice to meet you, though." He didn't slow down.

She fell into step beside him, talking animatedly about some girlfriend named Moolan who'd cut off all her hair and played with knives.

"They have school counselors for that kind of behavior."

Alison giggled and kept talking.

Joe climbed the porch steps and opened his door. "Well, Alison, this is where—"

She darted past him and went inside.

"Alison," he said in a stern voice. "You need to leave now. It's inappropriate to—"

"Your house smells kinda funny." She sat on the sofa and bounced. "Who's the lady in all the pitchers?"

He turned his back on her for a second; when he looked again she was at the windowsill, pawing through the pictures.

"Put those down," he said more sharply than was necessary.

Frowning, she put it down. "I don't like to share my stuff, either." She glanced at the row of photographs. There were three of them along the living-room window and two on the mantel. Even a child recognized an obsession when she saw one.

"The woman in the pictures is my wife. Diana." It still hurt to say her name aloud. He hadn't learned yet to be casual about her.

"She's pretty."

He gazed at a small framed montage of shots on the table nearest him. Gina had taken those pictures at a New Year's Eve party. "Yes." He cleared his throat. It was 4:15 now. Getting late. "Don't you have someplace to be?"

"Yeah." She sighed dramatically. "I gotta go give Marybeth my Barbie. *Mine*."

"Why?"

"I broke the head off hers. Grandpa says I hafta 'pologize *and* give her my doll. It's 'posed to make me feel better."

He squatted down to be eye level with her. "Well, Ali Gator, I guess we have something in common, after all. I . . . broke something very special, too, and now I have to go apologize."

She sighed dejectedly. "Too bad."

He put his hands on his thighs and pushed to his feet. "So, I really need to get going."

"Okay, Joe." She walked over to the door and opened it, then looked back at him. "Do you think Marybeth will play with me again after I 'pologize?"

"I hope so," he said.

"Bye, Joe."

"See ya later, Ali Gator."

That made her giggle, and then she was gone.

Joe stood there a minute, staring at the closed door. Finally, he turned and headed down the hallway. For the next hour, as he shaved and showered and dressed in his cleanest worn clothes, he tried to string together the sentences he would need. He tried pretty words—*Diana's death ruined something inside me*; stark words—*I fucked up*; painful words—*I couldn't stand watching her die.*

But none of them were the whole of it, none of them expressed the truth of his emotions.

He still hadn't figured out what he would say, when he turned onto their road or, a few minutes later, when he came to their mailbox.

Dr. and Mrs. Henry Roloff.

Joe couldn't help touching it, letting his fingertips trace along the raised gold lettering on the side of the mailbox. There had been a mailbox in Bainbridge like this one; that one read: *Dr. and Mrs. Joe Wyatt.*

A lifetime ago.

He stared at his former in-laws' house. It looked exactly as it had on another June day, so long ago, when Joe and Di had gotten married in the backyard, surrounded by family and friends.

He almost gave in to panic, almost turned away.

But running away didn't help. He'd tried that route, and it had brought him back here, to this house, to these people whom he'd once loved so keenly, to say—

I'm sorry.

Just that.

He walked up the intricately patterned brick path, toward the white-pillared house that Mrs. Roloff had designed to look like Tara. There were roses and sculpted hedges on both sides of him, their scents a cloying sweetness. On either side of the front door stood a cast-iron lion.

Joe didn't let himself pause or think. He reached out and rang the bell.

A few moments later, the door opened. Henry Roloff stood there, pipe in hand, dressed in khaki pants and a navy turtleneck. "Can I—" At the sight of Joe, his smile fell. "Joey," he said, his pipe aflutter now in a trembling hand. "We'd heard you were back in town."

Joe tried like hell to smile.

"Who is it?" Tina called out from somewhere inside the house.

"You won't believe it," Henry said, his voice barely above a whisper.

"Henry?" she yelled again. "Who is it?"

Henry stepped back. A watery smile spilled across his face, wrinkled his cheeks. "He's home, Mother," he yelled. Then, softly, he said it again, his eyes filling with tears. "He's home."

"Are you sure this is tequila? It tastes like lighter fluid." Meghann heard the sloppy slur in her voice. She was past tipsy now, barreling toward plastered, and it felt good.

"It's *expensive* tequila. Only the best for my friend." Elizabeth leaned sideways for a piece of pizza. As she pulled it toward her, the cheese and topping slid off, landing in a gooey heap on the concrete deck. "Oops."

"Don't worry 'bout it." Meghann scooped up the mess and threw it overboard. "Pro'ly just killed a tourist."

"Are you kidding? It's ten o'clock. Seattle is empty."

"That's true."

Elizabeth took a bite of her crust. "So what's the problem, kiddo? Your messages lately sounded depressed. And you don't usually cry when I show up."

"Let me see, I hate my job. My client's husband tried to shoot me after I ruined him. My sister married a country singer who happens to be a felon." She looked up. "Shall I go on?"

"Please."

"I baby-sat my niece when Claire went on her honeymoon and now my house feels obscenely quiet. And I met this guy. . . ."

Elizabeth slowly put down the pizza.

Meghann looked at her best friend, feeling a sudden wave of helplessness. Softly, she dared to say, "There's something wrong with me, Birdie. Sometimes I wake up in the middle of the night and my cheeks are wet. I don't even know why I'm crying."

"Are you lonely yet?"

"What do you mean, yet?"

"Come on, Meg. We've been friends for more than twenty years. I remember when you were a quiet, way-too-young freshman at the UW. One of those genius kids who everyone believes will either kill themselves or cure cancer. You used to cry every night back then. My bed was next to yours on the sleeping porch, remember? It broke my heart, how quietly you cried."

"Is that why you started walking to class with me?"

"I wanted to take care of you—it's what we Southern women do, don't you know? I waited years for you to tell me why you cried."

"When did I stop? Crying, I mean."

"Junior year. By then, it was too late to ask. When you married Eric, I thought—I hoped—you'd finally be happy."

"That was a long time ago."

"I've waited for you to meet someone else, try again."

Meghann poured two more straight shots. Downing hers, she leaned back against the railing. Cool night air ruffled the fine hairs around her face. The sound of traffic drifted toward her. "I have . . . met someone."

"What's his name?"

"Joe. I don't even know his last name. How pathetic is that?"

"I thought you liked sex with strangers."

Meghann heard how hard Elizabeth was trying not to sound judgmental. "I like being in control and waking up alone and having my life exactly the way I want it."

"So what's the problem?"

Meghann felt that wave again, the feeling of being sucked under a heavy current. "Being in control . . . and waking up alone and having my life exactly the way I want it."

"So this Joe made you feel something."

"Maybe."

"I assume you haven't seen him since you realized that."

"Am I so obvious?"

Elizabeth laughed. "Just a little. This Joe scared you, so you ran. Tell me I'm wrong."

"You're a bitch, how's that?"

"A bitch who's right-on."

"Yeah. That kind of bitch. The worst kind."

"Do you remember my birthday last year?"

"Everything up until the third martini. After that, it gets fuzzy."

"I told you I didn't know if I loved Jack anymore. You told me to stay with him. Mentioned something about me losing everything and him marrying the salad-bar girl from Hooters."

Meghann rolled her eyes. "Another shining example of my humanity. You talk about love; I answer in settlement. I'm so proud."

"The point is, I was dying in my marriage. All the lies I'd been telling myself for years had worn thin. Everything poked through and hurt me."

"But it worked out. You and Jacko are like newlyweds again. It's frankly disgusting."

"Do you know how I fell back in love with him?"

"Medication?"

"I did the thing that scared me the most."

"You left him."

"I had never lived alone, Meg. *Never.* I was so scared of not having Jack, I couldn't breathe at first. But I did it—and you were there for me. That night you came down to the beach house, you literally saved my life."

"You were always stronger than you thought."

Elizabeth gave her a so-are-you look. "You have to quit being afraid of love. Maybe this Joe is the place to start."

"He's all wrong for me. I never sleep with men who have something to offer."

"You don't 'sleep' with men at all."

"The bitch returns."

"Why is he so wrong?"

"He's a mechanic in a small town. He lives in the run-down cabin that comes with the job. He cuts his hair with a pocket knife. Take your choice. Oh, and though he's not much on decoration, he has managed to fill his place with photos of the wife who divorced him."

Elizabeth looked at her, saying nothing.

"Okay, so I don't really care about that stuff. I mean the photos are creepy, but I don't care about his job. And I sort of like Hayden. It's a nice town, but . . ."

"But?"

In Elizabeth's gaze, Meghann saw a sad understanding; it comforted her. "I left town without a word. Not even a good-bye. You can't turn that around easily."

"You've never been one to go for the easy route."

"Except for sex."

"I never thought sex with strangers would be easy."

"It isn't," Meg said quietly.

"So, call him. Pretend you had business that called you away."

"I don't know his number."

"What about the garage?"

"Call him at work? I don't know. That seems kind of personal."

"I'm going to assume you gave this guy a blow job, but a phone call is too personal?"

Meghann laughed at that. She had to admit how weird it was. "I sound like a psycho."

"Yes. Okay, Meghann. Here's what we're going to do. And I mean it. You and I are going to drive up to the Salish Lodge tomorrow, where I've scheduled some spa treatments for us. We will talk and drink and laugh and plan a strategy. Before you complain, let me tell you that I've already called Julie and told her you'd be out of the office. When I leave, you're going to drop me off at the airport and then head north. You will not stop until you reach Joe's front door. Am I understood?"

"I don't know if I have the guts."

"Do you want me to come with you? So help me, I will."

"This is why they call you women steel magnolias."

Elizabeth laughed. "Honey, you better believe it. You don't *evah* want to tell a Southern girl that you won't go after a good-looking man."

"I love you, you know."

Elizabeth reached for the pizza. "You just remember that phrase, Meg. Sooner or later, it's going to come in handy again. Now, tell me about Claire's wedding. I can't believe she let *you* plan it."

CHAPTER
TWENTY-FOUR

"$\mathcal{T}$HIS IS THE CLUB WHERE GARTH BROOKS WAS DISCOVERED."

Claire smiled at Kent Ames, the grand Pooh-Bah of Down Home Records in Nashville, and his assistant, Ryan Turner. Each one of them had imparted this pearl of information to her three times in the past hour. She wasn't sure if they had the memory of gnats or if they thought she was too stupid to understand their words the first time.

She and Bobby had been in Nashville for two days now. It ought to have been perfect. Their room at the Loews Hotel was breathtakingly beautiful. They'd splurged on romantic dinners in the restaurant and eaten breakfast in bed. They'd toured Opryland and seen the Country Music Hall of Fame. Most important, Bobby had aced his auditions. All four of them. His first had been in a dank, windowless office, with a low-level executive listening. Bobby had come home depressed, complaining that his big shot had been heard by a kid with acne and a poor sense of style. That night, they'd drunk champagne and tried to pretend it didn't matter. Claire had held him close and told him how much she loved him.

The callback had come at 8:45 the next morning, and it had been a Ferris wheel of opportunity since then. He'd sung his songs for one executive after another until he'd finally found himself in the big corner office that overlooked the street of Country and Western dreams: Music Row. Each new executive had introduced "his" discovery to the man above him.

Their lives had changed in the last twenty-four hours. Bobby was "someone." A guy who was "going places."

Now, they sat at a front table in a small, unassuming nightclub, she and the executives and her husband. In less than an hour, Bobby was scheduled to take the stage. It was a chance to "show his concert stuff" to the executives.

Bobby had no trouble talking to the men. Among them, there was rarely a pause. They talked about people and things Claire knew nothing about—demo records and studio time and royalty rates and contract provisions.

She wanted to keep it all straight. In her fantasies, she was Bobby's partner as well as his wife, but she couldn't seem to concentrate. The endless flight from Kauai to Oahu to Seattle to Memphis to Nashville had left its mark in a dull headache that wouldn't go away. And she kept remembering how disappointed Ali had been that Mommy wasn't coming home on time.

The smoke in the club didn't help. Neither did the thudding music or the shouting conversation. She clung to Bobby's hand, nodding when one of the executives spoke to her, hoping her smile wasn't as fragile as it felt.

Kent Ames smiled at her. "Bobby goes on in forty-five minutes. Usually it takes years to get a spot on this stage."

She nodded, widening her smile.

"This is where Garth Brooks was discovered, you know. Not by me, damn it."

Claire felt an odd tingling sensation in her right hand. It took her two tries to reach out for her margarita. When she took hold, she drank the whole thing, hoping it would ease her headache.

It didn't. Instead, it made her sick to her stomach. She slid off the bar stool and stood there, surprised to find that she was unsteady on her feet. She must have had one too many drinks.

"I'm sorry," she realized that she had interrupted a conversation when the men looked up at her.

"Claire?" Bobby got to his feet.

She pulled up a smile. It felt a little weak, one sided. "I'm sorry, Bobby. My headache is worse. I think I need to lie down." She kissed his cheek, whispered, "Knock 'em dead, baby."

He put his arm around her, held her close. "I'll walk her back to the hotel."

Ryan frowned. "But your set—"

"I had to call in a favor to get you this opportunity," Kent said stonily.

"I'll be back in time," Bobby said. Keeping a close hold, he maneuvered her out of the club and onto the loud, busy street.

"You don't have to escort me, Bobby. Really."

"Nothing matters more than you. Nothing. Those guys might as well know my priorities right off the bat."

"Someone's getting a little cocky." She leaned against him as they walked down the street.

"Luck's been on my side lately. Ever since I took the stage at Cowboy Bob's."

They hurried through the lobby and rode the elevator to their floor. In their room, Bobby gently undressed her and put her to bed, making sure she had water and aspirin on the night table.

"Go to sleep, my love," he whispered, kissing her forehead.

"Good luck, baby. I love you."

"That's exactly why I don't need luck."

She knew when he was gone. There was a click of the door and the room felt colder, emptier. Claire roused herself enough to call home. She tried to sound upbeat as she told Ali and Sam about the exciting day and reminded them that she'd be home in two days. After she hung up, she sighed heavily and closed her eyes.

When Claire woke up the next morning, her headache was gone. She felt sluggish and tired, but it was easy to smile when Bobby told her how it had gone.

"I blew them away, Claire. No kidding. Kent Ames was salivating over my future. He offered us a contract. Can you believe it?"

They were curled up in their suite's window seat, both wearing the ultrasoft robes provided by the hotel. Bright morning sunlight pushed through the window; Bobby looked so handsome he took Claire's breath away. "Of course I can believe it. I've heard you sing. You deserve to be a superstar. How does it all work?"

"They think it'll take a month or so in Nashville. Finding material, putting a backup band together, that sort of thing. Kent said it isn't unusual to go through three thousand songs to find the right one. After we make the demo, they'll start promoting me. They want me to tour through September and October. Alan Jackson needs an opening act. *Alan Jackson.* But don't worry. I told them we'd have to work out a schedule that was good for the family."

Claire loved him more in that moment than she would have imagined was possible. She grabbed his robe and pulled him close. "You will *only* have men and ugly women on your bus. I've seen movies about those tours."

He kissed her, long and slow and hard. When he drew back, she was dizzy. "What did I ever do to deserve you, Claire?"

"You loved me," she answered, reaching into his robe. "Now take me to bed and love me again."

Meghann was not relaxed by her day at the spa. Between massages, facials, and Jacuzzi tub soaks, she and Elizabeth had talked endlessly. No matter how often Meghann tried to control the direction of their discussions, one topic kept reemerging.

Joe.

Elizabeth had been relentless. For the first time, Meghann knew how it felt to be pummeled by someone else's opinions.

Call him. Quit being such a chicken. The advice had come in dozens of ways and hundreds of different sentences, but it all boiled down to the same thing:

Contact him.

Honestly, Meghann was glad to take her friend to the airport. The silence came as a sweet relief. But then Meghann returned to her silent condo and found that Elizabeth's voice had remained behind and so, she'd kept busy. For dinner, she bought a slice of pizza and walked along the wharf, window shopping with the steady stream of tourists that came off the ferries and spilled down the hilly streets from the Public Market.

It was 8:30 by the time she got home.

Once again, the quiet of her home was the only greeting that came her way.

"I need to get a cat," she said aloud, tossing her handbag onto the sofa. Instead, she watched *Sex and the City,* then a rerun of *The Practice* (Bobby Donnell was crying again). She turned it off in disgust.

Yeah. Male defense lawyers are a weepy set.

She went to bed.

And lay there, eyes wide open, for the rest of the night.

Call him, you chicken.

At 6:30 the next morning, she rolled out of bed, took a shower, and dressed in a plain black suit with a lavender silk shell.

One look in the mirror reminded her that she hadn't slept more than two hours the night before. As if she needed to notice her wrinkles to remember *that.*

She was at her desk by 7:30, highlighting the Pernod deposition.

Every fifteen minutes, she glanced at her phone.

Call him.

Finally, at 10:00, she gave up and buzzed her secretary.

"Yes, Ms. Dontess?"

"I need the number for a garage in Hayden, Washington."

"What garage?"

"I don't know the name or the address. But it's across the street from Riverfront Park. On Front Street."

"I'm going to need—"

"—to be resourceful. It's a small town. Everybody knows everybody."

"But—"

"Thanks." Meghann hung up.

Ten long minutes passed. Finally Rhona buzzed on line one.

"Here's the number. It's called Smitty's Garage."

Meghann wrote down the number and stared at it. Her heart was beating quickly.

"This is ridiculous." She picked up the phone and dialed. With every ring, she had to fight the urge to hang up.

"Smitty's Garage."

Meghann swallowed hard. "Is Joe there?"

"Just a sec. Joe!"

The phone clanged down, then was picked up. "Hello?"

"Joe? It's Meghann."

There was a long pause. "I thought I'd seen the last of you."

"I guess it won't be that easy." But the joke fell into silence. "I . . . uh . . . I have a deposition in Snohomish County on Friday afternoon. I'm sure you won't want to . . . I shouldn't have called, but I thought you might like to get together for dinner."

He didn't answer.

"Forget it. I'm an idiot. I'll hang up now."

"I could pick up a couple of steaks and borrow Smitty's barbecue."

"You mean it?"

He laughed softly, and the sound of it released that achy tension in her neck. "Why not?"

"I'll be there about six. Is that okay?"

"Perfect."

"I'll bring wine and dessert."

Meghann was smiling when she hung up. Ten minutes later, Rhona buzzed her again.

"Ms. Dontess, your sister is on line two. She says it's urgent."

"Thanks." Meg put on her headset and pushed the button. "Hey, Claire. Welcome back. Your flight must have been on time. Amazing. How was—?"

"I'm at the airport. I didn't know who else to call." Claire's voice was shaky; it almost sounded as if she was crying.

"What's going on, Claire?"

"I don't remember the flight from Nashville. I also don't remember getting my luggage, but it's right here. I don't remember getting my keys or walking through the garage, but I'm sitting in my car."

"I don't understand."

"Neither do I, damn it," Claire screamed, then she started to sob. "I can't remember how to get home."

"Oh, my God." Instead of panicking, Meghann took charge. "Do you have a piece of paper?"

"Yes. Right here."

"A pen?"

"Yes." Her sobs slowed down. "I'm scared, Meg."

"Write this down. Eight twenty-nine Post Alley. Do you have that?"

"I'm holding it."

"Keep holding it. Now get out of your car and walk toward the terminal."

"I'm scared."

"I'll stay on the phone with you." She heard Claire slam the car door shut. The rolling thump of luggage followed her.

"Wait. I don't know which way—"

"Is there a covered walkway in front of you, with airlines listed above it?"

"Yes. It says Alaska and Horizon."

"Go that way. I'm right here, Claire. I'm not going anywhere. Take the escalator down one floor. You see it?"

"Yes."

She sounded so weak. It scared the hell out of Meghann. "Go outside. Pick up the phone that says *Taxi*. What's the number above the door you just came through?"

"Twelve."

"Tell the cab driver to pick you up at door twelve, that you're going downtown."

"Hold on."

Meghann heard her talking.

Then Claire said, "Okay." She was crying again.

"I'm right here, Claire. Everything is going to be okay."

"Who is this?"

Meghann felt an icy rush of fear. "It's Meghann. Your sister."

"I don't remember calling you."

Oh, Jesus. Meghann closed her eyes. It took an act of will to find her voice. "Is there a cab in front of you?"

"Yes. Why is it here?"

"It's there for you. Get in the backseat. Give him the piece of paper in your hand."

"Oh God, Meg. How did you know I had this paper? What's wrong with me?"

"It's okay, Claire. I'm here. Get in the cab. He'll drop you off at my building. I'll be waiting for you."

The cab pulled along the curb and stopped. Before Claire could even say thank you, the front passenger-side door opened. Meghann threw a wad of bills at the driver, then slammed the door shut.

Claire's door opened.

Meghann was there. "Hey, Claire, come on out."

Claire grabbed her handbag and climbed out of the cab. She felt shaky, confused.

"Where's your luggage?"

Claire looked around. "I must have left it in my car at the

airport." She laughed, though it sounded weak, even to her. "Look, Meg, I'm feeling a lot better now. I don't know . . . I just spazzed out for a minute. The plane ride was awful, and they practically strip-searched me in Memphis. I'm already missing Bobby, and he's going to be down there for the next few weeks. I guess I had a panic attack or something. Just take me to a quiet restaurant for a cup of coffee. I probably just need to sleep."

Meg looked at her as if she were a science experiment gone bad. "Are you kidding me? A panic attack? Believe me, Claire, I know panic attacks, and you don't forget how to get home."

"Right. And you know everything." The stress of her . . . thing . . . snapped cleanly, left her exhausted. "I don't want to fight with you."

"You're not going to. We're getting in that car and going to the hospital."

"I'm fine now. Really. I'm probably getting a sinus infection. I'll see my doctor at home."

Meghann took a step toward her. "There are two ways this can go down. You can get nicely in the car and we can leave. Or I can make a scene. You *know* I can."

"Fine. Take me to the hospital, where we can spend the whole day and two hundred dollars to find out that I have a sinus infection that was exacerbated by air travel."

Meg took her arm and guided her into the cushy black interior of a Lincoln Town Car.

"A limo to the emergency room. How chic."

"It's not a limo." Meg studied her. "Are you okay now, really?"

Claire heard the concern in her sister's voice, and it touched her. She remembered suddenly that Meg always got loud and angry when she was frightened. It had been that way since childhood. "I'm sorry I scared you."

Meg finally smiled. Leaning back in the seat, she said quietly, "You did."

They exchanged looks then, and Claire felt herself relaxing. "Bobby aced the auditions. They offered him a big fat contract."

"He won't sign it until I review it, right?"

"The standard response is: *Congratulations*."

Meghann had the grace to blush. "Congratulations. That's really something."

"I believe it belongs in *Ripley's Believe It or Not!* under the headline *Eliana Sullivan Does Good Deed*."

"A good deed that benefits her. A famous son-in-law puts the spotlight on her, too, you know. Just think of the I-discovered-him-and-changed-his-life interviews." Meg pressed a hand to her breast, and said, "I'm so bighearted when it comes to family" in a gooey Southern drawl.

Claire started to laugh. Then she noticed that the tingling in her right hand was back. As she stared down at her hand, her fingers curled into a kind of hook. For a split second, she couldn't open it. She panicked. *Please, God—*

The spasm ended.

The car pulled up in front of the hospital and let them out.

At the emergency room's reception desk, a heavyset young woman with green hair and a nose ring looked up at them. "Can I help you?"

"I'm here to see a doctor."

"What's the problem?"

"I have a killer headache."

Meghann leaned over the desk. "Write this down: *Severe headache. Short-term memory loss*."

"That's right. I forgot." Claire smiled weakly.

The receptionist frowned at that and shoved a clipboard across the desk. "Fill that out and give me your insurance card."

Claire retrieved the card from her wallet and handed it to the receptionist. "My family doctor thinks I need to exercise more."

"They all say that," the receptionist said with a little laugh. "Take a seat until we call for you."

An hour later they were still waiting. Meghann was fit to be tied. She'd yelled at the receptionist three times and in the last twenty minutes, she'd been throwing around the word *lawsuit*.

"They've got a lot of nerve calling this an *emergency* room."

"Look at the bright side. They must not think I'm very sick."

"Forget the headache. We'll both be dead from old age by the time they see you. *Damn* it." Meghann popped to her feet and started pacing.

Claire considered trying to calm her sister down, but the effort was too much. Her headache had gotten worse, which she definitely did not reveal to Meghann.

"Claire Austin," called out a blue-scrubbed nurse.

"It's about fucking time." Meghann stopped pacing long enough to help Claire to her feet.

"You're a real comfort, Meg," Claire said, leaning against her sister.

"It's a gift," Meg said, guiding her toward the tiny, birdlike nurse who stood in front of the white double doors of the ER.

Bird Woman looked up. "Claire Austin?"

"That's me."

To Meg, the nurse said, "You can wait out here."

"No."

"Excuse me?"

"I'm coming with my sister. If the doctor asks me to leave for the exam, I will."

Claire knew she should be angry. Meg was being herself—pushing in where she didn't belong—but truthfully, Claire didn't want to be alone.

"Very well."

Claire clung to her sister's hand as they pushed through the double doors and entered the frightening white world that smelled of disinfectant. In a small exam room, Claire changed into a flimsy hospital gown, answered a few questions for the nurse, relinquished her arm for a blood pressure test and her vein for a blood test.

Then, again, they waited.

"If I were really sick, they'd rush to take care of me," Claire said after a while. "So this waiting is probably a good thing."

Meghann stood with her back to the wall. Her arms were crossed tightly, as if she were afraid she'd punch something if she moved. "You're right." Under her breath, she said, "Shitheads."

"Did you ever consider a career in health care? You've got quite a bedside manner. God knows you're calming me down."

"I'm sorry. We all know how patient I am."

Claire leaned back on the paper-covered exam table and stared up at the acoustical tile ceiling.

Finally, someone knocked, then the door opened.

In walked a teenage boy in a white coat. "I'm Dr. Lannigan. What seems to be the problem?"

Meghann groaned.

Claire sat up. "Hello, doctor. I really don't need to be here, I'm sure. I have a headache and my sister thinks a migraine is emergency-room-worthy. After a long flight, I had some kind of panic attack."

"Where she forgot how to get home," Meghann added.

The doctor didn't look at Meghann. He didn't look at Claire, either. Instead, he studied the chart in his hands. Then he asked her to perform a few functions—lift one arm, then the other, turn her head, blink—and answer some easy questions—what year it is, who the president is. That sort of thing. When he finished, he asked, "Do you often get headaches?"

"Yes, when I get stressed-out. More lately, though," she had to admit.

"Have you made any big changes in your life recently?"

Claire laughed. "Plenty. I just got married for the first time. My husband is going to be gone for a month. He's in Nashville, making a record."

"Ah." He smiled. "Well, Mrs. Austin, your blood work is all normal, as are your pulse and your blood pressure, and your temperature.

I'm sure this is all stress. I could run some expensive tests, but I don't think it's necessary. I'll write you a prescription for a migraine medication. When you feel one coming on, take two tablets with plenty of water." He smiled. "If the headaches persist, however, I'd recommend that you see a neurologist."

Claire nodded, relieved. "Thank you, doctor."

"Oh, no. *So* no." Meghann pulled away from the wall and moved toward the doctor. "That's not good enough."

He blinked at her, stepping back as she invaded his personal space.

"I watch *ER*. She needs a CAT scan, at the very least. Or an MRI or an EKG. Some damn initial test. At the very least, she'll take that neurology consult now."

He frowned. "Those are costly tests. We can hardly run a CAT scan on every patient who complains of a headache, but if you'd like, I'll recommend a neurologist. You can make an appointment to see him."

"How long have you been a doctor?"

"I'm in my first year of residency."

"Would you like to do a second year?"

"Of course. I don't see—"

"Get your supervisor in here. Now. We didn't spend three hours here so that an almost-doctor could tell us that Claire is under stress. I'm under stress; you're under stress. We manage to remember our way home. Get a real doctor in here. A neurologist. We are not making an appointment. We'll see a specialist *now*."

"I'll go get a consult." He clutched his clipboard and hurried out.

Claire sighed. "You're being you again. It *is* stress."

"I hope it is, too, but I'm not taking the prom king's word for it."

A few moments later, the nurse was back. This time her smile looked forced. "Dr. Kensington has reviewed your material for Dr. Lannigan. She'd like you to have a CAT scan."

"She. Thank God," Meghann said.

The nurse nodded. "You can come with me," she said to Claire.

Claire looked to Meghann, who smiled and took her arm. "Think of us as conjoined."

The nurse walked out in front of them.

Claire clung to Meghann's hand. The walk seemed to last forever, down one corridor and another, up the elevator and down another hallway, until they arrived at the Center for Nuclear Medicine.

Nuclear. Claire felt Meghann's grip tighten.

"Here we are." The nurse paused outside yet another closed door. She turned to Meghann. "There's a chair right there. You can't come in, but I'll take good care of her, okay?"

Meghann hesitated, then slowly nodded. "I'll be here, Claire."

Claire followed the nurse through the door, then down another short hallway and into a room that was dominated by a huge machine that looked like a white doughnut. Claire let herself be positioned on the narrow bed that intersected the doughnut hole.

There, she waited. And waited. Periodically, the nurse came back, muttered something about the doctor, and disappeared again.

Claire started to get cold. The fear she'd worked so hard to keep at bay crept back. It was impossible not to fear the worst here.

Finally, the door opened and a man in a white coat walked in. "Sorry to keep you waiting. Something came up. I'm Dr. Cole, your radiologist. You just lie perfectly still and we'll have you out of here in no time."

Claire forced herself to smile. She refused to think about the fact that everyone else wore lead aprons in the room, while she lay with only the thinnest sheet of cotton to protect her.

"You're done. Fine job," he said when it was finally over.

Claire was so thankful she almost forgot the headache that had steadily increased as she lay in the machine.

In the hallway, Meghann looked angry. "What happened? They said it would take an hour."

"And it did, once they corraled a doctor."

"Shitheads."

Claire laughed. Already she felt better with that behind her. "They certainly teach you lawyers to be precise with your language."

"You don't want to hear precisely what I think of this place."

They followed the nurse to another exam room.

"Should I get dressed?" Claire asked.

"Not yet. The doctor will be here soon."

"I'll bet," Meghann said under her breath.

Thirty minutes later, the nurse was back. "The doctor has ordered another test. An MRI. Follow me."

"What's an MRI?" Claire asked, feeling anxious again.

"Magnetic resonance imaging. It's a clearer picture of what's going on. Very standard."

Another hallway, another long walk toward a closed door. Again, Meg waited outside.

This time, Claire had to remove her wedding ring, her earrings, her necklace, and even her barrette. The technician asked her if she had any steel surgical staples or a pacemaker. When she said no and asked why, he said, "Well, we'd hate to see 'em fly outta you when this thing starts up."

"That's a lovely image," Claire muttered. "I hope my fillings are safe."

The tech laughed as he helped her into the coffinlike machine. She found it difficult to breathe evenly. The bed was cold and hard; it curved up uncomfortably and pinched her upper back. The technician strapped her in. "You need to lie perfectly still."

Claire closed her eyes. The room was cold and she was freezing, but she lay still.

When the machine started it sounded like a jackhammer on a city street.

Quiet, Claire. Still. Perfectly still. She closed her eyes and barely breathed. She didn't realize she was crying until she felt the moisture drip down her temple.

The one-hour test lasted for two. Halfway through, they stopped and set up an IV. The needle pinched her arm; dye bled through her system, feeling ice-cold. She swore she could feel it pump into her brain. Finally, she was let go. She and Meghann returned to an examination room in the Nuclear Medicine Wing, where Claire's clothes were hanging. Then they went to another waiting room.

"Of course," Meg grumbled.

They were there another hour. Finally, a tall, tired-looking woman in a lab coat came into the waiting room. "Claire Austin?"

Claire stood up. At the suddenness of the movement, she almost fell. Meg steadied her.

The woman smiled. "I'm Dr. Sheri Kensington, chief of Neurology."

"Claire Austin. This is my sister, Meghann."

"It's nice to meet you. Come this way." Dr. Kensington led them down a short hallway and into an office that was lined with books, diplomas, and children's artwork. Behind her, a set of X-ray–like images glowed against the bright white backlighting boxes.

Claire stared at them, wondering what there was to see.

The doctor sat down at her desk and indicated that Claire and Meghann should sit opposite her. "I'm sorry you had problems with Dr. Lannigan. This is, as I'm sure you know, a teaching hospital, and sometimes our residents are not as thorough as we would wish. Your demand for a higher level of care was a much-needed wake-up call for Dr. Lannigan."

Claire nodded. "Meghann is good at getting what she wants. Do I have a sinus infection?"

"No, Claire. You have a mass in your brain."

"What?"

"You have a mass. A tumor. In your brain." Dr. Kensington rose slowly and went to the X rays, pointing to a white spot. "It appears to be about the size of a golf ball, and located in the right frontal lobe, crossing the midline."

Tumor.

Claire felt as if she'd just been shoved out of an airplane. She couldn't breathe; the ground was rushing up to meet her.

"I'm sorry to say this," Dr. Kensington went on, "but I've consulted with a neurosurgeon and we believe it's inoperable. You'll want second opinions, of course. You'll need to see an oncologist, also."

Smack.

Meghann was on her feet, pressed against the desk as if she were going to grab the doctor's throat. "You're saying she has a brain tumor?"

"Yes." The doctor went back to the desk and sat down.

"And that you can't do anything about it?"

"We believe it's inoperable, yes, but I didn't say we can't do anything."

"Meg, please," Claire was absurdly afraid that her sister was going to make it worse. She looked pleadingly at the doctor. "Are you . . . saying I might die?"

"We'll need more tests to determine the exact nature of your tumor, but—given the size and placement of the mass—it's not a good outlook."

"Inoperable means *you* won't operate," Meg said in a don't-screw-with-me voice that was almost a growl.

Dr. Kensington looked surprised. "I don't believe anyone will. I consulted with our top neurosurgeon on this. He agrees with my diagnosis. The procedure would be too dangerous."

"Oh, really? It might kill her, huh?" Meg looked disgusted. "Who *will* do this kind of operation?"

"No one in this hospital."

Meg grabbed her handbag off the floor. "Come on, Claire. We're in the wrong hospital."

Claire looked helplessly from Dr. Kensington to her sister. "Meg," she pleaded, "you don't know everything. Please . . ."

Meg went to her, knelt in front of her. "I know I don't know everything, Claire, and I know I'm a blowhard. I even know I've let you down in the past, but none of that matters now. From this second on, all that matters is your life."

Claire felt herself starting to cry. She hated how fragile she felt, but there it was. Suddenly she *felt* like she was dying.

"Lean on me, Claire."

Claire gazed into her sister's eyes and remembered how Meg had once been her whole world. Slowly, she nodded. She needed a big sister again.

Meghann helped her to her feet, then she turned to the doctor. "You go ahead and teach Dr. Lannigan how to read a thermometer. We're going to find a doctor who can save her life."

CHAPTER
TWENTY-FIVE

A FEW YEARS AGO, CLAIRE HAD GONE THROUGH A FOREIGN-FILM phase. Every Saturday night, she'd handed Alison to Dad, gotten in her car, and driven to a small, beautifully decorated old movie house, where she'd lost herself in the gray-and-black images on screen.

That was how she felt right now: A colorless character walking through an unfamiliar gray world. The sounds of the city felt muted and far away; all she could really hear was the thudding, even beat of her heart.

How could something like this happen to her?

Outside the hospital, the real world came at her hard. Sirens and horns and screeching brakes. She fought the urge to cover her ears.

Meghann helped her into the car. The blessed silence made her sigh.

"Are you okay?" Meghann asked, and Claire had the impression that her sister had asked this question more than once. Her voice was spiked and anxious.

She looked at Meg. "Do I have cancer? Is that what a tumor is?"

"We don't know what the hell you have. Certainly those dipshit doctors don't know."

"Did you see the shadow on that X ray, Meg? It was *huge*." Claire felt tired suddenly. She wanted to close her eyes and sleep. Maybe in the morning things would look different. Maybe she'd find out it was all a mistake.

Meghann grabbed her, shook her hard. "Listen to me, damn it. You need to be tough now. No getting by, no giving up. This isn't like cosmetology school or college, you can't take the easy road and walk away."

"I've got a brain tumor, and you throw quitting college at me. You're amazing." Claire wanted to be angry, but her emotions felt distant. It was hard to think. "I don't even feel sick. Everybody gets headaches, don't they?"

"Tomorrow we'll start getting second opinions. First we'll go to Johns Hopkins. Then we'll try Sloan-Kettering in New York. There's got to be a surgeon who has some balls." Meghann's eyes welled up, her voice broke.

Somehow that frightened Claire even more, seeing Meg crack. "It's going to be okay," she said automatically; comforting others was easier than thinking. "You'll see. We just need to keep positive."

"Faith. Yes," Meghann said after a long pause. "You hold on to the faith and I'll start finding out everything there is to know about your condition. That way we'll have all the bases covered. God and science."

"You mean be a team?"

"Someone has to be there for you through this."

"But . . . you?"

The whole of their childhood was between them suddenly, all the good times and, more important, the bad.

Claire stared at her sister. "If you start this thing with me, you have to stick around if things get tough."

Meg glanced out the window at a passing motorist. "You can count on me."

Claire touched her sister's chin, made her turn to make eye contact. "Look at me when you say that."

Meg looked at her. "Trust me."

"I must be near death if I agree to *this*. God help me." Claire frowned. "I don't want to tell anyone."

"Why should we say anything until we know for sure?"

"It'll just worry Dad and make Bobby come home." She paused, swallowed hard. "I don't even want to think about telling Ali."

"We'll tell everyone I'm taking you to a spa for a week. Will they believe that?"

"Bobby will. And Ali. Dad . . . I don't know. Maybe if I tell him we need time together. He's wanted us to reconcile for years. Yeah. He'd buy that."

Joe had read once about a species of frog that lived on the Serengeti Plain in Africa. These frogs, it seemed, laid their eggs on muddy riverbanks in the monsoon season when the earth was black and oozing with moisture. But the wet season turned dry in time, and on the Serengeti a drought could go on and on. The eggs could lay trapped in the arid, hard-packed ground for years. Amazingly, when the rains finally returned, newborn frogs would come bubbling up through the mud and go in search of mates, to begin the cycle of life again.

Impossible, he'd thought at the time, for life to adapt to such conditions.

And yet, he felt a little like that now. The meeting with Diana's parents had released something in him. Not the guilt, or not all of it, certainly, but their forgiveness, their understanding, had eased his burdens. For the first time since his wife's death, he could stand straight again. He could believe that there was a way out for him. Not medicine. He could never go through that again, never watch death up close. But something . . .

And there was Meghann. To his disbelief, she'd called. Asked him on a date. His first real date with a woman in more than fifteen years.

He wasn't sure even how to prepare for it.

She wasn't like Diana. There was no softness in Meghann. No single moment with her promised anything—least of all another moment. Even when they were at their most intimate, when he was inside of her, she sometimes turned her face away from him.

He knew it would be smart to forget her and the desires she'd rekindled. Smart, but impossible. That would be like expecting those frogs to feel the sweet rainwater and stay hidden in the safety of their riverbank. Thousands of years of evolution had honed certain instincts to the point where they couldn't be ignored.

Meghann, perhaps even more so than the Roloffs' forgiveness, had brought Joe back to life. He couldn't turn away from her now.

It was because of her that he dared—at last—to go to town. On his lunch break, he strode down Main Street, head down, face partially obscured by a baseball cap. He walked past the two old men sitting outside the Loose Screw Hardware Shop, past a woman dragging two small children out of the ice-cream store. He was aware of people pointing at him and whispering. He kept moving.

Finally, he ducked into the old barber shop and climbed up into the empty chair. "I could use a haircut," he said, not making eye contact with Frank Hill, who'd first cut Joe's hair for the fourth-grade class photo.

"You sure could." Frank finished sweeping the floor, then grabbed a comb and some scissors. After pinning a bib in place, he started combing Joe's hair. "Head up."

Joe slowly lifted his head. Across the room a mirror held his reflection. He saw the imprint of the last few years. Sadness and guilt had left their mark in the lines around his eyes and the silver in his hair. He sat still for the next thirty minutes, his stomach clenched, his hands fisted, waiting for Frank to recognize him.

When it was over and he'd paid Frank for the haircut, he headed for the door. He'd just opened it when Frank said, "You come on back and see me anytime, Joe. You still have friends in this town."

That welcome gave Joe the courage to walk down to Swain's Mercantile, where he bought new clothes. Several old acquaintances smiled at him.

He made it back to the garage by 1:00 and worked for the rest of the day.

"That's about the tenth time you've looked at that clock in the past half an hour," Smitty said at 4:30. He was at the workbench, putting together a skateboard for his grandson's birthday.

"I've . . . uh . . . got someplace to be," Joe said.

Smitty reached for a wrench. "No kidding."

Joe slammed the truck's hood down. "I thought maybe I'd leave a couple of minutes early."

"Wouldn't hurt my feelings none."

"Thanks." Joe looked down at his hands; they were black with grease. He couldn't see touching Meghann with these hands, though the grease under his fingernails certainly hadn't bothered her in the past. It was one of the things he liked about her. The women he'd known in his previous life looked down on men like the one he'd become.

"Whatcha got going on—if you don't mind me asking," Smitty asked, moving toward him.

"A friend is coming over for dinner."

"This friend drive a Porsche?"

"Yeah."

Smitty smiled. "Maybe you want to borrow the barbecue. Cut a few flowers from Helga's garden?"

"I didn't know how to ask."

"Hell, Joe, you just do. Open your mouth and say please. That's part of being neighbors and coworkers."

"Thank you."

"Helga made a cheesecake last night. I'll bet she has a few extra pieces."

"My friend is bringing dessert."

"Ah. Sort of a potluck, huh? That isn't how we did it in my day. 'Course in my day, us men never cooked a thing." He winked. "Not on the stove, anyway. Have a nice night, Joe." Humming a jaunty tune, he headed back to the workbench.

Joe shoved the oily rag in his back pocket and left the shop. On his way to his cabin, he stopped by Smitty's house, talked to Helga for a few minutes, and left carrying a small hibachi. He set up the barbecue on the front porch, filling the black hole with briquettes that he'd bought that morning at Swain's.

Inside the house, he looked around, making a mental list of things to be done.

Oil, wrap, and stab the potatoes.

Shuck the corn.

Season the steaks.

Arrange the flowers in the water pitcher.

Set the table.

He looked at the clock.

She'd be there in ninety minutes.

He showered and shaved, then dressed in his new clothes and headed for the kitchen.

For the next hour, he moved from one chore to the next, until the potatoes were in the oven, the corn was on the stove, the flowers were on the table, and the candles were lit.

Finally, everything was ready. He poured himself a glass of red wine and went into the living room to wait for her.

He sat down on the sofa and stretched out his legs.

From her place on the mantel, Diana smiled down at him.

He felt a flash of guilt, as if he'd done something wrong. That was stupid; he wasn't being unfaithful.

Still . . .

He set his glass down on the coffee table and went to her. "Hey, Di," he whispered, reaching for the photograph. This was one of his favorites, taken on New Year's Eve at Whistler Mountain. She wore a white fur hat and a silvery parka. She looked impossibly young and beautiful.

For three years, he'd poured his heart out to her, told her everything; suddenly he couldn't think of a thing to say. Behind him, candles flickered on the table set for two.

He touched the photo. The glass felt cold and slick. "I'll always love you."

It was true. Diana would always be his first—maybe his best—love.

But he had to try again.

He collected the photographs, one by one, leaving a single framed picture on the end table. Just one. All the rest, he took into the bedroom and carefully put away. Later, he'd return a few of them to his sister's house.

When he went back into the living room and sat down, he smiled, thinking of Meghann. Anticipating the evening.

By 9:30, his smile had faded.

He sat alone on the couch, half drunk now with an empty bottle of wine beside him. The potatoes had long ago cooked down to nothing and the candles had burned themselves out. The front door stood open, welcoming, but the street in front was empty.

At midnight, he went to bed alone.

In the past nine days, Meghann and Claire had seen several specialists. It was amazing how fast doctors would see you if you had a brain tumor and plenty of money. Neurologists. Neurosurgeons. Neuro-oncologists. Radiologists. They went from Johns Hopkins to Sloan-Kettering to Scripps. When they weren't on airplanes, they were in hospital waiting rooms or doctors' offices. They learned dozens of frightening new words. *Glioblastoma. Anaplastic astrocytoma. Craniotomy.* Some of the doctors were caring and compassionate; more were cold and distant and too busy to talk for long. They outlined treatment models that were all depressingly alike and stacked them on statistics that offered little hope.

They each said the same thing: *inoperable*. It didn't matter if Claire's tumor was malignant or benign; either way it could be deadly. Most of the specialists believed Claire's tumor to be a glioblastoma multiforme. A kind they called the terminator. Ha-ha.

Each time they left a city, Meghann pinned her hopes on the next destination.

Until a neurologist at Scripps took her aside. "Look," the doctor said, "you're using up valuable time. Radiation is your sister's best hope right now. Twenty-five percent of brain tumors respond positively to the treatment. If it shrinks enough, perhaps it will be operable. Take her home. Stop fighting the diagnosis and start fighting the tumor."

Claire had agreed, and so they'd gone home. The next day, Meghann had taken her sister to Swedish Hospital, where yet another neuro-oncologist had said the same thing, his opinion bolstered by yet another radiologist. They'd agreed to begin radiation treatment the next day.

Once a day for four weeks.

"I'll need to stay here for the treatments," Claire said as she sat on the cold stone fireplace in Meghann's condo. "Hayden's too far away."

"Of course. I'll call Julie and take some more time off of work."

"You don't have to do that. I can take the bus to the hospital."

"I'm not going to dignify that with an answer. Even *I* am not that big a bitch."

Claire looked out the window. "A friend of mine went through chemo and radiation. . . ." She stared at the sparkling city, but all she really saw was Diana wasting away, losing her soul along with her hair. In the end, all those treatments hadn't helped at all. "I don't want Ali to see me like that. She can stay with Dad. We'll visit every weekend."

"I'll rent a car for Bobby. That way you guys can drive back and forth."

"I'm not going to tell Bobby . . . yet."

Meghann frowned. "What?"

"I am not going to call my brand-new husband and tell him I have a brain tumor. He'll come home, and I couldn't stand that." Claire looked at her. "He's waited his whole life for this break. I don't want to ruin it for him."

"But if he loves you—"

"He *does* love me," she answered fiercely. "That's the point. And

I love him. I want him to have his chance. Besides, there's nothing he can do but hold my hand."

"I thought the point of love was holding each other up through the hard times."

"That's what I'm doing."

"Really? It sounds to me like you're afraid he won't want to come."

"Shut up."

Meghann went to her sister then, sat down beside her. "I know you're scared, Claire. And I know Mama and I left you a long time ago. I know . . . we hurt you. But you have to give Bobby the chance to—"

"This isn't about the past."

"My shrink says everything is about our past, and I'm beginning to agree with her. The point is—"

"Do *not* tell me the point of my own life. Please." Claire's voice cracked. "I'm the one who has a tumor. Me. You don't get to organize or critique my choices, okay? I love Bobby and I am *not* going to ask him to sacrifice everything for me." Claire stood up. "We better get going. I need to tell Dad what's going on."

"What about Mama?"

"What about her?"

"You want to call her?"

"And hear her say she's too busy picking out sofa fabrics to visit her sick daughter? No, thanks. I'll call her if I get worse. You know how she hates unnecessary scenes. Now let's go."

Two hours later, Meg turned onto River Road and they were there. Late-afternoon sunlight drizzled down the yellow clapboard sides, caught the blooming pink roses and turned them orange. The garden was a riot of color. A small bicycle with training wheels lay on its side in the overgrown grass.

Claire whispered, "Oh, man . . ."

"You can do it," Meg said. "Radiation can save you. Just like we talked about. I'll help you."

Claire's smile was wobbly. "I need to do this alone."

Meg understood. This was Claire's family, not hers. "Okay."

Claire got out of the car and walked haltingly up the path. Meg fell in step beside her, offering a solid arm for support.

At the front door, Claire paused, drew in a deep breath. "I can do this. Mommy's sick."

"And the doctors are going to make her better."

She looked helplessly at Meghann. "How do I promise that? What if—"

"We talked about this, Claire. You promise it. We'll worry about what if later."

Claire nodded. "You're right." Forcing a smile, she opened the door.

Sam sat on the sofa, wearing a pair of faded overalls and a smile. "Hey, you two, you're late. How was the spa week?" Halfway through the sentence, his smile faded. He looked to Claire, then to Meghann. Slowly, he got to his feet. "What's going on?"

Alison was on the floor, playing with a Fisher-Price barnyard set. "Mommy!" she said, scrambling to her feet and running for them.

Claire dropped to her knees and scooped Alison into her arms.

Meghann saw the way her sister was trembling, and she longed to reach out to her, to hold her as she had when they were kids. She felt a fresh surge of rage. How could this happen to *Claire*? How could her sister possibly look into her daughter's eyes and say *I'm sick* without breaking like finely spun sugar?

"Mommy," Alison said at last, "you're *squishing* me." She wiggled out of her mother's arms. "Did you bring me home a present? Can we all go to Hawaii for Christmas? Grandpa says—"

Claire stood up. She glanced nervously back at Meghann. "Pick me up at six, okay?" Then, smiling, Claire faced her father and daughter. "I need to talk to you two."

Meghann had never seen such bravery.

I need to do this alone.

She backed out of the door, ran for the safety of her car, and drove away.

She didn't even know where she was going until she was there.

The cabin looked dark, unoccupied.

She parked out front and killed the engine. Leaving her purse in the car, she headed across the street and walked up to the front door.

She knocked.

He opened the door. "You have got to be kidding me."

That was when she remembered their date. Last Friday. She was supposed to bring the wine and dessert. It felt like decades ago. She looked past him, saw a dying bouquet of flowers on the coffee table, and hoped he hadn't bought them for their date. But of course he had. How long had he waited, she wondered, before he ate his dinner alone? "I'm sorry. I forgot."

"Give me one good reason not to slam the door in your face."

She looked up at him, feeling so fragile she could barely breathe. "My sister has a brain tumor."

His expression changed slowly. A look came into his eyes, a kind of harrowing understanding that made her wonder at the dark roads that had traversed his life. "Oh, Jesus."

He opened his arms and she walked into his embrace. For the first time, she let herself really cry.

Joe stood on the porch, staring out at the falling night. At the park across the street, a baseball game was being played. An occasional roar of the crowd erupted through the silence. Otherwise, there was only the sound of a cool breeze rustling the honeysuckle leaves.

It had been better, he now understood, to be angry at Meghann, to write her off for standing him up. When she stepped into his arms and looked up at him with tears in her eyes, he'd wanted desperately to help her.

My sister has a brain tumor.

He closed his eyes, not wanting to remember, not wanting to feel the way he did.

He'd held Meghann for almost an hour. She'd cried until there were no tears left inside her, and then she'd fallen into a troubled sleep. He imagined that it was her first sleep in days.

He knew. After a diagnosis like that, sleep either came to a person too much or not at all.

They hadn't spoken of anything that mattered. He'd simply stroked her hair and kissed her forehead and let her cry in his arms.

He couldn't think of it without shame.

Behind him, the screen door screeched open and banged shut. He stiffened, unable to turn around and face her. When he did, he saw that she was embarrassed.

Her cheeks were pink, and that gorgeous hair of hers was a fuzzy mess. She tried to smile, and the attempt tore at him. "I'll put you in for a Purple Heart."

He wanted to take her in his arms again, but he didn't dare. Things were different between them now, though she didn't know it. Hospitals. Tumors. Death and dying and disease.

He couldn't be a part of all that again. He had only just begun to survive his last round of it. "There's nothing wrong with crying."

"I suppose not. It doesn't help much, though." She moved toward him; he wondered if she knew that she was wringing her hands.

He got the sense that the time in his arms had both soothed and upset her. As if maybe she hated to admit a need. He'd been alone long enough to understand.

"I want to thank you for . . . I don't know. Being there. I shouldn't have busted in on you."

He knew she was waiting for an argument, waiting for him to say *I'm glad you're here.*

At his silence, she stepped back, frowning. "Too much too soon, I guess. I completely understand. I hate needy people, too. Well. I better go. Claire starts radiation tomorrow."

He couldn't help himself. "Where?"

She paused, turned back toward him. "Swedish Hospital."

"Did you get second opinions?"

"Are you kidding? We got opinions from the best people in the country. They didn't agree on everything, but *inoperable* was a favorite."

"There's a guy. A neurosurgeon at UCLA. Stu Weissman. He's good."

Meghann was watching him. "They're all good. And they all agree. How do you know Weissman?"

"I went to school with him."

"College?"

"Don't sound so surprised. Just because I live like this now doesn't mean I always did. I have a degree in American lit."

"We know nothing about each other."

"Maybe it's better that way."

"Normally I'd have a funny comeback to that. But I'm a little slow today. Having a sister with a brain tumor will do that to a girl. Pretend I was witty." Her voice cracked a little. She turned and walked away.

With every step she took, he wanted to go after her, apologize and tell her the truth, who he was and what he'd been through. Then, perhaps, she'd understand why there were places he couldn't go. But he didn't move.

When he went back inside the house, he saw the last remaining picture of Diana staring at him from the mantel. For the first time he noticed the accusing glint in her eyes.

"What?" he said. "There's nothing I can do."

Alison listened carefully to Claire's explanation of a golf-ball-size "owie" in her brain.

"A golf ball is little," she said at last.

Claire nodded, smiling. "Yes. Yes it is."

"And a special gun is gonna shoot magic rays at it until it disappears? Like rubbing Aladdin's lamp?"

"Exactly like that."

"How come you hafta live with Aunt Meg?"

"It's a long drive to the hospital. I can't go back and forth every day."

Finally, Ali said, "Okay." Then she got to her feet and ran upstairs. "I'll be right back, Mommy!" she yelled down.

"You haven't looked at me," Dad said when Ali was gone.

"I know."

He got up and crossed the room, then sat down beside her. She felt the comforting, familiar heat of him as he put an arm around her, pulled her close. She rested her head on the hard ledge of his shoulder. She felt a splash of tears on her face and knew he was crying.

"I'd drive you back and forth, you know," he said softly, and she loved him for it. But she didn't want to grow weak in front of him. She and Meghann had read about radiation; when it was focused on the brain it could really make a person sick. It would take everything she had to stay strong through the treatments. She couldn't come home every night and see herself through her dad's eyes. "I know that. You've always been there for me."

He sighed heavily, wiping his eyes. "Have you told Bobby?"

"Not yet."

"But you will?"

"Of course. As soon as he's finished in Nashville—"

"Don't."

She looked at him, confused by the sudden harshness of his voice. "What?"

"I didn't know your Mama was pregnant, did I ever tell you that?"

"You told me."

"I left one night to run to the store and when I got back, she'd left me. I tried to get ahold of her, but you know Ellie, when she's gone, she's gone. I went back to my job at the paper plant and tried to forget her. It took a long time."

Claire put her hand on his. "I know all this."

"You don't know all of it. When Meg called me to come get you, I went from alone in the world to father of a nine-year-old in one phone call. I hated Ellie then like you can't believe. It took years before I stopped hating her for denying me your childhood. All I could think about was what I'd missed—your birth, your first words, your first steps. I never got to hold all of you in my arms, not really."

"What does this have to do with Bobby?"

"You can't make decisions for other people, Claire, especially not for people who love you."

"But you can sacrifice for them. Isn't that what love is?"

"You see it as sacrifice? What if he sees it as selfishness? If . . . the worst happens, you've denied him the one thing that matters. Time."

Claire looked at him. "I can't tell him, Dad. I can't."

"I could kill her for what she did to you and Meg."

"This isn't about Mama dumping us," Claire said, believing it. "This is about how much I love Bobby. I won't make him give up his big break for me."

Before Dad could say anything else, Alison bounded into the room, dragging her worn, stained baby blanket, the one she'd slept with every single night of her life. "Here, Mommy," she said, "you can have my wubbie till you get all better."

Claire took the grayed pink blanket in her hands. She couldn't help herself; she held it to her face and smelled the little-girl sweetness of it. "Thanks, Ali," she said in a throaty voice.

Alison crawled up into her arms and hugged her. "It's okay, Mommy. Don't cry. I'm a big girl. I can sleep without my wubbie."

CHAPTER
TWENTY-SIX

ℳEGHANN SAT IN THE WAITING ROOM, TRYING TO READ THE newest issue of *People* magazine. It was the "Best- and Worst-Dressed" issue. Honest to God, she couldn't tell the difference. Finally, she tossed the magazine on the cheap wooden table beside her. The wall clock ticked past another minute.

She went up to the desk again. "It's been more than an hour. Are you sure everything is okay with my sister? Claire—"

"Austin, I know. I spoke with radiology five minutes ago. She's almost finished."

Meghann refrained from pointing out that she'd received the same answer fifteen minutes earlier. Instead, she sighed heavily and went back to her seat. The only magazine left to read was *Field & Stream.* She ignored it.

Finally, Claire came out.

Meghann rose slowly. On the right side of her sister's head was a small area that had been shaved. "How was it?"

Claire touched her bald spot, feeling it. "They tattooed me. I feel like Damien—that kid from *The Omen*."

Meg looked at the tiny black dots on the pale, shaved shin. "I could fix your hair so you couldn't even see the . . . you know."

"Bald spot? That would be great."

They looked at each other for a minute or so. "Well, let's go, then," Meghann finally said.

They walked through the hospital and out to the parking garage.

On the short drive home, Meghann kept trying to think of what to say. She had to be careful from now on, had to say the right thing. Whatever *that* was.

"It didn't hurt," Claire said.

"Really? That's good."

"It was hard to keep still, though."

"Oh . . . yeah. It would be."

"I closed my eyes and imagined the rays were sunlight. Healing me. Like that article you gave me."

Meg had given her sister a stack of literature on positive thinking and visualization. She hadn't known if Claire had read them until just now. "I'm glad it helped. The lady at Fred Hutch is supposed to be sending me another box of stuff."

Claire leaned back in her seat and looked out the window.

From this side, she looked perfectly normal. Meghann wished she could say something that mattered; so much was unsaid between them.

With a sigh, she pulled into the underground lot and parked in her space.

Still silent, they went upstairs. In the condo, Meghann turned to Claire. She stared at the bald spot for a second too long. "Do you want something to eat?"

"No." Claire touched her briefly, her fingers were icy cold. "Thanks for coming with me today. It helped not to be alone."

Their gazes met. Once again, Meghann felt the weight of their distance.

"I think I'll lie down. I didn't sleep well last night."

So they'd both been awake, staring at their separate ceilings from their separate rooms. Meghann wished she'd gone to Claire last night, sat on her bed, and talked about the things that mattered. "Me, either."

Claire nodded. She waited a second longer, then turned and headed for the bedroom.

Meghann watched the door slowly close between them. She stood there, listening to her sister's shuffling footsteps beyond the door. She wondered if Claire was moving slower in there, if fear clouded her eyes. Or if she was staring at that small, tattooed pink patch of skin in the mirror. Did Claire's brave front crumble in the privacy of that room?

Meg prayed not, as she went to the condo's third bedroom, which was set up as an in-home office. Once, files and briefs and depositions had cluttered the glass desk. Now it was buried beneath medical books, memoirs, JAMA articles, and clinical trials literature. Every day, boxes from Barnes & Noble.com and Amazon arrived.

Meghann sat down at her desk. Her current reading material was a book on coping with cancer. It lay open to a chapter called "Don't Stop Talking Just When You Need to Start."

She read: *This time of tragedy can be one of growth and opportunity, too. Not only for the patient, but for the family as well. It can be a time that draws you and your loved ones closer.*

Meghann closed the book and reached for a JAMA article about the potential benefits of tamoxifen to shrink tumors.

She opened a yellow legal pad and began to take notes. She worked furiously, writing, writing. Hours later, when she looked up, Claire was standing in the doorway, smiling at her. "Why do I think you're planning to do the surgery yourself?"

"I already know more about your condition than that first idiot we saw."

Claire came into the room, carefully stepping over the empty Amazon boxes and the magazines that had been discarded. She stared down at the filled legal pads and inkless pens. "No wonder you're the best lawyer in the city."

"I research well. I'm really starting to understand your condition. I've made you a kind of abstract—a synopsis of everything I've read."

"I think I better read it for myself, don't you?"

"Some of it's . . . hard."

Claire reached for the standing file on the left side of the desk. In it was a manila file with the word *Hope* emblazoned in red ink on the notched label. She picked it up.

"Don't," Meg said. "I've just started."

Claire opened the file. It was empty. She looked down at Meghann.

"This goes in it," Meg said quickly, ripping several pages out of her notebook. "Tamoxifen."

"Drugs?"

"There must be people who beat brain tumors," Meghann said fiercely. "I'll find every damn one and put their stories in there. That's what the file is for."

Claire leaned over, picked up a blank piece of paper. On it, she wrote her name, then she placed the paper in the file and returned the file to its stand.

Meg stared up at her sister in awe. "You're really something. You know that?"

"We Sullivan girls are tough."

"We had to be."

Meg smiled. For the first time all day, she felt as if she could draw an easy breath. "You want to watch a movie?"

"Anything except *Love Story.*"

Meg started to rise.

The doorbell rang.

She frowned. "Who could that be?"

"You act like no one ever visits you."

Meghann sidled past Claire and walked to the door. By the time she got there, the bell had rung another eight times. "Damn good doorman," she muttered, opening the door.

Gina, Charlotte, and Karen stood clustered together.

"Where's our girl?" Karen cried out.

Claire appeared and the screaming began. Karen and Charlotte surged forward, mumbling hello to Meghann, then enfolding Claire in their arms.

"Sam called us," Gina said when she and Meghann were alone in the hallway. "How is she?"

"Okay, I guess. The radiation went well, I think. She goes every day for four weeks." At Gina's frightened look, Meghann added, "She didn't want to worry you guys."

"Yeah, right. She can't be alone for a thing like this."

"I'm here," Meghann answered, stung.

Gina squeezed her arm. "She'll need all of us."

Meghann nodded. Then she and Gina looked at each other.

"You call me. Whenever," Gina said quietly.

"Thanks."

After that, Gina eased past Meg and went into the living room, saying loudly. "Okay, we've got spas-in-a-bucket, gooey popcorn balls, hilarious movies, and, of course, games. What should we do first?"

Meghann watched the four best friends come together; they were all talking at once. She didn't move toward them, and they didn't call out to her.

Finally, she went back to her office and shut the door. As she sat there, reading the latest literature on chemotherapy and the blood-brain barrier, she heard the high, clear sound of her sister's laughter.

She picked up the phone and called Elizabeth.

"Hey," Meg said softly when her friend answered.

"What is it?" Elizabeth asked. "You're too quiet."

"Claire," was all she could say before the tears came.

Joe sat sprawled across the sofa, drinking a beer. His third. Mostly, he was trying not to think.

The ephemeral chance for redemption—the one that only last week had glittered in front of him like a desert oasis beside a long, hot highway—had vanished. He should have known it was a mirage.

There would be no starting over. He didn't have the guts for it. He'd thought, hoped, that with Meg he'd be stronger.

"Meg," he said her name softly, closed his eyes. He said a prayer for her and her sister. It was all he could really do now.

Meg.

She wouldn't clear out of his mind. He kept thinking of her, remembering, wanting. It was what had sent him reaching for the bottles of beer.

It wasn't that he missed her, precisely. Hell, he didn't even know her last name. Didn't know where she lived or what she did in her spare time.

What he grieved for was the *idea* of her. For those few moments—unexpected and sweet—he'd dared to step onto old roads. He'd let himself want someone, let himself believe in a new future.

He took a long drink. It didn't help.

In the kitchen, the phone rang. He got slowly to his feet and started that way. It was probably Gina, calling to make sure he was okay. He had no idea what he'd tell her.

But it wasn't Gina. It was Henry Roloff, sounding hurried. "Joe? Could you meet me for a cup of coffee? Say in an hour?"

"Is everything okay?"

"How about the Whitewater Diner? Three o'clock?"

Joe hoped he could walk straight. "Sure." He hung up the phone and headed for the shower.

An hour later he was dressed in his new clothes and walking down Main Street. He still felt a faint buzz from the beer, but that was probably a good thing. Already he could feel the way people were staring after him, whispering about him.

It took an act of will to keep smiling as the hostess—a woman he didn't know, thank God—showed him to a booth.

Henry was already there. "Hey, Joe. Thanks for coming so quickly."

"It's not like I was busy. It's Saturday. The garage is closed." He slid into the booth.

Henry talked for a few minutes about Tina's garden and the vacation they'd taken to St. Croix last winter, but Joe knew it was all leading up to something. He found himself tensing up, straightening.

Finally, he couldn't take the suspense. "What is it, Henry?" he asked.

Henry stopped midsentence and looked up. "I want to ask a favor of you."

"I'd do anything for you, Henry. You know that. What do you need?"

Henry reached down under the table and brought out a big manila envelope.

Joe knew what it was. He leaned back, put his hands out as if to ward off a blow. "Anything but that, Henry," he said. "I can't go back to that."

"I just want you to look at this. The patient is—" Henry's beeper went off. "Just a minute." Henry pulled out his cell phone and punched in a number.

Joe stared down at the envelope. Someone's medical charts. A record of pain and suffering.

He couldn't go back to that world. No way. When a man had lost his faith and his confidence as profoundly as Joe had, there was no going back. Besides, he couldn't practice medicine anymore. He'd let his license lapse.

He got to his feet. "Sorry, Henry," he said, interrupting Henry's phone call. "My consulting days are over."

"Wait," Henry said, raising a hand.

Joe backed away from the table, then turned and walked out of the restaurant.

Though the radiation treatments themselves lasted only a few minutes a day, they monopolized Claire's life. By the fourth day, she was tired and nauseated. But the side effects weren't half as bad as the phone calls.

Every day, she called home at precisely noon. Ali always

answered on the first ring and asked if the owie was all better yet, then Dad got on the phone and asked the same question in a different way. The strength it took to pretend was already waning.

Meghann stood beside her for every call. She hardly went to the office anymore. Maybe three hours a day, tops. The rest of the time, she spent huddled over books and articles, or glued to the Internet. She attacked the issue of a tumor the way she'd once gone after deadbeat dads.

Claire appreciated it; she read everything that Meghann handed her. She'd even consented to drink the "BTC"—brain tumor cocktail—Meghann had devised based on her research. It contained all kinds of vitamins and minerals.

They talked daily about treatments and prognoses and trials. What they didn't talk about was the future. Claire couldn't find the courage to say, *I'm afraid,* and Meg never asked the question.

The only time Meg seemed willing to disappear into the woodwork was at 2:00. The designated Bobby Phone Call time.

Now, Claire was alone in the living room. In the kitchen, the 2:00 buzzer was beeping. As usual, Meg had heard it and made an excuse to leave the room.

Claire picked up the phone and dialed Bobby's new cell phone number.

He picked up on the first ring. "Hey, baby," he said. "You're two minutes late." Bobby's voice poured through her cold, cold body, warming her.

She leaned back into the sofa's downy cushions. "Tell me about your day." She'd found that it was easier to listen than to talk. At first, she'd been able to laugh at his stories and make up pretty lies. Lately, though, her mind was a little foggy, and the exhaustion was almost unbearable. She wondered how long it would be before he noticed that she spent their conversations listening to him, or that her voice almost always broke when she said, *I love you.*

"I met George Strait today. Can you believe it? He passed on a song—one called "Dark Country Corners"—and then mentioned that it'd be a good match with my voice. I listened to the song and it was great." He started to sing to her.

A sob caught in her throat. She had to stop him before she burst into tears. "That's beautiful. Top 10 for sure."

"Are you okay, baby?"

"I'm fine. Everyone here is fine. Meg and I have been spending a lot of time together; you'd be surprised. And Ali and Sam send their love."

"Slap 'em right back with mine. I miss you, Claire."

"I miss you, too. But it's only a few more weeks."

"Kent thinks we should have all the songs chosen by next week. Then it's into the studio. Do you think you could come down for that? I'd love to sing the songs to you."

"Maybe," she said, wondering what lie she'd come up with when the time came. She was too exhausted to think of one now. "Are you loving every minute down there?"

"As much as I can love anything without you. But, yeah."

She was doing the right thing. She *was*. "Well, babe, I've got to run. Meg is taking me out to lunch. Then we're getting manicures at the Gene Juarez Spa."

"I thought you got a manicure yesterday?"

Claire winced. "Uh. Those were pedicures. I love you."

"I love you, too, Claire. Is . . . is everything okay?"

She felt the sting of tears again. "Everything's perfect."

"I made us a picnic lunch," Meghann said the next morning after another treatment.

"I'm not very hungry," Claire answered.

"I know that. I just thought . . ."

Claire hauled up the will to think about someone else. Sadly, that was becoming difficult, too. "You're right. It's a beautiful day."

Meghann led her to the car. Within minutes they were on the freeway. To their left, Lake Union sparkled in the sunlight. They passed the Gothic brick buildings of the University of Washington, then raced over the floating bridge.

Lake Washington was busy today. Boats zipped back and forth, hauling skiers in their wake.

On Mercer Island, Meghann exited the freeway and turned onto a narrow, tree-lined drive. At a beautiful, gray-shingled house, she parked. "This is my partner's house. She said we were welcome to spend the afternoon here."

"I'm surprised she hasn't fired you, with all the time you've taken off lately."

Meghann helped Claire out of the car and down the grassy lawn to the silvery wooden dock that cut into the blue water. "Remember Lake Winobee?" she said, guiding Claire to the end of the dock, helping her sit down without falling.

"The summer I got that pink bathing suit?"

Meghann set the picnic basket down, then sat beside her sister. They both dangled their feet over the edge. Water slapped against the pilings. Beside them, a varnished wooden sailboat called *The Defense Rests* bobbed easily from side to side, its lines screeching with each movement.

"I stole that bikini," Meghann said. "From Fred Meyer. When I got home, I was so scared I threw up. Mama didn't care; she just looked up from *Variety* and said, 'Sticky fingers will get a girl in trouble.' "

Claire turned to her sister, studying her profile. "I waited for you to come back, you know. Dad always said, 'Don't worry, Claire-Bear, she's your sister, she'll be back.' I waited and waited. What happened?"

Meghann sighed heavily, as if she'd known this conversation couldn't be avoided anymore. "Remember when Mama went down for the *Starbase IV* audition?"

"Yes."

"She didn't come back. I was used to her being gone for a day or two, but after about five days, I started to panic. There wasn't any money left. We were hungry. Then Social Services started sniffing around. I was scared they'd put us in the system. So I called Sam."

"I know all this, Meg."

Meghann didn't seem to have heard her. "He said he'd take us both in."

"And he did."

"But he wasn't *my* father. I tried to fit in to Hayden; what a joke. I got in with a bad crowd and started screwing up. A therapist would call it acting out. Trying to get attention. Every time I looked at you and Sam together . . ." She shrugged. "I felt left out, I guess. You were all I really had, and then I didn't have you. One night I came home drunk and Sam exploded. He called me a piss-poor excuse for a big sister and told me to shape up or get out."

"So you got out. Where did you go?"

"I bummed around Seattle for a while, feeling sorry for myself. I slept in doorways and empty buildings, did things I'm not proud of. It didn't take long to hit rock bottom. Then one day I remembered a teacher who'd taken an interest in me, Mr. Earhart. He was the one who bumped me up a grade, back when we lived in Barstow. He convinced me that education was the way out of Mama's trailer-trash life. That's why I always got straight As. Anyway, I gave him a call— thank God he was still at the same school. He arranged for me to graduate high school early and take the SAT, which I aced. Perfect score. The UW offered me a full scholarship. You know the rest."

"My genius sister," Claire said. For once, there was pride in her voice instead of bitterness.

"I told myself it was the best thing for you, that you didn't need your big sister anymore. But . . . I knew how much I'd hurt you. It was easier to keep my distance, I guess. I believed you'd never forgive me. So I didn't give you the chance." Meg finally looked at her. She offered a small smile. "I'll have to tell my shrink I finally got my money's worth. It cost me about ten thousand dollars to be able to tell you that."

"The only thing you did wrong was stay away," Claire said gently.

"I'm here now."

"I know." Claire looked out to the sparkling blue water. "I couldn't have done all this without you."

"That's not true. You're the bravest person I ever met."

"I'm not so brave, believe me."

Meghann leaned back to open the picnic basket. "I've been waiting for just the right time to give you this." She withdrew a manila folder and handed it to Claire. "Here."

"Not now, Meg. I'm tired."

"Please."

Claire took the folder with a sigh. It was the one labeled *Hope*. She looked sharply at Meg, but didn't say anything. Her hands trembled as she opened the file.

In it were almost a dozen personal accounts of people who had had glioblastoma multiforme tumors. Each of them had been given less than a year to live—at least seven years ago.

Claire squeezed her eyes shut, but the tears came anyway. "I needed this today."

"I thought so."

She swallowed hard, then dared to look at her sister. "I've been so afraid." It felt good, finally admitting it.

"Me, too," Meg answered quietly. Then she leaned forward and took Claire in her arms.

For the first time since childhood, Claire was held by her big sister. Meghann stroked her hair, the way she'd done when Claire was young.

A handful of hair fell out at Meghann's touch, floated between them.

Claire drew back, saw the pile of her pretty blond hair in Meghann's hand. Strands drifted down to the water, where they looked like nothing at all. She stared down at the hair floating away on the current. "I didn't want to tell you it's been falling out. Every morning I wake up on a hairy pillow."

"Maybe we should go home," Meg said finally.

"I *am* tired."

Meghann helped Claire to her feet. Slowly they made their way back to the car. Claire's steps were shuffling and uncertain now, and she leaned heavily on Meg's arm.

All the way home, Claire stared out the window.

Back in the condo, Meghann helped Claire change into her flannel pajamas and climb into bed.

"It's just hair," Claire said as she leaned back against a pile of pillows.

Meghann set the *Hope* file on the nightstand. "It'll grow back."

"Yeah." Claire sighed and closed her eyes.

Meghann backed out of the room. At the doorway, she stopped.

Her sister lay there, barely breathing it seemed, with her eyes closed. Strands of hair decorated her pillow. Very slowly, still not opening her eyes, Claire brought her hands up and started touching her wedding ring. Tears leaked down the sides of her face, leaving tiny gray splotches on the pillow.

And Meghann knew what she had to do.

She closed the door and went to the phone. All of Claire's emergency numbers were on a notepad beside it. Including Bobby's.

Meghann dialed Bobby's number and waited impatiently for him to answer.

In the past twenty-four hours, Claire had lost almost half of her hair. The bare skin that showed through was an angry, scaly red. This morning, as she got ready for her appointment, she spent nearly thirty minutes wrapping a silk scarf around her head.

"Quit fussing with it," Meghann said when they arrived at the Nuclear Medicine waiting room. "You look fine."

"I look like a Gypsy fortune-teller. And I don't know why you made me wear makeup. My skin is so red I look like Martha Phillips."

"Who is that?"

"In the eighth grade. She fell asleep under a sunlamp. We called her Tomato Face for two weeks."

"Kids are so kind."

Claire left for her treatment and was back in the waiting room thirty minutes later. She didn't bother putting the scarf back on. Her scalp was tender.

"Let's go out for coffee," she said when Meghann stood up to greet her.

"Coffee makes you puke."

"What doesn't? Let's go anyway."

"I have to go into the office today. I've got a deposition sched-uled."

"Oh." Claire followed Meghann down the hospital corridor, try-ing to keep up. Lately, she was so tired it was hard not to shuffle like an old woman. She practically fell asleep in the car.

At the condo door, Meghann paused, key in hand, and looked at her. "I'm trying to do what's right for you. What's best."

"I know that."

"Sometimes I screw up. I tend to think I know everything."

Claire smiled. "Are you waiting for an argument?"

"I just want you to remember that. I'm trying to do the right thing."

"Okay, Meg. I'll remember. Now go to work. I don't want to miss *Judge Judy*. She reminds me of you."

"Smart-ass." Meg looked at her a moment longer, then opened the condo door. "Bye."

"This is the longest farewell in history. Bye, Meg. Go to work."

Meghann nodded and walked away.

When Claire heard the ping of the elevator, she went into the condo, closing the door behind her.

Inside, the stereo was on. Dwight Yoakam's "Pocket of a Clown" pumped through the speakers.

Claire turned the corner and there he was.

Bobby.

Her hand flew to her bald spot.

She ran to the bathroom, flipped open the toilet lid, and threw up.

He was behind her, holding what was left of her hair back, telling her it was okay. "I'm here now, Claire. I'm here."

She closed her eyes, holding back tears of humiliation one breath at a time.

He rubbed her back.

Finally, she went to the sink and brushed her teeth. When she turned to face him, she was trying to smile. "Welcome to my nightmare."

He came toward her, and the love in his eyes made her want to weep. "Our nightmare, Claire."

She didn't know what to say. She was afraid that if she opened her mouth, she'd burst into tears, and she wanted to look strong for him.

"You had no right to keep this from me."

"I didn't want to ruin everything. And I thought . . . I'd get better. You'd dreamed of singing for so long."

"I dreamed of being a star, yeah. I like singing, but I *love* you. I can't believe you'd hide this from me. What if . . ."

Claire caught her lip between her teeth. "I'm sorry."

"You didn't trust me. Do you know how that feels?" His voice was tight, not his voice at all.

"I was just trying to love you."

"I wonder if you even know what love is. *I'm in the hospital every day, honey, battling for my life, but don't you worry about it, just sing your stupid songs.* What kind of man do you think I am?"

"I'm sorry, Bobby. I just . . ." She stared at him, shaking her head.

He grabbed her, pulled her toward him, and held her so tightly it made her gasp. "I love you, Claire. I *love* you," he said fiercely. "When are you going to get that through your head?"

She wrapped her arms around him, clung to him as if she might fall without him. "I guess my tumor got in the way. But I get it now, Bobby. I get it."

Hours later, when Meghann returned to the condo, the lights were off. She tiptoed through the darkness.

When she reached the living room, a light clicked on.

Claire and Bobby lay together on the sofa, their bodies entwined. He was snoring gently.

"I waited up for you," Claire said.

Meghann tossed her briefcase on the chair. "I had to call him, Claire."

"How did you know what he'd do?"

Meghann looked down at Bobby. "He was in the recording studio when I called. Actually recording a song. Honestly, I didn't think he'd come."

Claire glanced down at her sleeping husband, then up at Meg. A look passed between the sisters; in it was the sad residue of their childhood. "Yeah," she said softly, "neither did I."

"He didn't hesitate for a second, Claire. Not a second. He said— and I quote—'Fuck the song. I'll be there tomorrow.' "

"This is the second time you've called a man to come save me."

"You're lucky to be so loved."

Claire's gaze was steady. "Yeah," she said, smiling at her sister. "I am."

CHAPTER TWENTY-SEVEN

$\mathcal{J}$OE WAS SITTING ON THE SOFA, STARING AT THE SMALL BLACK-AND-white television screen.

He was so caught up in the show, it was a moment before he noticed the footsteps outside.

He tensed, sat up.

A key rattled in the lock, then the door swung open. Gina stood in the opening, her fists on her hips. "Hey, big brother. Nice way you have of calling people."

He sighed. "Smitty gave you a key."

"We were worried about you."

"I've been busy."

She looked at the stack of beer cans and pizza boxes and smiled grimly. "Come on. You're coming home with me. I have a roast in the oven and I rented *Ruthless People*. We are going to drink wine and laugh." Her voice softened. "I could use a laugh."

Something about the way she said it shamed him. He'd forgotten about her troubles. He'd been too busy swimming in the pool of his own. "Are you okay?"

"Come on," she said, avoiding the question. "Smitty told me to drag your sorry ass out of here—his words. I intend to do just that."

He knew there was no point in fighting with her—she had that look on her face—and, truthfully, he didn't want to. He was tired of being alone. "Okay."

He followed her out to her car; within minutes, they were in her bright, airy kitchen.

She handed him a glass of Merlot.

While she basted the roast and turned the potatoes, Joe wandered around the great room. In the corner, he found a sewing machine set up. A pile of bold, beautiful fabric lay heaped beside it. He picked up the garment she'd made, ready to compliment her, when he saw what it was. There was no mistaking the slit back.

"It's a hospital gown," Gina said, coming up behind him. "I should have put that stuff away. I forgot. I'm sorry."

He remembered the day Gina had come to his house, bearing pretty designer hospital gowns just like this one.

You shouldn't have to look like everyone else, she'd said to Diana, who'd wept at the gift.

Those gowns had meant so much to Diana. It didn't seem like a big deal—just a change of fabric—but it had brought back her smile. "Who are they for?"

"Claire. She's undergoing radiation right now."

"Claire," he said her name softly, feeling sick. Life was so damn unfair sometimes. "She just got married."

"I didn't tell you because . . . well . . . I knew it would bring up memories."

"Where's she getting the radiation?"

"Swedish."

"That's the best place for her. Good." *Radiation.* He remembered all of it—the sunburned-looking skin, the puffiness, the way Diana's hair started to fall out. In strands at first, then in handfuls.

He and Gina had spent their fair share of time in the cancer end zone. He couldn't imagine how Gina could handle it again.

"Claire flew all around the country seeing the best doctors. I know she's going to get better. It won't be like . . . you know."

"Like Diana," he said into the uncomfortable silence.

Gina came up behind him, touched his shoulder. "I tried to protect you from this. I'm sorry."

He stared out the window at the backyard designed for children. Once, he and Diana had dreamed of bringing their babies here to play.

"Maybe you'd like to go see Claire."

"No," he said so quickly, he knew Gina understood. "My time in hospitals is done."

"Yeah," Gina said, "now let's go watch a funny movie."

He slipped an arm around his sister and pulled her in close. "I could use a laugh."

Meghann sat in the chair that had once felt so comfortable and stared at Dr. Bloom.

"It was all bullshit," she said bitterly. "All my appointments with you. They were just a way for a self-obsessed woman to vent about the mistakes she'd made in her life. Why didn't you ever tell me that none of it mattered?"

"Because it does matter."

"No. I was sixteen years old when all that happened. Sixteen. None of it matters—my fear, my guilt, her resentment. Who cares?"

"Why doesn't it matter anymore?"

Meghann closed her eyes, reaching for a bitterness that had moved on. All she felt was tired, lost. "She's sick."

"Oh." The word was a sigh. "I'm sorry."

"I'm afraid, Harriet," Meghann finally admitted. "What if . . . I can't do it?"

"Do what?"

"Stand by her bed and hold her hand and watch her die? I'm terrified I'll let her down again."

"You won't."

"How do you know that?"

"Ah, Meghann. The only person you ever let down is yourself. You'll be there for Claire. You always have been."

It wasn't entirely true. She wished it were. She wanted to be the kind of person who could be depended upon.

"If I were ill, there's no one I'd rather have in my corner, Meghann. You're so busy swimming in old sorrows that you haven't bothered to come up for air. You've made up with Claire, whether you two have said the words or not. You're her sister again. Forgive yourself and go forward."

Meghann let the advice sink in. Then, slowly, she smiled. It was true. This wasn't the time for fear and regret; she'd spent too many years on that already. These were days that called for hope and, for once, she was going to be strong enough to believe in a happy ending for Claire. No running away from potential heartache. That was the mistake Meg had made in her marriage. She'd feared a broken heart so keenly that she'd never given the whole of her love to Eric.

"Thanks, Harriet," she said at last. "I could have bought a Mercedes for what you charged me, but you've helped."

Harriet smiled. It surprised Meg, made her realize that she'd never seen her doctor smile before. "You're welcome."

Meghann stood up. "So. I'll see you next week, same time?"

"Of course."

She walked out of the office, went down the elevator, and emerged into the July sunlight.

Slinging her handbag over her shoulder, she headed for home.

She was almost there when she happened to look up. Across the street, the small park near the Public Market was a hive of activity. College-age kids playing hackey sack, tourists feeding the dive-bombing seagulls, shoppers taking a rest. She wasn't sure what had caught her eye and made her look.

Then she saw him, standing at the railing. His back was to her, but she recognized his faded jeans and denim shirt. He was probably the only man in downtown Seattle to wear a cowboy hat on a sunny day.

She crossed the street and walked up to him. "Hey, Bobby."

He didn't look at her. "Meg."

"What are you doing out here?"

"She's sleeping." Finally, he turned. His eyes were watery, red. "She threw up for almost an hour. Even when there was nothing left to vomit. Don't worry, I cleaned it up."

"I wasn't worried," Meg said.

"She looks bad today."

"Some days are worse than others. I bet Nashville looks pretty good about now," she said, trying to lighten his mood.

"Is that supposed to be funny? My wife is puking and her hair is falling out. You think I'm worried about my career?"

"I'm sorry." She touched him. "I've always been as sensitive as a serial killer."

He sighed. "No, I'm sorry. I needed someone to yell at."

"I'll always give you a reason, don't worry."

He smiled, but it was tired and worn. "I'm just . . . scared shitless, that's all. And I don't want her to know."

"I know." Meghann smiled up at him. Her sister was lucky to be loved by such a man. For no apparent reason, that made her think of Joe, of the day she'd found him weeping over his divorce. Joe was the kind of man who knew how to love, too. "You're a good man, Bobby Jack Tom Dick. I was wrong about you."

He laughed. "And you're not half the bitch I thought you were."

Meghann slipped an arm around him. "I'm going to pretend that was a compliment."

"It was."

"Good. Now let's go make Claire smile."

The days passed slowly; each new morning found Claire a little more tired than the night before. She strove to keep a positive attitude but her health was deteriorating rapidly. She visualized rays of sunlight instead of radiation. She meditated for an hour a day, imagined herself in a beautiful forest or seated beside her beloved river. She ate the macrobiotic diet that Meghann swore would help heal her body.

The Bluesers came down often, separately and together, doing their best to keep Claire's spirits up. Meg's friend Elizabeth had even come for a few days, and the visit helped her sister immensely. The hardest times were weekends, when they went to Hayden; Claire tried to pretend that everything was okay for Ali.

In the evenings, though, it was just the three of them—Claire, Meg, and Bobby—in that too-quiet apartment. Mostly, they watched movies together. At first, when Bobby arrived, they'd tried to spend the evening talking or playing cards, but that had proved difficult. Too many dangerous subjects. None of them could mention the future without flinching, without thinking, *Will there be a Christmas together? A Thanksgiving? A next summer??* So, by tacit agreement, they'd let the television become their nighttime soundtrack. Claire was grateful; it gave her several hours where she could sit quietly, without having to pretend.

Finally, the radiation ended.

The following morning Claire got up early. She dressed and showered and drank her coffee out on the deck overlooking the Sound. It amazed her that so many people were already up, going about their ordinary lives on this day that would define her future.

"Today's the day," Meg said, stepping out onto the deck.

Claire forced a smile. "Yep."

"Are you okay?"

God, how she'd come to despise that question. "Perfect."

"Did you sleep last night?" Meg asked, coming up beside her.

"No. You?"

"No." Meg slipped an arm around her, held her tightly.

Claire tensed, waiting for the pep talk, but her sister said nothing.

Behind them, the glass door opened. "Morning, ladies." Bobby came up behind Claire, slid his arms around her, and kissed the back of her neck.

They stood there a minute longer, no one speaking, then they turned together and left the condo.

In no time, they were at Swedish Hospital. As they entered the Nuclear Medicine waiting room, Claire noticed the other patients who wore hats and scarves. When their gazes met, a sad understanding passed between them. They were members of a club you didn't want to join. Claire wished now that she hadn't bothered with the scarf. Baldness had a boldness to it that she wanted to embrace.

There was no waiting today, not on this day that would answer all the questions. She checked in and went right to the MRI. Within moments, she was pumped full of dye and stuck in the loud machine.

When she was finished, she returned to the waiting room and sat between Meghann and Bobby, who both reached out for her. She held their hands.

Finally, they called her name.

Claire rose.

Bobby steadied her. "I'm right here, babe."

The three of them began the long hallway-to-hallway walk, ending finally in Dr. Sussman's office. The plaque on the door read: *Chief of Neurology*. Dr. McGrail, the chief of radiology, was also there.

"Hello, Claire. Meghann," Dr. Sussman said. "Bobby."

"Well?" Meghann demanded.

"The tumor responded to radiation. It's about twelve percent smaller," Dr. McGrail reported.

"That's great," Meg said.

The doctors exchanged a look. Then Dr. Sussman went to the viewbox, switched it on, and there they were, the gray-and-white pictures of Claire's brain. And there was the stain. He finally turned to Claire. "The decrease has bought you some time. Unfortunately, the tumor is still inoperable. I'm sorry."

Sorry.

Claire sat down in the leather chair. She didn't think her legs would hold her up.

"But it worked," Meg said. "It worked, right? Maybe a little more radiation. Or a round of chemo. I read that some are crossing the blood-brain barrier now—"

"Enough," Claire said. She'd meant to say it softly, but her voice was loud. She looked at the neurologist. "How long do I have?"

Dr. Sussman's voice was gentle. "The survival rates aren't good, I'm afraid, for a tumor of this size and placement. Some patients live as long as a year. Perhaps a bit longer."

"And the rest?"

"Six to nine months."

Claire stared down at her brand-new wedding ring, the one Grandma Myrtle had worn for six decades.

Meghann went to Claire then, dropped to her knees in front of her. "We won't believe it. The files—"

"Don't," she said softly, shaking her head, thinking about Ali. She saw her baby's eyes, the sunburst smile that was missing the front teeth, heard her say, *You can sleep with my wubbie, Mommy,* and it ruined her. Tears ran down her cheeks. She felt Bobby beside her, felt the way his fingers were digging into her hard, and she knew he was crying, too. She wiped her eyes, looked up at the doctor. "What's next?"

Meghann jerked to her feet and began pacing the room, studying the pictures and diplomas on the walls. Claire knew her sister was scared and, thus, angry.

Dr. Sussman pulled a chair around and sat down opposite Claire. "We have some options. None too good, I'm afraid, but—"

"Who is this?" It was Meghann's voice but she sounded shrill and desperate. She was holding a framed photograph she'd taken off the wall.

Dr. Sussman frowned. "That's a group of us from medical school." He turned back to Claire.

Meghann slammed the photograph on the desk so hard the glass cracked. She pointed at someone in the picture. "Who's that guy?"

Dr. Sussman leaned forward. "Joe Wyatt."

"He's a *doctor?*"

Claire looked at her sister. "You know Joe?"

"*You* know Joe?" Meghann said sharply.

"He's a radiologist, actually." It was Dr. McGrail who answered. "One of the best in the country. At least he was. He was a legend with MRIs. He saw things—possibilities—no one else did."

Claire frowned. "Meghann, let go of it. We're long past the need for a radiologist. And believe me, Joe wouldn't be the one to ask for help. What I needed was a miracle."

Meghann looked steadily at Dr. McGrail. She wasn't even listening to Claire. "What do you mean he *was* the best?"

"He quit. Disappeared, in fact."

"Why?"

"He killed his wife."

CHAPTER
TWENTY-EIGHT

THE RIDE HOME SEEMED TO LAST FOREVER. NO ONE SPOKE. WHEN they got back to the condo, Bobby held Claire so tightly she couldn't breathe, then stumbled back from her. "I need to take a shower," he said in a broken voice.

She let him go, knowing what he needed. She'd cried a few tears of her own in Meghann's expensive glass-block shower.

She went to the sofa, collapsed on it. She was tired and dizzy. There was a ringing in her ears and a tingling in her right hand, but she couldn't admit any of that to Meghann, who had that bulldog don't-quit look in her eyes.

Meg sat down on the coffee table, angled toward her. "There are all kinds of clinical trials going on. There's that doctor in Houston—"

"The one the government tried to prosecute?"

"That doesn't mean he's a fraud. His patients—"

Claire held up a hand for silence. "Can we be real for just a minute?"

Meghann looked so stricken that Claire had to laugh.

"What?" Meg demanded.

"When I was little, I used to dream about getting some rare illness that would bring you and Mama to my bedside. I imagined you crying over my death."

"Please, don't . . ."

Claire stared at her sister, so pale now, and shaky. "I don't want you to cry over it."

Meg stood up so abruptly she banged her shin on the coffee table and swore harshly. "I . . . can't talk about you dying. I can't." She couldn't get out of the room fast enough.

"But I need you to," Claire said to the empty room. A headache started behind her eyes again. It had been lurking nearby all day.

She started to lean back into the sofa when the pain hit. She gasped at it, tried to cry out. Her head felt as if it were exploding.

She couldn't move, couldn't breathe. She tried to scream her sister's name.

But the stereo was playing "Thunder Road" and the music swallowed her tiny voice.

Alison, she thought.

Then everything went dark.

Meghann stood by her sister's bed, holding on to the metal bed rails. "Is the medication helping?"

Claire looked small in the hospital bed, delicate, with her pale, pale skin and patchy hair. Her attempt at a smile was heartrending. "Yeah. A grand mal seizure. Welcome to my new world. I guess the good news is I didn't have a heart attack, too. How long will I be here?"

"A few days."

"It's time to call Mama."

Meghann flinched. Her mouth trembled traitorously. "Okay."

"Tell Dad and Ali and the Bluesers they can come down to see me, too. Gina can always make me laugh."

Meghann heard the defeat in her sister's voice; even worse was the acceptance. She wanted to disagree, to make her sister angry enough to fight, but her voice had abandoned her. She shook her head.

"Yes, Meg," Claire said with a resolve that surprised Meg. "And now I'm going to go to sleep. I'm tired."

"It's the meds."

"Is it?" Claire smiled knowingly. "Good night. And take care of Bobby tonight, okay? Don't cut out on him. He's not as strong as he looks." Then she closed her eyes.

Meghann reached out. Being careful not to disturb the IV in Claire's arm, she held her hand. "You're going to be okay." She said it at least a dozen times; every time she expected a response, but one never came. A few minutes later, Bobby walked into the room, looking haggard. His eyes were red and swollen.

"She woke up," Meghann said gently. "And went back to sleep."

"Damn it." He took Claire's hand in his and squeezed it. "Hey, baby. I'm back. I just went for a cup of coffee." He sighed, said quietly, "She's giving up."

"I know. She wants me to call everyone. Tell them to come see her. How do we tell Ali this?" Tears stung her eyes as she looked up at Bobby.

"I'll tell her," Claire said quietly, opening her eyes. She smiled tiredly at her husband. "Bobby," she breathed, reaching for him. "I love you."

Meghann couldn't stand there another second. Every breath her sister exhaled seemed to whisper good-bye. "I've got phone calls to make. Bye." She raced from the room.

Anything was better than standing there, trying to smile when it felt as if someone were ripping her heart apart. Even calling Mama.

It was late now; the night shift was on duty and the hallways were quiet. She went to the bank of pay phones and dialed Mama's number.

Mama herself answered, sounding boozy and loud. "Hello, Frank?"

"It's me, Mama. Meghann."

"Meggy? I thought you prowled the bars this time of night."

"Claire's sick."

"She's on her honeymoon."

"That was a month ago, Mama. Now she's in the hospital."

"This better not be one of your stunts, Meggy. Like the time you called me at work 'cause Claire had fallen out of bed and you thought she was paralyzed. I lost forty dollars in tips to find out she was asleep."

"I was eleven years old when that happened."

"Still and all."

"She has a brain tumor, Mama. The radiation treatments didn't work and no one has the guts to operate on her."

There was a long pause on the other end; then, "Will she be okay?"

"Yes," Meghann said because she couldn't imagine any other response. Then, very softly, she said, "Maybe not. You should come see her."

"I've got a *Starbase IV* event tomorrow at two, and a—"

"Be here tomorrow or I call *People* magazine and tell them you didn't visit your daughter who has a brain tumor."

It was a long moment before Mama said, "I'm no good with this sort of thing."

"None of us are, Mama." Meghann hung up without saying good-bye, then punched in the 800 number on her calling card and dialed Sam. The phone rang once and she lost her nerve. She couldn't tell Sam this over the phone.

She slammed the receiver onto the hook and went back to her sister's room.

Bobby stood by the bed, singing softly to Claire, who snored gently. It brought Meghann up short.

Bobby looked up at her. Tears glistened on his cheeks. "She hasn't opened her eyes again."

"She will. Keep singing. I'm sure she loves it."

"Yeah." His voice cracked.

Meg had never seen a man in so much pain; she knew the look in Bobby's eyes matched her own. "I'm going to go tell Sam in person. I can't give him this news over the phone. If Claire wakes up—" She caught herself. "*When* Claire wakes up, tell her I love her and I'll be back soon. Do you have your keys to my place?"

"I'll sleep here tonight."

"Okay." Meghann wanted to say something else but didn't know what. So she left the room. She practically ran for her car. Once inside, she hit the gas and headed north.

Ninety minutes later, she reached Hayden. She slowed down through town, stopped at the light.

And there it was: the silver Quonset hut.

Joe Wyatt.

He's a radiologist. Probably one of the best in the country. It came rushing back to her now, the stunning news that had been lost somehow, buried beneath a thick layer of grief.

Dr. Joseph Wyatt. Of course. No wonder he'd looked familiar. His trial had been front-page news. She and her colleagues had speculated about his fate over many a beer. She'd been firmly in his camp, certain he'd be acquitted. It had never occurred to her to wonder what had become of him after the trial.

Now she knew. He'd run away, hidden out. But he was still one of the best radiologists in the country. *He saw things—possibilities— no one else did.*

Yet when she'd come to him, sobbing about her sick sister, he'd done nothing. Nothing.

And he *knew* Claire.

"Son of a bitch." She glanced sideways. The envelope from the hospital was on the passenger seat.

She turned the wheel hard and slammed on the brakes, parking along the curb. Then she grabbed the envelope and marched toward the cabin.

She pounded on the door, screaming, until she heard footsteps coming from inside.

When he opened the door, saw her, and said "What—?" she shoved him in the chest so hard he stumbled backward.

"Hey, Joe. Invite me in." She kicked the door shut behind her.

"It's practically midnight."

"So it is, *Doctor* Wyatt."

He sank onto the sofa and looked up at her.

"You held me. You let me cry in your arms." Her voice trembled; the ache in her heart only made her madder. "And you offered a *referral*. What kind of man are you?"

"The kind who knows his hero days are behind him. If you know who I am, you know what I did."

"You killed your wife." At his flinch, she went on. "If I'd known your last name, I would have remembered. Your trial was a big deal in Seattle. The prosecution of the doctor who euthanized his dying wife."

"Euthanasia is a prettier word than manslaughter."

Some of the steam went out of her at the soft sadness in his voice. She'd learned about that kind of sorrow in the past month. "Look, Joe. In an ordinary world, I'd talk to you about what you did. I might even take you in my arms and tell you that I understand, that anyone with a drop of compassion in their soul would have done the same thing. That's what your acquittal meant. I might even ask you about the road you've been on, the journey that led one of the country's best radiologists to this place. But it's not an ordinary world for me right now. My sister is dying." She tripped over the word, felt the sting of tears. She tossed the oversize manila envelope on the coffee table in front of him. "These are her MRI films. Maybe you can help her."

"I let my license lapse. I can't practice medicine anymore. I'm sorry."

"Sorry? *Sorry?* You have the power to save people's lives and you hide out in this dump of a cabin drinking cheap scotch and feeling sorry for yourself? You selfish son of a bitch." She stared down at him, wanting to hate him, hurt him, but she couldn't imagine how to do either one. "I *cared* about you."

"I'm sorry," he said again.

"I'll send you an invitation to the funeral." She turned on her heel and headed for the door.

"Take this with you."

She stopped, gave him one last withering look. "No, Joe. You'll have to touch them. Throw them in the trash yourself. Try looking in the mirror after that."

Then she left. She made it all the way to her car before she started to cry.

Outside the trailer, Meg sat in her car, trying to compose herself. Every time she opened her compact to fix her makeup, she looked at her watery eyes and it made her cry all over again.

She wasn't sure how long she'd sat there, but at some point it started to rain. Drops thumped on the convertible's soft top and tapped on the windshield.

Finally, she got out of the car and walked up to the trailer.

Sam opened the door before she even knocked. He stood there, frowning, his eyes already watery. "I wondered how long you were going to sit out there."

"I thought you didn't know I was here."

He tried to smile. "You always did think you were smarter than me."

"Not just you, Sam. I think I'm smarter than everyone." She wanted to smile but couldn't.

"How bad is it?"

"Bad." When she said it, the tears came back. She wiped them away.

"Come here," Sam said gently, opening his arms.

Meg hesitated.

"Come on."

She surged forward, let him hold her. She couldn't seem to stop crying. Then he was crying, too.

When they finally drew back, they stared at each other. Meg had no idea what to say.

Suddenly there were footsteps in the hallway. Ali came running out, dressed in pink footed pajamas, carrying her Groovy Girl. She looked up at Meg. "Do we get to go see Mommy now? Is she all better?"

Meg knelt down and pulled her niece into her arms, holding her tightly. "Yeah," she said in a throaty voice. "You get to see Mommy tomorrow."

Meghann tossed and turned all night, finally falling into a troubled sleep around dawn. When she woke up again, bleary-eyed and exhausted, she was surprised to see that it was 9:30. A quick check of the condo told her that Sam and Ali had already gone to the hospital. Bobby hadn't come home last night. She forced herself out of bed and stumbled into the shower. By the time she got to the hospital and parked, it was 10:00.

The waiting room was already full.

Gina sat in a chair by the windows, knitting a delicate pink blanket. Beside her, Karen and Charlotte were playing cribbage. Bobby stood at the window, staring out. At Meghann's entrance, he looked up. She could tell by his eyes that Claire had had a bad night. Ali sat at his feet, coloring.

"Aunt Meg," the little girl cried out, scampering to her feet.

Meghann scooped her niece into her arms and hugged her.

"Grandpa's in with Mommy. Can I go now? Can I?"

Meg looked at Bobby, who sighed and shrugged, as if to say, *I can't take her*.

"Sure," Meg said. Slowly, dreading every step, she carried Ali down the long hallway.

At the closed door, she paused, pulled up a bright smile, and went inside.

Sam stood by Claire's bedside. He was crying and holding her hand.

Ali wiggled out of Meg's arms and slid to the floor. She immediately went to her grandfather, who picked her up. "What's the matter, Grandpa? Do you have something in your eye? One time Sammy Chan got poked in the eye and then Eliot Zane called him a crybaby."

Meghann and Claire exchanged a look.

"Leave my baby with me," Claire said, opening her arms. Ali didn't notice the way her mother winced at every movement, every touch.

Sam wiped his eyes and managed a smile. "I better go call that plumber. The pool filter sounds bad."

Ali nodded. "Like shit."

Claire smiled. Tears glittered in her eyes. "Alison Katherine, I've told you not to copy Grandpa's bad language."

"Oops." Ali grinned.

Sam and Meg looked at each other, and a question hung between them, clear as a sunny day. *Who will tell Ali things like that . . . ?*

Meg backed out of the room, left the three of them alone. She went back to the waiting room and thumbed through a magazine.

An hour or so later, a commotion in the hall got her attention. She looked up.

Mama had arrived. Sheathed in elegant, flowing black, she marched forward carrying a tiny dog in a beaded carrier and leading the way. Behind her was a cluster of people; one of them was snapping photographs.

Mama came to the waiting room and looked around. When she saw Meghann, she burst into tears. "How is our girl?" She pulled a silk handkerchief out of her sleeve and dabbed her eyes.

A photographer flashed a photo.

Mama offered a brave smile. "This is m'other daughter, Meghann Dontess. D-O-N-T-E-S-S. She's twenty-nine years old."

Meghann counted silently to ten. Then, in a steady voice, she said, "Dogs aren't allowed in the hospital."

"I know. I had to sneak him in. You know, Elvis, he—"

"Elvis is going to be as dead as his namesake in about ten seconds." At Mama's affronted gasp, Meghann looked at the man standing slightly apart from the crowd. Dressed in black, neckless, he looked like a WWF combatant. "You. Mr. Bodyguard. Take the dog to the car."

"The hotel," Mama said with a dramatic, suffering sigh. "The suite has plenty of room."

"Yes, ma'am." Neckless took the dog carrier and walked away.

That left just Mama, the photographer, and a thin, mouse-faced man with a tape recorder. The reporter.

"Excuse me," Meghann said to the men as she grabbed Mama's arm and pulled her into a quiet corner. "What did you do, hire a publicist?"

Mama drew herself up to her full height and sniffed. "I was talking to her on the other line when you called. What was I supposed to tell her? It's hardly *my* fault that *Us* magazine wanted to cover my visit to my gravely ill daughter. I am, after all, news. Celebrity can be such a burden."

Meghann frowned. She should have been mad as hell right now, ready to deep-fry Mama in some down-home chicken grease. But when she looked into her mother's heavily made-up eyes, she saw something that surprised her.

"You're afraid," she said softly. "That's why you brought the entourage. So it would be a performance."

Mama rolled her eyes. "Nothing scares me. I just . . . just . . ."

"What?"

"It's Claire," Mama finally answered, looking away. "*Claire.*" Her voice thickened, and Meghann saw something honest for once. "Can I see her?"

"Not if you're bringing the circus with you."

Mama said quietly, "Will you go in with me?"

Meghann was surprised by that. She'd always imagined Mama to be shallow as a pie pan and tough as nails, a woman who knew what she wanted in life and made a beeline for it, the kind of woman who would cross police tape and step over a body if it was in her way. Now, she wondered if she'd been wrong, if Mama had always been this weak and frightened.

She wondered if it was all an act. Fear was something Meghann understood. Especially when it grew out of guilt.

"Of course I'll come with you."

They went over to the magazine people. Mama made a teary plea for privacy in this difficult time, then recommended a restaurant across the street for the rest of the interview.

Mama's high heels clacked on the linoleum floor. The sound seemed designed to draw attention, but no one noticed.

At Claire's room, Meghann stopped. "You ready?"

Mama pulled up a smile, nodded, and swept into the room like Auntie Mame, her long black sleeves fluttering out behind her. "Claire, darlin', it's Mama."

Claire tried to smile, but against the white mound of pillows and industrial gray blankets, she looked worn, impossibly pale. The patch of baldness gave her an odd, lopsided look. "Hey, Mama. You just missed Sam and Ali. They went down to the cafeteria."

Mama stumbled, her arms lowered. She glanced back at Meghann.

"I know I look like shit, Mama," Claire said, trying for a laugh.

Mama moved slowly this time. "Why, darlin', that isn't true at all. You're lovely." She pulled up a chair and sat down beside the bed. "Why, I remember an episode of *Starbase IV*. It was called 'Attack Buffet,' remember that? I ate a bad bit of space food and all m'hair fell out." She smiled. "I sent that episode in to the Emmy voters. 'Course it didn't work. Too much politics. I sort of liked the freedom of no hair."

"It was a rubber skullcap, Mama."

"Still. It makes a woman's eyes look beautiful. I do wish I'd brought my makeup though. You *could* use a little blush, maybe a touch of liner. Meghann should have told me. And I'll pick you up a pretty little bed jacket. Maybe with some fur around the collar. I remember a dress I once wore to the—"

"Mama." Claire tried to lean forward. The effort clearly cost her. "There's a tumor eating through my brain."

Mama's smile fluttered. "That's awfully *graphic* of you, darlin'. We Southern women—"

"Please, Mama. *Please.*"

Mama sank into her chair. She seemed to lose mass somehow, become smaller, ordinary, until the flapping black outfit swallowed her up, leaving behind a thin, heavily made-up woman who'd had one too many face-lifts. "I don't know what you want from me."

It was the first time in twenty years Meghann had heard her mother's real voice. Instead of the sweet lilt of the South, it had the pinched flatness of the Midwest.

"Oh, Mama," Claire said, "of course you don't. You never wanted children. You wanted an audience. I'm sorry. I'm too tired to be polite. I want you to know that I love you, Mama. I always did. Even when you . . . looked away."

Looked away.

That was how Mama always put it: *I was standing there one day, takin' care of my babies, then I looked away for a minute, and they were both gone.*

It had been easier, Meghann thought, than confronting the fact that Mama had simply let Claire go.

"Sam was a good man," Mama said so softly they had to strain to hear it. "The only good one I ever found."

"Yes, he was," Claire agreed.

Mama waved her hand airily. "But y'all know me. I'm not one to go pickin' through the past." The accent was back. "I keep movin'. That's always been my way."

They'd lost Mama; whatever opportunity had been opened by the sight of Claire's illness had closed. Mama had rallied. She stood up. "I don't want to tire you out. I'm goin' to run over to Nordstrom and buy y'all some makeup. Would you mind if a friend of mine took a little picture of us together?"

"Mama—" Meghann warned.

"Sure," Claire said, sagging back into the pillows. "Meghann, would you send Bobby and Ali in? I want to kiss them before I take another nap."

Mama bent down and kissed Claire's forehead, then barreled out of the room. Meghann almost fell into her when she left. Mama was standing in the hallway.

"Makeup, Mama?"

"I don't care if she is dyin', there's no need to let herself go like that." Mama's composure cracked.

Meghann reached out.

"Don't you dare touch me, Meggy. I couldn't take it." She turned and walked away, skirts flapping behind her, heels clattering on the floor.

There wasn't a single person who didn't look at her as she passed.

Claire grew weaker. By her second day in the hospital, she wanted simply to sleep.

Her friends and family had begun to exhaust her. They'd shown up religiously. All of them. The Bluesers had descended on her tiny hospital room, bringing life and laughter, flowers and fattening food, and Claire's favorite movies. They talked and told jokes and re-membered old times. Only Gina had had the guts to brave the harsh, icy landscape of Claire's fear.

"I'll always be there for Ali, you know," she said when everyone else had gone to the cafeteria.

Claire had never loved her friend as much as in that moment. No wartime charge ever took more courage. "Thank you," was all she'd been able to say. Then, softly, "I haven't been able to tell her yet."

"How could you?"

Gina's eyes met hers, filling slowly with tears. They'd both been thinking about how a woman said good-bye to her five-year-old daughter. After a long pause, Gina smiled. "So. What are we going to do about your hair?"

"I thought I'd cut it off. Maybe dye what's left of it platinum."

"Very chic. We'll all look like old housewives next to you."

"That's my dream now," Claire said, unable to help herself. "Becoming an old housewife."

Ultimately, as much as she loved to see her friends, she was glad when they went home. Late that night, in the quiet darkness, she gave in to the meds and fell asleep.

She woke with a start.

Her heart was pounding too fast, skipping beats. She couldn't seem to breathe, couldn't sit up. Something was wrong.

"Claire, are you okay?" It was Bobby. He was sitting beside her bed. He'd obviously been sleeping. Rubbing his eyes, he stood up, came to her bedside. For a second, she thought it was a hallucination, that the Pacman tumor had eaten through the good parts of her brain and left her crazy. Then he moved closer to the bed, and she heard the jingle of the keys.

"Bobby," she whispered, trying in vain to lift her heavy, heavy arms.

"I'm right here, baby."

It took effort, a painful amount, but she reached up and touched his wet cheek. "I love you, Robert Jackson Austin. More than anything in the world except my Ali Gator.

"Come," she said. "Get into bed with me."

He looked at all the machines, the IVs, the tubes and cords. "Oh, baby . . ." He leaned down and kissed her instead.

The sweet pressure of his lips felt so good. She closed her eyes, feeling herself sinking into the pillows. "Ali," she whispered. "I need my baby—"

Pain exploded behind her right eye.

Beside her bed, an alarm went off.

• • •

There is no pain. No ache. She feels for the dry, itchy patch of skin on her head and feels long, beautiful hair instead.

She sits up. The tubes that connect her to the machines are gone. She wants to shout out that she is better, but there are people in her room. Too many of them, all dressed in white. They're crowding her, talking all at once so she can't understand.

She realizes suddenly that she is watching herself from above—in the air somewhere—watching the doctors work on her body. They've ripped open her gown and are ramming something on her chest.

"Clear!" one yells.

There is such relief in being here, above them, where there is no pain . . .

"Clear."

Then she thinks of her daughter, her precious baby girl whom she didn't hold one last time.

Her baby, who will have to be told that Mommy has gone away.

The doctor stepped back. "She's gone."

Meghann ran to the bed, screaming. "Don't you do it, Claire. Come back. Come back, damn it."

Someone tried to pull her away. She elbowed him hard. "I mean it, Claire. You come back. Alison is in the waiting room. You cannot run out on her this way. You haven't told her good-bye. She deserves that, damn it. Come back." She grabbed Claire's shoulders, shook her hard. "Don't you *dare* do this to Alison and me."

"We have a heartbeat," someone cried out.

Meghann was pushed aside. She stumbled back into the corner of the room, watching, praying, as they stabilized her sister.

Finally, the doctors left, dragging their crash cart with them. Except for the buzz and beep of machines, the room was quiet.

She stared at Claire's chest, watching it rise and fall. It was a moment before she realized that she was breathing intently, trying to will her sister's body to keep up the rhythm.

"I heard you, you know."

At Claire's voice, Meg pulled away from the wall and moved forward.

There was Claire, half bald, pale as parchment, smiling up at her. "I thought: *Christ, I'm dead and she's still yelling at me.*"

CHAPTER
TWENTY-NINE

*J*OE HAD TRIED TO THROW OUT THE DAMN ENVELOPE AT LEAST a dozen times. The problem was, he couldn't bring himself to touch it.

Coward.

He heard the word so clearly he looked up. The cabin was empty. He stared at Diana, who looked back at him from her place on the mantel.

He closed his eyes, wishing she'd come to him again, maybe sit down on the bed beside him and whisper, *You break my heart, Joey,* the way she used to.

But she hadn't come to him in so long that he'd forgotten how those hallucinations felt. Although he didn't need to conjure her image to know what her words would be right now.

She would be ashamed of him, as ashamed as he was of himself. She would remind him that he'd once taken an oath to help people.

And not just anyone, either. This was Claire Cavenaugh, the woman who'd sat by Diana's bedside hour after hour when she was ill, playing dirty-word Scrabble and watching soap operas. Joe remembered one night in particular. He'd worked all day, then headed for Diana's hospital room, exhausted by the prospect of another evening spent beside his dying wife. When he'd opened the door, Claire was there, wearing nothing but her bra and panties, dancing. Diana, who hadn't smiled in weeks, was laughing so hard there were tears on her cheeks.

No way, Claire had laughed when he asked what was going on. *We are not going to tell you what we were doing.*

A girl has to have some *secrets,* Diana had said, *even from the love of her life.*

Now it was Claire in a bed like that, in a room that smelled of despair and looked out on graying skies even in the height of summer.

There was probably nothing he could do for her, but how could he live with himself if he didn't try? Maybe this was God's way of reminding him that a man couldn't hold on to old fears if he wanted to start over.

If she were here right now, Diana would have told him that chances didn't come any plainer than this. It was one thing to run away from nothing. It was quite another to turn your back on a set of films with a friend's name in the corner.

You're killing her, and this time no pretty word like euthanasia *will fit.*

He released a heavy breath and reached out, pretending not to notice that his hands were shaking and that he was suddenly desperate for a drink.

He pulled out the films and took them into the kitchen, where full sunlight streamed through the window above the sink.

He studied the first one, then went through the rest of them. Adrenaline made his heart speed up.

He knew why everyone had diagnosed this tumor as inoperable. The amount of skill needed to perform the surgery was almost unheard-of. It would require a neurosurgeon with godlike hands and an ego to match. One who wasn't afraid to fail.

But with a careful resection . . . there might be a chance. It was possible—just possible—that this one thin shadow wasn't tumor, that it was tissue responding to the tumor.

There was no doubt about what he had to do next.

He took a long, hot shower, then dressed in the blue shirt he'd recently bought and the new jeans, wishing he had better clothes, accepting that he didn't. Then he retrieved the film, put it back in the envelope, and walked over to Smitty's house. Helga was in the kitchen, making lunch. Smitty was in the living room, watching *Judge Judy*. At Joe's knock, he looked up. "Hey, Joe."

"I know this is irregular, but could I borrow the truck? I need to drive to Seattle. I may have to stay overnight."

Smitty dug in his pocket for the keys, then tossed them.

"Thanks." Joe went to the rusty old '73 Ford pickup and got inside. The door clanged shut behind him.

He stared at the dashboard. It had been years since he'd been in the driver's seat. He started the engine and hit the gas.

Two hours later, he parked in the underground lot on Madison and Broadway and walked into the lobby of his old life.

The painting of Elmer Nordstrom was still there, presiding over the sleek black high-rise that bore his family name.

Joe kept his head down as he walked toward the elevators. There, making eye contact with no one, his heart hammering, he pushed the up button.

When the doors pinged open, he stepped inside. Two white-coated people crowded beside him. They were talking about lab results. They got off on the third floor—the floor that led to the sky bridge that connected this office building to Swedish Hospital.

He couldn't help remembering when he'd walked through this building with his head held high; a man certain of his place in the world.

On the fourteenth floor, the doors opened.

He stood there a half second too long, staring at the gilt-edged black letters on the glass doors across the hall.

Seattle Nuclear Specialists. The business he'd started on his own.

There were seven or eight doctors listed below. Joe's name wasn't there.

Of course it wasn't.

At the last second, as the doors were closing, he stepped out of the elevators and crossed the hall. In the office, there were several patients in the waiting room—none of which he knew, thank God—and two women working the reception desk. Both of them were new.

He considered walking straight down to Li's office, but he didn't have the guts. Instead, he went to the desk.

The woman—Imogene, according to her name tag—looked up at him. "Can I help you?"

"I'd like to see Dr. Li Chinn."

"And your name?"

"Tell him an out-of-town doctor is here for an emergency consult. I've come a long way to see him."

Imogene studied Joe, no doubt noticing his cheap clothes and small-town haircut. Frowning, she buzzed Li's office, gave him the message. A moment later, she hung up. "He can see you in fifteen minutes. Take a seat."

Joe went to one of the chairs in the waiting room, remembering that Diana had picked the fabric and colors for the office. There had been a time when their home had been wall-to-wall samples.

I want it just right, she'd said when he made fun of her. *Your job is the only thing you love more than me.*

He wished he could smile at the memory; it was a good one.

"Doctor? Doctor?"

He looked up, startled. That was a word he hadn't heard directed at him for a long time. "Yes?" He stood.

"Dr. Chinn will see you now. Go down the hall and turn right—"

"I know where his office is." He went to the door, stood there, trying to breathe evenly. He was sweating and his palms were damp. His fingerprints would be all over the envelope.

"Doctor? Are you okay?"

He released a heavy sigh and opened the door.

The interior hallways and offices were filled with familiar faces. Nurses, physician's assistants, radiology techs.

He forced his chin up.

One by one, the people he'd known made eye contact, recognized him, and looked quickly away. A few of them smiled awkwardly or waved, but no one spoke to him. He felt like a ghost passing through the land of the living. No one wanted to admit they'd seen him.

Some of the gazes were frankly condemning; that was the look he remembered, the one that had sent him running in the first place. Others, though, seemed embarrassed to be seen looking at him, confused by his sudden appearance. What did you say to a man you'd once admired who'd been prosecuted for killing his wife and then vanished for three years?

He walked past the row of women in hospital gowns waiting for mammograms, past the second waiting room, then turned onto another, quieter hallway. In the far end, he came to a closed door. He took a deep breath and knocked.

"Come in," said a familiar voice.

Joe entered the big corner office that had once been his. Huge picture windows framed the Seattle high-rise view.

Li Chinn was at his desk, reading. At Joe's entrance, he glanced up. An almost comical look of surprise overtook his normally impassive face. "I don't believe it," he said, remaining in his seat.

"Hey, Li."

Li looked awkward, uncertain of how to proceed, what to say. "It's been a long time, Joe."

"Three years."

"Where did you go?"

"Does it matter? I meant to come by here and tell you I was leaving. But—" he sighed, hearing how pathetic he sounded "—I didn't have the guts."

"I kept your name on the door for nearly a year."

"I'm sorry, Li. It was probably bad for business."

Li nodded; this time his dark eyes were sad. "Yes."

"I have some film I'd like you to look at." At Li's nod, Joe went to the viewbox and put the film up.

Li came closer, studying it. For a long moment, he said nothing. Then, "You see something I do not?"

He pointed. "There."

Li crossed his arms, frowned. "Not many surgeons would attempt such a thing. The risks are grave."

"She's going to die without the surgery."

"She may die because of the surgery."

"You think it's worth a try?"

Li looked at him, his frown deepening. "The old Joe Wyatt never asked for other men's opinions."

"Things change," he said simply.

"Do you know a surgeon who would do it? Who *could* do it?"

"Stu Weissman at UCLA."

"Ah. The cowboy. Yes, maybe."

"I can't practice. I've let my license lapse. Could you send Stu the film? I'll call him."

Li flicked off the light. "I will. You know, it's an easy thing to re-instate your license."

"Yes." Joe stood there a moment longer. Silence spread like a stain between the men. "Well. I should go call Stu." He started to leave.

"Wait."

He turned back around.

"Did any of the staff speak to you?"

"No. It's hard to know what to say to a murderer."

Li moved toward him. "A few believed that of you, yes. Most . . . of us . . . just don't know what to say. Privately, many of us would have wanted to do the same thing. Diana was in terrible pain, everyone knew that, and there was no hope. We thank God that we were not in your shoes."

Joe had no answer to that.

"You have a gift, Joe," Li said slowly. "Losing it would be a crime, too. When you're ready—if you ever are—you come back to see me.

This office is in the business of saving lives, not worrying about old gossip."

"Thank you." They were small words, too small to express his gratitude. Embarrassed by the depth of his emotion, Joe mumbled thanks again, and left the office.

Downstairs, in the lobby, he found a bank of pay phones and called Stu Weissman.

"Joe Wyatt," Stu said loudly. "How the hell are you? I thought you fell off the face of the earth. Damn shame, that hell you went through."

Joe didn't want to waste time with the where-have-you-been stuff. There would be time for that when Stu got up here. So he said, "I have a surgery I want you to do. It's risky as hell. You're the only man I know who is good enough." Stu was a sucker for compliments.

"Talk to me."

Joe explained what he knew of Claire's history, told him the current diagnosis, and outlined what he'd seen on the film.

"And you think there's something I can do."

"Only you."

"Well, Joe. Your eyes are the best in the business. Send me the film. If I see what you do, I'll be on the next plane. But you make sure the patient understands the risks. I don't want to get there and have to turn around."

"You got it. Thanks, Stu."

"Good to hear from you," Stu said, then hung up.

Joe replaced the receiver. Now all he had to do was speak to Claire.

He went back to the elevators, then crossed the sky bridge and headed into Swedish Hospital. He kept his gaze pinned on the floor. A few people frowned in recognition, a few more whispered behind him. He ignored them and kept moving. No one had the guts to actually speak to him or ask why he was back here, until he reached the ICU.

There someone said, "Dr. Wyatt?"

He turned slowly. It was Trish Bey, the head ICU nurse. They'd worked together for years. She and Diana had become close friends at the end. "Hello, Trish."

She smiled. "It's good to see you back here. We missed you."

His shoulders relaxed. He almost smiled in return. "Thanks." They stood there, staring at each other for an awkward moment, then he nodded, said good-bye, and headed for Claire's room.

He knocked quietly and opened the door.

She was sitting up in bed, asleep, her head cocked to one side. The patchy hairless area made her look impossibly young.

He moved toward her, trying not to remember when Diana had looked like this. Pale and fragile, her hair thinning to the point where she looked like an antique doll that had been loved too hard and then discarded.

She blinked awake, stared at him. "Joey," she whispered, smiling tiredly. "I heard you were home. Welcome back."

He pulled a chair over and sat down beside her bed. "Hey, Claire."

"I know. I've looked better."

"You're beautiful. You always have been."

"Bless you, Joe. I'll tell Di hi for you." She closed her eyes. "I'm sorry, but I'm tired."

"Don't be in such a hurry to see my wife."

Slowly, she opened her eyes. It seemed to take her a minute to focus on him. "There's no hope, Joe. You of all people know what that's like. It hurts too much to pretend. Okay?"

"I see it . . . differently."

"You think the white coats are wrong?"

"I don't want to give you false hope, Claire, but yeah, maybe."

"Are you sure?"

"No one is ever sure."

"I'm not asking anyone else's opinion. I want yours, Joey. Are you telling me I shouldn't give up?"

"Surgery might save you. But there could be bad side effects, Claire. Paralysis. Loss of motor skills. Brain damage."

At that, she smiled. "Do you know what I was thinking about just before you got here?"

"No."

"How to tell Ali Kat that Mommy is going to die. I'd take any risk, Joe. Anything so I don't have to kiss Ali good-bye." Her voice cracked, and he saw the depth of her pain. Her courage amazed him.

"I've sent your films to a friend of mine. If he agrees with my diagnosis, he'll operate."

"Thank you, Joe," she said softly, then closed her eyes again.

He could see how tired she was. He leaned down and kissed her forehead. "Bye, Claire."

He was almost to the door when she said, "Joe?"

He turned. "Yeah?"

She was awake again, barely, and looking at him. "She shouldn't have asked it of you."

"Who?" he asked, but he knew.

"Diana. I would never ask such a thing of Bobby. I know what it would do to him."

Joe had no answer to that. It was the same thing Gina always said. He left the room and closed the door behind him. With a sigh, he leaned back against the wall and closed his eyes.

She shouldn't have asked it of you.

"Joe?"

He opened his eyes and stumbled away from the wall. Meghann stood a few feet away, staring up at him. Her cheeks and eyes were reddened and moist.

He had a nearly irresistible urge to wipe the residue of tears from her eyes.

She walked toward him. "Tell me you found a way to help her."

He was afraid to answer. He knew, better that most, the double edge of hope. Nothing hit you harder than the fall from faith. "I've spoken to a colleague at UCLA. If he agrees with me, he'll operate, but—"

Meghann launched herself at him, clung to him. "Thank you."

"It's risky as hell, Meg. She might not survive the surgery."

Meghann drew back, blinked her tears away impatiently. "We Sullivan girls would rather go down fighting. Thank you, Joe. And . . . I'm sorry for the things I said to you. I can be a real bitch."

"The warning comes a little late."

She smiled, wiped her eyes again. "You should have told me about your wife, you know."

"In one of our heart-to-heart talks?"

"Yeah. In one of those."

"It's hardly good between-the-sheets conversation. How do you make love to a woman, then tell her that you killed your wife?"

"You didn't kill her. Cancer killed her. You ended her suffering."

"And her breathing."

Meghann looked up at him steadily. "If Claire asked it of me, I'd do it. I'd be willing to go to prison for it, too. I wouldn't let her suffer."

"Pray to God you never have to find out." He heard the way his voice broke. Once, he would have been ashamed by such obvious vulnerability; those were the days when he'd believed in himself, when he'd thought he was a demigod at least.

"What do we do now?" she said into the silence that felt suddenly awkward. "For Claire, I mean." She stepped back from him, put some distance between them.

"We wait to hear from Stu Weissnar. And we pray he agrees with my assessment."

Joe was at the front door when he heard his name called. He stopped, turned.

Gina stood there. "I hear my brother is acting like a doctor again."

"All I did was call Stu."

She came closer, smiling now. "You gave her a chance, Joe."

"We'll see what Stu says, but yeah. Maybe. I hope so."

Gina touched his arm. "Diana would be proud of you. So am I."

"Thanks."

"Come sit with us in the waiting room. You've been alone long enough. It's time to start your new life."

"There's something I need to take care of first."

"Promise me you'll come back."

"I promise."

An hour later, he was on the ferry headed to Bainbridge Island. He stood at the railing on the upper deck as the ferry turned into Eagle Harbor. The pretty little bay seemed to welcome him, with all its well-maintained homes and the sailboats clustered at the marina. He was glad to see that it looked the same; still more trees than houses, and the beachfront hadn't been cut into narrow lots.

This is it, Joey. This is where I want to raise our kids.

His fingers tightened around the railing. That day hadn't been so long ago—maybe ten years—but it felt like forever. He and Diana had been so young and hope-filled. It had never occurred to either one of them that they wouldn't be together forever.

That one of them would have to go on alone.

The ferry honked its horn.

Joe returned to his truck, below deck. When the boat docked, he drove off.

Memories came at him from every street corner and sign.

Pick up that armoire for me, won't you, Joey, it's at Bad Blanche's.

Let's go to the winery today. I want to smell the grapes.

Forget dinner, Joey, take me to bed or lose me.

He turned onto his old road. The trees were huge here; they towered in the air and blocked out the sun. The quiet road lay shadowed and still. There wasn't a house to be seen out here, just mailboxes and driveways that led off to the right.

At the last one, he slowed down.

Their mailbox was still there. Dr. and Mrs. Joe Wyatt. It had been one of Diana's first purchases after they'd closed on the house.

He drove down his long, tree-lined driveway. The house—his house—sat in a patch of grassy sunlight beside a wide gravel beach.

It was a pretty little Cape Cod–style home with cedar shingles and glossy white trim.

The wisteria had gone wild, he noticed, growing thick and green along the porch railings, around the posts and up some of the exterior walls.

He was moving slowly now, breathing hard, as he left the safety of his car and walked toward the house.

The first thing he noticed was the smell. The salty tang of sea air mixed with the sweetness of blooming roses.

He found the key in his wallet—the one he'd kept especially for this day.

In truth, there had been weeks, months even, when he'd never believed he'd find the guts to reach for it again.

The key fit the lock, clicked.

Joe opened the door—

Honey, I'm home

—and went inside.

The place looked exactly as he'd left it. He still remembered the day he'd come home from court—supposedly an innocent man (no, a not-guilty one)—and packed a suitcase. The only phone call he'd made had been to Gina. *I'm sorry,* he'd said, too tired to be eloquent. *I need to go.*

I'll take care of the place, she'd answered, crying. *You'll be back.*

I don't know, he'd said. *How can I?*

And yet, here he was. True to her word, Gina had taken care of the place. She'd paid the taxes and the bills from the money he'd left in a special account. No dust collected on the furniture or windowsills, no spiderwebs hung from the high pitched ceilings.

He walked from room to room, touching things, remembering. Every stick of furniture reminded him of a time and place.

This chair is perfect, Joey, don't you think? You can sit in it to watch TV.

Every knickknack had a story. Like a blind man, he moved

slowly, putting his hands on everything, as if somehow touch elicited the memories more than sight.

Finally, he was in the master bedroom. The sight of it was almost too much. He forced himself to go forward. It was all still there. The big antique bed they'd gotten from Mom and Dad as a wedding present, the beautiful quilt that had come to them on Dad's death. The old nightstands that had once been piled with books—romance novels on her side, military histories on his. Even the tiny needlepoint pillow that Diana had made when she first got sick.

He sat down on the bed and picked up the pillow, seeing the tiny brown spots that marred the fabric.

I don't think needlework is a good therapy. I'm losing so much blood I'm getting light-headed.

"Hey, Diana," he said, wishing for the days when he'd been able to conjure her image. He stroked the pillow, trying to remember how it had felt to touch her. "I was at the hospital today. It felt good."

He knew what she'd say to that. But he didn't really know if he was ready to go back. His life had changed so much, degraded somehow into tiny bits that might not fit together again.

He hadn't forgotten the way people looked at him at his old office. They saw him and wondered, *Is that what a murderer looks like?*

He stared down at the pillow, stroking it. "You shouldn't have asked it of me, Di. It . . . ruined me.

"Well . . . maybe I ruined me, too," he admitted quietly. He should have stayed here, in this community he'd cared so much for. His mistake had been in running away.

It was time to quit hiding and running. Time to stand up to the people who judged him poorly and say, *No more.*

Time to take his life back.

Slowly, he got up and went to the closet, opening the louvered doors.

Diana's clothes filled two-thirds of the space.

Three years ago, he'd tried to box them up and give them away. He'd folded one pink cashmere sweater and been done for.

He reached out for a beige angora turtleneck that had been her favorite. He eased it off of the white plastic hanger and brought it to his face. The barest remnant of her scent lingered. Tears stung his eyes. "Good-bye, Diana," he whispered.

Then he went in search of a box.

CHAPTER THIRTY

$\mathcal{T}$HE NEXT MORNING STU WEISSMAN CALLED CLAIRE. HE SPOKE IN clipped, rushed sentences. She was so groggy and disoriented, it took her several seconds to understand him.

"Wait a minute," she finally said, sitting up. "Are you saying you'll do the surgery?"

"Yes. But this thing will be a bear cat. Could be a bad outlook all the way around. You could end up paralyzed or brain damaged or worse."

"Worse sooner, you mean."

He laughed at that. "Yes."

"I'll take the chance."

"Then I will, too. I'll be there tonight. I've scheduled the surgery for eight A.M. tomorrow." His voice softened. "I don't mean to be negative, Claire. But you should put your affairs in order today. If you know what I mean."

"I know what you mean. Thank you, Dr. Weissman."

• • •

All that day, Claire said good-bye to her friends. She did it one at a time, feeling that each of them deserved that kind of attention.

To Karen, she joked about the gray hairs Willie was sure to cause her in the upcoming years and begged her friend to make this third marriage work. To Charlotte, she said, *Don't give up on babies; they're the mark we leave in this world. If you can't have one of your own, find one to adopt and love her with all you've got.* Gina was more difficult. For almost an hour they were together, Claire dozing off every now and then, Gina standing by the bedside, trying not to cry.

Take care of my family, Claire said at last, fighting to keep her eyes open.

Take care of them yourself, Gina had responded, her voice spiking for humor that it couldn't reach. Then, softly, she said, *You know I will.*

They were awkward, painful partings, full of things unsaid and boundaries upheld. They all pretended Claire would still be here to-morrow night, laughing and screwing up as she always had. She left her friends with that faith, and though she wanted to own it for her-self, hope felt like a borrowed sweater that didn't quite fit.

She was bone tired, but most of all, she was afraid. Dr. Weissman had been guarded in his optimism and blunt in his assessment of the risk. *A bad outlook all the way around,* he'd said. The worst part of her fear was how alone it made her feel. There was no one she could tell.

Time and again throughout the long, drawn-out day, she found herself wishing that she'd died already, simply floated from this world unexpectedly. There was no way to be stealthy now, not with all her loved ones in the waiting room, praying for her, and the thought of the good-byes she still had left was devastating. Bobby and Sam would hold her and cry; she'd have to be ready for that. Meg would get angry and loud.

And then there was Ali. How could Claire possibly get through *that?*

• • •

The hospital had a small nondenominational chapel on the second floor.

Meghann stood outside it, paused in the open doorway. It had been years since she'd gone to a church in search of comfort; decades, in fact.

Slowly, she went inside, let the door ease shut behind her. Her footsteps were hushed and even on the mustard-colored carpet. She slid into the middle pew and knelt on the floor. There was no cushion for her knees, but she knelt anyway. It seemed right to be on her knees when she asked for a miracle.

She clasped her hands together and bowed her head. "I'm Meghann Dontess," she said by way of introduction. "I'm sure you've forgotten me. I haven't talked to you since . . . oh . . . the ninth grade, I think. That's when I prayed for enough money to get Claire ballet lessons. Then Mama got fired again and we moved on. I . . . stopped believing you could help." She thought of Claire upstairs, so pale and tired-looking in that hospital bed, and of the risks the surgery entailed. "She's one of the good ones, God. Please. Protect her. Don't let Ali grow up without her mom."

She squeezed her eyes shut. Tears slid down her cheeks and plopped on her hands. She wanted to say more, maybe find a way to bargain, but she had nothing to offer beyond desperation.

Behind her, the door opened, closed. Someone walked down the aisle.

Meghann wiped her eyes and eased back onto the pew.

"Meg?"

She looked up, surprised. Sam stood beside her, his big body hunched in defeat, his eyes a watery red. "She's saying good-bye to her girlfriends."

"I know."

"I can't stand watching each one come out of her room. The minute they close the door, their smiles fade and the crying starts."

Meghann had run from the same thing. "She's lucky to have so many friends."

"Yeah. Can I join you?"

She sidled to the right, making room. He sat down beside her. He was close enough that she could feel the heat of his body, but they didn't touch, didn't speak.

Finally Sam said, "I was thirty years old when you called me."

She frowned. "Oh." What did he want her to say?

"I had no brothers and sisters and no other children."

"I know that, Sam. You pointed it out every time I screwed up."

He sighed. "I was pissed at Eliana. She'd denied me my daughter's childhood. All those years I'd been alone when I didn't have to be . . . and the way you and Claire lived from hand to mouth. I couldn't stand it."

"I know that."

He twisted around to face her. "Claire was easy. She looked up at me with those big, trusting eyes and said, *Hi, Daddy*; just like that, I fell in love. But you." He shook his head. "You scared the shit out of me. You were tough and mouthy and you thought everything I said to Claire was wrong. I didn't know you were just being a teenager. I thought you were like . . ."

"Mama."

"Yeah. And I didn't want Claire to be hurt. It took me a while—years—to see that you weren't like Ellie. By then it was too late."

"Maybe I *am* like Mama," she said quietly.

"No," he said fiercely. "You've been Claire's rock through this nightmare. You have the kind of heart that saves people, even if you don't believe it. And I'm sorry I didn't see that when I was younger."

"A lot of things have become clearer lately."

"Yeah." He sat back in the pew. "I don't see how I'll get through this," Sam said.

Meghann had no answer. How could she, when the question haunted her as well?

A few minutes later, the door opened again. This time it was Bobby. He looked terrible.

"She wants to see Ali," he whispered harshly. "I can't do it."

Sam made a fluttery sound. "Oh, God."

"I'll do it," Meg said, slowly rising.

• • •

Claire must have fallen asleep again. When she woke, the sunlight outside had faded, leaving the room a soft, silvery color.

"Mommy's awake."

She saw her daughter then. Ali clung to Meghann like a little monkey, arms wrapped around her aunt's neck, feet locked around her waist.

Claire made a quiet, whimpering sound before she rallied and pulled out a tired smile. The only way to get through this moment was to pretend there would be another. For Ali, she had to believe in a miracle.

"Hey there, Ali Kat. I hear you're eating all the cinnamon rolls in the cafeteria."

Alison giggled. "Only three, Mommy. Aunt Meg said if I had one more I'd throw up."

Claire opened her arms. "Come here, baby."

Meg leaned forward and gently deposited Ali into Claire's thin arms. She hugged her daughter tightly, couldn't seem to let go. She was battling tears and hanging on to her smile by a thread when she whispered into her daughter's tiny, shell-pink ear, "You remember how much I love you."

"I know, Mommy," Ali said, burrowing closer. She lay still as a sleeping baby, quieter than she'd lain in years. That was when Claire knew that Ali understood, but when her daughter leaned closer to say, "I told God I'd never ask for Cap'n Crunch again if He made you all better," Claire felt something inside her tear away. She clung to her daughter for as long as she could. "Take her home," she finally said when the pain became more than she could bear.

Meghann was there instantly, pulling Ali into her arms again.

But Ali wiggled out of Meg's grasp and slithered to the molded plastic chair beside the bed. She stood there, on the wobbly chair, staring at Claire.

"I don't want you to die, Mommy," she said in a husky little voice.

It hurt too much even to cry. Claire looked at her precious baby and managed a smile. "I know that, punkin, and I love you more than all the stars in the sky. Now you skedaddle on home with Grandpa and Bobby. I hear they're going to take you to see a movie."

Meghann picked Ali up again. Claire could see that she was near tears, too. "Make Bobby go home," she said to her sister. "He's been here every night. Tell him I said Ali needs him tonight."

Meg reached out, squeezed her hand. "We need *you*."

Claire sighed. "I need to sleep now" was all she could think of to say.

Hours later, Claire came awake with a start. Her heart was pounding so hard she felt light-headed. For a split second, she didn't know where she was. Then she saw the flowers and the machines. If she squinted, she could make out the wall clock. Moonlight glinted on the domed glass face. It was 4:00.

In a few hours, they'd crack her skull open.

She started to panic, then saw Meg was in the corner, sprawled in one of those uncomfortable chairs, sleeping.

"Meg," she whispered, hitting her control button; the bed tilted upward. The buzzing of the machinery sounded loud, but Meghann didn't wake.

"Meg," she said in a louder voice.

Meghann sat upright and looked around. "Did I miss the test?"

"Over here."

Meghann blinked, pushed a hand through her wild, tangled hair. "Is it time?"

"No. We have four more hours."

Meghann got up, dragged the chair over to the bed. "Did you sleep?"

"Off and on. The prospect of someone cracking your skull open keeps a girl wideawake." Claire glanced out the window at the moonlight. Suddenly, she was so afraid, she was shaking. All the veneer of bravery she'd applied for her family and friends had worn off, leaving her vulnerable. "Do you remember what I used to do when I had a nightmare?"

"You used to crawl into bed with me."

"Yeah. That old cot in the trailer's living room." Claire smiled. "It smelled like spilled bourbon and cigarette smoke, and it was too small for the two of us. But when I got into bed and you hugged me, I thought nothing could hurt me." She looked up at Meghann, then very gently peeled back the blanket.

Meghann hesitated, then climbed into bed with Claire, drawing her close. If she noticed how thin Claire had gotten, she didn't comment on it.

"How come we forgot all the things that mattered?"

"I was an idiot."

"We wasted a lot of time."

"I'm sorry," Meg said. "I should have said that a long time ago."

Claire reached for Meg's hand, held it. "I'm going to ask you something, Meg, and I don't want any of your bullshit to get in the way. I can't ask this twice; saying each word is like swallowing broken glass. If the worst happens, I want you to be a part of Ali's life. She'll need a mother."

Meg squeezed Claire's hand so tightly it cut off the blood flow to her fingers. Long seconds passed before she answered in a throaty voice, "I'll make sure she always remembers you."

Claire nodded; she couldn't speak.

After that, they lay in the darkness, each holding the other one together until dawn lit the room and the doctors took Claire away.

Meghann stood at the window, staring out at the jumble of beige buildings across the street. In the three hours since they'd taken Claire to surgery, Meghann had counted every window and every door in this view. Twenty-three people had passed the corner of Broadway and James. Another sixteen had stood in line outside the tiny Starbucks.

Someone tugged on her sleeve. Meghann looked down. There was Alison, staring up at her. "I'm thirsty."

Meghann stared into those bright green eyes and almost burst into tears. "Okay, honey," she said instead, scooping Ali into her arms. Forcing herself not to squeeze the girl too hard, she carried her down to the cafeteria.

"I want a Pepsi Blue. That's what you got me last time."

"It's only eleven in the morning. Juice is better for you."

"You sound like Mommy."

Meg swallowed hard. "Did you know your Mommy loved Tab when she was little? And Fresca. But I made her drink orange juice."

Meghann paid for the juice, then carried Alison back to the waiting room. But when she leaned over to put Ali down, the girl squeezed harder.

"Oh, Ali," Meg said, holding her niece. She wanted to promise that Mommy would be better, but the words caught in her throat.

She sat down, still holding Ali, and stroked her hair. Within minutes, the child was asleep.

From across the room, Gina looked up, saw her holding Ali, then went back to her crossword puzzle. Sam, Mama, Bobby, Karen, and Charlotte were playing cards. Joe sat off in the corner, reading a magazine. He hadn't looked up in hours, hadn't spoken to anyone. But then, none of them had spoken much. What was there to say?

Around noon, the surgical nurse came out, told them all that it would be several more hours.

"You should get something to eat," she said, shaking her head. "It won't help Claire if you all pass out."

Sam nodded, stood up. "Come on," he said to everyone. "Let's get out of here for a while. Lunch is on me."

"I'll stay here," Meghann said. Food was the last thing on her mind. "Ali needs the sleep."

Bobby squeezed her shoulder. "You want us to bring you something back?"

"Maybe a sandwich for Ali—peanut butter and jelly."

"You got it."

When they'd gone, Meghann leaned back in her chair, rested her head against the wall. In her arms, Ali snored quietly. It seemed like yesterday that Meg had held Claire this way, telling her baby sister that everything would be okay.

"It's been almost four hours, damn it. What're they all doin' in there, anyway?"

Meg looked up. Mama stood there, holding an unlit Virginia Slims cigarette. Her makeup had faded a little, been smudged off in places, and without it, she looked faded, too. "I thought you went out for lunch with everyone."

"Eat *cafeteria* food? I don't think so. I'll eat an early dinner in my hotel suite."

"Have a seat, Mama."

Her mother collapsed into the molded plastic chair beside her. "This is the worst day of my life, honest to God. An that's sayin' something."

"It's hard. Waiting."

"I should go find Sam. Maybe he'll want to play cards or somethin'."

"Why did you leave him, Mama?"

"He's a good man" was all Mama said.

At first, Meghann thought it wasn't an answer. Then she understood.

Mama had run away *because* Sam was a good man. Meghann could relate to that kind of fear.

"There are things I should have said," Mama whispered, gesturing impatiently with her unlit cigarette. "But I never was too good without a script."

"None of us talks really well."

"And thank God. Talkin' doesn't change a thing." Mama stood up suddenly. "Talkin' to reporters always cheers me up. Bye, Meggy. I'll be across the street when"—her voice trembled—"y'all hear that she's fine." With that, she sailed out of the waiting room, her smile Hollywood bright.

• • •

One hour bled into the next until finally, around 4:00, Dr. Weiss-man came into the waiting room. Meghann was the first to see him. She tightened her hold on Ali and got to her feet. Bobby stood next; then Sam and Mama; then Joe, Gina, Karen, and Charlotte. In a silent group, they moved toward the doctor, who rubbed a hand through his thinning hair and managed a tired smile.

"The surgery went well."

"Thank God," they whispered together.

"But she's a long way from out of the woods. The tumor was more invasive than we thought." He looked up at Joe. "The next few hours will tell us more."

CHAPTER
THIRTY-ONE

*C*LAIRE WOKE UP IN RECOVERY FEELING GROGGY AND CONFUSED. A headache pounded behind her eyes. She was about to hit her call button and ask for an Advil when it struck her.

She was alive.

She tested her memory by counting to one hundred and trying to list all the towns she'd lived in as a child, but she'd only made it to Barstow when the first of the nurses came in. After that, she was poked and prodded and tested until she couldn't think.

Her family took turns sitting with her. Two of her most vivid postsurgery memories were of Bobby, sitting by her bed, holding an ice pack to her head for hours at a time, and of her dad, feeding her ice chips when she got thirsty. Meghann had brought in Ali's newest drawing; this one was three brightly colored stick figures standing by a river. In an uncertain scrawl across the bottom it read: *I love you Momy.*

By the second full postop day, Claire had become irritable. She hurt now; her body ached everywhere and the bruises on her forehead from the iron halo had begun to throb like hell. They wouldn't give her much in the way of pain medication because they didn't want to mask any surgical aftereffects.

"I feel like shit," she said to Meghann, who sat in the chair by the window.

"You look like shit."

Claire managed to smile. "Again with the bedside manner. Do you think they'll come soon?"

Meghann looked up from her book, which Claire noticed was upside down. "I'll check again." Meg put the book down and stood up as the door opened.

Claire's day-shift nurse, Dolores, walked into the room, smiling. She was pushing an empty wheelchair. "It's time for your MRI."

Claire panicked. Suddenly she didn't want to go, didn't want to know. She felt better. That was good enough—

Meghann came to her side, squeezed her hand. The touch was enough to get Claire over the hump. "Okay, Dolores. Take me away."

When they rolled into the hallway, Bobby was there, waiting for them. "Is it time?"

It was Meghann who answered. "It is."

Bobby held Claire's hand all the way to Nuclear Medicine. It took an act of will to leave them behind and go down that familiar white hallway alone.

A few minutes later, as she lay once again in the jackhammer coffin of the MRI, she visualized a clean, clear scan of her brain, saw it so clearly that by the time it was over, her temples were wet with tears.

Bobby, Meghann, and Dolores were waiting for her when she was finished.

Dolores helped Claire into the wheelchair, then positioned her slippered feet on the footrests. Back to the room they went.

After that, the waiting was unbearable. Meghann paced the small hospital room; Bobby squeezed Claire's hand so tightly she lost all feeling in her fingers. Sam came in every few minutes.

Finally, Dolores returned. "The docs are ready for you, Claire."

Little things got Claire through the wheelchair ride without screaming—the warm pressure of Bobby's hand on her shoulder, the easy patter of Dolores's monologue, the way Meghann stayed close.

"Well. Here we are." Dolores stopped at the office door and knocked.

Someone called out, "Come in."

Dolores patted Claire's shoulder. "We're praying for you, sweetie."

"Thanks."

Meghann took control of the wheelchair and guided Claire into the office. There were several doctors in the room. Dr. Weissman was the first to speak. "Good morning, Claire."

"Good morning," she answered, trying not to tense up. The men waited for Meghann to sit down. Finally they realized that she wasn't going to.

Dr. Weissman clicked on the viewbox. There were Claire's films. Her brain. She grabbed the wheels and rolled forward.

She studied the film, then looked up at the men. "I don't see any tumor."

Dr. Weissman smiled. "I don't, either. I think we got it all, Claire."

"Oh my God." She'd hoped for this, prayed for it. She'd even worked to believe it, but now she saw that her belief had stood on a shaky foundation.

"Initial lab reports indicate that it was a low-grade astrocytoma," he said.

"Not a glioblastoma multiforme? Thank God."

"Yes, that was good news. Also, it was benign," Dr. Weissman said.

One of the other doctors stepped forward. "You are a very lucky woman, Mrs. Austin. Dr. Weissman did an incredible job. However, as you know, most brain tumors will regenerate. Twenty-eight percent of all—"

"Stop!" Claire didn't realize that she'd yelled out the word until she saw the startled looks on the doctors' faces. She glanced at Meg, who nodded encouragingly. "I don't want to hear your statistics. It was benign, right?"

"Yes," the doctor said, "but benign in the brain is a rather misleading term. All brain tumors can ultimately be fatal, benign or not."

"Yeah. Yeah. Limited space in the head and all that," Claire said. "But it's not a cancer that's going to spread through my body, right?"

"Correct."

"So it's gone now and it was benign. That's all I want to hear. You can talk to me about treatments from here on, but not about chances and survival rates. My sister immersed herself in your numbers." She smiled at Meg. "She thought I wasn't listening, but I was. She had a file that she kept on the kitchen counter—a file she labeled *Hope*. In it, there were dozens of personal accounts of people who'd been diagnosed with brain tumors more than seven years ago and were still alive. You know what they all had in common?"

Only Dr. Weissman was smiling.

"They'd all been told they'd live less than six months. You guys are like Seattle weathermen in June. All you ever predict is rain. But I'm not taking an umbrella with me. My future is sunny."

Dr. Weissman's smile grew. He crossed the room and bent down to her ear. "Good for you."

She looked up at him. "There are no words to thank you."

"Joe Wyatt is the man you should thank. Good luck to you, Claire."

As soon as she was back in her room, Claire broke down and cried. She couldn't seem to stop. Bobby held her tightly, kissing her bald head, until finally she looked up at him. "I love you, Bobby."

He kissed her fiercely.

She clung to him, then whispered in his ear, "Go get our little girl. I want to tell her Mommy's going to be okay."

He hurried out.

"You were amazing in there," Meg said when they were alone.

"My new motto is: *Don't screw with Baldie.*"

"I won't," Meg grinned.

Claire reached for her sister's hand, held it. "Thanks."

Meg kissed Claire's screw-marked forehead and whispered, "We're sisters." It was answer enough. "I'll go get Mama now. She'll probably bring a film crew." With a smile, Meghann left the room.

"The tumor is gone," Claire practiced saying aloud to the empty room.

Then she laughed.

Meghann found everyone in the cafeteria. Bobby was already there, talking to Sam. Mama was at the food line, signing autographs. The Bluesers and Alison were sitting in the corner, talking quietly among themselves. The only one missing was Joe.

"And there I was," Mama was saying to a rapt audience, "all ready to take the stage in a dress that wouldn't zip up. I am *not*," she said, laughing prettily, "a flat-chested woman, so y'all can imagine—"

"Mama?" Meghann said, touching her arm.

Mama spun around. When she saw Meghann, her painted smile faded. For a moment, she looked smaller, vulnerable. Little Joanie Jojovitch from the wrong side of the tracks in Detroit. "Well?" she whispered.

"Go on up, Mama. It's good news."

Mama sighed heavily. "Of *course* it is. Y'all were so dramatic." She turned back to her audience. "I hate to leave in the middle of a story, but it seems my daughter has made a miraculous recovery. I am reminded of a television movie I once did, where. . . ."

Meghann walked away.

"Auntie Meg!" Alison said, jumping up, throwing herself at Meg, who scooped her up and gave her a kiss. "My mommy is all better!"

At that, another whoop went up from the Bluesers. "Come on," Gina said to her friends. "Let's go see Claire."

Bobby walked up to Meghann. "Come on, Ali Gator," he said, pulling the little girl into his arms. "Let's go kiss Mommy." He started to walk away, then paused and turned back. Very gently, he kissed Meghann's cheek, whispered, "Thank you."

Meghann closed her eyes, surprised by the depth of her emotion. When she looked up again, through a blur of tears, Sam was coming toward her.

He moved slowly, as if he were afraid his legs would give out. He reached out, touched her cheek.

It was a long moment before he said softly, "I'll expect you at the house this Thanksgiving. None of your lame-ass excuses. We're family."

Meg thought of all the years she'd declined Claire's offer, and all the years one hadn't been extended. Then she thought of last Thanksgiving, when she'd eaten Raisin Bran for dinner by herself. All that time, she'd pretended that she wasn't lonely. No more pretending for her, and no more being alone when she had a family to be with. "Just try and keep me away."

Sam nodded and kept walking. She saw that he looped over by the food line and grabbed Mama's arm, dragging her away from the crowd. She blew air-kisses as she stumbled along beside him.

Meghann stood there a minute longer, uncertain of where she should go.

Joe.

She ran through the hallways, smiling and giving thumbs-ups to the nurses and aides who had become more than friends in the past few weeks.

In the waiting room, she skidded to a stop.

It was empty. The magazine he'd been reading lay, still open, on the table.

She glanced back down the corridor, but Claire didn't need her right now. There would be time for them later, when the excitement had dimmed and real life returned. There was a lifetime left for them. Right now, what Claire needed was clothes to wear home from the hospital.

Meghann went to the elevators and rode down to the lobby, then headed outside. She couldn't wait to call Elizabeth with the news.

It was a glorious, sunny day. Everything about the city felt sharper, cleaner. The distant Sound shone silvery blue between the gray high-rises. She walked downhill, thinking about so many things—her life, her job, her family.

Maybe she'd change her career, practice a different kind of law. Or maybe she'd start a business, sort of an informational clearing-house for people with brain tumors; maybe she could find a disillusioned doctor to partner with her. Or maybe a charitable company, one that helped finance the best of care in the worst of times. The world seemed wide-open to her now, full of new possibilities.

It took her less than a half an hour to walk home. She was just about to cross the street when she saw him, standing outside the front door of her building.

When he saw her, Joe pulled away from the wall he'd been leaning against and crossed the street. "Gina told me where you lived."

"Stu told you about the MRI?"

"I spent the last hour with him. It looks good for Claire."

"Yeah."

He moved toward her. "I'm tired of not caring, Meg," he said softly. "And I'm tired of pretending I died when Diana did."

She looked up at him. They were close now, close enough so that he could kiss her if he chose. "What chance do we have, a couple like us?"

"We have a chance. It's all any of us gets."

"We could get hurt."

"We've survived it before." He touched her face tenderly; it made her want to cry. No man had ever been so gentle with her. "And maybe we could fall in love."

She gazed up into his eyes and saw a hope for the future. More than that, even. She saw a little of the love he was talking about and, for the first time, she believed in it. If Claire could get well, anything was possible. She put her arms around him and pressed onto her toes. Just before she kissed him she dared to whisper, "Maybe we already have."

ƐPILOGUE

One Year Later

THE NOISE WAS DEAFENING—THE FAIRGROUNDS WERE JAMMED with people; kids screaming from the carnival rides, parents yelling after them, carnies barking out enticements to play the games, the musical cadence of the calliope.

Alison was up ahead, dragging Joe from ride to ride. Meghann and Claire walked along behind, talking softly, carrying the collection of cheesy stuffed animals and cheap glass trinkets that Joe had won. Claire's limp was the only physical reminder of her ordeal, and it was getting less pronounced each day. Her hair had grown out; it was curlier and blonder than before.

"It's time," Claire said, signaling to Joe. The four of them fell in line together, walking past the refreshment stand and turning left toward the fairgrounds' bleachers.

"There's a crowd already," Claire said. She sounded nervous.

"Of course there is," Meghann said.

"Hurry, Mommy, hurry!" Alison was bouncing up and down. At the special side door, Claire showed her backstage pass. They made their way through the staging area, past the musicians and singers who were warming up.

Bobby saw them coming and waved. Alison ran for him. He scooped her into his arms and twirled her around. "My daddy's gonna sing tonight," she said loud enough for everyone to hear.

"I sure am." Bobby looped an arm around Claire and pulled her in for a kiss. "Wish me luck."

"You don't need it."

They talked to him for a few more minutes, then left him to get ready.

They climbed the bleachers and found their seats in the fourth row. Meghann helped Claire sit down; her sister was still unsteady sometimes.

"Kent Ames called last week," Claire said. "Mama ripped him a new one for canceling Bobby's contract."

"She's been cussing him out for months."

"I know. Last week she told him she'd gotten Bobby an audition at Mercury Records. Kent Ames threw a fit. It seems he wants to give Bobby another chance, after all. Said he hopes Bobby's *priorities* are straight this time." Claire smiled.

A man took the stage and announced, "Bob-by Jack Austin!"

The crowd applauded politely.

Alison jumped up and down, screaming, "Yay, Daddy!"

Bobby leaped up onstage with his guitar. He scanned the audience, found Claire, and blew her a kiss. "This song is for my wife, who taught me about love and courage. I love you, baby." He strummed the guitar and started to sing. His clear, beautiful voice wrapped around the music and mesmerized the crowd. He sang about finding the woman of his dreams and falling in love with her, about standing by her side in dark times. In the final stanza, his voice fell to a throaty whisper; the crowd leaned forward to hear the words.

When I saw you stumble
over rocks along the way
I learned the truth of real love
and the gift of one more day.

The applause this time was explosive. Half the women in the audience were weeping.

Meghann put an arm around her sister. "I *told* you he'd make a great husband. I liked that guy from the first moment I saw him."

Claire laughed. "Yeah, right. And what about you and Joe? You guys are practically living together. It looks to me like maybe there's a prenuptial agreement in your future."

Meghann looked at Joe, who was on his feet, clapping. Alison was in his arms. Since he'd started practicing medicine again, he said anything was possible. They'd taught each other to believe in love again. "A prenup? Me? No way. We were thinking about a small wedding. Outside—"

"Where it rains? Where bugs breed? *That* outside?"

"Maybe with hamburgers and hot dogs and—"

"Gina's potato salad."

They both said it at the same time and laughed.

"Yeah," Meghann said, leaning against her sister. "That kind of wedding."